Invincible Defeat

All the Best
[signature]

**By
Peter Fergus**

This book is a work of fiction. People, places, events, and situations are the product of the author's imagination. Any resemblance to actual persons, living or dead, or historical events, is purely coincidental.

© 2011 Peter Fergus. All rights reserved.

No part of this book may be reproduced, stored in a retrieval system, or transmitted by any means without the written permission of the author.

First published 06/07/2011

Published by adVenture

ISBN: 978-0-9570041-0-8

Printed in the United Kingdom By Book Printing UK

For Teresa

Chapter One

We pulled down the anchor line guided by the vertical shafts of sunlight that pierced the water like shimmering spears, above us a trail of silver bubbles danced and mushroomed their way to the surface. The rope gave way to links of galvanised chain and then twisted shapes slowly became clearer. We settled down on a large cylindrical object and after adjusting our equipment I gazed into Jenny's mask, her eyes were wide with excitement. I patted what was left of a ship's boiler. Like Jenny the excitement was building inside me. I forced myself to calm down to avoid hyperventilating. 'Jen, it's a bloody shipwreck'. I shouted the best I could through my mouthpiece, 'A wreck… a virgin shipwreck!'

The abundance of sea life was mesmerising. The wreck, having lain undetected since secretly settling on the seabed decades ago, had never been disturbed or fished. Large shimmering walls of Pouting passed gracefully only inches away in synchronized slow motion. Even the seabed appeared to be alive, as weed of all colours swayed back and forth in the invisible current. Small creatures darted in and out of crevices avoiding Conger eels whose grey heads poked out from their dark lairs. A shoal of silver Pollock hung motionless above us, like sentinels guarding their realm. We were being watched by thousands of hidden eyes.

Jenny gave an enthusiastic OK signal, which I returned and then we glided effortlessly over the lumps of wreckage that looked as if they were growing out of the seabed.

I lifted a brass porthole that had turned green from a pile of twisted steel plating and propped it upright, Jenny fumbled with a plastic bag, which held bread. She was quickly joined by lots of brightly marked Cuckoo Wrasse and striped Pouting. They rapidly took full advantage of this easy meal and within a minute she looked like a victim of a Piranha attack. She was cocooned in a ball of darting colour from her waist upwards.

After twenty minutes of exploring the broken wreckage we returned to the anchor line, I secured the porthole I'd found to the chain and then we made our slow ascent back to the warm sunlight. Jenny's friends had their dive and by chance returned with a silver fork, which they gave me to help identify this lost forgotten ship.

Steaming back home I noticed Jenny was maintaining an almost childlike grin. 'What are you grinning about then, Ginge?' I received an expected scowl. Then she looked back at me, while keeping her mouth smugly closed, her eyebrows rose and her head rocked from side to side.

'Come on then, what's made you so bloody cocky?'

'Look what I found.' She held a coin up and waved it in front of me then quickly returned it to her pocket and then pushed her tongue out at me. It was obvious by the sparkle it reflected in the sunlight that it was gold.

Back in the harbour Jenny's friends finished unloading their equipment.

'Thanks for taking us out,' said Dave who was accompanied by his bubbly girlfriend Carol.

'Yeah, thanks a lot, it was a brilliant dive,' she added with a warm smile.

'That's all right. You're welcome anytime.'

As the car doors closed with muffled thuds my attention turned to Jenny. She disregarded my glance, but couldn't hide the excitement rising inside. She was smiling like a lottery winner.

Overstated humming took over from the low sound of Dave's car purring away.

I turned again to Jenny. 'Come on, let's have a proper look, you little tease.' She squeezed her hand into her tight jeans pocket and held the coin up between her thumb and finger.

'Well, what do you think?'

I rubbed the shiny coin under fresh water which revealed Saint George slaying an aggressive looking dragon. 'It's a sovereign, a gold sovereign.'

'Is it worth much?'

'Well it is dated 1902 and it has Edward the V11 on the face, it's got to be valuable, they were sort of international currency in the old days.'

'Like Krugerrand's are now?'

'Yeah, I suppose. This is worth a few hundred quid, it has to be.'

'Hundreds,' Jenny said in a raised voice. 'Fantastic!'

'Can you remember where you found it?'

'Yeah, I think so, yeah, it was near a long… thingy sort of thing.'

'A long… thingy thing.' I shook my head. 'Only a woman could describe a piece of wreckage that way.'

'Hey buster a woman found it.' She grabbed the coin and studied it while rolling her head from side to side. 'Shall we sell it then?' She looked so youthful and enthusiastic. 'We could have a big posh meal and some bubbly.'

'Not so hasty, there might be some more down there. If word got out there would be a gold rush. You know how greedy people are; it would be like that scene from Jaws, when everyone was trying to kill the shark to collect the bounty. It was shrewd of you not to tell your college mates about it.'

She uplifted her eyes. 'I go to a university not a college; there is a big difference you know!'

'Yeah, yeah, they're all just nerdy hangouts.'

'So I've done something right, then…for a nerd that is?'

'You certainly have, Jenny Dean.' I put my hand on her shoulder, 'Partners then?'

She flicked the coin and asked heads or tails, I said heads and she peeped at the coin …through her fingers I could just make out the dragon. 'You're lucky. Partners we are, then.'

Three days of unsettled weather followed our wreck discovery, which somewhat diluted all the initial excitement. Jenny had reluctantly returned to college, so I used up the two days servicing my boat *Westwind*. I glanced from the window of my warm cosy study. The strong wind was forcing the taller of the silver birches to bend in defiance, as it tried to steal their leaves, while above, blackened clouds sped across the grey sky. A slight swell had forced its way down the river causing the moored boats to nod up and down like feeding birds. It was going to a few days before the sea would allow us to pry into her secrets again.

Piles of books lay spread around the large oak table that adjoined the big bookshelf which covered the entire wall. Several were open, a few acted as tablemats to crumb-filled plates and empty cups. I brooded over them for a few minutes, then sat upright and sighed. I glanced at the silver fork that was tantalising me. For the hundredth time I studied it with a magnifying glass. Sand had eroded a crest or emblem that was once stamped on the back of the handle. Just an S' about three o'clock on a circular shape, and the letters 'IRA' on the bottom of the shape could be distinguished. I put the fork down and again pondered what it could mean; while in the background the old clock ticked deep and methodical giving the room a heartbeat.

'Got to go back,' I told myself out loud. The sovereign was in front of me, its presence was eerie, it was dominating the table like a glinting, staring eye. Could it have been in someone's pocket while they struggled in the cold dark water prior to being dragged to their doom, then over the decades the sea dissolved the poor soul into obscurity leaving the coin as the only trace of their existence? Could there be more sovereigns, maybe a large consignment, a fortune, waiting to be found?'

I shook the mouse and the computer woke up displaying the latest weather forecast. It read 'S - SW Gale Eight.' Not a chance, I cursed to myself.

Moving to a drawer I sifted through a collection of sea charts, pulling out several. I placed them on the table. The charts went back to the nineteen twenties, none of them showed the unknown wreck, but it was after all in an area that is dominated by boulders as big as buses and strewn with deep gullies. Day dreaming over the charts with a teacup in both hands, I suddenly remembered the porthole.

Inside the old garage that always felt warm and silent when entering, I donned a pair of rubber gauntlets. A bluebottle buzzed annoyingly in my face then crashed into a large and perfectly made spider's web in the corner of the window. I watched on in anticipation, the feeling of excitement and fear reminded me when I worked offshore at night and large moving shapes appeared on the edge of the lighted area. I shuddered as a mean looking spider appeared from a tunnel in a millisecond and sunk its fangs into the struggling fly.

   I fished into the large blue drum that held diluted acid and pulled out the porthole and placed it in a tub of fresh water. The stiff brush made easy work of the dissolved calcium growth, and within minutes of scrubbing a number 'six' appeared as clear as the day it had been stamped into the heavy brass frame. I scrubbed further, and letters started appearing from the grime. 'John Royal, RAINHILL.' I knew Rainhill was a place just outside of Liverpool and the makers name 'John Royal' should be easy to trace; at least we now knew we had found a British built ship. I lowered it back into the tub of fresh water and wiped my hands, out of the corner of my eye I noticed the spider with the fly, it was now just a pellet of silk and for a later meal. A shiver ran down my spine as I shut the door.

Back in The Lodge I looked at the pile of open books spread on the table, sat down and drew a deep breath, our search for treasure was underway.

Chapter Two

I dragged the noisy phone from the bedside unit and juggled with the handset.

'Hi, Kris.'

'God, what time is it?' I cleared my throat and brushed the hair from my forehead.

'Nine thirty,' Jenny replied. 'Are you still in bed?'

'Yeah I, err, stayed up late trying to find some information about the wreck.'

'Lazy bones. Did you find anything?'

I sat up and rubbed my eyes back to life. 'No, I've been over the old charts, right through all my books and on the Internet. I did find one reference to a ship carrying gold sovereigns, but it was on the other side of the Atlantic and couldn't be ours.'

'Ours, I like the sound of that.'

'Technically we are 'the salvers in possession,' but if we can't make a positive identity, any more gold we find would become treasure trove.'

A stifled giggle squeaked from the mouthpiece. 'Sorry. What does all that mean in English?'

I cleared the gravel from my throat again. 'If we cannot find the owner, or the insurance underwriters, the government will only award us a percentage of the value. Like the things treasure hunters find with metal detectors. It's all classed as treasure trove.'

'What sort of percentage?'

'It all depends. Sovereigns aren't really national heritage although they could be worth more if the wreck was well known or had an interesting providence, but we will never know if we don't identify it positively. Any more coins we find would become hard currency and the Chancellor would want his split. That's of course if there is more down there.'

'Kris, how do you know all this?'

'Wreck salvage was a good earner for the daring or the crazy when navigation aids first became available to smaller boats. Obtain a boat and go and get what you can. That's how it was back then, and a lot of scrap men became involved, due to the quantity of non-ferrous metal that the steamships had fitted to them. There were hundreds of wrecks off the coast where I lived.' I grinned unreservedly. 'I stiffed a few of those would be salvers by finding what they were searching for before they could organise themselves.'

'So you were a real pirate then?'

I grinned and lifted my eyes. 'Not really, but I got closer than most people.'

'When do you think we can go back to our wreck?'

'The weather is getting better on Sunday so we could go have a look on Monday, all being well.'

'What about tomorrow?'

'Hell no, you know we've got dive charters over the weekends. Anyway if anyone saw us on the site, which they are more likely to on a busy weekend, they would steal our position and every man and his parrot would be diving it the next day.'

'You mean dog?'

'No, that's the marine version. How are you fixed for Monday?'

'I've got an exam on Monday, but I suppose I could…?'

'Don't even think about missing it, Jenny. I won't take you if you cop out.'

'It'll have to be Tuesday then I suppose.' Her defiant reply was punctuated with several huffs.

'OK, Tuesday. Here at eight?'

'I could come Monday night if you wanted, you know, bring a bottle or two.'

I paused in silence, I was almost drawn to say yes, but our sixteen-year age gap curtailed the temptation that suddenly confused me.

'No, Jenny. We need early nights. We can't drink the night before diving anyway. A few silent seconds passed.

'Aye, aye, shipmate. It only be a suggestion so it be, Tuesday so be it. Ah, ah.'

'Yeah OK, you nutcase, that'll be fine, weather permitting. I'll call you if it's off.'

'See you…shipmate.' A few more seconds of silence prevailed.

'Bye then,' she said softly or was it sadly?

'Jenny. Jenny,' I called out, but she'd gone. I placed the handset down gently as a hollow feeling of loneliness crept inside me.

Westwind rose up and down in the majestic Atlantic swell. Jenny placed the heavy cylinder onto the engine box with a dull thump.

'Don't forget, take your time and try to remember where you found the coin. Just get yourself orientated first. Remember, the last dive, we started from the boiler and swam off in a northerly direction.' I helped her put her arms into the shoulder straps.

'You mean that big round rusty thing with the holes.'

'Yeah, yeah, that big round broiler thing with the holes is the ships boiler.'

Her head flicked up and she tutted, shot a smile at me through the mask and then rolled over the gunwale disappearing in a neat splash.

I paced up and down as her bubbles moved all over on the rising and falling swells. Her movement told me that she was searching randomly around, and obviously hadn't found the long thingy thing. I felt a little disappointed. Planning salvage in the comfort of an armchair was a far cry from actually being out at sea.

A further twenty minutes passed then her red sausage shaped marker buoy appeared amongst a ring of foamy bubbles, about twenty metres from the boat. It repeatedly bobbed vertically, then fell flat on the surface as Jenny pulled on it while ascending.

I moved *Westwind* slowly alongside where I now could see Jenny's white cylinder through the rising bubbles. She eventually got closer and a hand like the lady of the lake appeared from the water. As soon as her head broke the surface she dragged off her mask.

'The bell, I've found it. I've found a bell!' she shouted, while gasping for breath between the small choppy waves.

'You sound like Quasimodo. You've what?' I shouted back in disbelief.

'Honest, I've found a golden bell. I scratched it. It's solid gold, Kris.'

Unable to stop myself grinning, I shouted. 'It'll be made of brass, you nugget.'

I patted her shoulder as I helped her back into the boat. 'Well done, partner.'

After she calmed down I began to coil the length of rope neatly on the deck, to recover the bell with. She was placing her dive gear tidily in a pile, which caused her thick red hair to fall scruffily. She looked up at me while parting it from her face. I noticed her brown eyes were on fire, she was beaming with pure exhilaration.

'You got the anchor chain right on the top of that broiler thingy, you bighead. The fish were still there patrolling like before, they're everywhere. It's really hard to know where you are with all the disordered broken bits and pieces that are strewn everywhere, and the visibility wasn't good. I was dashing around like a loony and got out of breath. The thought of you making fun out of me panicked me. It's so frustrating when you get los- err, disorientated.' She looked awkwardly at me. 'I only had one minute left and was leaving the bottom when I noticed a lone dark shape in a patch of sand so I had a quick look. I couldn't believe what I saw.' She caught her breath. 'A bell, little Nerdy me has found the ship's bell.'

'So you got lost and lucky eh?'

'Kris, don't take it so badly, you'll just have to look harder that's all.'

I could only grin at her. She was high on self-achievement, which was great. 'You can't buy this anywhere, kid.' I caught her gaze.

'What's that?' She gasped while panting softly with excitement. I looked out to the horizon and smiled…'Real adventure.'

I swam down Jenny's thin white line that held her marker buoy. In my right hand I tightly held on to the thicker rope. I could hardly bear the anticipation as the light began to dim and the seabed rose up to meet me. It was my turn now to hear and feel my own heart beating as I pulled the bell from the coarse sand that had been its home for decades. I quickly secured the rope through its hanging hole. Rolling it around I rubbed at it to see if I could find a name. I smiled as I saw the small scratch that Jenny had made on its hanging hole. Gold! I laughed inwardly. The bell was about eighteen inches high, beautifully shaped and about twelve inches wide at its base. I rubbed it again where I could see engraved letters, but years on the bottom of the sea had left a hard crust of marine concretion making it impossible to read, so I surfaced as fast as safety would permit.

'Ready?'

'Yeah,' Jenny replied, holding the rope in both hands.

We pulled hard like two grinning children until the bell appeared, then we lifted it carefully onto the deck.

'You're a beauty, a gorgeous,' I looked at Jenny…'Brass beauty!' I bent down to her and gave her a peck on the cheek. She was preoccupied; carefully picking up tiny crustaceans that had fallen from the bell and were struggling for their lives on the hot deck. She affectionately identified every one as she carefully released them back into the sea. She even had silly little names for them like 'Len the Lobster' and 'Chris the Crab'. I watched her, intrigued by her gentleness. After all the years of working offshore I must have been witness to the demise of millions of similar little creatures, I mused. I hadn't even noticed one of them.

She bounced to her feet and brushed her hands together then turned to me looking quite serious, almost aggressive. She then held my chin and pressed her lips firmly to mine. Her kiss was hard and hungry, it totally captivated me. She ended the kiss then pressed her lips briefly to mine again. They felt so warm and soft, so soft that our lips stuck slightly as she pulled away, I stood speechless. Uplifting her attractive brown eyes she gave the most seductive smile I'd seen for years. 'Hmmm got you that time… salty lips.'

I stepped into the wheelhouse with a child-like feeling of anticipation, despite my ideals about our age difference.

As we steamed back home the GPS indicated our speed as twenty-two knots. I felt that my heart was doing fifty. We didn't talk. The bell had left us deep in thought. The identity of the wreck would soon be known. If we were lucky, the secrets of its cargo would also be revealed. The kiss was on both our minds, I'm sure; it had been more than just a friendly peck this time. I felt strong passion and a rising desire during it, a feeling I had suppressed for far too long.

Laughter broke the energised silence as the tender drew near to The Lodge. I was rowing more strongly which made the small boat spin completely round on several occasions. Within minutes of reaching the steps the bell was introduced to the acid bath and was left slowly fizzling away.

Twisting the wire while Jenny washed, I restrained the cork causing the bottle to make a lengthy hiss.

'Congratulations, partner!' We chinked glasses and sipped the fizzy wine while interrogating each other's faces.

'How long do you think it'll take to dissolve the gunge off the bell?'

'Well, we don't want to chip or mark it. I once sent a bell up to the surface using a lifting bag. Unfortunately the idiots in the boat decided to chip off the crud with diving knifes so they could read the name. They left marks all over it! I reckon tomorrow morning, at the earliest.'

The stir-fry I knocked up was demolished quickly. We were starving. The last of the prawn crackers were eagerly washed down with a second bottle of bubbly. As the night progressed Jenny warmed herself in front of the crackling log fire and we talked about the prospect of discovering more sovereigns. Eventually we started dropping off, helped by the log fire, and no doubt the wine.

I turned on the shower and leant against the glass with my hand testing the temperature. The familiar warmth of the water caressed me as it splashed from my face and ran generously down my body. After a few minutes the liquid spell was broken by a metallic click as the shower door opened.

Jenny stood naked; she slowly uplifted her head, revealing an uncertain smile. 'Can I come in? The shower in my room is all cold, and I've brought some soap with me.' Her face anxiously searched mine for approval. In response I held out my arms, which caused her smile to transform into a serious look of desire as her beautifully curved body slowly approached me like a predatory animal. I embraced her. I was full of trepidation, but as soon as our bodies touched I was desperately lost in her. She moaned softly causing her hot breath to caress my neck, as she poured herself on me like warm honey.

The corridor had become a vertical shaft no larger than an average garage door, in which thirty or more crowded bodies screamed and cried hysterically as they frantically tried clinging to each other under the ghastly blanket of darkness. Some were already dead or injured from the people that had fallen from above them when they could no longer hold on to the hand rails; they bobbed and spun like big apples in a barrel as Vicky clawed at them. She was holding little Jane tightly to her as she gasped for breath, unaware that the small body was limp and lifeless. All around her invisible hands pushed her deeper and deeper. She fought valiantly to keep their heads above the numbing water along with the frenzied souls that struggled beside her, but the brutal kicks she was receiving viciously jolted her small frame until she could take no more.

I awoke abruptly; soaked in sweat and then light filled the room. I turned. Jenny was sat upright.

'Kris, you're soaked. You were tossing and turning and shouting for someone called Vicky over and over again. What is it, what's wrong?'

A feeling of pure desperation overwhelmed me I clasped my hands around my knees and dropped my head. She put her arm around me and rested her head on my shoulder as my pounding heart began to slow down.

Jenny smiled at me then she gave a long wiggly stretch, which made her disappear under the quilt, I left her to wake up and went to shower.

A bit later, wearing an oversize dressing gown, she entered the kitchen scratching her mass of curly red locks.

'Good morning again,' she said through a yawn.

'Good morning. I've set the table under the window. Go and sit down, I won't be a minute, oh, and could you check on the coffee percolator please?'

'Hmm, you're posh. Percolator indeed, I thought only Nerds had stuff like that.' She turned then glanced cheekily from the corner of her eyes. I don't think she was thinking about the percolator. I wasn't either. I felt different inside. Despite the return of the nightmare, a sort of feeling of contentment had replaced the feeling of emptiness that had been with me so long.

As she sat pouring the coffees, I noticed her mood change as her attentions turned to the fireplace. 'Last night…err, is that Vicky?' The picture on the stone mantel showed an attractive blonde woman with a small girl on her knee. She had long blonde pigtails and revealed a missing front tooth through a beaming grin.

I nodded. 'A memory.' I attempted a smile but failed, staring blankly at the picture, until I felt Jenny's hand rest on my shoulder.

After a rather quiet breakfast, full of stolen glances, we entered the garage. The bell emerged from the acid in a sorry looking state, so we placed it into the fresh water tub, and rubbed away the black and slimy dissolved calcium. I lifted it out and placed it on the bench, and started to read out 'SS MA.'

'*Madeira*,' Jenny burst out. 'It's called *Madeira*!' She jumped up and around clapping her hands together.

'1884,' I said levelly. 'Come on.'

We rushed into The Lodge and to the big oak bookshelf where I snatched out several books.

'Here, you look in this one.' I passed her one then opened another. '*M. M. Maddox* no, here it is, *Madeira*. Wait a minute. No this one is 1897 and sank in the Med.' I picked out another book. 'Here, here it is. Look.' I moved aside so she could see. '*Madeira, Elder Dempster & Co. 1884. This one sounds about right. Made by Barclay, Curle & Co. 1.773 tons. 300 x 36.2 x 19.9. 221 n.h.p. Compound Engines. Listen to this. The British cargo ship Madeira was last reported 35 miles west of Ushant on Wednesday 17 November 1914 while carrying a general cargo from the west coast of Africa to Liverpool. Heavy weather reported at the time may have caused the vessel to founder as no further reports were heard.*

'That's encouraging. It must have stayed afloat longer than they thought and drifted in the Gulf Stream and strong winds.' Jenny looked at me.

'But how could it have drifted all that way?' I replied.

'It must have, silly, or it wouldn't be here, would it?'

'What if another ship had rescued some of the crew and one of them carried the bell on board, then that ship sank here?' I puzzled.

'How could they have come by the bell though? I mean the *Madeira* sank without trace, didn't it?' Jenny said.

'Shit, yeah, but someone could have taken it off before it sank.' I shook my head.

Jenny stood up 'That's what I just said.'

We pondered in silence. Then I noticed the fork Dave had found lying on the table. The 'S' and 'IRA' made sense now, the taunting irony of hindsight.

'That's it, the fork! Someone could have taken a bell, it's the heart of the ship and unique, but who'd take a bloody fork?' Scousers sprang to mind, but on a serious note I felt confident now that we had found the lost steamship *Madeira*.

I picked up my cup and walked to my thinking place at the window. Jenny meanwhile buried her head in several books. One called 'Missing Treasure of Lost Shipwrecks' held her attention.

'My God,' she said softly and looked up at me. 'Look at this, Kris. Come here and have a look.' She glanced at me humbly, then down at her finger, which was pressed hard on the page.

*'SS MADEIRA Nov 17, 1914. Ship British. Built 1884. Last reported North West of Ushant. Rout West Africa to U.K. Cargo, **Gold specie.**'*

She looked at me again. 'Well, what do you think about that?'

I was lost in thought. Hell, this was getting big. Gold specie was money in the form of coins and these were gold coins. Surely they wouldn't list them as cargo unless there was a respectable quantity on board? I felt a rush of excitement flood through every vain.

After polishing the bell we sat staring at it.

'Shouldn't we report it to the receiver of wrecks?'

I thought for a while then gave my reply. 'We will in time, but not just yet. We've got to confirm its identity all over again. You would think with the gold coin and a named bell it would be a definite, but as we said, if the bell was cargo and someone had lost the coin you found, we could be barking up the wrong tree altogether.'

'What can we do then?'

'We'll have to get the specifications from the builders if we can. The boiler size and type, or a maker's name plate off the engine or something like that. It's back to searching.'

'I'm at university till the weekend, but I could help you in the evenings. After all, we are partners in this.'

'No problem.'

'No problem?' She pulled a face.

'I'm sorry. Of course I would like you to come around.'

'Fine then.' She picked up her keys. 'I'll see you in the week.' She winked then was gone, leaving only the provocative aroma of her perfume.

I sat in thought. She's such a good kid; but I shouldn't have got involved. She made all the moves though. I smiled as I reflected on our erotic encounter, which still felt like a breath of cool oxygen lingering inside me.

I had been on the phone all the next day but had gleaned no useful information. The records of the ship builders were eluding me. Most of them were long gone along with their records, destroyed by wartime bombing raids and fires. My search eventually led me to the library at the University of Glasgow where I received the first positive response. They had lots of records from the busy Clyde side shipbuilding days. Two choices remained. Go to Glasgow, or to contact the Salvage Association, which works in alliance with marine insurance underwriters. The problem with showing our hand so early worried me, as a lot of interested parties closely monitor such organisations to get information on such sites. If there was a lot of gold down there and news leaked, we would be watched day and night. Also if someone got a sniff of our interest in the *Madeira* they might draw up a salvage contract with the underwriters and gain the rights to it themselves, despite not knowing where it sank. After explaining all that to Jenny, we decided to wait and dive the wreck again.

I stopped my old pickup outside the dive shop and started carrying the heavy cylinders inside. Rich, the dive shop owner, sat with his feet on the counter, reading a Bits magazine. He grinned. 'Hi mate, how's it going?'

'OK.' I placed two bottles down onto the chipped red painted concrete floor. 'Could you top these up for me?'

'Yeah, sure. Lurch? Lurch, get in here!' He shook his head. 'You just can't get the bloody staff.'

A tall big-framed youth burst through the dirty coloured strips of plastic that hung in the doorway. 'If I'm Lurch you must be the Thing.'

Rich rolled his magazine and it made a loud pop as it landed on the lad's head. 'So where have you been diving lately?'

'Ah, just the usual stuff.' I replied while looking down at the trendy coloured diving gear behind the glass counter.

'I hear that Ginger Jenny is… well, you know.'

I looked up. 'Nah, she's only crewing for me.'

A voice from the back shouted, 'Bloody baby snatcher!' I looked at Rich.

'He's has always fancied her you know. Anyway, you should know you can't shag a skate around here without everyone knowing about it. Is she as fit as she looks, then?' He pulled a stupid smile.

'Leave it out, pal,' I snapped. 'I told you. She's crewing.'

'Crewing, screwing…whatever?' He raised his eyebrows.

'You're vulgar imagination must be quite a handicap when you're mixing gasses. A shapely arse passes by and someone gets a death mix. Anyway, how much do I owe you?'

'Nothing, just keep the punters coming this way for their air fills.'

'Cheers. There's another twelve coming this weekend.'

'Good.' Rich smiled while rubbing his hands together. 'Send them in. What's she like then?' He winked.

I shook my head. 'You don't give up do you?'

'It's official, mate. Ferret told us.'

'That cretin. How can you believe anything he tells you? He has trouble timing his breathing!'

'The car mate, her old banger is always in your drive. You can see it when you pass The Lodge.' He looked at me. 'All hours apparently. Are you doing a bit of night diving together?' He chuckled, I remained silent.

Then a voice from the back shouted, 'Has she got a ginger minge then?'

Rich burst into laughter. I shook my head, but failed to contain a smirk.

Rich raised his eyebrows again. 'It's OK mate. It'll be our secret.'

As I loaded the last bottle onto the pickup the local rogue, Ferret, appeared near the van. I noticed him sniff the air like a nervous rodent. He enquired in a deep local accent.

'Where you diving to? Seen any Pollock out there, Bass?'

I looked down at him. 'Not a lot.'

'I seen you with that Jenny.'

'You've seen me with Jenny? Course you have you silly bugger, she's my crew girl.'

'All right, all right, what's your problem?'

'You are, spreading around false rumours about us.'

'I seen her car there.' He wiped his nose on his cuff then smiled like Steptoe's dad. 'Like em young, do ya?'

'I told you, she's my crew. She's parking there, you moron.' I brushed him aside to open the door. He squinted and sniffed loudly several times.

'I knows where ya diving to.'

'So does half the country. I run a dive charter boat, or haven't you sussed that one out yet?'

He frowned suspiciously at me with his mouth-hung open. 'Clear off and get a bath, or something, better still, jump in the harbour. You stink like a boiled crab!' I climbed into the van and drove off. Looking into the mirror I could see him mumbling to himself while scratching his stringy beard.

The weekend's chartering passed successfully without incident so we had an early night, as the forecast was favourable to dive the next day. It was perfect weather so we hastily prepared to dive the wreck site again.

Leaving at first light, to avoid being seen by anyone, we slipped the mooring and proceeded out to sea. I dived first and secured the anchor line onto the boiler so we could use it as a reference point.

The water was rather cloudy caused probably by the storm and subsequent swell, which made locating Jenny's 'long thingy thing' difficult. Searching in a northerly direction for about twenty minutes, I ended up at a large fan shaped piece of steel. Lying next to it was a large rusty iron propeller. Although disguised heavily with sponges and anemones I could clearly distinguish the shapes of its blades.

'Yes,' I said to myself as I scanned the pile of twisted metal for clues, and after ten minutes searching the remains of the stern, I found something interesting. It was a round shaped object. It had a flat top and was clearly made of brass as the swirling sand had worn one side of it, like it had been polished every day. It was about twelve inches across, but try as I might I couldn't pull it out. I cursed myself for not bringing a crowbar. Finally after a great deal of physical exertion, which left me breathless and with stars darting in my eyes, the object gave a puff of black silt, as it reluctantly broke free.

Now I had to get it to the anchor line. I pulled and pulled but it wouldn't move, so I had a closer look and found a shaft about fifty millimetres thick connected to its base.

A shrill beeping sound made me swear even more as my decompression computer sounded again. I quickly tied my reel to the find, and then made my way back to the anchor. I secured the line tied to the find to the anchor chain then I began my ascent.

I swore more repeatedly out of frustration as I told Jenny about the dive. Jenny passed me a hot drink.

'Don't worry, Cock, I'll get it for you,' she mocked in a Yorkshire accent, as if relishing the challenge that had just beaten me. She picked up the hacksaw.

'Do you know how to use one of those?'

'Yes, of course I do, we do commercial work at the University as well as academic work you know.'

I grinned and shook my head.

'And what's that stupid smirk supposed to mean?'

I backed off. 'You'd better take…'

She interrupted. 'A spare blade?' She pushed the hacksaw into my view and pointed at the spare blade taped to it.

'I don't know a Nerds work is never done.' She inserted her mouthpiece, gave a little wave and rolled over the side.

Jenny must have made light work of the shaft, and in a little while obviously had the object rolling along the seabed towards the anchor line, I could see her bubbles slowly advancing towards it.

With Jenny and the object safely on board I moved *Westwind*, snapping the thin sacrificial line that connected the tripped anchor to the boiler. As we drifted slowly in the tide Jenny got changed while I got on with a well-practised ritual of making the bacon and egg sandwiches.

'Who's this?' Jenny shouted as she rose to her feet half-dressed, revealing skimpy pink pants. I stood up. About ten metres away and approaching directly on our bow was Ferret's small open boat.

'The shifty bastard,' I cursed. 'He's sneaked up on us from out of the sun.'

'Good morning,' Ferret shouted and waved as he passed several metres away.

'What on earth is he doing?'

'He's trying to mark our position on his plotter, the scavenger. It's a good job we've drifted in the tide well away from the wreck; otherwise he would have found all the fish shoals with his echo sounder.'

'He must suspect that we've found something.'

'Yeah. Obviously he's after the fish and shellfish. He'd lay so many crab pots and nets on it; it would be equivalent to erecting a neon sign saying 'New Wreck Here.' He's not as daft as people make him out.'

'He's lived here all his life,' Jenny mumbled, having a mouth full of sandwich. She raised her hand to her mouth in embarrassment.

I laughed at her then my face changed to a mean glare as I turned my attention to the sly intruder who was busily staring at his navigation instruments in an attempt to locate our wreck site.

Back at The Lodge, I plugged the angle grinder into the socket. The grime filled the air as the wire brush turned the calcium into obnoxious dust, making us cough and splutter in chorus. Then the letters started to appear. 'John Hastie & Co Ltd. Greenock, No 3516.'' 'Excellent, we've got you now.'

After cleaning ourselves up we examined the object and with the help of one of my books identified it as being the head of an emergency steering binnacle that would have been fitted on the stern of the vessel, directly above the rudderstock.

'God, this is getting really exciting. I'm going to take a few days out to help with the search.'

'No, you can't do that Jenny,' I replied, which caused her head to snap around.

'Is that it? Just...' no, you can't do that,' she said with a look of indignation.

'Yeah, well you can't.' There was an uncomfortable silence. 'Look, all this could be one big goose chase. Even big salvage firms have poor success rates and take a long time. We've got a long way to go yet. You just don't give up years of studying on a hunch like this.'

She stood up. 'Is this a hunch then?' She held up the sovereign then dashed to the book stamping her finger on it so hard that it was bending back on itself. She cleared away her hair, as her temper rose. 'And this, oh and the bell I found and that round thing we got today,' she pointed to the steering head. 'There's a lot of hard facts in our hunch don't you think?' She was getting fired up standing with her hands on her hips eyes staring wide. 'Well? Well?' she shouted through her now gritted teeth.

'Jenny calm down for God's sake, it could take years before we find anything, it could be ten metres below the sand, that's if there is anything there.'

'You can't push me out now!'

'You've got to go to college.'

'Ugh' She clenched her fists. 'How many times, it's a university I go to, not a duff fucking college.'

'OK, OK, but you still have to go.' I looked down, avoiding her angry eyes. 'You're doing so well. Your studies are more important than a hit and miss treasure hunt. Christ, you're gifted with a brain that could stop a watch and you want to waste it on a long shot. It's your whole future at stake here, all the studying you've done. You can't re sit exams this time. The wreck will still be there next week.' Her face gave me a stern (Shut the fuck up) look.

'A few days off won't matter. It's not a big deal. What if someone else found it while I was sat in a classroom sniffing mud? How would you feel then?'

I stared out of the window in silence.

'Loads of students take time out, everybody does it, everyone, hell, how many people find gold…and treasure every day?' She slumped onto a chair.

'This is a really important year for you, Jenny. I won't be responsible for you blowing it on …on a long shot that I've instigated.'

'God, you sound just like my fucking dad.'

I closed my eyes and drew a deep breath as her words battered me.

She bounced up and turned to me. 'I'm sorry, I'm so sorry I should never have said that. I just get so angry sometimes, I've got such a short temper and I want this more than anything.'

'I think you'd better go, Jenny. It's getting late now.'

She stood with her hands hung by her side looking helpless. I broke the painful stand off by turning to the window again. She snatched her coat from the back of the chair, making it bounce noisily on the stone floor. 'And my name isn't fucking Uri Geller.'

The door banged shut. I swore out loud as the stem of my glass smashed off from banging it down onto the fireplace. Outside in the lane I could hear Jenny fumble clumsily with the gear stick while crunching the gears. She stalled the car and I saw her beating the wheel through the small tower window

The weekend charter was really hard without Jenny helping. Despite leaving several messages on her answer machine in an attempt to put things right, she had not been in touch, she was one stubborn girl. She had unwittingly become more than 'just crew' but everything felt wrong. I knew if I kept encouraging her, I could mess her life up big time. Sixteen years, sixteen years, how many times had I heard that in my mind? In two years' time I would be forty. She would be only twenty-four and in her prime.

Chapter Three

Dear Mr Woods,

Thank you for your enquiry. Unfortunately our records of the maritime industry for Clydebank are vast and as yet have not been fully indexed. However we would have no objections should you wish to visit our records department. If you would contact me through the reception, I will gladly arrange a date and assistance for you on your visit.

Yours sincerely,
Barbara Sutton.

The old pick up was fine for running around locally, but a trip hundreds of miles to Glasgow would be taking the proverbial piss, and I'd probably end up leaving it steaming its heart out in some isolated lay-by, and have the police tracing me for abandoning it. Or I'd end up paying a small fortune for a tow off the motorway to the scrap yard, where some guy sucking through his teeth would tell me it would cost thirty quid to dispose of it in an environmentally friendly way. So I decided to go into the town and enquire about hiring a car for the long journey.

Walking up the steep tree-lined lane that led to the local hive of civilisation my mind wandered. What if there is a lot of gold on the wreck? What would I do with the money? I didn't owe anything on my property, or the boat. I had some savings left, part of which was from the compensation from the disaster, but I secretly despised it and preferred to live off the charter work.

The roar of modern life gradually became louder as I entered the maze of narrow built-up streets. It was another world compared to my tranquil home. Jenny was the first woman I'd been with since Vicky. I had succumbed to the girls of the night for comfort during the early days of drunken despair, and got all the way into a bedroom once, but it all felt so false and phoney. I shied away at the last minute, paid the girl and ended up slobbering over a KFC in a shop doorway, analysing myself.

A pinkish Ford Ka was all that was available from the only hire company I could find. I went through the procedures and paid the money, then drove out of the forecourt feeling slightly embarrassed.

The clouds had cleared away and there was little wind penetrating the narrow street and the sun blazed down relentlessly. Stuck in a queue of holiday traffic while following the overloaded one-way system my eyes locked onto a shapely girl who was walking along the pavement. She was dressed in the shortest of skirts and had lovely sculptured legs. I was getting replays of her each time I caught up to her up in the slow moving column of cars. I was approaching her again when a loud jolting bang rudely interrupted me.

What a Muppet! I cursed myself for not paying enough attention on the car in front. 'Shit,' I snapped then stared, taken aback as Jenny rushed out from her dented red Clio.

She glared, and started tapping aggressively with her key on the half open window. I rolled the window down and she followed it.

'You stupid fool! Err…' Her face changed from anger to total surprise. 'Kris?'

'I'm sorry, Jenny,' I replied. She paused for a few seconds then glared at me.

'You're sorry for what?'

'Sorry for hitting your car.'

'Fuck the car!' I reeled back at her aggressive response. Her clear brown eyes stared wide open at me, her pose demanded an answer. Seconds passed then horns started to sound.

'You're sorry for…?'

I sighed. 'I'm sorry for being a sanctimonious prick. I suppose.'

'Apology accepted,' she replied with indulgence then stood upright and frowned.

'What are you doing in that gay little car?'

The busy reception bustled with people of all shapes and sizes as they hurried around with armfuls of books and papers. We were lead to a large fusty smelling room, and introduced to a Miss Gallbraith. Her voice didn't fit her features: she was small and thin, with beady eyes and a pointed nose. She looked like she'd survived an undernourished life.

'John Hastie & Co Ltd,' she repeated nonchalantly, in a hard Glaswegian accent. 'Follow me.' Tons of papers in cardboard boxes filled the tall shelves all the way up to the ceiling, and our voices sounded subdued by the strange acoustics. The place smelled extraordinarily stale.

'This lot.' Miss Gallbraith gesticulated with her hands to a wall of boxes.

'There's hundreds!' Jenny said in awe.

She cocked her head and stared like a witch. 'Not enough for you?'

'No, no, I mean they're all records from the one company?'

'No,' she answered in a patronising tone. 'Start from the top, mind, or you'll get buried alive. Call me if you need assistance.'

'Holy shit.' I looked at Jenny. 'I had no idea there would be this much.'

'That's why it's not catalogued. It would take a decade.' She looked up and around. 'See, I knew you would need a hand. Come on then,' Jenny said as she pulled the wheeled steps into place. 'Let's make a start.'

At four-thirty Miss Gallbraith appeared as if on wheels, floating ghostlike in her floor sweeping skirt. 'Have you found what you're looking for, yet?'

'No,' we sighed in harmony. She grinned back in a satanic way, paused and peered over her glasses. 'Some spend weeks in here before giving up.'

'That's encouraging,' Jenny said as she stood upright, dusting off her hands.

I slid a box back in its place and descended the steps. 'Can we return tomorrow please?'

'Aye lassie, nine-thirty the doors open.' She held both hands together in a furtive manner. 'I'll be here, I always am.'

'She's so spooky,' Jenny complained as we walked to the car park. 'Did you feel her eyes piercing the back of your head?'

'Yeah,' I agreed. 'She makes you feel like it's her personal records we're going through.'

Miss Gallbraith was at her sentry post, which was an old oak desk that could have been used as part of the set in a Dickens play. A pen and clerical stuff was laid out perfectly symmetrical on it. She'd probably worked here all her life.

'Good morning to you.' She followed us closely. 'What exactly are you looking for?' We hurried to the steps feeling we were being chased.

'Just some information on something we found on a shipwreck.' Jenny replied over her shoulder.

'Is it for salvage of valuables or book research?' We stopped and turned to her with a surprised look. 'Ah, you've found something.'

'What makes you ask that?' Jenny replied leaning forward holding both hands on her hips in a defiant manner.

'I can tell. Book researchers study in detail just about everything they find and copy each find meticulously. You're looking for one thing and there's always a reason for that.' She turned and walked back to her sentry post. 'Always a reason,' she repeated in a distant mumble.

Jenny turned to me. 'Hell, she is a bloody witch.'

'Not as daft as she first appears,' I added, as I cast a suspicious glance in her direction. 'We better be discreet here. She's too nosy, I don't trust her.' Jenny nodded in agreement.

All day we searched to no avail.

'Still no luck then? I flinched notably as Gallbraith materialised from nowhere. 'Tell me what you're looking for. I might be able to help.' I turned. Behind her Jenny was vigorously shaking her head.

'We've found some information, thank you very much. We'll pop back again tomorrow morning if that's all right.' The old woman just nodded in silence.

Jenny shivered noticeably as she sat in the car. 'She's so creepy.'

'As I said, too bloody nosy, hell, I thought you were going to kick off for a moment when I saw your hands go on your hips and you started swaying.' Jenny remained silent.

'I've got an idea.'

'You surprise me.'

'Cheeky sod. An old mate of mine, Ronny, lives near here. We could look him up and have a few beers.'

'Yeah,' Jenny replied with enthusiasm. 'That would be great. Who's Ronny?'

'We were working together for a few years. No! On the second thought he'll probably be away.'

She nodded in thought then turned to me. 'What were you working on?'

We were saturation divers working offshore, real deep work.'

Jenny smiled.

'What?'

She smiled again. 'You don't often mention your past. That's good, Kris.'

'You're studying Marine Biology, not psychology.'

'Men are really just like crabs you know.'

'What?'

'They are tough outside, but squishy inside.'

That evening we ate at the hotel. Jenny turned in early while I had a few drinks at the bar. I had decided to cool our relationship which seemed to be accelerating a little too fast. I couldn't accept the age gap and especially being labelled a baby snatcher. I arrived at the room to find her fast asleep so I slipped quietly into the bed.

I woke with a start again and Jenny called out to me. I'd been suffering from the nightmare again; maybe sharing a bed after being alone so long was affecting my subconscious and screwing with my head. I lay sweating and breathless.

Jenny clunked around the mini bar and returned with two glasses of brandy. 'Sit up Kris, I think you need to talk. Those nightmares aren't going away. You were shouting her name repeatedly.' She passed a glass and sat on the bed.

I took a laboured breath. 'I was working in the Dutch sector on a construction rig. We had a few days leave ashore so they flew out to meet me. We had a wonderful time, you know, on the joy rides, teddy bears, candy floss and stuff like that.'

I paused, as Jenny's small hand moved on to mine. 'I... err... I couldn't get a convenient flight home for them, so I put them on a ferry.' Jenny's eyes widened as did her mouth. I turned to her with an unfocused gaze.

'Not the Herald of Free…? Oh my god.' She gasped.

I was defenceless; tears rolled down my face. 'I should have been there… I - I could have done something if I'd been with them. Water's my job, all my life I've... I know I could have saved them. Hell, it's been almost three years and it's still shredding my insides like a razor.'

I couldn't stop my hands from shaking. Jenny noticed and moved closer. I took a gulp and stared into the glass. 'I was one day into a ten-day saturation dive, quite a deep one. When back on the rig, in-between shifts, a small portable TV used to get shoved against one of the portholes of the accommodation chamber so we could see the news and soaps. I'll never forget the sight of the ferry as it lay on its side. We crammed our heads together to get a closer look at the little screen, and then one of the lads spoke out its name. I sat in silence as I worked out the time of events. As hard as I tried not to, I kept coming to the same conclusion. I didn't tell anyone. I don't know why. I suppose I was wishing away the inevitable, but there was so much coverage about it on the news and with divers being called in from all over to help search for survivors, it was of interest to everyone. Being a member of a close team I was soon sussed out. I eventually cracked up and got changed out. I was in no fit state to dive and had become a liability. The two-day decompression was the longest two days of my life, knowing what was waiting for me outside of the little world I was cocooned in. A cold feeling stalked and eventually took over me, I knew it, I felt it… I would never see them again, shiny eyes, the smiles that stir up your insides and make you feel all is worthwhile, I just knew that they were gone… no more hugs and all that good stuff that made my life complete, committed to a life of memories…oh fucking hell… why me?'

I gathered myself. 'I learned later from one of the salvage divers working for Smit International that they had to prise my little girl from her mother's arms. I see them in the dream; I try to pull them out, but can't reach them. I fail them every time.'

Jenny rose onto her knees and held me to her chest, taken aback in silence as suppressed emotion flooded from me. I'd lost the plot completely and sobbed like a kid.

'You have to let go Kris, you've got to put it behind you, they wouldn't want you to suffer like this anymore. Give them smiles not tears, think of the good times. If they could look down and see you like this, how would they feel?' I noticed her eyes were glistening; she sniffed and drew an uneven breath and smiled bravely forcing tears to run down her freckles, then she started talking about the wreck and the bell. I must have fallen asleep in her arms.

Gallbraith lowered her gaze from the old clock on the wall.
'Losing interest are we?'
'No, we just had a cosy cuddle in our king sized bed.' Jenny replied in a flippant manor. Gallbraith glanced at Jenny's bare finger, presumably for a ring then clucked disapproval.

It was approaching two p.m. when Jenny whispered, 'Kris, Kris, look at this.'

I moved to her. Still whispering she continued, 'Barclay, Curle & Co. Look it's the right year.'

I held the thick folder of hand-written papers that were tied together with a red ribbon and hastily untied the bow.

'Look for any mention of John Hastie of Greenock.' Shuffling through the neatly written pages, which mostly contained lists of parts and order requisitions, I uncontrollably hissed with excitement. 'I've found it.'

An order list detailing twenty or more brass auxiliary steering columns complete with direction indicators and eight-spoke mahogany wheels, all fitted with a brass hub, lay before us. Each one had the maker's number and which ship they were ordered for. It stuck out of the page as if it was embossed an inch high. No: 3516. Ship *SS Madeira*. Barclay, Curle & Co. The year was 1884. We looked at each other with contagious smiles.

'You've found what you're looking for, I presume?'

We turned in shock like surprised kids. She must have materialised from the dust.

'Hmm.' she looked at the open documents. 'Do you want those copying?'

'Err, please just this one.' I replied feeling guilty, having avoided confiding in her. 'You're not the first to look up that file you know. Ships that were built in our yards and then later sank, while carrying valuables are tracked down to here. There is two of interest in this file, if I'm correct. I think I can guess which one you're interested in. If you had mentioned the name *Madeira* you could have saved yourselves three days. As I said before, all the book researchers, whose work probably enticed you here, visit regularly.' We looked each other in shock, feeling totally stupid.

'People don't take into consideration that I've been here all my working life. Still, what would an old woman like me know about,' her eyes turned sinister, 'deep sea treasure hunting?'

After escaping Gallbraith's tongue whipping and piercing hawk eyes we retreated to the car.

'Bollocks, three days wasted.' I gasped as I slammed the door and slumped into the seat.

'How the hell did she know?'

'Simple, I suppose. She probably remembers it being built. No seriously, we've just walked a well-trodden path and she noticed us on it.'

Jenny huffed. 'She made us look so stupid.'

'I feel bloody stupid.'

'Yeah, I bet she loves doing that to everyone. She had the last laugh all right.'

'Hmm, I bet the old bag was dripping with excitement like a George Forman grill.'

Jenny screwed her face. 'That's an awful thing to say.'

I grinned and turned the ignition key.

I passed the glass to Jenny and we drank a toast. 'The *Madeira*.' Jenny gazed at her fizzing drink. 'Do you really think there could be lots of gold down there?'

'Well things are looking a lot more positive, yeah I reckon there could be enough to see us all right. That old crow might have found us out, but we know where she sank and no one else does.'

Chapter Four

It was almost two weeks since our Scottish experience. We were desperate to get out to the wreck, but had to honour the dive charters. This particular weeklong charter was now at its end and after the last divers had finished removing the final bits of kit from *Westwind* her deck came clean and uncluttered once again.

We sat on the gunwale with our legs dangling over the side, tired but glad to be alone after a week of ear bashing. We pulled the ring pulls together and nursed our cold tins of cider as the divers' small convoy of vans and cars headed back to take on the M25 car park and their crowded city existence.

I sighed. 'Was that hard work or what?'

'They were,' Jenny grumbled. 'Five days of molly-coddling all those novices.' She took a swig, but was cut short.

'Twelve pool hardy nuggets.' I added.

'You have to take the rough with the smooth,' Rich joined the conversation as he approached us.

'You said they were all experienced.'

'Padi divers get signed up in all liquids, you should know that.' Rich grinned as he pulled out a wad of notes then began to pay us in cash.

'It was their first bloody sea dives,' I grumbled. 'They trained inland, in a quarry.'

Rich made a feeble attempt to look surprised. 'It wasn't, was it?'

'You knew it was,' Jenny interrupted. 'You trained them. So what was your cut, you haven't earned the nickname, 'Richey Rich' for nothing.'

'She's a fine boat,' Rich said, changing the subject. Then he looked seriously at me. 'You know when you went away a couple of weeks ago. I don't want to appear nosy, but was it to plan a salvage operation?' Jenny's head turned, I stopped counting and looked up at him.

'No why?'

'It might be nothing, but most of the dive shop owners down the coast have had calls from some geezer asking who, around these parts, has got a boat capable of working offshore. The thing is, Kris, he's asking particularly for a six-foot, fair-haired guy with blue eyes, who's accompanied with a younger ginger girl with a distinctive Devon accent and a bit gobby apparently.' He grinned at Jenny. 'Does anyone spring to mind?'

We looked at each other speechless then Jenny glared at Richey and pulled at her hair. 'It's called auburn, stupid.'

'Just thought I would let you know mate, in case you can think of any folk who fit that description.' Pushing upright and holding on to the shiny rail, he looked at the money he'd just passed me. 'It's all there, skipper.' He nodded. 'Less my ten percent of course. See you guys later.'

'What was his name?'

'Wouldn't say mate, but he was pushy, oh yeah, sounded a bit like you. A Northern terrier I think.' He grinned back at us. 'Keep sending in the punters, mate. Be seeing you.'

We moved into the wheelhouse.

'How the hell could this happen?' I said as I paced up and down, 'I've told no one. You haven't. It must be that old hag from Glasgow. She must be getting paid for spilling information on people researching there. I knew she was fishing for information.' Jenny remained silent and looked a little uncomfortable.

'The old crow! I said she was weird.' I continued then noticed Jenny wasn't facing me.

'Jenny?' She turned. 'What is it?'

'It was me. I said something to my mum.'

'You, what do you mean?'

'When we had words I was upset and in my room, crying. Mum comforted me and I told her everything. I was so upset at the thought of us falling out after all we'd done together. I didn't mean to do any harm.'

'Your mum wouldn't have said anything, surely?' I noticed she cast an empty glance at the deck.

'Tell me Jenny.'

'I'm a local here. Ferret was once married to an auntie of mine. I told her to say nothing to anyone, but she thought I was upset because of you, and she does gossip a lot at the bingo hall.'

'What time is it?' I looked at the clock. 'Shit, it's too late.'

'Too late for what?'

'Contact the Salvage Association. It's the only thing we can do now, that's if our mystery man hasn't already.'

She looked confused. 'Already what?'

'Gained a salvage contract to work the *Madeira*, you know like I mentioned before.'

'Could they do that?'

'Yeah, of course. All they have to do is select an area to search and agree a share percentage and the underwriters will grant them a note of authority. They have nothing to lose and everything to gain, and it would shut us out.'

'Yes, but we can dive our wreck while they are searching miles away.'

'No, no Jenny. They must know from the witch that we were looking to identify the steering head; they will know now that we have found it, and about your sovereign. All they have to do is watch us and wait. Doing that could save them thousands and lead them straight to the wreck.'

'Yeah, but we're sort of hidden here aren't we?' Her searching expression waited for a hopeful reply.

It's probably leaked out of the village by now. Everybody involved in salvage knows what the others are up to. They make it their business to know.'

She moved close to me with a small child troubled look and before I could say more she said quietly. 'Sorry,' she rested her head against my chest.

Our cuddly moment was crudely interrupted by a loud air horn. Ferret bobbed his head up and down as he slowly passed us, and then waved grinning with satisfaction at catching us together.

I slammed the phone down so hard it bounced off its base and on to the floor. 'How dare they do it, the bastards!'

Jenny rushed into the room. 'What is it?'

'International Salvage and Recovery, they call themselves. It's just as I feared. They have already approached the SA for a contract.'

'Oh no, Kris. It's not fair.'

'There's nothing fair in this corrupt world, especially in this country. They agreed a contract yesterday. Yesterday! What a fucking bonehead! Why didn't I do it earlier?'

'I haven't seen you this angry before.' Jenny looked unsettled.

'You've seen nothing yet.' I picked up the phone again. I heard Jenny turn off the shower; she obviously had heard me talking, she appeared wrapped in a towel and stood listening.

'Get this down on paper please, yes now, yes, when he comes back into the office, please give him it personally. *We* have found and have proved the identity of the SS *Madeira*, which sank Nov 17 1914. Whoever calls themselves International Salvage and Recovery are lying to you and trying to defraud us, we have removed a sample gold sovereign and declare ourselves the Salvers in possession…yes, Kris Woods and Jenny Dean. Yes, yes. Thank you.'

I turned to Jenny. 'Well that's that. We can't do any more for the moment. Our cards are open and on the table. There's only Ferret that has an inkling of where we've been diving. Let's hope he doesn't link up with the other guy who's interested in the wreck and the Salvage Association contacts us sooner rather than later, or we could be watching the find of a lifetime sail past.' I nodded across the room 'Past that very bloody window.'

Two frustrating days passed and then a call came in.

'Jenny, they just called. The Salvage Association, they want a meeting to see our proof and if we convince them, they'll award the contract to us and cancel the note of authority they issued to those con merchants.'

She gave a screech down the phone and then went silent. 'But, but what about the others? They won't be well pleased with us…'

'Yeah, they will no doubt spit there dummies out and tell everyone that we stole their wreck, and eventually believe it themselves. Tough shit, we found it first,' I sneered. 'Bloody chancers, they just hang around like vultures waiting for people to do all the work for them, and then move in for the rewards.'

'Ah but we'll have the law on our side soon, won't we?'

'Yes we will Jenny, but how many police cars do you see eight miles out at sea?'

We were seated at the end of the largest gleaming walnut table I'd ever seen. It must have taken a small forest to make it. At the opposite end to us huddled an ever-increasing group of pinstripe suits. As each new entrant approached they suspiciously inspected our credence, first the Bell, then the steering head along with its builder's notes, but it was Jenny's gold sovereign that clearly thrilled them.

I whispered to her. 'The gold is attracting them like bees to honey.' She nodded in silence without taking her eyes of the group of executives, totally bewitched by there presence.

We were taken to an old gentlemen's club after they had satisfied themselves that our evidence was genuine, we were wined and dined like VIPs. We struggled with more cutlery than I had in my kitchen drawer, while our hosts downed enough brandy to keep Father Christmas going for the next fifty years.

We later returned to the big table, and were seated I reckon about thirty foot away from ten rich and powerful men. Maybe keeping us at a distance made them feel superior. I couldn't help noticing that they all had shiny well-fed faces, busting bellies and soft hands that had never experienced manual labour. The smell of brandy was so conspicuous if I had thrown a match at them I reckon they'd have gone up in blue flames.

'Is this the only sovereign you have recovered?' The one who appeared to be their chairman enquired loudly in a well spoken manner.

'Yes it is the only one.' I replied equally loudly. There was silence.

'How can we be sure?'

'You can't, but our being here alone proves our desire to be trusted and to be given a chance.' Jenny turned to me and smiled.

'You have obviously spent much time researching the history of this loss. What of its cargo?'

'We do have scant information that it was carrying specie, err…gold coins. You have the record that's why we're here, to find out.'

'Could you carry out a safe and legal salvage operation, within the required parameters?'

'Of course. We have a registered workboat available, we can recruit suitable personnel and I am experienced and qualified to oversee and supervise the whole operation.'

'The operation would require Submariners and R.O.V. Pilots. How large is your vessel?'

'No, you're misinformed. It is not a deep-water recovery.' I sat back down.

'That's got the buggers going,' Jenny chuckled under her breath.

'Steady,' I said quietly. 'We don't want them to think we're taking the piss.'

They conferred noisily with each other. At the same time they studied several documents. When the discussion abated the chairman stood up and turned to us.

'Our records unequivocally place this loss in an area where the depth is at least one hundred metres.' He superciliously glared at me for my reply.

I stood up. 'Well gentlemen, your records,' I paused holding their attention, 'unequivocally, are a pile of crap, wouldn't you agree, considering our firm evidence?'

They resumed their debate, hissing whispers to each other. Jenny turned to me pulling a disapproving face. 'I can't believe you just said: 'A pile of crap!'

'Mr Woods and Miss...' the man looked embarrassed.

'Dean' Jenny's voice sounded distinctly soft and feminine amid the loud male voices echoing around the big room.

He continued, 'We must agree that your evidence is undeniable by its presence. Does your trust extend as far by informing us where exactly you found these items?' The suit gesticulated with his hands at the evidence laid before him on the table.

'That request is inappropriate prior to an offer of contract,' I replied assertively. 'Nevertheless, gentlemen, I can guarantee you the wreck is not in the area where you think it is and we could conduct a quick and cost effective recovery of your gold.'

Their spokesman looked to his right hand man who paused in confusion then nodded. 'Very well, we will adjourn to consider an offer.' They all stood up. 'We will resume this meeting at eleven a.m. tomorrow.' They waddled out and no doubt headed straight for their expensive crystal decanters.

I shook my head. 'They arrogantly assume we have the day off tomorrow without asking us. Don't they just piss you off?'

'God, they're like barristers.'

'He probably is one,' I smiled. 'Do you know I've got a good feeling about this now, Jenny? They're holding back and trying to glean information from us. I bet there's a bob or two on the *Madeira*.'

The coughing slowly faded like it does at the final frame of a televised snooker tournament then the spokesman slammed his big briefcase on the table scaring everyone into silence.

'Good morning, gentlemen.' He rummaged in his briefcase for a few seconds then looked up at us.

'And ladies,' I interrupted loudly, pissing on his bonfire.

'My sincere apologies my dear, we…we are rarely graced by the fairer sex, here in this establishment. Please accept my apologies once again.' Jenny gave him a polite smile.

'The steam ship *Madeira,* which you have no doubt found and identified, was carrying fifty thousand gold sovereigns at the time of its loss. It was returning from Africa. There could possibly be uninsured items on board but we have only speculation and rumours about that,' he coughed. 'We feel an offer of sixty-forty in favour of the underwriters, subsequent to a secure and complete recovery is a more than generous offer.'

Jenny was traumatised. As her mouth fell open she slowly turned her head. 'Shit! Tell me I'm not dreaming.' I ignored her while absorbedly jabbing my fingers on the big red and yellow calculator I'd bought from Mothercare. It was the only one I could find on the way here, but it was capable of calculating the offer into a figure I could relate to. I wrote down the results, and then stood up, causing an abrupt silence. I looked at my paper.

'With all respect, we feel the offer should be in our favour. We say this after taking into consideration all the risks and the costs of mobilisation, plant, personnel, standby rates and marine insurance, which ironically happens to be a cartel, controlled by yourselves.'

My reply was met with suppressed frustration, as they again busily conspired among themselves like a pit full of politicians. Then after ten minutes we were offered fifty percent, which we eagerly accepted.

The loud scream caused all heads to stare as Jenny ran around the busy street with her hands waving in the air. After restraining her we sat silently in a coffee bar. Jenny was still in a daze when I returned to my kiddie calculator.

'It's not a fortune.'

'Sorry?' Jenny replied.

'Well, it's not what I secretly hoped.'

'Tell meeeeeeee!' she said through gritted teeth.

I read from the piece of paper. 'After tax our share could be just short of two hundred and fifty grand.'

Jenny banged her fists and stamped her feet while staring wildly at me like a loony.

'That's each,' I added.

'What!' she shouted and then jumped to her feet knocking the table and spilling coffee from the cups, which ran from full saucers, instantly discolouring the posh white cotton tablecloth. 'Yes!' she repeated loudly.

I grabbed her arm and rushed her out of the shop as she continued her verbal orgasm. All eyes fell on this mad redhead as she cast an overstated smile around the surprised diners.

I braked hard on the steep incline as we approached the gate at the end of the track. Jenny leapt from the car and ran in front, arms flailing around like an excited kid returning from a holiday. She abruptly stopped and placed her hands to her mouth.

I climbed out of the car expecting to see a dead cat nailed to the door or abuse splattered on the wall.

She turned to me with a painful gaze. 'The door's wide open, Kris.'

Inside the cottage I looked around in despair. Everything was on the floor; all my precious books were thrown around, some were torn. My best crystal glass set crunched under our feet as we carefully stepped over my scattered possessions. The bedrooms were also turned upside down; almost everything was smashed and strewn around. I stood with my hands by my side and gave a heavy sigh.

From behind, Jenny's arms embraced me.

'We'll soon sort this out, come on, let's get started.'

'Just a minute,' I replied and hurried to the garage. I shook my head with anguish as I saw the slashed tyres on the old pickup, then snatched the short ladder and banged it against one of the roof joists, I opened up what looked like an owl box, and after a few clicks climbed down holding a videocassette.

'You're full of surprises,' she said.

'Someone's going to get more than a surprise for doing this.' After finding the video player and repairing the broken lead, I reassembled the system and pushed in the tape. We couldn't see their faces as they entered through the door, only their backs.

'So there were three of them,' Jenny said in a low voice. I jogged the frames as they reappeared, leaving through the same door.

Jenny shouted, 'Oh no, that's Ferret.'

'Have you seen the other two before?'

'She held her hair back as she leaned closer to the screen, shaking her head. 'Sorry.' I stared at the paused frame. 'Who the hell is that?' I stood up and looked again at the partly visible face on the screen.

'What is it Kris?'

'I'm not sure.'

'Sure of what?'

'That one there,' I pointed at the face. 'I'm sure I've seen him somewhere, but I can't remember when or where. I just have a weird feeling about him. At least we know that lowlife Ferret knows who they are. He's made the biggest bloody mistake of his life. I'm going to pull his head off and strangle him with his spinal column.'

'Seriously Kris, what are we going to do?'

'That company who tried to deny us gaining a contract may not know about our deal just yet, but if they knew it was inevitable we would get our own contract having found hard evidence, this break-in could have been an attempt to find the wreck's position.'

'And assisted by Ferret who knows his way around here,' Jenny added.

'Christ!' I suddenly rushed towards the door. 'The boat.'

We hurried to the jetty to find the tender missing, looked at each other and then hastily stripped to our underwear and dived into the cold water.

Swimming fast and frantically, it was plain to see that *Westwind* was very heavy in the water her white load line was well below the surface.

'What's that whirling sound?' asked Jenny as soon as she climbed on board. The padlock that secured the port engine boxes had been smashed off. I heaved the heavily insulated lid open.

'Hell, what have they done?' I drove my hand into the water that completely filled the bilge and was almost covering the gearbox.

'The intake pipe has been cut. Get pumping with the manual bilge pump quickly.' Jenny started pushing the handle backwards and forwards as if her life depended on it. I hastily turned off the seawater intake and started pumping like mad at the second pump. Slowly but surly the level dropped and after an arm-aching half hour the pumps started to make loud sucking noises as air mixed with the last of the water.

'Shit,' I gasped as I slid onto my knees. 'Another hour and she'd have gone.'

'What is that whirling noise? I thought it might be a bomb.'

'That's what saved her. The noise is the electric bilge pumps dying as the batteries weakened. They must have been running for ages to flatten such a big battery bank. They saved her all right.' I gave a sigh and wiped sweat from my brow.

'Kris, the wheelhouse door is open.'

'For fuck's sake…what next?' I gasped. Before I even entered I could see that the navigation plotter had been torn from its bracket.

'Oh Kris,' Jenny stood dejected, her hands to her mouth as she sighed in desperation. They'll have all the positions and information. We'll lose everything, Kris.'

I coldly shook my head. 'No we won't.' I produced a memory disk from a hidden panel. 'There's also a copy in my wallet, it's all on here.' I waved the disk. 'I might be a…' I looked her in the face, 'sanctimonious prick, but I'm not that bloody stupid. I cleared the memory from all the electronics before we left. Come on, we'd better get ashore and get warmed up,' I looked her over; she had no bra, only a skimpy thong, she looked so sexy despite her uncontrollable shivering. I felt a little embarrassed ogling her. 'Hell, you're all goose pimpled.' She had sussed me out and frowned at me. 'We'll get the flat batteries ashore in the morning.'

Jenny wiped away the tears that hung on her cheeks as she sniffed then smiled.

'Aye, aye, Captain, you can warm me up, and then we'll fight on and crush them bad pirates.' Then she nimbly stepped onto the gunwale and dived in.

Jenny crunched the toast, sipped the coffee and looked up at me. The flames from the fire flickered and danced in her eyes. I was placing the last of the books on the shelf.

'I thought everything would be simple. We'd dive the wreck, find the gold, hand it over, receive a cheque and then retire heroes.'

I hunched my shoulders as I blew air from my nose. 'If only it was that simple. Someone knows that there is one-and-a-half million up for grabs, and untraceable.' I knelt beside her. 'We have to be very careful, Jenny Dean. I don't want you out of my sight. How long is it before you have to return to college?'

She rolled her eyes. 'Its university, how many times....' She shook her head and stared with a face full of youth.

'Yeah, whatever.'

'I've a few weeks left.'

'If we could find out exactly where they stored the sovereigns in the ship from its cargo manifest, if we could get the builders' plans, we could probably recover all of the sovereigns in one go, but we would only get one shot at it before gold fever took over.' We sat up late into the night with a bottle of rum, planning our next and probably last chance to explore the Madeira wreck.

Fish boxes flew high into the air as the pick up crashed its way along the jetty before skidding completely sideways in a screeching halt. I dashed from the cab leaving the door wide open. Sprinting around the van I jumped over the pile of trawl nets then ran towards the group of fisherman who were mending their gear on the quayside. Several were pushed into their nets as I tore through them ignoring their objecting shouts.

I was gaining on him as I saw him jump on to a trawler. It was the inside boat of six that were moored against the harbour wall. My rigger boots hit the same deck shortly after with a heavy metallic thump. Ferret leaped onto the next boat and then the next until he could run no further. He was on the last boat, and I had him trapped.

Jenny stopped running and watched the scene unfold. Then to her dismay, she recognised the trawler we were on. She jumped up and down shouting and waving her arms into the air. 'Kris, no come back, come back.' I did not register her calls; my adrenalin was pumping too much.

Ferret snatched up a long machete knife that was near the main winch. He turned his back to the wheelhouse door and started hammering it with his foot while shouting, 'Get up here, Get up here.'

I grabbed a thick rope strop that had a big rusty hook spliced on its end, then approached Ferret. Suddenly two hefty fishermen pushed through the door and instantly assessed the scene.

'Get the bastard with me!' Ferret screamed.

'Leave while you can lad,' one of the men threatened, half-heartedly.

'I've got unfinished business with this thieving shit,' I cursed.

Ferret grinned. 'You haven't met me in-laws, have ya?' There was a short stand off.

'He burgled and wrecked my house and tried sinking my boat, I'm going nowhere without some answers from this shit.' The men stared hesitatingly at Ferret then at me. Ferret then moved closer waving the machete.

'What you gonna do now, eh?' He lunged with the big knife, making me jump back. He chuckled sadistically, and then looked at the fishermen. 'Come and hold him for me,' he shouted spitefully through drawn back lips. 'I'm gonna put a big scar on this northern bastard.'

The fishermen approached cautiously, and then one picked up a metal pipe as Ferret again lunged at me laughing and snarling like a demented dog.

I retaliated by landing the hook hard against the shoulder of the nearest man. He dropped the bar as he fell to his knees holding his smashed collarbone. Ferret glanced at him then at the other man.

I made another attack, and the fisherman reeled backwards before leaping onto the next boat to make his escape.

'Come back ya fat chicken bastard,' Ferret shouted at the fleeing man.

He stood panting heavily while shooting desperate glances around. Through the corner of my eye I noticed the injured fisherman crawling towards the stern. He was also attempting an escape. They didn't want to know. It was one to one now.

'Family's not so loyal eh, or maybe not as stupid as you.'

He lunged forward again. I tried to swing the strop but the hook cruelly caught in a net that lay on the deck. I snatched in desperation, trying to free it. Ferret's face instantly transformed from one of fear to delight.

'Now what ya gonna do, ya northern bastard?' He swung the big blade from side to side in slow motion and then made another swipe at me. I dodged sideways, which caused my boot to slip on the worn timber deck as I avoided the deadly blade. Now within range Ferret started a frenzied attack. I held up the thick orange nylon rope between my hands, blocking the savage hacks, but one blow landed on the rope at an angle, which made the blade slide along and into my clenched hand. I didn't feel any pain, just rage as my blood oozed freely over my wrist and into my sleeve. Ferret gurgled saliva through his missing teeth as he realised his success then he pointed the blade at my face moving it slowly closer and closer.

I dropped the rope and pressed my finger to my cheek. 'Cut here mate.' His weather-beaten wrinkled face took on a bewildered sneer then he moved closer. I swung my steel toecap upwards with all my strength into his balls; he gave out a sort of big hiccup as the machete fell to the deck, then his chin pressed against his chest as his face contorted with pain. I was on my feet in an instant; his hands were on his crotch now, I seized him firmly by his scrawny neck and I forced him to the gunwale.

Jenny watched helplessly as both of us rolled over the side in a ball of flailing arms and legs, disappearing with a mighty splash. As soon as I hit the water I pulled down, hard and away from the boat. When I surfaced my strong uncut hand still gripped Ferret's thin weathered neck; I could feel his stubble pricking my skin.

'You're in my world now,' I shouted into his fear struck face, then pulled him below the surface. I stared coldly at him below the water, watching him struggle, and gag, then resurface.

As he gasped for his life I levelly told him, 'Now I'm going to drown you.' I dragged him down again; he struggled hard but in vain as he convulsed and jerked wide-eyed and frantic as his lungs burned for air.

A desperate loud gasp echoed across the still water as Ferret's head popped up after almost a full minute. Onlookers starred in disbelief while being serenaded by Ferret's coughing and retching as he tried pleading for mercy.

'Who was it?' I shouted, 'Who was it?' Again I submerged his face, his hands desperately thrashed against my arms. He sucked a life saving lung full of air as his gasping mouth met the surface once again.

'For the last time, who was with you?' I shouted through gritted teeth.

'That… that salvage company,' he spoke between gasps with his lips extended fully, trying to suck in more air.

'A name, give me a name damn it, you fucking rat.'

'T…Tony Banks,' he murmured. My head must have snapped around as if I had been stuck with a cattle prod.

'Again, say the name again,' I slapped him hard on the face. Trembling and cowering again he murmured the name, 'Tony Banks.

'The other man, who was he?'

'I…. I don't know, I don't, honest.'

'Don't 'honest' me you bastard,' I pushed him under again. Through my peripheral vision I could see blue flashing lights, and there was a crowd gathering on the harbour wall. More deep gasps and spluttering poured from Ferret as he hung limp and spent from my arms.

'If I let go of you you'll sink and be dead in minutes. Who was the other man?'

'A Canadian I think, that's all I know. Please help me.' I dragged him to a mooring buoy, which he eagerly grabbed; I then pulled smoothly to the ladder where Jenny was waiting.

I received twelve stitches to my hand between my thumb and finger. Thankfully there was no serious damage done, as the area cut was just muscle. Jenny passed me a hot drink laced with a more than generous measure of my old mate, Captain Morgan.

'You're a dark horse, you are.'

'What do you mean?'

'The way you handled yourself. God, you bust them up like a pro.'

'I haven't been hidden away in this cottage all my life you know.'

'That's quite apparent.' She turned her eyes to mine. 'So what do we do now?'

'Well, we've called the police about the break-in. With them involved it should make things harder for Banks and Co to run amok, which could help give us the time we need.' We were suddenly interrupted by a sharp knock on the door. We turned in surprise, looking at the door.

'Hello, I'm from the Western News. Can I ask you a few questions?'

'Sorry mate, not now.'

'Are the rumours true about you finding an old shipwreck and a fortune in gold?'

'I wish! Where did you hear that?' I replied while laughing.

'We received a phone call.'

'Don't tell me, it was anonymous.' I gave the reporter a patronising stare. 'Someone's pulling your string, mate. We take sports divers out for a living. Here, take one of our cards. Someone's wasting your time. Did the caller by any chance have a northern accent?'

'Yes as a matter of fact, he did,' the reporter answered. He looked confused. Jenny flashed me a glance.

'That's our kid,' my brother. I shook my head grinning. 'We always play practical jokes on each other. I'm sorry your time has been wasted.'

A police car pulled up to the gate and two officers got out. I looked at the reporter.

'We got burgled when we were on holiday, if you don't mind.'

The police asked their obligatory questions, but soon left when they had no more biscuits left to dip into their tea.

What really concerned us right now was how much Banks had got to know. Just his presence on our doorstep was a major worry, but now things were getting personal we had no choice but to take drastic and risky action.

Chapter Five

I guided the big yellow road compressor with a rope as it swung on the crane's hook towards the flat space at the stern of the *Scorpion*. After much debating we decided to play it extra safe and leave *Westwind* on her mooring. We left The Lodge after dusk in the pick up. Jenny's car was left in its normal place and the usual lights were left on in The Lodge. We'd prearranged to hire *Scorpion* for a twenty-four hour bare-boat charter; she was a thirty-eight foot Aquastar workboat, which belonged to a friend and fellow charter operator who worked out of Plymouth, called Dave.

The large volume road compressor fitted snugly and we secured it with cargo webbing and ratchets. We needed the compressor to power the airlift, which if all went well, would suck away the sands of time that had built up on the site over eighty odd years. Our next stop would be the wreck.

The Salvage Association, as promised, had sent by courier a copy of the contract, which we signed and returned via the same courier. Along with the contract were the all-important ship's manifest and builder's plans, which showed the strong room. I now knew exactly to the nearest foot where to excavate for the sovereigns.

As darkness fell *Scorpion* slipped unseen out of Plymouth harbour and headed for the western side of the breakwater. If anyone was watching us hopefully taking the western end of the sound would cause confusion, but I felt sure our plan had fooled Banks and his cronies.

We steered due south and when we were ten miles out to sea, and out of range of all but military radar, we turned east putting the famous Eddystone reef and the reassuring flashing lighthouse on our starboard side.

We maintained a distance of ten miles offshore and after a six-hour steam and in total darkness without showing any navigation lights, we approached the wreck site from due south. *Madeira* lying almost eight miles from the coast made me confident that any one watching from the cliffs would be left disappointed, as the night was quite misty. I carefully checked the radar for other vessels in the area but there was nothing within miles of us. I prepared the big steel grapnel hook and laid the rope carefully to avoid knots and twists, which would only cause delays.

We approached dead slowly. 'Now,' I shouted to Jenny as the plotter's cursor occupied the same place as the mark on the screen. At the same time the wreck appeared on the echo sounder. She immediately threw the heavy grapnel into the blackness.

Scorpion wallowed for a minute then swung around and settled in the gentle tide run.

I kitted up as quickly as I could in the dim moonlight that shone down on us.

Being first down the line I had to find the number two hold just aft of the bulkhead that lay, according to the plans, about two metres forward from the boilers.

Once located, I then had to swim the anchor to the search area and secure the mooring line there.

Everything went to plan and within ten minutes I gave Jenny two sharp pulls, the signal for her to pay out slack on the mooring line.

Twenty-five metres below her, I dragged the heavy anchor to the boilers and secured it by wrapping the chain around a protruding flange face half a dozen times.

Resting for a minute on the north end of the boiler I shone my torch on the seabed and could just make out a rusty line made by the partly dissolved bulkhead. I marked the area with light sticks, snapping them to life with loud crunches and then made my ascent tying a light stick every ten metres along the anchor line.

Jenny I knew would be transfixed to the down line and waiting for a bright ball of light to appear.

'Everything's all right?' Jenny asked in a desperate whisper.

'Yeah, fine. We're on the job.'

Back on deck I helped her kit up. 'I think your long thingy thing is the remains of the number two holds bulkhead, the strong room according to the plans was located directly above. I've marked off the area to excavate with a ring of light sticks. Get the airlift down as quickly as you can, and if you have any bottom time left give me five bells on the air line and I'll turn the air on.'

She turned to me and I noticed with concern that her face was full of apprehension, almost scared; again I became aware just how young she was.

'Are you OK?'

'Hmm,' she nodded nervously.

'Listen, you keep on the line, it's easy. The torch is powerful. It's just a normal dive. You be careful, kid.' I gave her arm a double squeeze.

Her white teeth gave away her smile, then, in a gush of bubbles, she was gone, leaving me alone and fidgeting with sudden apprehension.

Jenny would see the light sticks appearing then fading into the scary darkness. They would reassure her as she struggled with the heavy airlift, which would be sparkling with green phosphorescence in the obscurity, as if it were electrified. She would have to lift the loop that held the airlift over every light stick, enabling it to slide down the mooring line. Gradually she would see the welcoming green fairy ring of light appear out of the blackness.

I could visualise her every move. She would be turning on the torch about now and positioning its beam on the seabed, and then she would, as I always did, sort her weight belt and bottle straps out and get herself into a comfortable position. My thoughts were pleasantly interrupted by five double tugs on the airline, so I slowly turned on the air and with nagging anxiety I watched and listened.

She would now be waiting apprehensively and looking around at the wall of darkness, conger eels could be feet from her without her knowing. She would be imagining that unseen monsters were stalking her and probably shuddering and gasping heavily through her mouthpiece then the airline would all of a sudden become ridged as it filled with air and hopefully would take her mind off the surrounding hunters.

On the surface the sea suddenly hissed and erupted into a large mushroom of turbulent bubbles, making me even more anxious. I waited in trepidation, repeatedly glancing at my watch; I was taking a big risk. Although Jenny was a competent diver I couldn't tell, due to all the bubbles, if she was in trouble.

Ten minutes passed then the noisy air compressor shook into a quiet tick-over and the boiling sea calmed into whispering hissing bubbles, which soon disappeared leaving only a small group of saucer sized ones. Why she had stopped airlifting concerned me and I could see that her bubbles were erratic, she was surfacing.

I was even more worried when Jenny made surface. She was screaming and shouting so much that I couldn't understand her. I speedily helped her up the dive ladder as she panted and murmured something that I couldn't make out. On the deck she stood shivering uncontrollably while staring wildly at me.

'Are you OK?'

She pushed her clenched fists towards me while nodding. I put out my hands and she opened her fists dropping several glistening gold sovereigns into my hands. I looked to her face; it was pulsating and shaking with pure excitement as she pushed her fingers into her mouth and nodded, powerless to speak.

Then she burst into tears. 'I've found them, we've found them,' she repeated over and over, in-between tears and gasps of joy.

I stood grinning at her, relishing every second of her accomplishment as she described her dive while sipping a mug of hot chocolate.

'I stabbed the prongs of the dredge into the sand then carefully turned the valve handle. The whole thing shook and banged as the air rushed through it and the sand appeared to come alive as it disappeared into the tube. It made a really strange gritty sound; I focused on the streaming sand that looked almost liquid. It was mesmerising me as it ran from all directions like a big egg timer. Then totally unexpectedly, as if by magic, the corner of a worm eaten box appeared. I turned off the airlift and froze in total astonishment as a river of shiny coins streamed into the excavation hole blanketing the seabed with gold. Oh Kris, it was the most wonderful thing I've ever seen. My heart started pounding so hard it caused my body to throb as I scooped the coins into a bag, but when I turned to pull myself up the rope the bag was far too heavy to lift. Then I ran out of bottom time and had to leave it.'

Jenny had hardly excavated below thirty centimetres when she uncovered the box. The corrosive seawater had eroded and dissolved the ship over the decades and the sand over the years had levelled over what was left of the wreck. Ironically Jenny's long thingy thing was within a few metres of the boilers all along.

I cut the light sticks from the line on my way down then settled into the pleasant task of carefully filling each bag with a comfortable amount of coins before attaching an airbag. When inflated each bag slowly rode up the line to Jenny's eagerly awaiting hands. Regardless of the tide, we used our dive computers to calculate the amount of bottom time we had on each dive to frantically scoop up the alluring coins.

We dived every two hours and as each dive ended we sucked pure oxygen for five minutes to allow for the physical exertion and the overwhelming excitement we were experiencing.

Dawn arrived too soon, making us feel desperately vulnerable as we stuck out on the calm water like a big blackhead on a baby's nose.

We had recovered thousands of sovereigns by the time the sun smiled over the horizon; we stored them in upturned lifting bags, which were almost splitting at their seams under the weight.

The last bag of coins thumped onto the deck as several black dots appeared on the distant horizon.

'That's the lot,' I said as I dried my hair with a towel. 'The remains of the wooden boards that lined the bottom of the ship are clean as a whistle. We've missed sweet…Fu…nothing.'

Jenny grinned. 'There's more than fifty thousand, I'm sure of it.'

I rubbed my hands together. 'What will you do with yours?'

'Get mum and dad out of that grubby council house for a start, go on holiday with you and get a flash car and a house and err, err, anything I want! I might even marry you.'

Woo! Not so fast Ginge.' She smiled a lovely smile. I spurted out. 'Thank you steamship *Madeira*,' I saluted the water. Then I engaged the engines.

A few miles behind us, a big orange, Humber ridged inflatable appeared as if from nowhere. It had a large forward wheelhouse and it stopped exactly where we had been. It was followed by a slower, larger workboat.

'Look,' I pointed. 'There they are.'

'How can they do that?' Jenny said.

'Radar and plotter, simply place your cursor on the target and read off the position.'

'As easy as that?'

'Yeah, they located us at first light and now they think they've cracked it, that's why we had to make a move, and what a move eh? Night time, they didn't anticipate that we might work this site in the dark, with another boat… Dickheads, they couldn't get their arses out of bed.'

'Well, they will be a bit disappointed, don't you think?'

'Not really,' I laughed. 'I left one for them.'

'You didn't.'

'Yeah right in the middle on one of the planks at the bottom of the hole we dug.'

'Who is this Tony Banks geezer anyway?'

'I looked at my watch. 'Are you sitting comfortably?'

She dropped on to a bag full of gold and drew her legs around it. 'Very comfortably thank you, I'm sitting on a fortune.'

I'm sure the corners of my mouth hinted a smile as I restrained the rude comments that were resting on the tip of my tongue. 'Tony Banks. Hmm, his reputation among the cut-throat world of what are basically underwater scrap men, was, and still is, notorious. Nothing short of a gangster, he was responsible for crudely tearing historic and archaeological treasures to pieces with ten-ton grabs, operated from his former world war two-tank landing craft *Retainer*. He likes to think he is a salvage expert, when in all truth; he's just a chancer who got lucky. He started tatting wrecks in the middle seventies before everyone got in on the act, he used scuba divers as cheap labour on the strength they got free dives, but he lost at least two. You have to give him his due; he did find lots of copper and some tin, and that was when the prices for scrap were the highest ever. He's dabbled in buying and selling vessels, bodged commercial contracts, dodgy deals and night clubs. You know the usual things crooks get into.'

'Why did he call that paper then?'

'Probably to force us out and to make a rushed attempt which would give him the wreck's position, like he's just done now! Then he would have forced us off it with meatheads. They will have been watching our every move. Also, I didn't want to alarm you but they even bugged my telephone when they smashed up the lodge. That's how they got to know so much. They have been ready and waiting all right. That's Banks on the site right now.'

'How on earth do you know all this? It's like something you see on the telly, telephone bugs and gangsters.' She shook her head in disbelief.

'I come from the same town as him and knew him reasonably well. I had a boat too. We were rivals in a sense. We've played this cat and mouse game in the past. I got a chance to work offshore and left, but I kept up-to-date on what was going on in the game, out of interest really.'

'So that's how you know all about the Salvage Association and all that.'

'Yeah, it's a long time ago, but Banks I never trusted, no one in their right mind would, and I know for sure he doesn't give a shit about anyone. Missing out on this will truly piss him off; especially knowing it's me who beat him again, I'll have to watch my back for a while. Bastards like him are convinced they are elite.'

'Bollocks to them,' Jenny said, attempting to look angry but failed by grinning as she scooped a handful of sovereigns, then let them slowly fall noisily back into the bag. 'We're in the money, we're in the money.' She sang sweetly while nodding her head from side to side and smiling.

Jenny stared silently as I loaded the shotgun. I told her to stay on *Scorpion* with the engines running, while I checked around The Lodge. I knew they were probably on the wreck right now and targeting all their resources on it, but I wanted to be certain. One thing that was for sure was they would be throwing their dummies overboard in fits of rage, having being denied hours earlier, by just one guy and his twenty-two-year-old crew girl. Over one-and-a-half million pounds lost is a big 'ouch' to say the least. I didn't think they would have come near The Lodge after the police were called, but these thick-skinned bastards know no bounds. I wasn't taking any chances and wouldn't hesitate to shoot one of their feet off then kick them screaming into the sea in the name of self-defence.

The Lodge was safe, and after spending the remainder of the morning counting the coins and packing them into nylon sandbags, the security van arrived midday at the gate as planned. The two guards sealed each bag with security tape, placed them into a strong steel box and then secured the lid. Within less than an hour the coins were safely on their way to the Salvage Association in London and we felt a lot less vulnerable.

Dave arrived soon after. I paid him in cash and he left in his boat five hundred pounds better off, wearing a fixed smile.

The phone rang at five forty five p.m. I placed the receiver down and turned to Jenny. 'They've got them, thank God. They are over the moon with praise, they couldn't believe that we've done it so soon; they had two observers all briefed and ready to join us. Several weeks they presumed it would take. They don't care how we did it any more, or where the wreck is. They have what they wanted and without any fuss.'

'What about our share?'

'We will get a cheque in due course, that's after the government has taken its toll.'

'We've still got these.' Jenny patted the bag containing over four hundred coins; let's bury them in the woods, just in case, you know pirate treasure.' She brought her fists to her chin in excitement.

'Yeah, let's do that. It can be our little secret,' I passed her a large sparkling glass of champagne. 'To our secret,' I winked while we chinked glasses.

The banging on the door abruptly woke me. I dragged my dressing gown on and rushed to the door. I opened it gingerly and was dazzled by bright flashes then crowds of people pushed towards me firing questions, lots of questions all at once like you see on the TV.

'Is it true that you have recovered two million in gold? Is there more left out there?'

'Where did you find it? What have you done with it? Can we see some?'

'Where's the girl who found the gold?'

'Wait, wait,' I held my hands up and then Jenny appeared.

'Is this the girl who was with you when you found the treasure?'

I gave up trying to avoid them. 'She found it.' I said as I placed my arm around her.

After dozens of questions the flashes gradually ceased and the press people melted away leaving a pile of cards.

'Hell, I didn't expect that,' Jenny scratched her head.

'Neither did I, still it'll stop all the nosy villagers whispering behind our backs and spreading rumours.'

> *Goldilocks finds two million in gold sovereigns.*
>
> *'Twenty-two-year-old blonde marine-biology student, Jenny Dean, struck gold while diving on an unknown shipwreck off the Devon coast. Along with her thirty-eight year old 'Prince Charming' the love-struck adventurers scooped the find of the century from right under the noses of the country's leading salvage experts.'*

'I'm not even blonde. They get everything bloody wrong. Idiots.' She threw the paper on to the pile.

'What does that one say?'

'Ah, nothing,' she replied as she folded it tightly and pressed her foot on it. 'It's all rubbish.' I agreed, and dropped the paper with the rest on to the floor.

As Jenny left for home I cleared the pile of tabloids from the floor and carried them to the bin. Something caught my eye. I paused, then carefully picked one out and unfolded it.

> *'Stunning twenty-two-year-old student finds her thirty-eight-year-old sugar daddy a fortune in gold.'*

'Bastards! So that was what Jenny had tried to hide from me. The rotten bastards!' I slammed down the dustbin lid causing the resident doves to burst into flight.

Exactly one week from acknowledging safe delivery of the coins a cheque for five hundred thousand pounds lay on my oak table. I sat staring at it. It all seemed too easy, when was the leveller going to strike me again, I pondered. I was pleased for Jenny, what a good start for her, but what about her? I should let her mix with her own age group; I was annoyed at my weakness, and how readily my ideals selfishly melted away by her presence, or from just one smile from her.

'I've just got a bank statement, my mind's in a spin. Kris, my life has changed overnight!'

I sat down holding the telephone. 'Hey, you have to be careful, once it's gone, it's gone. You've got to invest some of it.'

'I know, but I'm going to get ourselves a nice house when I come home.'

'How's your studying going?'

'I've been dissecting bloody molluscs for days. It gets pretty boring. They stink.'

'When you have a good job that holds respect and pays well you won't complain.'

'Oh, I miss you so much, Kris.'

'Come on Jenny, don't do this. I saw what that paper said, the one you tried hiding from me. It's true Jenny, you need to be with people your own age.'

'I said I miss you.... something rotten.'

'Where are you?'

'Sat looking over the Sound. Even the sea reminds me of you. Everything reminds me of you, Kris, don't you know that...I love you.' I remained silent.

'Did you hear what I just said?'

I paused stuck for words; I was flapping like an idiot, I'd messed her up by letting 'us' go too far, it was entirely my fault and now anything I did now would be bad for her in the end. I had to cool things.

'Do you want me to come home tonight?'

'No, err, I don't mean to sound square, but you get on with your studies.'

'I feel like packing it in and doing the charters with you. As soon as I leave you Kris, I want to come straight back to you.'

'That's the last thing I want to hear, Jenny. The money won't last.'

'All that money, and I'm stuck in a room with sea slugs. Shall I?'

'What?'

'Come round now, we could go straight to bed.'

'No, no Jenny. I'm going out.'

'No you're not. You never go out, and I know how you like to…go to bed with me.'

'I, I don't want to see you, I mean like that. You know, any more.'

'What are you babbling on about, I know you, don't forget?'

'We've got to stop seeing each other.'

'No, Kris, don't start all that age difference crap again.'

'It's not crap. All I'm doing is stopping you from getting on with your life.'

'How can you say that? It's because of you I'm happy and rich and my life is great. You made me a real pirate,'

'It won't last forever.'

'We can go back to the wreck. Those men said there could be uninsured items on it.
We'd be in a real life adventure again. I'm not bothered what people think about us, sod them Kris, no… fuck them, all of them, they can go to hell, it's you I want, I just told you that I love you, I really do, Kris.'

Normally Jenny's temper would be on one by now, and dishing out abuse big style, but this time she sounded so sad, which was making things even harder for me.

'Listen, you won't want me in ten years from now! I'll be bloody forty-eight you silly sod, can't you see that? We wouldn't work; you'll want kids one day? You'd be looking after an old man when you're in your prime. Oh shit, Jenny, don't make this any harder. Please…. Jenny, are you there?'

After a long silence she softly spoke. 'You truly mean this, don't you? I just can't believe your so stupid, I, oh Kris, please?'

'The last thing I want is to hurt you.'

'You are doing Kris, big style.' She sounded so sad; I could hear her sniffing back tears.

'We can still be friends you know, go diving still…and err.' I was hopelessly waffling.

'Bye, Kris.' The phone clicked like a switch that instantly filled me with regret, as the phone's empty impersonal tone replaced her familiar voice. I placed the receiver down as a remorseful sensation of loss grew inside me. What the hell did I do that for? She was rejoicing and I've just flattened her. I walked over to the window and gazed out through foggy eyes. Reluctantly deep inside I knew it was right.

It had been weeks since that heartbreaking conversation with Jenny. The weekend charters continued without incident, but I felt something was missing, the adventure rush that we had shared so intimately now felt just like one of those fleeting dreams that leaves you sad and wanting when you wake up to reality. I missed her badly and regretted my actions.

Charter days were ordinary without Jenny on board, casting her youthful smiles. The money didn't matter right now, it felt almost crude and irrelevant, but I continued week after week, mainly not to let the divers down. Even they sensed my mood and would regularly tell me to cheer up.

Sat with a Captain Morgan after a routine day's maintenance, watching the boats pass, I felt that hollow worthlessness seeping into my life again. I was drinking far too much and knew it but really didn't give a shit anymore. Again I had lost someone special; maybe I was destined to be alone with only memories.

Then an unexpected phone call coaxed me into the town.

'Hello stranger.' Mike the barman sarcastically greeted me. 'I thought we weren't good enough for you, since you became rich and famous.'

'Pint of dry cider, please mate, and one for you.'

'An American couple has been asking around for you. They're in the snug.'

'Yeah, I know about them. Cheers mate,' I replied then walked, sipping the brimming pint.

The two strangers turned and looked expectantly towards me as I entered the small room. I instantly noticed the smell of expensive perfume dominating the regular smell of spilt ale.

'We spoke on the phone, I believe.'

The well-dressed man spoke in a strident American accent; he stood up and stretched out his hand. 'I'm Larry Stevens, pleased to meet you.'

I couldn't help staring at the beautiful woman that accompanied him. He looked far too ugly and old to be with one so stunning.

'Kris Woods.' We shook hands. His hand was big and strong.

'This is my wife, Laura,' he said, closely watching my reaction, which I sensed he had probably done before. I goggled at the goddess who smiled openly at me. I must have looked like a young squaddie at his first brothel. I felt like one in her presence.

'Pleased to meet you, Kris,' she said provocatively. Her distinctive high cheekbones and full red lips made her film star smile unique.

'And you.' I nodded, unable to take my eyes from her.

'Please sit down,' Larry requested, 'another drink?' He smiled showing his long nicotine stained horse-like teeth as he picked up his empty glass.

I thought about the saying, 'pet owners look like their pets'. Larry must have a chain smoking bloodhound. 'Yes please,' I accepted.

As Larry disappeared to the bar Laura quizzed me with her emerald cat-like eyes.

'This is a lovely part of England, Kris. Were you brought up in these parts?'

'No, I was born up north, but I've worked all over.' I felt unusually nervous during the following few minutes of silence, as the beautiful Laura studied me like a shrink would a patient. She had an air of superiority about her.

'There you go fella,' Larry smiled down at me. Mike the barman followed with Laura's drink, but caught the glass stem on the table, which caused some wine to splash on to Laura's leg. She sprang up,

'You stupid fool! Do you realise how much these pants cost?' The poor man flinched at her fierceness.

'That's a real Cornish drink, I believe,' Larry cooled the mood. He was at least six foot two; his arms were long and gangly like his face, his hands told me he'd never worked manually, but smoked heavily. He scraped his chair while sitting back down. Mike the barman made a hasty retreat as Laura continued to beat him up with her enraged glare.

'Kris, the guy who runs the dive store recommended you to us. He said you have the best dive boat around here.' A few nosy heads turned, listening in on Larry's side of our conversation.

'It's not bad,' I replied, becoming slightly annoyed at Larry's unnecessary brashness, which fell on all ears in the room.

'Kris, we want to hire you and your boat for a week's diving around the Channel Islands.'

Laura, now chilled, leant forward on her elbows and rested her chin slowly on to her hands, displaying her long perfect fingernails; she stared, smiling at me in anticipation.

'Yeah, I can see no problem, but it would have to be midweek. I'm booked over the weekends, and the tides are really strong there, its neap tides next week, but we would still have to dive the slack waters.'

Laura relaxed her pose, obviously pleased to hear my positive reply. 'When can we go?' she asked, and then slowly sipped her drink while maintaining her green eye contact.

'It would have to be Monday. I'll have to charge for the full boat, you understand.'

'Yeah, not a problem, Kris. We'll fly over and book into a hotel. Can you supply some dive gear?' Larry asked. 'We have suits and hoods only.'

'I can hire some from the dive shop for you,' I said, nodding while sneaking a look at Laura's fantastic model figure as she stood up.

'Yeah, you do that, Kris. We'll sort out all the finances when you arrive in Guernsey.'

'I'll leave on Sunday night so you can have two dives on Monday. I'll be on the visitors' pontoon at the Victoria Marina first thing Monday morning. That's in St Peter's Port.'

'That's fine, perfect,' Larry looked at Laura. 'Didn't I tell you we would find the right captain, my dear?' Laura directed her distinguished smile longingly at me, which made me think that her pet had to be a pampered Siamese cat.

After they left I returned to the bar, a little confused at their odd approach.

'What did they want then?' asked Mike.

'I just got a full week's dive charter off them.'

'What an evil, nasty temper she's got,' he gasped then bent over to me, 'Still, I wouldn't mind spending a week watching her getting her kit off. She looks like one of those models you see in those top shelf magazines.'

'So it's you who buys them all?' He went slightly red. 'Perks of the job, mate. I'll snatch a photo of her changing if you want.'

'Hey would you?' I started laughing at him as he realised I was taking the piss, but then my laughter abruptly died as I saw the big red hair.

'Jenny?' I said in a whisper.

The barman looked over his shoulder. 'So you two are history now? Money's a strange thing.'

He blabbed on like a radio through a wall as I watched her discreetly. She was with a group of young people; one lad kept putting his arm around her shoulder causing Jenny to repeatedly twist her body to dislodge it. A rush of jealously hit me and for a moment I wanted to head into the lounge and snot the guy who was pushing himself on her, then Jenny's laugh found my ears. She suddenly turned, somehow sensing I was there. Her stare was expressionless for a few seconds then it melted into a melancholy smile and she tilted her head at me. It gave me the urge to dash over the bar, hold her tightly to me and snuggle into her. Instead I lowered my head and reluctantly walked from the room, ending our brief contact as my insides began churning wildly with regret.

The crossing to Guernsey went well. *Westwind* skipped across the unseen waves at twenty knots making the journey last only four hours. On arrival I moored her safely on the visitors' pontoon at the Victoria Marina. The weather was fine and the moored yachts' rigging was pleasantly silent for a change. I poured a generous Captain Morgan and made a cheese and tomato sandwich. Ten minutes later I climbed into my cosy familiar bunk.

Ten a.m. exactly the Stevens appeared walking along the pontoon towards *Westwind*. Larry was several steps ahead of Laura whose presence transformed the wooden pontoon into catwalk.

'Hi Kris,' she smiled. 'Nice boat.' She stroked the rail while locking her gaze on me.

'Good morning. Yeah she is.'

Larry's voice suddenly boomed out. 'Sure is a fine day for scuba diving!' He threw two diving suits on to the deck. I placed them with the gear I had hired from the Aquanaut dive centre back in Plymouth.

They didn't speak much as *Westwind* slowly passed the Herm rocks. I stopped at the Little Russel reef for their first dive. The water was crystal clear and they could be seen unmistakably as they descended down the anchor line. I tidied the deck then placed the kettle on to the cooker. Jenny's 'Keep it Clean or Else' notice troubled me as I fought with the all too familiar regret.

Because it was shallow water their dive lasted well over an hour. I recovered the anchor. My experience helped me maintain contact with their steady stream of bubbles that gave away their presence. The sun was high and I soaked it all in. The cries of the gulls along with the sounds of the waves dashing on the rocks made me feel at ease in this beautiful place. Eventually they surfaced and signalled to be picked up. Back on board they remained restrained, almost disappointed.

'Did you not enjoy your dive?'

'Fine,' Laura answered while towelling her silky ash blonde hair.

'Yeah, it was beautiful down there, so much life, like a flooded garden,' Larry shouted. I acknowledged him with thumbs up then we headed back to port.

The Stevens disappeared for lunch as soon as the boat touched the jetty. I snatched beans on toast and then washed them down with a mug of tea.

Two hours later I woke to the sound of voices. 'Hello again captain Kris.' Laura smiled as she climbed aboard. My eyes secretly followed her around the deck, hidden behind my Ray Ban glasses that had been left on board by some wealthy nugget. Bent over, sifting through the dive gear, she looked so provocative. Her see-through costume left little to the imagination. Sod Mike the barman, I considered taking a photo of her for myself.

'Had the boat long?' she asked.

'Two years this month.'

'I bet she's worth a few dollars.'

'Yeah, she is. I got her brand new.' I paused. 'She's my life now.' I suddenly saw Jenny's wild hair in my mind.

'Kris is there not a woman in your life?' I got up and folded the chair away.

'Not really at the moment.'

'Ah,' she pulled her hands through her blonde bob, emphasising her perfect breasts. 'A sore point eh?'

I smiled at her, well at her breasts. 'You don't strike me as the diving type.' She turned a wily glare at me that felt intimidating. 'You'd be surprised what type I am, Kris.'

'What are you two talking about?' Larry broke the moment in his typical brash manner causing me to visualise his pet Bloodhound wearing a Texan hat.

'You're not sweet talking my woman are you now?' I smiled politely. 'She's a doll don't you think?' Larry bestowed a kiss on her cheek while holding her slim waist with his gibbon-like arm.

I entered the wheelhouse feeling slightly jealous and strangely, a little inferior. I wonder if they would mind a threesome, I joked to myself.

The afternoon's dive on the Les Fryttes rock pinnacle went well and we were moored on the jetty within ninety minutes of leaving.

Larry produced a litre bottle of Jack Daniels. 'Have you got three glasses, captain?' He twisted off the lid and dropped it on the deck, I moved to pick it up, but he crushed it with his size twelve. I looked up at him and received an unnerving toothy, almost challenging smile. I obligingly produced the glasses, which were generously filled to the tops. For the first time since meeting them I felt at ease and was starting to enjoy their company, the whisky was breaking the ice.

The following day I took them to the Hanois reef for the first dive, then to Point Robert for a second one. Back in port, the whisky appeared and again I took full advantage of Laura floating around me, dressed in the skimpiest of bikinis. She flirted more and more as the Jack Daniels wisdom ran high. She effortlessly oozed femininity.

Larry almost paraded Laura, and seemed to enjoy me stealing glimpses of her. He knocked down the drink eagerly and within half an hour was heavily snoring.

'Why don't you chill out, Kris, have another?' She filled my glass then entered the wheelhouse.

'The sun's gone down, it's become a bit chilly.' She felt inside her holdall, causing her breasts to almost fall out. She reached behind her back to unclip her top. I courteously turned away, while swaying from the whisky.

'Can you help me with this please, Kris?' I turned to face her; she turned around just as the bikini top fell into her arms.

'I've caught you looking at me.' I moved to go out. 'Stay,' she snapped. Taking my hands she placed them over her flat stomach and around her slim waist, her perfect breasts pressed into my chest.

'Pull them down if you want, Kris.' My pulse rose as I registered her warm sweet aroma; I could feel myself tingling uncontrollably. She pulled up my tee shirt and pressed her hand hard against my jeans.

'My, you're nice and horny.' A glass smashed loudly as Larry's hand relaxed its grip.

'Are you OK?' I asked as Larry's glazed eyes blinked in confusion. He gasped. 'Hell, it wasn't full was it?'

'I don't think so.' The forced smile fell from my face and I swallowed heavily while from the corner of my eyes I watched Laura peel off her bikini bottom, revealing a neatly trimmed thin strip of blonde pubic hair nestled on her naked mound. She kept a serious gaze on me as she slowly finished dressing.

'I think we'll be on our way,' Larry slurred as he swayed with J.D. 'Laura, are you ready?' he said while staring wildly around with his jaw open, gasping air like a fish out of water. She glided past me, showing the whites of her eyes as her pupils locked on to mine.

In the galley and with shaking hands I removed the cling film from the whisky bottle and poured myself another drink. 'Shit,' I cursed loudly. You don't bang the client's wife, for Gods sake; but I felt my body betraying me again, I couldn't stop visualising her enticing nudity.

It was now Thursday and shortly after the sun chased away the mist my guests arrived. I had taken them to a wreck the previous day, and had deliberately avoided a drinking session while filling the dive cylinders. Like the previous morning Laura was avoiding me so I got on with my job and credited our erotic encounter to the drink.

The day was gorgeous, with no wind or clouds, just a clear blue void that dissolved into the smooth blue sea, leaving only the rocky islands to betray the horizon. We decided to visit the rugged coast of Alderney.

The diving was excellent and Larry and Laura returned to the boat with two good-sized lobsters.

'Can we barbie them when we get back to port?' Larry enquired.

'No problem,' I said as I pushed the throttles forward. On return to the mooring they left me to light the BBQ while they visited the shops. Suddenly the boat's radio caught my attention. One of the local skippers was calling me, *Vagabond*. '*Vagabond,* this is *Westwind*,' I replied. 'Were you calling me, Alan?'

'Kris how are you doing mate? Yeah err, were you off the Casquets today?'

'Yeah, we were there with some divers.'

'Did you lose a dive hood over the side?'

'What colour is it?'

'It's blue with a black centre stripe.' I looked at their suits laid in a pile on the engine box. 'Yeah, sounds like one of ours, mate.'

'Well you know where it is; I'll keep it on board for you.'

'Yeah, thanks for that Alan, you must have eyes like a shitehawk, I owe you a pint Al. I'll catch you later, thanks, cheers and gone.'

Larry passed the full shopping bags that had French sticks poking from them over to me as Laura jumped aboard.

'Here's to our first class captain.' The half-pint tumblers chinked as we joined glasses. I tried to avoid the whisky, but my glass was being constantly topped up. The lobster was eagerly devoured along with the fresh salad and washed down with wine and afterwards, plenty more J.D. I steadied myself with one arm on the toilet bulkhead. I was half pissed and it was still quite early.

On returning to the party I was surprised to see Larry opening yet another bottle of whisky.

'Here's to the *Westwind*,' he slurred and predictably crushed the bottle top with his clown size foot. Laura shook her head grinned and downed her drink in one.

'Come on, Kris where's your spunk?' I looked at her confused, which caused her to laugh and put her hand to her mouth.

'I've just remembered we're in England. She deliberately widened her eyes at me.

Four drinks later as if on cue, Larry slid sideways on the seat and started snoring loudly. Laura lifted his head and placed a folded jacket underneath, then dropped it down deliberately hard, but Larry was away with J.D. and just snored back at her.

'That's that, then,' she staggered sideways intentionally making me catch her. She moved her hands from my face on to my shoulders.

'I really like you Kris, you feel so strong and firm.' Her arms gripped and her sea green eyes widened. 'Captain Kris…we've got unfinished business.'

She led me into the wheelhouse then down into the accommodation, I felt like that fly being taken by the spider back at the lodge. She locked the door and turned like a predator.

'You left me so wet and horny. He's old and always pissed.' She tore at my belt and jeans then she knelt down to me.

'God, I'm gonna enjoy this,' she gasped out. Holding me with both hands she pulled me to her mouth.

I snatched an uncontrolled shuddering breath and grabbed her soft warm hair as my initial nervousness quickly transformed into raw lust. This felt too good to refuse.

Chapter Six

I turned over then sighed holding my pounding head with both hands.

'Oh shit,' I gasped as the confused jigsaw of the previous evening's events started falling into place. I rolled over and arched my back in pain and then slipped off the wrecked bunk, I turned in front of the mirror, scratches and nips covered most of my back and I had several teeth marks on my shoulders. Bloody hell, the wild bitch had torn me to pieces.

After tidying the galley I moved to the deck. 'Christ.' I said out loud as I saw the empty bottles.

'Some party.' One of the marina workers chuckled as he passed.

I shook my head without replying.

One hour later my customers delicately stepped on to the now clear deck. 'Morning Kris, sorry we are late,' Larry said, surprisingly quiet.

Laura just pouted at me like a little girl. I felt strangely uncomfortable with her sulky glances.

Hardly a word was exchanged as *Westwind* droned towards the Banc De La Shoal, a shallow rocky reef that lay between the islands.

I sat in the galley trying to avoid them. I felt exceptionally rough, almost sick and could still taste the whisky.

'Have you seen Laura's hood?' Larry asked.

'Oh yeah, I forgot to tell you. I think it must have fallen over the side yesterday, I've got this one for her to use.'

'I don't fucking believe this,' he exploded. 'I want her damn hood.' I reeled back at his aggression.

'I didn't lose it, you must have. There's nothing wrong with this one,' I held up my own hood. Larry snatched it from me like a spoilt brat.

'I'll make us a coffee,' said Laura, cooling the scene while appeasing Larry.

I remained angry but silent. I could smack him and chuck him off for talking to me like that, but that wasn't an option after all the time and effort. I wanted to get paid. I attributed his mood to his hangover.

Westwind sat at anchor, close to the small breakers that danced around the top of the reef.

'You've only got about forty minutes of slack water here, so don't hang around. I'll pick you up at the North end.' I briefed them as they prepared to dive.

'Bye, Kris.' Laura said, slowly uplifting her eyes she turned away and picked her mask from the bucket of water, shaking out the water. She shot me a strange almost unnerving gaze then hid it behind her mask. She fitted her mouthpiece and disappeared over the side.

I sat at the helm watching their bubbles breaking the calm surface as they moved from the anchor towards the reef. 'Bye Kris,' echoed through my mind, it was the last thing Jenny had said to me, and sadly Vicky.

I finished my pint mug of strong black coffee and stood at the stern watching their bubbles a few feet away. I suddenly began to feel strange, I was well hung over from the marathon drinking session that witnessed the sun peeping over the horizon, but this was something different, I started shaking and my vision was becoming distorted. I staggered into the wheelhouse and grabbed for the radio, but I fell onto the bench seat my body was invaded by tremors, then I sank on to my side, unable to move. Was I having a stroke?

'Bye Kris, bye Kris, bye Kris,' echoed over in my mind, as dark shapes moved around me like demons. I tried to lift my head as more dark shapes surrounded me; but the pain in my neck prevented me from moving. I felt paralysed mentally and physically. My shirt was soaked in dribble and I felt sticky and freezing cold. I must have wet myself.

'You bastard...you drunken bastard.' I vaguely recognised the deep voice, but everything was spinning in my head. Two uniformed men seized me roughly and dragged me off the long seat. I fell heavily, as my arms and legs weren't responding. They dragged me out and on to the deck.

'Larry is that you?' I thought then tried to say, but my words wouldn't come out properly. A sharp blow to my stomach made me retch and vomit on myself, but I couldn't feel myself do it.

'You fucking murderer, you murdering drunken bastard!' Someone threw several buckets of seawater hard in my face as Larry screamed obscenities at me then fell to his knees sobbing. My mouth was numb as if I'd been to the dentist.

'I, I don't understand,' I tried to say, but only garbled slurs escaped from my non-responding mouth.

'He's been in the water for over six hours, you pisshead!'

I shook my pounding head as my nose began to bleed heavy.

'She's lost. His wife is missing, probably drowned by now. She was swept away in the tide. Can't you remember a thing?'

'Fix… h…urs? T… Thas im…imp… inos…sible,' is all I could say. I could hear them shouting at me clearly, but still my own words came out garbled and incoherent. I felt dizzy one second. I had tunnel vision the next. I could see nothing but dull shapes. My body was going into spasms, I felt I was dying and they didn't even know I was ill.

A policeman came out from the wheelhouse holding an almost empty bottle of whisky then he looked into the bin and clanked the empty bottles loudly. 'I think your problem has reached its climax. He's obviously suffering from alcohol poisoning, take him to the station.'

The breath test that took me almost an hour to complete proved positive. The policeman coldly rose to his feet.

'Kristopher Woods, I am arresting you for being under the influence of alcohol while in charge of a licensed passenger vessel and subsequently causing the death of Laura Stevens. You do not have to say anything, but it may harm your defence if you fail to mention when questioned something, which you later rely on in court. Anything you do say will be given in evidence.'

I collapsed on to the floor.

I lay in the dark cell, shivering uncontrollably, as my mind struggled to make sense of what was happening to me. It was all a blank that I couldn't understand. Six hours, I tried repeating out loud to myself, but I couldn't even do that. I remembered one time I had been given gas as an anaesthetic at the dentist's. I was told not to drive afterwards, but I did and I found it hard to concentrate because I was drifting in and out of reality. I felt like that right now, but ten times worse. I had never in my life lost so much time and sensibility. Even during those drunken days in the badlands of grief I could still recollect every minute. I closed my watering eyes and returned to the peace of sleep.

The next day I felt a little better physically, despite spending a night full of vivid scary hallucinations of every description.

The solicitor, or advocate as they call themselves on Guernsey, was as transparent as glass. He asked futile questions and I was distinctly aware of his poorly hidden contempt.

I was still drifting into blank moments when my mind felt as though it was on pause, which wasn't helping and I must have looked as if I'd spent a week on the piss with Oliver Reed.

'It doesn't look very good, I'm afraid. They were in your care and you got drunk.'

'I didn't drink on the boat. I never drink while actively working at sea, never.' I stamped my fists on the table. 'There's something wrong with me, something happened to my mind.'

The advocate closed the thin file that looked empty, then stood up. 'You will have to attend the magistrate's court sometime tomorrow. We will of course apply for bail. Have you any funds or property?'

'Yeah.'

'Your boat has been seized as evidence; you cannot use it for bail security.'

'I have funds.'

'In the region of, say a hundred thousand pounds?' I could tell by his smug look he expected me to say, 'not that much'.

I sternly looked him in the eyes. 'Yes,' I gasped then asked for a bucket. I felt terribly sick again.

As the advocate left to the noise of me retching into the tin bucket, the accompanying policeman held me by the arm. I pulled away from him before being escorted back to the cell, still with my head staring at the yellow bile.

The thin mattress offered little comfort as I tossed and turned during the night, aware of every hour. Then the light spilled through the small window, but this dawn was full of gloom and despair, as the true reality of my situation roosted inside me. I stared at the ceiling for hours, going over and over what had happened. The breath test would have proved positive. Hell, I drank almost a full bloody bottle of J.D and didn't turn in till after dawn, I think. I was feeling stronger, but why won't they get me a doctor?

I pictured Laura's distinct smile, why had she repeatedly told me she really did like me? I then thought of our lustful encounter, why had she behaved so aggressively, she was almost unstable, wildly thrusting her heavenly body against me like a woman possessed. The scratches she left on my back were still sore and weeping and then, the next day, she all but ignored me.

A bang, then rattling keys made the graffiti-covered door swing open. 'You are at the magistrate's court at one thirty.' The policeman spoke dispassionately as he dropped a tray on the seat. Before I could reply the door closed noisily.

The food was stone cold; I dropped an anaemic sausage back on to the hard grease mould I had prised it from and sat staring at the wall.

The Paras was hard, but you had buddies, even if you were caught on an escape and evasion exercise, you weren't alone. Like being caned as a kid, it was never as bad when someone else was being punished with you. I felt alone here more than I had ever been in my life.

I looked at the messages left on the wall, written probably by pissed up holidaymakers. Stare as I might I couldn't read them. I had been in that position for nearly two hours with my mind somersaulting in confusion. Then the keys rattled me back to reality.

The advocate was sitting at the table. He had a younger man with him this time, no doubt a trainee, just here to gloat.

'Mr Woods. Good morning.' They both rose to their feet. I ignored them, sat down and placed my hands together on the table before looking up to them.

'You're at a magistrate's hearing this afternoon. Unfortunately I cannot attend, so Mr Hooper will be representing you.'

'He's still wet behind the ears for God's sake,' I said wearily.

'I beg your pardon sir, Mr Hooper is a valued member of our firm.'

'Yeah, right,' I sighed. 'I need to get out of here. I've got to find out what really happened.'

'You got hammered,' the attending policeman quipped.

'I wasn't drunk; I had a drink the night before, but not at work, never at sea.'

The young whatever wriggled nervously in his chair then broke the silence.

'It doesn't look good at all.'

'Tell me about it, pal.' I looked coldly into the young man's eyes. He escaped my hard unshaven face by blinking at the table.

'Your statement,' he shook his head and looked at his colleague. 'It, It…Your statement even makes you well, sound like you were still drunk at the time you made it. It's vague and incoherent.' He finished the sentence with a nervous stare around the room.

'That's because he was wrecked out of his skull,' the policeman butted in again.

'Shut it, fatty,' I snapped, with frustration. 'If you're so intelligent why didn't you get me a doctor and take a blood test, isn't that procedure?'

'We didn't need a blood test to find out which cloud you were on. You almost melted the breathalyser, when you eventually managed to finish it. Even your clothes still stink of the stuff,' the policeman said sarcastically. 'That poor girl was slowly drowning while you and Jack Daniels had a party. You make me sick,' he said shaking his head.

'Thank you officer, that's quite enough,' the advocate protested.

Staring aggressively at the policeman I asked levelly. 'Will I get bail?'

'I don't know, it's hard to say.'

'How long before…I get out, if I don't get bail?'

'You may get bail, but quite honestly it is extremely doubtful.'

'What's the worst that could happen?' I asked staring at my clenched hands.

'Placed on remand, the Quarter Sessions, the Royal Court here or a Crown Court on the mainland, possibly a conviction for manslaughter and a jail sentence. I'm afraid no one will show much compassion, considering the circumstances.'

I folded my arms.

'Have you a criminal record?'

'No.'

'Have you had a problem with alcohol in the past?'

'No,' I hesitated. 'Well I did go on a long bender a few years ago, after a personal tragedy. My wife and daughter were drowned.

'Diving off your boat, were they?' The policeman again quipped sarcastically.

I sprang of the chair and gripped his windpipe and his hat fell off. 'There was no need for that.'

Chairs scraped as they stood up 'Gentlemen, please.'

I held the choking man for a few further seconds then released him. Coughing and gasping he rolled against the wall and out of the room.

'Err, yes well, where were we? Oh, yes, you err, haven't been in any trouble previously have you?' he gasped and looked nervously past me.

They soon dried up as fast as the shell on a boiled egg and the meeting fizzled into taut silence. They hung around a bit longer to ensure an extra hour's pay then left smiling out 'Cheerios' as two policemen, now carrying batons, roughly escorted me back to the cell.

Three proud ambassadors of the community sat behind the bench. Two overfed women wearing horn rimmed glasses and dressed in flowery frocks sat either side of a man who had the appearance of a retired army officer. He had a large handlebar moustache, which looked like it was stuck on his face with super glue.

They glanced repeatedly at me. I knew from past experience that only sad people like these who don't have real lives can be bothered to get involved in what they think is an elite position. Sadly, they are totally unaware that no real person would be seen dead sucking up to the system like they eagerly do, for the meagre reward of publicly showing off their blind arrogance.

I stood with a policeman in this court of fools, feeling like a mass murderer. After lots of loud whispers the jester with the moustache cleared his throat with a cough then stood up.

'Kristopher Woods, you are attending this magistrate's court today with serious charges set against you. We have read your statement, albeit vague and brief. We have also read Mr Steven's statement, and in all my years of serving on this bench, I have never been so deeply touched by such sadness.

Mr Stevens, a guest to our shores experienced true despair as he feebly held on to his beloved wife for hours until eventually he become too weak, and sadly could no longer hold on to her. She was cruelly torn from his arms, Mr Woods,' he said in a highly raised voice. 'At the same time you were drinking yourself into an oblivious stupor. If it were not for a passing vessel I have no doubt the same fate would have befallen him.'

The two women on the bench stared at me scornfully through slit like eyes.

'As yet no body has been found, but 'lost at sea presumed dead' is a statement that sums up the true gravity of this incident, and sadly, is one this island has heard all too often! You were responsible for these poor souls but you showed no care or consideration for their safety, your attention or lack of it was elsewhere…' he paused looking around the court then snapped his head accusingly like an actor delivering his major line. 'Staring at the bottom of a whisky bottle! Society bestows great trust in people in your vocation, but you have blatantly failed in your duties. Because of the severity and consequences of this failure we are placing you on remand. You will appear at the next Quarter Sessions. Your application for bail is refused.'

I stood silent, as the knot in my stomach started to tighten, spreading through the whole of my body. I felt desperately trapped with no escape from this living and ever spiralling nightmare.

A hand gripped around my arm and pulled at me. 'Back to the cell for you, me lad.'

I stared down at the lad who called himself a solicitor. He just shrugged his shoulders as if condoning the result.

During the journey to the remand centre I was locked in one of eight man-sized cages within the Sherpa van. I was the only one in the vehicle, which rattled and banged relentlessly, ensuring I got no rest.

The van left the ferry and drove somewhere inland, causing the air to change from fresh and sea smelling to something I was not used to.

On arrival I was ushered through a labyrinth of locked doors to a small room with a hatch. A face appeared and looked me up and down, then a few minutes later the face returned.

'Shoe size?' was the question. Then after answering the face, a pile of brown clothes with a pair of canvas slip-on shoes flopped on to the scratched wooden counter.

'Remove all your own clothes and put these on,' the face requested coldly. I stood in the ill-fitting jacket and trousers and was led through more doors, into a cell that had two sets of bunk beds. In the middle of the small dull cell was a toilet that had fixed strips of hardwood screwed to it. The whole place smelled of piss, sweat and stale tobacco. A few possessions lay on three of the beds, toothbrushes, washing stuff and some paperbacks.

I walked to the small heavily barred window and stretched to look out. I could only see a red brick wall which had a thin covering of green moss, where water had leaked from the gutters somewhere above. I heard noises and banging. The voices became louder and suddenly the keys rattled and the green door swung open.

'What have we here then?' A youth of about twenty stopped in the doorway. Two other heads appeared at either side of his.

'I think it's me granddad,' the skinhead said without cracking his face. 'That's my fucking bed yer leaning on, granddad,' he said as he pushed his way in, past the other two.

'I'll leave you lot to get acquainted,' the warder sneered sarcastically, as he slammed the big green door shut.

'So who the fuck are you, then?' the tall thin skinhead asked in a broad Scouser accent. I only stared back at him. 'Do ya smoke then?' I shook my head. 'You don't say a fucking lot do ya, granddad?'

'No,' I replied.

'What are you in for?' asked the smaller, chubby inmate.

'A total cock up.' I sighed as I sat down on the bottom left hand bunk.

'Don't tell me… and you're innocent.' They all laughed openly then the skinhead's face hardened.

'Who the fuck said you could sit there?' He pointed at me aggressively.

'Leave it out, pal, not now.'

'Think ya fucking hard do ya? Fancy ya self do ya?' He stood over me.

'Yeah, who said that was your bunk anyway, granddad?' the black kid with orange hair joined in while blowing stale smoke in my face. I said nothing; the last thing I wanted right now was a fight. The door opened and the stand off melted away as the two mouthy cellmates quickly left.

I looked at the chubby lad. 'What was that all about?'

'Scouser's the cock of this place, he controls the cigs and dope in here, and he'll want your cigs.'

'He's welcome to them,' I said while standing up. 'So what do you all do in here?'

'Telly, ping-pong, you know, stuff like that.'

'Is it all mainly kids in here?' I looked at the lad who had spots erupting from his young face.

'Mostly,' he replied

'Woods,' the warder said loudly, from outside, 'Come with me.' I walked ahead of the warder to a small counter where a packet of cigarettes, chocolate bars and washing kit was laid out.

'Sign here.' I signed for the stuff then was escorted back to the cell. I was pleased I was alone again. I moved to the small square hole in the wall and tried to look out but all I could see was bricks.

Severe shaking on my shoulder rudely awoke me. 'Where's the cigs?' I turned over facing the wall. 'I said, where's me fucking cigs, granddad?' I rubbed my eyes back to life as I faced the reality; this moron wasn't going to disappear. I reluctantly got to my feet. The Scouser was about the same height as me, tattoos covered most of his lean muscular body and his face bore the scars of a hard life, and probably lots of fights.

'I've decided to start smoking,' I said calmly while staring unblinking into his cold, dull, grey eyes.

The Scouser spun around to speak to Orange Hair. 'This old man doesn't fucking get it, does he?' He ranted on like Lily Savage.

How arrogant, I thought, he's turned his back on me, totally confident that I'm going to wait for him to turn around and hit me. I quickly adjusted my feet. The chubby lad noticed I had changed my stance; his eyes started darting around the glazed brick walls.

I connected a sharp right cross into the kidneys of the Scouser. He turned, doubled over and shot a savage glance at me. I was already bringing a hammer blow to his temple. Orange Hair shot his hand under his mattress as my foot found the Scouser's groin.

'Look out!' Chubby screamed as Orange Hair thrust the sharpened hacksaw blade into my side. A searing pain shot through and down my right side as I turned to my attacker. I grabbed his ears and pulled his head sharply down onto my rising knee, a sickening crunch filled the cell as his nose shattered. I felt the blade protruding from my side then my warm blood oozed down over my protecting hand. Chubby, having stepped over the writhing bodies, banged noisily on the door and screamed for a warder.

A sparrow chirped obliviously somewhere above my barred window. I held the paperback with my finger marking the page as I moved into the shaft of sunlight that invaded the small room at that time of day.

I had been moved into a single cell after my two-day hospital visit where I had received numerous stitches. The doctor said because of the blade's short length no vital organs were damaged. I closed the book with a snap. I had read almost half the pages, but couldn't remember a bloody thing about it.

Tomorrow would be Tuesday and my court appearance. Ten days since normality is how I looked back on those mind-crucifying days. How long I had sat, holding the book, I hadn't a clue, until a voice swam with my thoughts.

'You have a visitor. Are you all right?' the warder prodded me.

'What?' I squinted through half closed eyes.

'You have a visitor, come with me.' The first thing I noticed was the smell. The sweet smell filled my head and made me feel dizzy.

'Oh, Kris.' Jenny's embrace hit me with a wave of pleasure as she held me tightly.

I stood silent. 'Kris, what's happened?' She cleared her throat then her hair from her face. Seeing my attire she broke into a deluge of tears.

'I read it in the paper, they, they're saying horrible things about you being drunk and all that. If I had been with you this would never have happened. It's my entire fault,' she wept openly.

I held her memorable curves, gave a deep sigh and looked around. 'I don't know what's happening to me Jenny I'm...I know I didn't drink on that day, I know I didn't, but I can't remember a single minute, I just can't explain, because I don't know how it happened.' She composed herself and half-smiled, biting the corner of her lip while sniffing uncontrollably between jerks.

'When can you come home? What are you doing in this horrible place anyway?'

'They refused my bail.'

'But, why Kris?' she asked naively.

'For God's sake, Jenny! I'm responsible for her death, its manslaughter.'

She burst into tears again.

'Please Jenny, don't do this.' She held a hanky shakily to her face and stared at me. The past again taunted me with unreachable memories.

'Come on, rainy face, don't spoil those lovely brown eyes,' I said, trying to sound strong but inside I felt I was being microwaved.

'What about the boat and all the charters?' asked Jenny in-between sniffles.

I gave a long blink, which ended in a hopeless sigh, as I thought about all the work that I had put in. 'Can you get my diary from The Lodge and contact them for me? Tell them the boat has problems, that the engines have blown up or it sank, something like that, please.'

'Do you want me to go and take the boat back?' Jenny asked.

'They're holding it as evidence for now. God damn it,' I cursed. 'I'm told jack shit in here, and the solicitors are a set of useless wankers.' She followed me around the small room with tearful eyes.

'I miss you so much, Kris. You're all I think about.'

'Did you get a house?' I asked, changing the subject.

'Yeah, a beauty, it's on Church Rise, it has brilliant views over the river.' She looked away and sniffed. 'But you aren't there and it feels so hollow.'

'I hope you have some money left.'

'I've got the house and furniture, a new red sports car and fifty thousand invested.'

'Well done Jenny Dean,' I said vaguely, as I pictured my own special home.

'What about you, Kris? What's going to happen?'

'The way my luck is going I'll get jailed, then struck by lightning the day I get released.'

'Oh Kris, please don't give up. I'll get a barrister from London.'

'No Jenny, I'm as guilty as sin in their eyes, and I dare say I can't blame them. I haven't got a chance in hell so why pay silly money to one of those exorbitant scoffing bastards. Anyway my court appearance is tomorrow.'

'Tomorrow' she looked troubled. 'Is there any thing I can do for you?'

'One kiss for old times' I asked, struggling to smile. Her soft lips fitted perfectly, just as I had dreamed of and for a second her tenderness washed over me like summer sunshine, until her tears on my face turned into winter rain and broke the spell.

I sat in the crowded court. The press filled most of the public gallery, but one face in the room cast haunting glances at me. Larry Stevens. He sat iron faced, dressed immaculately in black. He constantly stared accusingly across at me. Jenny couldn't be missed, despite being small and at the back of the crowd; her auburn hair was visible to me like a beacon of hope in the midst of a sea of hostility.

Larry Stevens spoke with cool composure as he told his tale of events. He kept repeating 'the struggle for life' like a well-rehearsed actor. His loud deep voice was like a Shakespearean actors and perfect for the role. He enthralled the room's listening heads and no one moved or made the slightest noise. Even I started hating the selfish carefree bastard he was describing.

I felt like one of the criminals at the Nuremberg war trials after Larry Stevens' damning thirty-minute account that was regularly interrupted by anguished pauses and tears, which prompted hankies to appear among the jurors. He even showed the jury a picture of Laura.

Now it was my turn despite knowing I was truly fucked. I looked gaunt and every bit the struggling drinker I was accused of being and expected no mercy from this lot. The public gallery even hissed at me as I stood up. In the back of my mind I thought about the damning things Stevens had said about me. Why was he lying so much? Perhaps he'd forgotten some details in the midst of his grief.

I told it as I remembered it. I was confused and scared and cast sorry eyes at the twelve cold faces of the jury. I was questioned, but had no decent answers, only that I couldn't and didn't know what had happened to me during those lost hours, which really was as good as saying, sod you all.

Looking down at Stevens I noticed his shiny shoe was tapping up and down quickly and in a way that could only be described as nervously.

The crunch of the many bottle tops sounded in my ear, that same foot that was now nervously tapping had crushed every single bottle top, and then I suddenly recalled the bottle that the policeman brought from the wheelhouse. That one still had its top on, and it was now sitting on a table in front of me as evidence.

'Mr Woods, do you find these proceedings somewhat boring?' the judge boomed across the polished benches. I snapped back to reality.

'Sorry?' I said, confused.

'I've heard little in your defence, and the damning evidence against you leaves me no choice but to conclude this hearing. I would normally guide a jury towards a just verdict, but in this case I feel you have steered a clear course for yourself.' How nautical, even the judge was taking the piss. 'I now call upon the jury to consider all the evidence set before this court.'

'All rise,' the clerk shouted. The jury obeyed, and shuffled away in silence. I was taken to another desolate box and left to stew in sorrow.

They no doubt had a unanimous vote of 'guilty' before the kettle had boiled; the rest of the hour they were out I assumed was occupied by them lazily stuffing their tea and sandwiches down their throats. Eventually they reappeared and shuffled themselves into the same seats in an unorganised, but polite manner. When they stopped moving and started coughing a voice spoke loudly.

'All rise.' They obeyed like a school assembly.

'Jury, have you made your decision?'

'Yes we have.' The foreman of the jury stood looking nervous.

'Have you reached a unanimous decision?'

He nodded. 'Yes.'

After a pause the clerk moved nearer to the foreman. 'Is your decision guilty, or not guilty?' asked the clerk of the court loudly.

My eyes uplifted from my bowed head.

'Guilty.'

Before the judge spoke I saw Larry Stevens smile openly at his barrister. It wasn't the smile of a grieving man at all. He looked like he'd just won the pools.

Chapter Seven

Dear Jenny,

Thanks for your support in the court. Having you there helped me more than you could imagine. I feel so frustrated not knowing why I felt like I did that day Laura disappeared. I must admit I drank a lot the night before, but I was fine in the morning. I can't go back, but I just don't see a way forward.

They say the first month in here is the worst, but I don't think any month in here could become easier on the mind. Two years for manslaughter is a respectable term and offence in here by all accounts. I feel like I've had my insides torn out and been made to eat them. I'm hollow and aching, and can't sleep, as everyone in the smelly cell snores loudly. I've lost almost a stone and feel lethargic and uninterested in everything. I have died inside.

How is your new home? I wonder sometimes if I'll ever see it. It seems years since I held you that night in the shower. It was incredibly exciting. A million thanks for giving me those sweet memories.

I'm number five-hundred-and-four. That's how you're identified in here, like a numbered sheep. Most of the men in here take drugs and smoke heavily, but at least there's a calmer feeling about this place, almost a feeling of acceptance like we're all broken inside and trying to get by each day without becoming further damaged. There are a few troublemakers, but generally everyone just tries to get by. I could get out within fourteen months if I keep my slate clean, so I've been told. Thanks for cancelling the charters and getting 'Westwind' back safely for me and for keeping things ticking over at The Lodge. Thank you for everything; you are a true friend,
Kris X

My Dear Kris,

I'm sorry my reply is late. Everything is fine here. I check the boat when I can, and The Lodge is safe and sound. The seagulls are roosting on the boat; they must know you're away. The gunge takes ages to remove after the sun has baked it almost to resin. I like to sit on the boat and daydream that nothing is wrong and you'll pop out from the wheelhouse giving orders at any minute. Then I sit at the window and have a little cry for you.

I've always got exams these days, but not going out much now gives me lots of time for studying. I hate weekends. It's now been nearly six months; but the time is flying by and before we know it we'll be throwing the anchor in some secluded spot and skinny-dipping for lobsters.

I'm back. I've just returned from Plymouth after a field trip. We were diving on a small reef counting species. Paul, my dive buddy is a scream; he jokes around a lot. I'm going to get a bath now so keep smiling No 504, soon you'll be home and we can catch up on all those cuddles.

Love,

Jenny.

Dear Jenny,

It was nice to hear from you again, it's getting cooler as the sun is lower in the sky now and not reaching my window anymore. I had some bad news yesterday; I received a letter from Stevens' legal team as they call themselves. It looks like he's suing me. I had a talk with one of the lads, a disbarred brief. God, I even talk like a crook now! Anyway he reckons Stevens has got a good case and could make a hefty claim against me for compensation considering the circumstances. It makes me feel so vulnerable now; knowing all I have accumulated through hard work and, sadly, misfortune could be lost. Being here with my hands tied makes things even worse for me.

I had a dream about you last night. I could smell you and feel your hair on my neck. I got all excited. When I was at The Lodge I used to have a feeling of excitement in the morning and couldn't wait to grasp the day ahead, but this morning in here I didn't want to wake up. I wanted to stay with you forever in that dream. I'm sorry I upset you so many times. I am slowly accepting the inevitable, the sea has given me so much over the years, but the heavy price it's taken back has outweighed everything. I feel empty and lonely, but worse than all that I've lost all self-respect and pride. If I could find a way I would certainly end this escalating torture.

Love,

Kris X

Dear Kris,

I find it really hard to write to you after your last letter. I don't know what to say. You are serving your punishment and now they are trying to take everything away from you, it's so unfair, but you must fight them. You need really good representation like a well-known barrister who would scare them away or something. There must be a way, there's always a way. You told me yourself. Can you remember those nights we were planning the dive on the Madeira, and we drank loads of rum and ended up diving into the river stark naked? I remember how warm your body was afterwards when we lay on the grass and you made love so gently and passionately that I felt I was floating around the garden. We had so much going I'm sure we can catch up when you come home.

Sorry, I had to leave you in the drawer for a few days; my mum invited her sister from over in Ireland to stay here in my very own posh and paid for brilliant new house.

The rabbits in the lane near the gate have grown to full size now and they fight with each other instead of playing. I put the heating on for a few days to warm and air in The Lodge, as it was feeling a bit damp. Westwind is fine. I run the engines every week to keep the batteries charged up, but she'll need a good scrub on her bum soon, as the weed is getting thicker and trailing from her stern. My Auntie Kath thinks you're a real dish. She saw that photo of us sitting on the sovereigns together. I've got to go now; we're all going to bingo. See you soon.
All my love
Jenny.

Dear Jenny,

I have been told that I could be freed in six months time. That's if I am granted parole. I have kept out of trouble and I think gained the respect of a few warders. There's bad news though. I got a letter from Stevens legal representative that's how they're describing themselves now. They should really call themselves legal parasites. Well, they have started proceedings. Billy the brief says it will be only a matter of weeks. So I got a solicitor, but I feel because I'm in here, they're taking the piss. Nodding and smiling like fucking politicians do on the telly, and he's charging a fortune per hour. Why is it that the people in this damn country always try to screw each other rather then the bastards who screw them? Anyway I should know my fate before I get out of here.

Do you know this place doesn't bother some men, the type of men who don't care about or understand the quality of life; cigs, drugs, a bed and a wank, and they're content! When you have been free in the sea and in control of your life this place is hell.

A seagull hung around for a few minutes this morning. The bread I put out of the window must have got his attention. He flew above the building for a while sussing out the possible meal. His call was music to my ears. I was lost in pleasant memories until someone in the cell dumped noisily, causing a smell that I couldn't begin to describe.

I see your face every time I close my eyes. Did you know you are haunting me, Jenny Dean? I lost so much when Vicky and Jane were cruelly ripped out of my life. I thought I would never survive to see another dawn and then you appeared through my mist of gloom and invigorated my life again.

I'm back; I had to leave you under my pillow. I hope you didn't mind being there for a full day, but you admitted to leaving me into your drawer for ages. Sorry for getting a bit heavy earlier. This place makes you store emotion, and when you find a source of release it flows uncontrollably from you. Thanks again for being my red haired supporter.

Dear Jenny,

Just a quickie, it's been nearly three weeks since your last letter. Is everything all right? Every day I long for a letter from you. The only letters I receive almost every bloody day are full of legal gobbledegook from those legal leeches. It looks like I'll lose everything; they must know how much I have in the bank. The bastards have audited me, and are after every single thing I own. Why does all this shit come my way? I've never killed a robin; I've always been fair and honest as the next man. Every dam politician in this country has soiled hands and they're all rich and smiling. It seems the biggest twats reign supreme in this sad world. If you find the time please write to me.

Dear Kris,

I'm so sorry I didn't write earlier. I've been in Scotland. We went to Fort William to do a commercial diving course and we dived to fifty metres. I'm a bit of a celebrity at the Uni. Having found treasure and being a pirate gives you real street cred, everybody thinks I'm stinking rich and I get lots of jealous looks from the other girls.

How can they sue you for just having a drink then making a silly mistake? It's really not fair.

I lowered the letter. She had just described the collapse of my world as 'a silly mistake.' I didn't read any further. As the sun was rising for Jenny it was setting for me. Even she viewed me as being guilty of getting wrecked and letting Laura Stevens drown.

The hollow intruder gnawed at me yet again. Freedom was so important, but freedom to struggle and find a home and a source of income wasn't something to look forward to, especially after being financially comfortable, living somewhere unique and in full control of my destiny.

The solicitor sighed ominously as he waded through the pile of official looking documents. 'Stevens' representatives have certainly done their homework, Mr Woods. They have seized all of your assets. I'm afraid his legal team has bulldozed their way through the courts and used every trick in the book. Due to the circumstances of his compensation claim, you really haven't got a hope in hell.'

'Can we appeal?'

'You wouldn't get legal aid for an appeal involving a civil claim, and to be frank you have no chance of winning the case. Don't forget, you are serving a sentence for his wife's manslaughter.'

'How the hell can I forget, but surely they can't take everything?'

'I'm afraid so, all of your assets.'

'Everything how can they do that? The boat's my living. They can't take your living from you, surely?' I turned to him for a hopeful response.

The solicitor sifted through his briefcase and produced a letter confirming that my Certificate of Competence had been revoked by the MCA.

'I see.' I sat heavily back onto the chair.

'What did you expect?' The solicitor tried to sound sympathetic, but all I could feel was despondency invading me from all angles.

'So what happens next?'

'They will sell your assets through a court-appointed agent; they have already frozen your bank accounts. I'm afraid it's the American way these days. The claim culture has crossed the Atlantic. You have to sign a few papers of release.' He pushed the documents across to me.

'And if I don't?'

'You will just be delaying the inevitable that's all. This way you make a clean break. I'm sure you wouldn't want them claiming against you in the future.'

I looked him in the eyes and sighed…. 'What future?'

I arrived back in the cell feeling mentally anaesthetised. My three cellmates instinctively sensed my plight and remained silent. It was all they could do.

'Everything I own,' I muttered. 'All I've worked for all my life has just been fucking ripped away from me again,' I slumped on to my bed and rested my head in my hands. No one in the dull room spoke. The casual shakes of their heads accepted impersonally a loss they could never comprehend. I accepted hollowly that I'd get no pity or support from anyone in here; they had their own problems.

I opened the double garage. In the corner were a few cardboard boxes that held the remnants of my life. I opened one to find my clothes all neatly folded. Another few were full of my beloved books. Jenny's mother watched me standing like a lost child ringing my hands, as I wrestled with emotions.

'I'll best be making us a drink,' she said in her soft Irish accent and made her escape. Her voice reminded me of an impressionable part of my past in Ulster when violence and death abruptly corrupted my ebbing adolescence at the grand old age of eighteen.

I sipped the tea and looked around the comfortably post war semi. Jenny's dad Bill folded up his paper and removed his glasses as I entered the large living room that had unspoiled views over the river.

Jenny had chosen well.

'Aye, it's been a bad affair lad,' Bill sighed. 'What are your plans now?'

I could see small parts of Jenny in his face. I shrugged. 'I have no skipper's licence now. I suppose I could go back diving or maybe get a job on a boat. I just don't know right now.'

'How's the flat? Jenny said it was small but cosy.'

'Yeah, she's done me proud, sorting everything out.'

'It's the least she could do, it's the least all of us could do after what you did for us. You'll always be welcome in this house, despite all that err....' There was an uncomfortable silence, Jenny's mum broke it.

'Oh Kris, Jenny asked me to give you this.' Jenny's mother passed me a heavy A4 envelope. She should be home in a couple of weeks. You'll like Paul; he's such a nice young man.' She didn't have to emphasise the 'young' word as much as she did, but Jenny was still her baby, and I had probably danced to the same music she had in her youth.

I loaded up Jenny's car, which I had borrowed, with the boxes, thanked them and left.

The flat Jenny had rented for me had a comfy bed and partial views of the harbour from the main living room. It was above a small gift shop run by an elderly couple, Mary and Joe. I hung my coat behind the door then sat at the table facing the envelope. A smile spread on my face as I pulled out the wads of twenty-pound notes. A card with a boat on the front accompanied the money.

> *Dear Kris,*
> *Sorry I'm not there for you, I do hope the flat is OK, I thought you would like the view. The money is from the extra sovereigns we buried in the garden. It should help you get on your feet, I'm so sorry things turned out this way; I hope you are happy for me. Paul is a great bloke, he's kind and considerate and we are studying the same subject, so it's really good for us. You will like him.*

> *I was so lonely when you were away. Please forgive me; I only did what you always told me, to find someone my own age. I will forever have special feelings for you; you made me so alive and grown up. I still want us to be good friends forever, Kris, regardless of whatever happens in our lives.*

I placed the card on the table smiling through watering eyes. However painful for me, it was right for Jenny and that's what really mattered. I spent the afternoon personalising my new home with my meagre belongings then ended the day with a plate of fish and chips and a pint.

Eight months had passed since moving into number fifty-five A, Harbour Road and I was starting to enjoy my uncomplicated new life.

My first meeting with Jenny and Paul was as cordial as if Saddam and Bush were sharing a table. The atmosphere was strained and all wrong. Jenny was trying hard to promote new friendships, but faltered in-between every sentence each time we made eye contact, which made things completely unworkable. Later Jenny kept in touch with odd postcards and the occasional polite letter; time as always was working its healing spell.

I was picking up the odd job on various pleasure craft, oil changes, hull scrubbing, and painting. I hadn't been near The Lodge since that fateful week and whenever I passed while crewing on a boat I had to look away until we were out of view. The original owners had bought it back and they were using the place as holiday accommodation.

Westwind had been auctioned by the evil legals and was working in Cornwall somewhere. No one had seen or heard of Ferret since his near drowning and Jenny had passed her degree with honours, and was now working on a research vessel somewhere in the mid Atlantic along with perfect Paul.

I had been crewing on one of the small boats that take holidaymakers on bird and sea life watching trips along the coast during the summer season. A casual relationship with a divorced local barmaid called Jayne sustained my desires on the odd evening, but she had grown kids living with her and I wasn't in the family mood. Most of my time I spent alone with Captain Morgan and the occasional book. Life was pretty simple for me until one Sunday afternoon.

Old Bill Clark, an ageless captain Birdseye character who owned *The Puffin* had asked me to come along as crew, which involved securing the ropes and making drinks for the trippers. I'd done this on several occasions and was familiar with the boat, which was a forty-five foot open decked pleasure vessel that specialised in scenic trips along the coast, encountering basking sharks and dolphins.

Puffin's skipper Bill was one of the old boys, fair and straightforward and expert at viewing his prey without causing them unnecessary hassle.

A mix of holidaymakers cheerfully boarded *The Puffin* and off we chugged at a gentle pace. I made the drinks as normal and the seabirds serenaded us as I busied myself passing the refreshments, while joking with the passengers.

The trip went as Bill planned. They even laughed at Bills well told joke. 'What bird is always out of breath?' He loved to tell them it was the Puffin. Everyone saw dolphins and seals and the noisy breeding seabirds. The clients all 'wooed' at the dramatic splendour of the coastline when we rounded each headland, and again when we closed on a family of basking sharks. Then I had to reluctantly endure more complimentary gasps and questions as we passed within metres of The Lodge as we returned up the river.

Safely back in the harbour I secured the boarding plank and the passengers started disembarking in an orderly fashion. As usual I assisted the more elderly up the steep walkway, which was at its steepest when the tide was low. As the last couple began to climb up the plank, I noticed by their voices that they were American. I held the elderly woman's arm as she giggled and swayed up the moving slope with her arms full of tourist leaflets and papers.

On the quayside she continued swaying, as many that have been to sea do, she grabbed a rail to steady herself, dropping all her papers on the floor.

'Oh, I'm so silly,' she said as she held tightly onto the rail with both hands. 'Jeez, I'm still rolling around,' she smiled out while looking at me through tired eyes that defiantly retained a flirty glint. I smiled back at her.

'It won't last long, look around at the buildings and you'll be fine in a minute or two.' Dropping to one knee I started gathering up her papers.

I suddenly froze in astonishment on the spot. The woman's husband noticed me and placed his hand on my shoulder.

'Are you all right, son?' I was clearly pale with shock and shook my head, then slowly raised myself, eyes still locked on the paper, inspecting the page more closely. I shook my head again in disbelief and then sank onto a pile of rope.

I was clearly trembling all over with doubt and hesitation as I held the paper closer. 'It's Larry Stevens,' I squinted at the old man then blurted out. 'It's him! It's unquestionably him!'
The American woman shook her head in confusion and said, 'Ah, you can keep the goddamn paper.' With that, the visitors walked away. Bill's voice interrupted me.

'Are you all right, son? You look like you've just seen a ghost.'
'I just have…. a ghost of the past.'
'Are you sure you're all right lad?' he repeated. Still riveted to the paper I nodded silently as he pushed a twenty-pound note into my breast pocket.

'I'll be in the *Mermaid*, lad if thee fancies a wet.' He left me staring vacantly down a tunnel of confusion.
I was looking at the face that had relentlessly haunted me for what seemed like a lifetime. Once again, those long cheekbones and distinctive big teeth. I had him in print.

I looked around, then back at the picture. It was grainy and creased. The text below was naming some politician and a group of high flyers that were promoting a new marine salvage business and looking for investors. The head of the man above the crowd without a doubt belonged to Larry, but my eyes were now playing tricks on me as the profile of a along his side made me tremble, was I now convincing myself?
I strained and scanned the picture closely, but inside I needed no convincing about that face and its smile. 'Bye Kris.' I could still

clearly see her in my mind's eye sitting on the gunwale of *Westwind*; her high cheekbones and Marilyn Monroe smile was scarred so deeply into my mind I'd have recognised her profile in a football crowd.

'The deceitful bitch,' I spat out in a hiss, releasing the tension that had suddenly built inside me. Several people stopped in their tracks looking at me as though I was a wino, who was on a high. I didn't give a toss.... I knew now, as my instinct had always told me that I was truly innocent, they had deceived me all along.

The police station was just a waiting room adorned with various old posters warning people about potato blight and rabies, in the centre of the wall opposite the door was a cubby hole protected with steel mesh. I was in a queue of three, an elderly man was complaining that his next door neighbour had parked his camper van outside his house and it was blocking his view of the street. He wanted the police to move it. The girl behind the mesh tried in vain to explain to him that the best option was to ask his neighbour politely to move it. The old guy just kept repeating himself and complained that he'd fought in the war and that he was being treated so bad that he would have been better off under Hitler's rule, which caused the waiting heads to shake in despair. Almost ninety minutes later and after more complaints about barking dogs and an encroaching privet hedge, it was my turn. 'Could I speak with a detective please?'

The young woman PC replied frigidly. 'What is it about?'

I unfolded my paper, fully aware of the group of people that had accumulated and were sat close behind, listening with interest of what crap I was going to come out with. I cleared my throat and said in a low voice. 'It's about this woman, I err…I was supposed to have…lost... her in the sea.'

The girl frowned and rolled her eyes. 'You want to report a missing person?'

'Well not exactly…can I talk somewhere less public, please?' I could feel her frustration rising and she deliberately wasn't hiding it.

'What exactly is your complaint, sir?' She spelled out her gruffness with a jolting fold of her arms.

I took a breath. 'I haven't come to complain. I need your help.

Look I was supposed to have lost this woman off my charter boat whilst diving off the Channel Islands.'

'You better go back there and sort it out then.'

'No you don't understand, I was charged for her drowning, she was lost at sea, you know manslaughter'. The conversation faded behind me, I suddenly had centre stage.

'So you're telling me you were charged for manslaughter, when was this?'

'I got sentenced for it over two years ago, but she's here look!' I held up the paper.

I was becoming aware how stupid I must be sounding. Look, this is a recent paper and she's here on it, this one here with white hair, well she's blonde really.' I pointed to Laura in the grainy picture; the guy next to her is called Larry Stevens and is her husband. 'I need to see a detective or somebody; I have to sort this out, please.'
The girl huffed and turned to leave, she mumbled. 'If she's dead how it can't be her?' She disappeared leaving me under a multitude of glances. A minute later a policeman arrived, he had three large white stripes. Duty Sergeant Willson, now what is this all about sir?'

I repeated my story and in return I received a wry smile. 'So you're an ex con than where did you serve the time?'

'Dartmoor, I served eighteen months of a two year sentence.'
The room's occupants were silent by now and totally engrossed.

'So you committed the crime and served the time.'

'I didn't commit the crime, I was set up, conned they ruined me, took everything.'

'Did you get a fair trial, a jury verdict?'

'Well obviously not because she's still alive isn't she!'

 Do you realize sir, it is a crime to waste police time,' He stood upright,' considering you're previous, a trip back to Dartmoor could be a distinct possibility.'
Combined sniggers sounded around the room.

'For fucks sake let me talk to a proper detective, I have a right as a rate payer!'
He disappeared and another door abruptly opened. The sergeant appeared with another PC and they grabbed my upper arms. 'Sir the only right you will have if you continue this behaviour is a right to

remain silent. Consider yourself lucky this time.' They lead me to the door and pushed me out.

'You don't understand.' I tried pleading.

'Another word out of you and you'll be in a cell cooling down for twenty four hours and likely charged for obscenity and wasting police time, now be off!' One of the people waiting behind me stepped outside; he gave me a glance and shook his head. I walked home feeling a so frustrated, but so angry and hopeless all at the same time.

Sitting at the table I swallowed the sweet heavy rum without taking my eyes away from the article and picture, which had now become the most important thing in my life. The implications were bombarding my mind like a severe headache as the true gravity of my situation started to sink home.

'I'm innocent.' I couldn't help repeating loudly. They must have faked everything to get my money. With the boat and house and all my savings they would have netted at least seven hundred thousand pounds, one point three million in American dollars, a clear profit for those conning bastards.

'Bastards,' I cursed loudly as rage filled my guts. The empty bottle rolled in a half circle as I drew my knees up. My breathing was heavy as I fell into the deep rum-assisted sleep; in my hand I held the newspaper close to my chest.

The next day I was sat in the reception the main Police headquarters. After explaining myself more successfully to three duty policemen I was lead to an interview room where I waited for at least half an hour before I was joined by a plain clothed middle aged woman. 'DI Spiller.' She sat opposite me and opened a thin A4 folder.

'I'm sorry for the delay in speaking with you, I've just contacted the Jersey police and they confirmed the events you describe.' She sniffed the air deftly. 'Have you still got a problem with alcohol Mr Woods?'

I instantly regretted having a couple of large rums the previous night. She eyed me with suspicion.

'Did you drive here Mr Woods?'

'No I got a train and walked and I haven't got a drink problem, despite what you are thinking, but I did celebrate after finding a real lead, which you can go on.'

'Well according to the report all your problems stemmed from your drinking issues.'

'Laura Stevens is alive and living in New York, look.' I passed her the paper.

She looked at it and smiled.

'There she is.' I pointed to the face on the picture. 'There's your proof.'

'Are you really sober Mr Wood's, you pick out a bearably distinguishable face in a crowd and expect to be taken seriously. Laura Stevens died as a result of your gross negligence. You served your custodial sentence, let it go Kristopher, don't carry the emotion of guilt with you and try to convince yourself it never actually happened.

'I know it is her, honestly I see her every day in my mind. Can't you get the police in New York to investigate for me, they completely ruined me, I need to clear my name'.

She gave me a sympathetic smile. 'I'm sorry Mr Woods it will never happen.'

'Just one phone call, surely you can make one call.'

'A call to whom, there are more than seven million people in New York Mr Woods.' She stood up and smiled haplessly. 'You must accept the facts I'm afraid. We are busy people, I'm sorry there is nothing we can do to help you.' She opened the door and all my built up hopes flooded out once more.

It was now time for payback, no more manners or decency, fuck them; I had to forget the system that helps no one but the rich and start listen to my gut feelings.

After a long and expensive phone call I found out that the New York Times had purchased the photo from an agency that in turn used freelance photographers. I had a large notepad and was adding to it by the hour.

The eight thousand pounds that lay on the table was enough to support me in my hunt for the Stevens.

I would need to hire a private detective, a good one. There was so much floating around in my head to take in all at once. I felt I was going to blow a fuse. I needed a structured plan but all I wanted to do was get my hands on those lying bastards and wring their necks.

I recalled the hisses and scowls I received while lying Larry had the gallery in tears. Ferret's disappearance was a puzzle. Why would someone so local suddenly disappear without a trace? His boat hadn't been used since. I must have been drugged while they somehow planted the whisky. That's why it had an intact top on it, so there must have been a third person. The implications were getting serious as the extent of the conspiracy unfolded more and more in my head. There was only one course I could take. I had to go to New York.

Chapter Eight

With dried nostrils and aching arse cheeks I sat patiently with the rest of the suffering passengers. My luck again was true to form I mused. The fatheaded toddler bounced up from between the head rests and blew spit at me, and then smiling like a devil screamed high pitched baby abuse at me. The parents dozed on oblivious, as the ugly brat repeatedly tore down my newspaper shield.

'Sod off,' I hissed at it but it just swore back at me in its own language.

Later into the flight I was woken as a half-gummed rusk biscuit hit me full in the face. Eventually the last passenger awake in my row started dozing; I slowly rolled up the paper and waited.

The flight was to take about seven hours. I had been to Colorado before but never The Big Apple. Nine hundred pounds was the cost of the flexi-economy flight; the flexi bit meant that I could return when I wished, being a visitor from the U.K. I had ninety days maximum in the States.

I had left Devon at five a.m. and boarded the big 747 at ten a.m. and this little bastard had started the moment I sat down. My jacket looked like a snail had been jogging around it. The warning juddering of the seat told me another spitting attack was imminent. A quick glance to both sides confirmed an all clear. Its black devilish eyes appeared again then slowly and deliberately it studied me, pushing its shiny lips in and out as it manipulated a slug of elastic spit for its next assault. Whack! The paper found its target and it fell back to its parents with a screech.

'Good shot, fella,' a man behind me whispered his support.

The engines changed tone as the plane lost altitude causing my stomach to go light and woolly. I glanced at the window as the plane banked, and between thinning puffs of clouds I could see wet grasslands. The wind must be from the north my seafaring mind told me, the grasslands must be the Jamaica Bay wildlife refuge I had read about while studying the New York City guide.

The plane's movements caused heightened activity as everyone busied themselves with various tasks. Women adjusted their flattened hair and almost every one of them produced little mirrors from nowhere like magicians and got on with the all important task of maintaining their faces. Then the 'Fasten Seat Belts' sign flashed and all the heads returned into their uniformed rows.

A pretty flying flirt strode like a model doing her skywalk down the aisle while checking the safety belts; her relentless smile looked like it had been applied medically. Another Barbie doll followed grinning vainly from all the eye attention she was receiving from the men.

I started to feel slightly apprehensive as the plane banked and dropped while making its approach, now I had it all to do. I had to clear my name and try and recover some of my finances if there was any left of them.

The look of pure anguish on every passenger's face melted away as the plane touched down safely. After the obligatory taxiing around the tarmac the plane stopped, then fresh air rushed in like pure oxygen as the door was opened. I would need an ice pick to clear my nose. It felt like I'd been snorting breadcrumbs for hours. Eventually I forcibly pushed into the shuffling queue in the aisle and felt instant relief as I got out of the knee trembler position. I approached the pretty hostesses who were still dishing out their generous well-practised smiles. I couldn't help grinning at their dedication.

It was early October and the temperature would be similar to the U.K this time of year, if not a little warmer, but that would soon change dramatically.

The New York Times building is on 43rd Street was in an area called Midtown West, so after studying the area I reserved a room. The Broadway Inn 264w 46th Street was described as a cosy reasonably priced bed and breakfast hotel, close to Times Square. This was an area where high flying con artists like Larry and Laura would probably congregate to find their victims, but until I had traced where the photo of her had been taken, and the person who took it, the whole search was vague and flawed, especially as more than six million people lived in this concrete jungle.

'Grand Central Station,' announced the tired looking neon sign with the odd flicker. I waited in the large impersonal queue that shuffled slowly like a column of refugees, as the fleet of airport buses efficiently whisked us away. Despite the thousands of people dashing around, I recognised a few faces from the flight. Fortunately the devil child wasn't one of them.

Sleepy Devon was just a memory now. I felt as if I had fallen asleep and woken up in some American film. The skyscrapers stole all the sun, and thousands of people rushed about like ants. I squinted and the people looked like flowing water pouring along the pavements while being serenaded by tooting car horns.

The first thing I noticed was that no-one made eye contact; on the occasions I tried I was nervously ignored, as if I was about to draw a gun or worse.

The bus stopped abruptly with a loud hiss and the tired doors rattled open. After evacuation I stood looking around trying to find the exit to 42nd Street, then realised it was the main one that everybody was filing through.

A feeling of vulnerability nagged me at the thought of a TV or armchair crashing down on me from above, the result of a domestic in the clouds. It didn't pay to look up unless you wanted to feel dizzy.

I walked west like a lost boy towards the bustling Times Square, passing buildings and parks I'd never seen, but their names were still familiar, like The Grace Buildings and Bryant Park. I turned north on to Seventh Avenue, again noticing the lack of eye contact from the people rushing past. Theatres made up most of this area and massive neon's flashed in competition with each other. I became aware of several South American looking youths watching me, so I hardened my expression and upped the pace towards the hotel.

After the somewhat rigid formalities of registering I entered the lift and headed for room 207. I unpacked and hung my clothes in the closet, which was large and brash and made my gear that occupied about five hangers look more like some unwanted items that had been abandoned.

I had a long hot shower then I cracked open the litre of Captain Morgan I got from the duty free shop in London. If I asked for a 'Captain Morgan' here in the 'Apple' they would no doubt think I was asking for a cop. I filled a tumbler full of ice and poured a long one that made the ice crack loudly. I retrieved the remainder of my sandwich, which tasted horrible, so I washed it down with a resounding 'Ah'.

I slowly woke and stared at the elaborate ornate plaster ceiling. It looked so unfamiliar, which totally confused me as I focused my eyes around the strange room, then slowly the ceaseless car horns reached my consciousness and reminded me where I was.

The New York Times Building on 43rd Street is a fine-looking structure with big globe lamps guarding it. I entered the elegant reception area, which was bustling with suits and walked across the big marbled floor towards the suspended enquiries sign. I stood glancing at one of three girls behind the counter.

'Can you help me please?' She looked South American; her hair was shiny black and had natural curls, a bit like Jenny's but tighter. She greeted me with a smile, revealing teeth you would kill for.

'If I can.' She cast another dazzling grin while cocking her head to one side.

I bent down and fumbled in my shoulder bag. A big security guard looked on with concern and turned to face me lowering his arms by his side. He returned his hands back in front of him as I produced the wrinkled and now old-looking newspaper.

'I'm trying to find out where this was taken and, and, err, possibly who took it?'

'You're Australian. Aren't you?' I shook my head with a smile. 'English.'

She gently pulled the paper from my hand then her eyes scanned the issue number and date. She dazzled me again with another smile, then walked to a screen and started tapping the keys.

I was casually flicking through one of the many papers on the desk.

'Mr?' She paused.

'Woods, Kris Woods.'

'Well Kris, the guy who could have told you is on vacation, but I can give the names of the agencies we use.'

'Yeah, anything would be appreciated.'

'A long lost friend?' She looked at me with a hint of sympathy.

'Hardly,' I sighed. She held her stare; she wasn't going to give up as her big dark, almost black eyes mesmerised me.

'We met in the U.K. and she sort of changed my life,' I replied, as if I was confiding in her.

'Oh I see,' she nodded as if sharing a secret with me.

I placed my elbow on the counter and leaned closer to her. 'Yes, I would really like to surprise her.' I smiled. *With a heavy baseball bat! I thought to myself.*

'Mr Woods.'

'It's Kris.'

'Well Kris, we normally don't give out information about our journalists. Most of them are freelance and submit their work through the agencies.'

I must have looked disappointed. She smiled and said in a low voice with a friendly nod.

'Here, these are the main ones we work with.' She passed me a sheet of paper.

'Hey thanks love, err, Patsy,' I said after reading her name badge. I felt myself begin to blush as all three girls broke into giggles.

'What's so funny?' I asked.

'It's just your accent, Kris, and no one calls anyone 'love' here in the Big Apple.'

'Well, thanks anyway, lo…' I paused, staring at her, 'Sorry, I mean Pats.' Her mouth opened with surprise and she huffed out, 'Pats?'

I turned and walked towards the exit. As I drew level with the doors I looked back. Patsy gave me a nice smiley wave.

The list she had given me had a ring around one of the names and addresses and she had added in pen, 'Try this one first.' Friendly girl I thought, as I read the circled text.

Mark Rees was the columnist's name. I studied my map under one of the large globe lights. 240 West 57th Street was Rees' address, up 8th and on the left.

I waved down a yellow medallion cab and jumped in. Thankfully the driver was an English speaker.

'Where to?' he asked, the moment my arse hit the seat.

'240 West 57th' I replied sounding confident.

'Hey, you're an Aussie.'

'English,' I sighed with a smile.

'Ah, a goddamn Limey,' he said with a broad grin, while observing my reaction in his mirror. He had the look of an ex boxer.

'Do you know how that name came about?' I asked. The cabby went silent for a few minutes then cursed another driver.

'Go on then, smart arse,' he bawled, annoyed for not knowing the answer.

I half-shouted over the traffic noise. 'When all you criminal buggers were deported over here, you were given lime juice every day to avoid the scurvy, hence the nickname 'Limes'. You're probably more of limey then me, mate.'

The big cabby laughed whole-heartedly at my robust and accurate answer all the way down 57th Avenue, then stopped his cab and blew his nose.

'Here we are fella, 240 West 57th.'

'Cheers pal.' I handed him six dollars. The cab disappeared, along with the laughter from its driver.

It wasn't what I expected. The hallway was cold and draughty and litter was strewn all over the big black and white chequered floor tiles and it smelt fusty. In its centre was a cage type lift with steel concertina doors that you had to slide sideways by hand. Thick dust and hairs coated the grease that must have been thrown all over the gates by the handful. It looked like a new life form had colonised it.

I entered and pressed the button for the twentieth floor. The lift jerked upwards and as it passed every floor the noise of babies crying and people shouting in Spanish or Portuguese rose and fell. Then the lift shook and stopped.

The decor wasn't as bad on this floor. It appeared that most of the rooms were used for business purposes. I reached number 2414. 'Mark Rees, Investigative Reporter' was engraved on a small brass plaque. I knocked.

'Yeah,' a voice shouted, so I knocked again.

'Yeah, yeah,' the voice shouted again this time louder so I opened the door.

'What's up, you hard of hearing or something?' The room was thick with cigar smoke and littered with coke cans and food wrappers. Behind a long desk sat squinting over his glasses was a man I hoped was Mark Rees. He looked a little confused, then in a coarse voice asked,

'Yeah, what do ya want?'

'Mark Rees?'

'Who's asking?' He looked more like an American cop than a writer.

'My name is Kris Woods. I've come over from England.' I paused. 'It's a bit of a long story. Do you want me to make an appointment? That is if you're busy right now.'

He seemed bemused by my politeness.

A humorous smile spread on his face. 'England you say, so why me?'

I pulled the newspaper from the inside of my bomber jacket. 'I believe you wrote this article.' I couldn't place it on his desk because it was full of papers and rubbish so I held it out to him.

'Yeah Bob Sumers with his entourage of parasites, he's pissed you off too? That guy needs a goddamn bullet.'

In the picture and barely distinguishable, due to the level of zoom, was a white haired man. Rees had spotted him instantly.

'Do you know who this woman is?' I felt my heartbeat increase; the next answer could change my life. Rees looked hard with a big squint.

'Not sure, but she's not the type a man couldn't forget. Quite a stunner, what I can make of her.'

'Tell me about it,' I sighed. Rees studied me once again as a policeman would a suspect. 'Who told you how to find me?'

'One of the receptionists at the Times building, a girl called Patsy.' Rees looked at the clock on the wall. 'Fancy a drink?' he asked as he stood up.

A crowd of banished smokers were huddled outside the dingy looking bar, they all acknowledged Rees as we approached, he was obviously well known.

'Nah,' Rees said to me as I produced a ten-dollar bill, 'I've a tab here, this is my real office.' Rees appeared to be chilling out and losing the aggression in his voice as we moved to a table.

'Bob God dam Sumers is as bent as a hog's dick.' He took a drink.

'So what's your beef with him?'

'Are you sitting comfortably?' My joke was lost on this New Yorker, and I received a thin smile. As I told my story Rees nodded, and listened more intently as the story unfolded. When I had finished Rees sat back and wiped the sweat from the back of his neck with a napkin.

'That's one hell of a story, boy. You're sure this is the same woman?' He pointed to the picture.

'One hundred percent, a million percent, as a matter of fact she haunts me.'

'You sure talk strange, but I hear where you're coming from.' Rees ordered more drinks and asked a lot more questions. Rees was, I estimated about fifty-three, five six and probably two stone overweight, his suit was getting a little small for him or rather he was getting too big for his suit. He had a southern twang to his New York accent. Bald but for two black strips of hair above his ears, made him the type of man who could easily disappear in a crowd. A lot of men I'd seen around looked like him, but he also had an inner confidence that was expressed through his probing, almost suspicious face. His distracted manner somehow strengthened his character.

'This Sumers guy, is he a local?'

'As local as poverty.'

I sighed. 'So where could I find him?' Rees took a long look at me, which ended with him shaking his head.

'So what's that suppose to mean?'

'Listen, boy.'

'Will you stop calling me boy?' I snapped.

Rees looked over his glasses. 'That there temper of yours is gonna get you into trouble over here' he deliberately emphasised the word 'boy'.

I apologised. I didn't want to cock up this major contact I'd been lucky to find so soon.

'Tomorrow we will call on Jimmy. He's the photographer who took this shot.' He looked down at the paper again and hissed, 'Sumers' then called for more drinks.

I awoke lying on top of my bed fully clothed. I remembered going for a meal with Rees, then entering another bar, where we met more New Yorkers, who also liked my Australian accent and their booze. The rest of the night had become a blurry blank.

As promised, Rees arrived outside the Broadway Inn, exactly at 13.00 hrs, tooting the horn of his black Lincoln. The car's interior looked like four teenagers lived in it, a total mess. He looked funny with his short legs poking from the bench seat fully exposing white socks that contrasted against his black shoes and trousers. He looked a bit like a Blues brother, the dumpy one.

'Climb in,' he shouted, then stuffed the fat soggy end of his cigar back in his mouth and wrestled with the column change. I cleared a space and got thrown into the seat before I could shut the door. 'Get a fucking life' was his favourite saying as he swerved in and out of the traffic, totally oblivious to the horns that blasted protests. He hung his head out of the window. 'If you can't drive it, park it, you moron!'

The Lincoln came to an abrupt halt and I stepped out, releasing a pile of litter and cans onto the pavement. I didn't have a clue where I was, but I recognised the smell of cooking garlic, which made my mouth water.

Cucina Della Fontana looked like a normal bar from the outside. I feared another drinking session was about to ensue, but I was pleasantly surprised as I followed Rees through the bar and to the back into a plant-filled area that was open to the skyline, tables nestled in a private recesses surrounded by shrubbery. It was also obvious by the amount of smoke rising from the shrubbery that it was an area where people could beat the smoking ban.

A young man dressed in an open flowery shirt that covered a white tee-shirt rose to meet Rees.

'Good to see you man.' He flung his arms around Rees who in turn patted him like a father.

'Jimmy, I want you to meet Kris Woods. He's over from England.'

'Good to meet you man.' Jimmy was about twenty-eight, good-looking with thin features and tight dark curly hair. He had a face that smiled all the time. Two expensive looking cameras hung from his neck.

As we sat down Jimmy unloaded his cameras and placed them

carefully out of sight at the base of a plant.

'Captain Rees,' the waiter shouted, as he approached with a handful of menus. Rees glanced at me as if I had just broken his cover. My mind started crunching away.

'Good to see you Pier, how is Melissa?'

'Ah, you know,' he threw his arms around in the air. 'Always a spending my money,' he gushed loudly.

'What will you have Captain Rees? We have some specials on today.'

'You choose, Pier.'

'Of course, Captain Rees.' He fussed with our glasses then disappeared inside.

'Captain?' I looked at Rees.

'Yeah, yeah, I was on the force.' The tone of his voice and his body language stopped me from asking further, but I didn't have to, after a few minutes of indifferent silence Rees blurted it out.

'They fucked me over big style,' he ranted. 'Me and Frank, unfortunately Frankie took it bad.' I sipped my red wine from the big balloon glass that almost covered my face and remained silent. 'Poor bastard died of lead poisoning.'

'What?'

'He had a .45 inserted into his skull. Ah,' he greeted Pier who arrived through the shrubs with an enormous plate of steaming pasta.

Talking with his mouth full of mince, which he was spitting all over the table, Rees cursed Sumers for causing his termination from New York's finest, as well as Frankie's demise. Further plates arrived and for the next twenty minutes food became the priority. Rees downed his claret in one slurp then gestured to me.

'Gimme your paper.' I pulled my treasured script from my pocket and placed it on the table.

'Enough to put you off your God damn food,' Rees cursed at the picture.

'Hey that's one of mine,' Jimmy said with pride. I hung on to his words like a lion about to pounce.

'Do you know who this woman is?' I remained tensed, 'Come on, say yes,' I pleaded inside. Jimmy shrugged his shoulders causing mine to sag. My shoulders straightened again as Jimmy spoke?

'I've seen her around though. A photographer doesn't forget a face like that, and those high cheek bones, yeah, I'm sure she's local.'

'What about him?' I pointed to the head that I suspected was Larry's.

'Give me a break dude; I'm not a clairvoyant.' I sagged again and Rees noticed.

'Hey, you're doing fine boy, you've got a lead within two days of arriving here. You now know they hang around with that scumbag Sumers.'

'It could be Larry Edwards.' I shot my eyes at Jimmy. Rees nodded at me.

'Some coincidence, don't you think?' Rees was still thinking like a cop and he knew that most false identities usually retain their forenames and so did I. Time in Belfast on stakeouts, hidden observation points and snatch squads had taught me the basics of clandestine activities.

'Who's Edwards? Are you sure it's him?'

'No, it's just a hunch, but I've seen this gang a few times and I never forget a face, it's the long features, it could be him. Those types hang around glitzy charity events to clock their marks, you know, the rich and stupid. I just steal their faces, not their cash like Edwards and co.'

'Well, what do you know about him?' I was again stalking Jimmy.

'Not much, just that he hangs around with the in, crowd the ones who never work, but always have dosh.'

'Have you seen him with her?' I jabbed my fingers at Laura's picture.

'Hey man I'm not sure, what's with the intense attitude, man? You need to chill out.'

'You'd be pretty intense Jimmy if what happened to Kris here, happened to you.' Rees looked at me. Jimmy rolled a joint then gasped smoke from his mouth and nose at the same time, which escaped into the skyline way above.

'Hey, I'm sorry man. My latest woman just bummed off with some wealthy dude again. It's always happening to me, there's not enough dosh in this game. I need a big break.'

There was a long silence then Pier appeared with his well-practised smile.

'Captain Rees.' I didn't hear the conversation. Rees was right though, I had done well; the name Larry for once was music to my ears and I had locals helping me.

Bob Sumers, I was fast learning, was a very controversial character and apparently incredibly dangerous. A political high flyer, he'd even run for Mayor once. Rees hated him so much that he couldn't finish a sentence about him without it degenerating in to swearing curses. Jimmy, however, after several joints, was as laid back as a well-fed cat basking in the small shaft of sunshine that was visiting us for a few minutes from between the skyscrapers way above.

Pier left us and Rees turned to me. 'Sumers is as bent as they come, involved with inner city development in conjunction with our Italian friends. He was accused a few years ago of being linked in an abduction and date rape, and there were rumours about a child porn ring, but the guy who was investigating him suddenly disappeared.' I nodded in silence. 'You'd better be careful, boy. If your friends are teamed up with him you could be walking into a lions' den.'

I looked at Rees and noticed the pistol grip of a Smith and Weston under his jacket.

'Insurance,' Rees said evenly with a squinty smile.

'So how did you get into writing?'

'Investigation is what I've done all my life. I've written so many goddamn reports I became a fiction writer. Now I write for the column inches, it's the same thing.'

'Yeah, I suppose it's the same sort of work.' I agreed, as an outsider I didn't have a clue where to start, and this contact was too good to screw up by asking too much too soon, but I soon went too far.

'So where does Sumers live then?' Rees looked at me. Then Jimmy interrupted.

'He's been keeping a low profile. I haven't seen him since Frank got plugged. No one knows where he is, but he's out there all right, no doubt controlling his puppets. He's even got the mob pissed with one of his crooked property deals, so I heard.'

'Why, that's a bit crazy, messing with those guys, isn't it?' Jimmy looked at Rees. The look they shared told me they both knew something.

'Sumers is crazy. He thinks he is beyond the law. One of the family's dons had a hit on him a few months ago. His eldest son caught the bullet and got wasted during the attempt. There never is a good time to piss the family off, especially at this moment in time. It would be suicidal after what just happened.' Jimmy sat back and looked at Rees.

'There's a big powder keg out there. Just one spark and the explosion will be felt by a lot of high rollers. They're all on edge and waiting for any excuse to retaliate.' Rees leant over to me. 'There are over eight million people in this here city, boy!' his eyes thinned. 'And each and every one will bite your hand off if you poke it in the wrong place, but there are a few that will cut off your head and stuff it up your butt without a second thought. Know where I'm coming from, boy?' I wanted to keep this experienced ex cop on my side so I nodded subserviently, yeah? I saw the Godfather film.'

I received another confused squint. 'I'll make a few calls and get back to you. Wanna lift?' he stood up and wrestled his sagging pants back over his stomach.

Rees drove New York style back to the Broadway Inn, leaving me on the pavement with ears ringing from his obscenities.

There were hundreds of Edwards in the massive telephone book. I sighed as I half-heartedly glanced through them. Stevens, Edwards...how many names does this bloody con artist have, and no doubt Laura would have changed her name? I thought of what I would say to her if I met her face to face. I couldn't prove a thing yet. At least Rees believed me, or was he only interested in getting revenge on Sumers for wasting his pal and costing him his career? I didn't even remember all the other things he held Somers responsible for. I felt mentally drained.

The car horns woke me; my illuminated wristwatch told me it was nine thirty p.m.
I showered then slipped on my new Levis and my comfy bomber jacket, then headed out to the roar of 47th street. Walking around in no particular direction I adjusted the mobile in my pocket, it hadn't

rung for ages. If I dropped dead right now nobody would care. Was this entire search going to be a waste of time?

I stopped at a window. The Collins Bar looked stylish. Inside small groups of people were laughing and generally having a good time. The right side wall had sports photos covering it, famous boxers and baseball players. Ironically I had heard of most of them, which gave me bizarre comfort. On the opposite wall was the most diverse jukebox I had ever seen. The atmosphere was relaxing, so I sat at the bar.

'Hi there, what can I get you?' the diminutive barmaid asked, with smiling eyes.

'Bud, please.'

'Are you Australian?'

I smiled while shaking my head. 'I'm from England.' I replied trying to look cool in the trendy surroundings and then I drew from the bottle. The froth expanded into my nose causing me to cough and splutter uncontrollably. 'Fuck it,' I cursed to myself as the barmaid passed me a handful of napkins.

'Sorry, it went down the wrong way,' I croaked. She smiled politely, which made me feel even more stupid.

I escaped to a table while clearing my throat to the sound of 'Pebbles on the Beach' by Paul Weller.

'Hi there.' The voice made me look up. It was the angel from the reception at the New York Times building.

'Hi,' I squeaked. I cleared my throat then tried again. 'Hi.' I paused searching my memory then nodded. 'Patsy isn't it?' She smiled back.

'Are you all alone here?'

I nodded. 'Yeah.'

'Why not join us?' I looked over where two black dudes sat staring with stone faces.

'Err, its OK.' Shit! I cursed myself, 'Get up you idiot!' Her enduring smile forced me up.

'Guys this is, sorry,' she tittered into her hand.

'Kris.'

'Kris is English.'

There was silence. These guys weren't going to jump up and hug me. They just rolled their eyes at me while Patsy pulled me on to a chair, and without further introductions started to fire questions at me. The two guys finished their beers and banged the bottles down and then left without a word, while eyeballing threats.

'Gee, thanks for that, Kris. That was my half cousin, the older one; he's always trying to pair his friend off with me.' I looked at her thinking what a knob I was for thinking she remotely fancied me.

'I can't blame him. I mean… err.' Patsy smiled then snatched my empty bottle, spun on her seat in quick time and made for the bar, swinging her shapely Levi clad bottom.

'There you go, it's the least I can do for saving me from Leroy.' She placed the bottle in front of me then sat down and counted her change. I felt embarrassed at being used to rid her of those guys, but at least I was sitting with a pretty girl and not alone.

Silence ensued then the big flashing box broke into Lou Reed's 'Perfect Day'. I drifted into the past. Perfect Day was Vicky's and my song; we played it at our wedding. I hadn't heard it for years and it suddenly overwhelmed me. Maybe it was delayed shock or something. I just felt really low. I was miles away in a strange place with no friends, just memories.

'Are you all right, Kris?'

My heavy eyes must have betrayed me as I sniffed. 'Yeah, yeah I'm fine.'

Patsy looked seriously at me. 'Do you wanna talk away those sad puppy dog eyes? I think you need to. I've got all the time in the world.'

I half smiled as Lou finished his song with 'You Only Reap Just What You Sow'. I'd sowed so much in my life and only reaped injustice.

After lots more buds and more melancholy songs from the big flashing box Patsy sat shaking her head slowly with disbelief. I had told her everything. It just poured out of me like water. She listened with genuine interest and compassion. After all, what harm could she do me?

'Jeez, that's some story,' she said shaking her head. 'So what... so what are you gonna do now?'

'Revenge' I said evenly, 'is high on the list, but I've got to be careful, I want my life back and I've got only one shot, it's got to be a....' As her hand closed onto mine I turned to her. 'A good one.' I smiled again; her eyes held their gaze and her hand held the squeeze.

'You should smile more often, Kris. You look cool when you smile.'

I enjoyed the moment, fully expecting her to get up and go at any second, leaving me staring into my beer, instead she stood up still holding my hand and I was truly shocked when she said.

'Shall we go now?'

I found it hard to shave. I was grinning like an asylum inmate as I called to mind the honesty of her big dark eyes, and the feel of her luscious curvy body, as we snogged like teenagers here in this room. It didn't go any further, but just holding her and receiving kisses from her had made me feel so much better and ready to speed up my mission. 'Wow,' I shouted and slapped aftershave on to my face, 'you lucky bastard,' I told myself through the mirror. My smile fell as the phone rang.

'It's Rees. I've been asking around. We need to meet.' A car horn sounded. 'Get a fucking life jerk. Pier's at 2.30,' Beep. Beep. 'And you, up your bucket ya big fruit.'

It was just after 10 a.m. Four-and-a-half hours to wait. The way Rees was raving off I wondered if his heart would last that long. I decided to walk as far as I could, firstly to get some exercise and secondly to pass some time, but speculating what Rees wanted or had found out was crowding my mind.

The sweet smell of flowers wafted into my nostrils displacing the smell of fumes for just a moment, reminding me of The Lodge for a few fleeting seconds. Ten minutes later, after leaving the flower shop, I was passing the big building where Patsy worked.

I hung around until a youth on a flowery decorated scooter pulled on to the kerb and removed a bouquet from his top box. I peeped through a small slit in the blind and watched Patsy and her friends fussing over them. I smiled to myself. It was the least I could have done for such an unselfish act, which had left me feeling a hundred times more confident. I only hoped it wasn't just a sympathy thing.

It didn't take as long as I anticipated getting to Bleecker Street where it joins Charles Street in a well-to-do area called West Village.

Pier eyed me with suspicion until I mentioned 'Captain Rees,' which jogged his memory and sent him dashing around the tables with handfuls of cutlery, like a clockwork mouse. I ordered a large glass of wine. Rees sounded well fed up on the phone and was probably ready for a session anyway, so I ordered a large carafe.

Despite the appalling traffic, Rees, as usual, arrived on time pulling up his battered Lincoln with loud tyre squeals. He deposited more rubbish into the gutter as he struggled like an upturned beetle to climb out.

'Fucking morons, all of them,' he ranted, breathless as he grabbed the wine and filled a glass until it overflowed onto the red tablecloth. 'If they don't know how to drive they should stay off the goddamn roads, fucking morons.' He flopped into a chair; exposing veins on his forehead that were close to bursting. Out came his hankie as almost on cue he wiped the sweat from the back of his neck. 'Well, boy, you've certainly found yourself a whole lot of shit.' He gulped the glass empty as if he was drinking water and then helped himself to another. 'The deeper I dig the more piles up, shit I mean.'

'Have you found out if it is Stevens, sorry I mean Edwards?'

'Gee whiz, if the guy you call Edwards is the same guy who we know in the precinct as Larry Retch then you've hit the bottom of the shit can.'

'Captain Rees, it's good to see you again so soon, what will you have today?' Pier nodded to me. 'And your Australian friend?'

'English, for Christ sake,' I protested in a deliberately strong Yorkshire accent.

'You prefer an English dish, huh?' He sounded disappointed. Pier was either winding me up or thought I was Crocodile Dundee.

'Gimme one of those seafood platters, you know that feeds two.' Rees butted in then looked at me.

I nodded eagerly. 'You like seafood?' I smiled thinking of Jenny ripping the tail from a large lobster and grinning up at me as she eagerly chewed it.

'Yeah,' I replied softly, still lost in seafood memories.

'You'll like this,' he nodded father like. 'Where was I?'

'What? Oh yeah,' I reached for my glass. 'The bottom of a shit can.'

Rees lit a big cigar and disappeared for a few seconds in the smoke.

'You see Sumers past is vague.' He wafted away the smoke to see me better. 'I uncovered quite a bit of dirt a few years ago, which cost me my badge when I tried to pin it to him. The ranks closed, and papers disappeared, you know the stuff. They pinned missing police funds on me. All a fucking set up. If Larry Retch is your man we will have to keep the lid tightly closed, for both our sakes. You hear where I'm coming from boy?'

I nodded.

'You see I know Retch and Sumers go back a long, long way. Professional scams, heists, embezzlements can be traced to Retch because he did time. I suspected Sumers was his old partner in crime, but there's no solid proof. If he did receive ill-gotten funds from Retch to boost his run up the political ladder, his career would be over in a cloud of shame. If any links could be made, the person pointing the finger would have to be careful and remain invisible.'

I was deep in thought. 'Stevens, no Retch I mean, if it is him, really conned me big time, but he did it through the courts, you know, properly. It's that scheming bitch I need to find.' For a second I was holding the baseball bat again and chasing her around Central Park.

'Good briefs make everything foggy to hide their client. That's what they did to you. A loner hasn't a chance in hell against them. They will both have numerous ID's which they switch whenever they want, bank accounts, driving licences and passports; you see you're dealing with true professionals here. They have lived on the edge of the law all their lives; they disappear and re-invent themselves as casually as other folk have haircuts.'

Pier appeared, struggling with a big silver tray. He lowered it carefully onto the table, revealing almost every fish and shellfish imaginable. It lay among tomatoes, cucumber and rosso lettuce, plus other stuff I'd never seen before. He stood proudly with hands on hips, beaming like a graphic on a restaurant window.

'Jesus, you could have stocked an aquarium with this lot.' I joked, but received no reply; Rees was all ready stuffing half a crayfish noisily into his mouth.

An hour later and after two more carafes of wine the table looked like a sea lion had thrown up on it. Rees was sitting back trying to avoid bursting out of his heavily stained shirt while belching for the USA.

'The woman, I've got to find her,' I said, in-between louder belches from Rees.

'If she's got a record and I reckon she will have, considering the company she keeps, it should be simple. I'm waiting for Jimmy to email a copy of the original shots he took then I will get it run through the computer.' He belched.

'What, the police database?'

'Yeah, old friends of mine, I'll call in a few favours and see if I can get more on Sumers,' he threw a twenty-dollar bill on the table. 'Got to go, wanna lift?'

'No thanks, I'll walk some of this food off.' The thought of projectile vomiting out of a car window while careering around Times Square didn't appeal to me. Anyway I was in no rush to go anywhere.

Chapter Nine

I had been in New York for four nights, and was in my fifth day. October was flying past. I felt a little despondent at not having the local knowledge to be able to get around the town freely, and ask the type of questions I was aching to ask. I was walking through Central Park along the Mall to pass a few hours before my two p.m. meet with Rees, when my mobile rang.

'Hello?'

'Hi Kris, it's Jenny.' A warm wave ran through me.

'Hi there, you're a voice I didn't expect to hear.'

'I went round to see you and they told me you were in America. What are you doing there?'

'Hell, it's all gone loopy, Jenny. Laura Stevens is still alive.'

There was silence. 'I don't understand, Kris. What do you mean, alive?' She must have thought I'd totally lost it and Laura had been found doing the breaststroke somewhere off the coast of France.

'Alive and in New York, well somewhere here, and with lying Larry.' There was still silence. 'They faked it all, you know, so they could sue me and get my assets and all my savings, including my sovereign money.'

'They found Ferret, Kris. A beam trawler off Guernsey trawled his body up. It's in all the papers. He was weighed down with an anchor chain, Kris. Mary, your landlady said the police are asking questions about your whereabouts. You know what she's like, she told them the truth, that you had gone to America, well, New York.'

Shit. My mind was racing.

'Jenny, are you at home for a few days?'

'Yes, for two weeks. The job's really great and the money is good. You were right all along, Kris.'

'I'm chuffed for you. How's Paul?'

'Fine. We're going out for a meal tomorrow, it's his birthday.'

'Good, look, I need time to think Jenny. Can I call you later on?'

'Yeah of course Kris, it's nice to hear your voice again.'

'Yours as well, catch you later. Bye, then.' She said softly, 'Take care, Kris.' There was a long silence. 'I still miss you.'

'I'm...' My battery gave its last dying beep and I lost her. 'Shit.' She'll think I cut her off, I didn't like fobbing her off like that but my thoughts were fizzing like uncorked champagne. I was seen publicly trying to drown Ferret one day, and now what is left of him has been trawled up, off the same island where I had, in their eyes, committed manslaughter. Even Inspector Clouseau would have got it in one. It couldn't get any worse. The hand of fate wasn't just slapping me in the face; it seemed to be putting the boot in as well. Then cold realism began to sink in. If I failed to expose these conning bastards, instead of sitting in my flat bitter and twisted, but free, I could be facing the rest of my days locked up for a murder I didn't commit. I felt close to slinking away somewhere obscure and becoming a silent illegal hermit in this big country. It was an option.

I walked for a while as joggers of all shapes and sizes hobbled past blowing steam into the cold air, which I noticed had dropped several degrees already since I had arrived here. My head felt full of dark ruins again. I couldn't even return home now, but if I hadn't come here I'd be locked away on a murder charge by now. I had to somehow expose the truth.

The room was if anything more untidy than on my first visit. Rees tried on several occasions to balance his fat cigar on the summit of stubs that filled his ashtray. Eventually he gave up and stuffed it into the side of his mouth and greeted me with a pat on the shoulder.

'How's it going, Kris?'

'Shit.' I couldn't hide how I felt.

His face turned into the cop again as he studied me. 'Bad news is it?'

'You could say. Have you heard from Jimmy? You know the photo?'

His sly smile made me feel reassured. He had some news. 'Laura Retch is her real name; she has got form, plenty of it.' He moved a brown A4 envelope that had 'Rees' scribbled on it and passed me a folder that was beneath it. It contained arrest sheets and had several mug shots of her holding up numbers. She was obviously younger and looked even more attractive than I remembered her. There were fingerprints on the photocopies of her arrest sheets, but it appeared she never served a sentence, having been awarded bail each time and always represented by some top notch brief. She'd got off every charge. They consisted of bribery, corruption and several confidence scams, which involved the old and ill, not at all a good résumé for one so elegant and attractive. Then I saw it. One of the proofs Jimmy had provided leapt out of the file as if on a cartoon spring. Larry, whatever his damn name was, had tried, as most of those in the photo had, to turn his back on the press, but Jimmy had caught his side profile, and the bastard's reflection could be seen in a nearby car window. Those long-recognisable features confirmed one hundred percent to me that it was hound faced Larry.

'Can I pay you for these? There could still be her fingerprints on my old boat and if the shit hits the fan these could be crucial to me.' Rees drew on his cigar while again interrogating me with his cop's eyes.

'No mention of me, boy, that's the way it's got to stay.' He paused and looked troubled. 'All you told me was the truth?'

'Of course it was, why?'

'A guy, I believe you called him some English rodent?'

'Ferret.' I knew what was coming next. Rees was still a cop and he certainly felt like one right now.

'Did you sink him?'

'I swear on my life, no.'

'It *is* your life now, boy! Your file is over here. It says that the chain found on Fred Ireland's body matches the stuff that's stored on your old boat.' He looked sternly at me, watching the hope the documents had brought me fading from my eyes.

He grunted as he snapped out of whatever he was thinking. 'I believe you, Kris. Everything else you told me figures out.' Those few words meant so much. 'I don't want you to contact me here anymore or call me from anything that resembles a telephone. Have you a mobile?' I nodded. 'Destroy it now.' I crushed the phone with my boot heel and suddenly felt even more isolated.

'What are you doing? I meant the sim card.' I looked at him speechless. He shook his head slowly.

'We have total access to all British security files in the U.S.A.

You will have to get out of your hotel immediately and find somewhere where they don't ask for papers. You're on the run now! Meet me at Pier's tomorrow at ten p.m.' He walked to the door and opened it while puffing out smoke. 'Keep your head down boy.'

I stood with my bag outside the hotel like a lost runaway not knowing which direction to take. I eventually ended up back in the Collins bar. I'd been there for about an hour, desperately rummaging through my New York City guide for some idea where to find dodgy digs. I wasn't having much success as the well-researched book didn't have a section that catered for fugitives. I was feeling totally depressed. Instead of getting revenge I was now being hunted for murder. Then a beer mat hit my head. I didn't look up. I hadn't done since I had arrived. Then another mat skimmed on to my table, which caused me to look up. As if things weren't bad enough, sat with about eight of his rapper mates was Leroy. The way he looked told me in no uncertain terms that he wasn't going to rush to the bar and get me another bud.

I called the waitress over. It was the same girl who witnessed me choking the other night. As she placed a chequered cloth on to the bar to free her hands I discreetly put all my cash into the green folder Rees had given to me, and folded the flap inside the folder, securing it the best I could like a big envelope. She came over.

'What can I get you?'

I nearly said, 'A shotgun.'

'Do you know Patsy who comes in here, she works for the Times.'

'Sure, I know little Patsy.'

'Could you do me a big favour and give her this for me?' I slipped her ten dollars and she returned to the bar with my only hope.

The boys were getting more impatient by the minute. They were flashing their eyes and teeth from the dark corner like a pack of hyenas. One of the rappers fell off his high stool and distracted the others. It was time.

I shot through the door, still gripping my bag and ran as fast as I could to nowhere. I could hear their shouts as they followed. My luck was on form. They were closing in on me. The fucking Harlem Globetrotters were chasing me, not a good thing at my age. I could hear a guy behind me. I was probably taking six strides to his one. He clipped my ankle like a footballer's foul, and I slapped onto the paving stones like a joint of beef. I remember seeing a dented coke can, and then lots of size twelve designer trainers, that was all I remembered.

Some kind taxi driver had taken me to the nearest A&E where I was cleaned up and made comfortable. As the morning shift started arriving I dressed and slipped painfully out and into the cold street.

I hobbled around most of the morning mainly to keep warm, then made my way back to the Collins bar using the Times building as my guide. I assumed the globetrotters had taken all my belongings; there was nothing beside my bed, but the clothes I'd got tackled in. Thankfully I still had my bomber jacket; although it was thin it still felt warm.

I snatched a glance at my reflection in an immaculate shiny window of some wealthy legal firm. My head and face were bigger than yesterday and patched up with stitches and butterfly dressings. Thankfully rappers don't wear Doc Martins.

As usual in the Big Apple no one stared or looked my way. If my head fell off I doubt anyone would have noticed. I cursed myself for not saving my passport and credit card, but they were no doubt stopped, or now could be instrumental in revealing my location. Hopefully my cash and files were safe. If they weren't, a quick jump off the nearest bridge would be my next move. At least the cold water would be familiar.

I entered the bar, which was almost empty. A youth was cleaning the big jukebox; he looked at me without a reaction. I waited for a waitress to come to me.

'Ish…err the girl with the pony tail on today?' I asked with a painful struggle through my bust lip.

'Joe's in the back. I'll get her.' Joe was probably in her early twenties, about Jenny's age. She reacted as though a pin had just pricked her when she saw me. 'Gee, I'm so sorry, I had no idea.' I shook my head. I was finding it too painful to talk unnecessarily.

'My folder. Is it?' she interrupted.

'I gave it to Patsy as you asked; she came here not long after you rushed out.' I struggled with a thank you as her expressions shared my pain.

I made my way the best I could to see Patsy. Limping across the marble floor I received sudden interest from the security men. I looked a total mess.

'Is Patsy av? I couldn't do 'available' so I ended with a gasping 'here?'

The girl looked at me with concern. 'I'm sorry. She's taken a vacation.' Shit, the bridge looked even closer now. 'She'll be back tomorrow.'

I couldn't hide my relief and I smiled. Well, I was going through the motions of a smile. I must have looked like Charles Laughton doing his best ever hunchback impression.

I had to walk to Piers. For the moment I was broke. If shapely Patsy had opened the file and clocked the wads of notes and shared them with lanky Leroy I was fucked, and it would be a lonely walk to the nearest bridge for me.

Rees was always punctual. As I turned the corner of the block the black Lincoln screeched to a halt in a blue haze of burning rubber.

'What the fuck has happened to you?' he gasped. 'You've been hit by a tram?' I didn't want to go into the nitty details about me trying to steal someone's ambition and them getting revenge, so I told him that I had been mugged, at least he might feel sorry for me and lend me a few dollars.

'Goddamn low lives,' he cursed, 'are you all right?' He looked me over, while noisily puffing his cigar, quick time.

'Yeah, just bruises.'

Sitting at the same table where we demolished half the Great Barrier Reef, Rees gave me the eye treatment. 'What are you gonna do boy? I mean, what are your plans? You have Jack shit to go on. You're the one who's under suspicion now, not them. You need hard evidence these days to get a DA to consider a case. Some English guy on the run with a bullshit tale like yours… sucks to say the least.'

I sat in silence. He was right, but I hadn't come this far to give up and get locked up.

'Come on, Rees, think of the story you would have. You said yourself that they were at the bottom of the shit pile. Surely we can find something more about them.'

'Have you found somewhere to stay yet?' I shook my head. 'Here's a key to Jimmy's apartment. It's in the Chelsea district, a few blocks north of here. West 21st off Ninth. Number 114. It's on the west side. Mind yer butt though, the area's full of faggots.'

'Jimmy's not, is he?' Rees grinned.

'Nah, Jimmy's straight as an arrow, his true love is his photography. He suggested you lie up there, he's hardly there anyway.'

I felt instantly relieved as the fear of roaming the streets like a vagrant suddenly evaporated.

'Here.' Rees passed me an envelope, which I opened. *'E 68th Off 5th Avenue, number 40.'* I looked up at him. He had his face almost inside a large glass of red wine and looked hideously distorted.

'What's this?'

He swallowed with a sigh. 'The Edwards, sorry, the Retch's are staying there, that's all I can get at the moment. I have lots of feelers out for you boy, just sit tight and hope that we dig something up soon. Oh, by the way, don't go bashing the door down like that James Bond guy of yours. I'm trying my best.'

'Thanks mate.' Rees must have liked being called mate. He nodded a warm smile at me then handed me twenty dollars.

'Get yourself some English tea, you look like you need it.' He grinned, amused at the state I was in, and I couldn't blame him.

Jimmy's apartment was functional. It was clean and tidy and thankfully had two bedrooms. It was obvious which one was the spare room. It was sparsely decorated with a mixture of furnishings from different eras. I didn't look into Jimmy's. It was good of him to trust me considering we had only met once. I made myself a drink while I ran the bath, which was a big deep cast iron one.

The main living room was quite unique. Every wall was covered in photographs. Hardly an inch of wallpaper could be seen. Just as well. It must have been brought over by those limey immigrants - it looked so ancient. I took my mug of PG tips into the bathroom and sank into warm soapy heaven.

Patsy had heard about my kicking. Thankfully she didn't approve, which was why she left the Collins bar almost as soon as she had arrived, mercifully with my folder. I shared Patsy's lunch hour with her while struggling with my cappuccino like a dribbling old man. I told her that I had moved out of the hotel and gave her Jimmy's telephone number. I didn't want to get too involved with Patsy despite her cracking good looks. It had painful complications, some I could feel right now. She had been kind to me and could be of help in the future, but as we parted I glanced back at Patsy and through the file of marching bodies I saw her watching me, she looked troubled and was wringing her hands.

I made my way to one of the most prosperous and respectable areas in town, 5th Avenue. I walked steadily north-east and joined 5th at the Rockefeller Centre. The whole area seemed to be well planned out with offices and architecture mixing together well. I passed some representations of 'Cubism' by famous artists; a bag of shit sprang to mind.

Then I noticed the area change to all out glamour as I approached Cartier, Gucci and Tiffany and Co. Posh limos were everywhere, some parked outside and others were cruising around waiting for their eccentric employers. Spoilt dogs waddled along wearing more jewellery than my poor old mother had gathered in her entire lifetime. It all looked bling and flash but fumes and bullshit is what I noticed the most.

I veered down a side avenue and found a motorcycle store, where I bought a full-face helmet that had a tinted slide-down visor and a leather jacket and gloves, to look like a biker. I would be able to get up close to anyone now without being clocked. As I walked out I noticed a row of flashy Peugeot scooters lining the footpath. It made me stop and think. Walking along the streets dressed like Robo-cop could encourage suspicion, despite witnessing some of the weirdest people I'd ever seen strutting along the footpaths or sidewalks as they are called here. One scooter was all black and pretty worn in places with big scratches. Nevertheless it would blend in anywhere nicely, and it was only $500.

I changed some cash, getting ripped off with the crap exchange rate then returned and bought the scooter for $475. Sod the legalities of insurance and all that stuff. After all, I was on the run now. Strangely I liked the feeling. It reminded me of youthful irresponsibility.

Number 40 East 68th was a big elegant colonial styled building with two driveways. One was signed 'Entrance' the other 'Exit Only'. It was immaculately painted brilliant white, and big pillars guarded its unnecessarily large shiny black doors. I passed the building a few times on my twist and go. The area between the entrances had trees and shrubs growing there. It was an ideal place to set up an observation point, as the thick shrubbery ran almost up to the big doors. I decided to stop and watch the exit driveway for a while and for the first time in ages my luck changed. It was in the form of a woman on foot leaving from the entrance drive. I instantly recognised her perfect catwalk movement. Butterflies swarmed around my stomach. It was Laura for sure.

I turned the small ignition key and my twist and go vibrated beneath me. I had to follow her carefully, with her form she must have been followed in the past, but she just sauntered along as if she didn't have a care in the world, while exhibiting her shapely arse, which I could still clearly remember lustfully cupping with both hands.

We slowly skirted the north edge of Central Park where dog walkers and joggers competed for space. She turned right at the Grand Army Plaza then continued south across the road and into a big building called the Plaza Hotel.

I stopped on the opposite side of Central Park South. The Plaza according to my new guidebook was expensive to say the least. Double rooms started at $365 a night, up to a celebratory price of $15,000 a night. What the hell was she doing in there? I couldn't imagine her having a part time cleaning job.

I sat looking at my guidebook and kept a watch on the hotel entrance in one of the scooter's small rear mirrors. In front of me people grabbed shit from the tired piss stained grass as joggers of all shapes and sizes dodged the crouched dogs.

Almost three hours and a full bin of dog muck later, Laura appeared at the doors, a young man in uniform rushed to open them. She adjusted herself, smiled her thanks then slinked down the marble stairs and headed in the same direction she had come from.

I was pleased with the scooter. It was perfect for nipping in and out of the traffic and blended almost invisibly with all the cars that crowded the roads. Laura disappeared back inside number 40. I waited for another two hours then returned to Jimmy's and parked the scooter in his hallway.

The next day I found a camping shop and purchased two green ground sheets, a green sleeping bag, and some thick warm gloves. I needed to talk to Jimmy about a suitable camera so I returned to his flat. I knew immediately that he was home as soon as I entered. The hallway no longer smelt of motor scooter, the distinct smell of dope had taken over.

'Hi man,' Jimmy greeted me, through a blue haze while making a coffee. 'Want one?'

'Cheers mate,' I accepted.

'How did you get to know Rees? He's a pretty elusive dude.'

'A girl called Patsy at the Times building. She's a receptionist there and a bit of a doll.'

'Gee man, you get around fast.' We laughed.

'Jimmy, if I wanted to take photos day and night, without a flash going off, which camera would you recommend?' I knew he was going to say an S.L.R. and he did, being a professional, with his own dark room.

'What about a digital camera?' I had one at home which you could download to send the pictures by e-mail, but it was dead basic.

'How much do you want to spend man?' My mind was whirling. If I got a decent digital camera I would be able to send proof of her existence directly to anyone anywhere. I was getting excited at that thought.

Jimmy was pleased to help me, and after our coffees he ushered me through parts of the City I'd never even heard of. I was amazed how many people knew him. I must have heard 'Hi Jimmy' dozens of times before I was marched into a big store called B&H Photo Video on 9th Avenue.

We were instantly greeted by more 'Hi Jimmy's, and even more at the end of every aisle. The place bristled with everything photographic. Jimmy roamed freely behind counters and into display cabinets as if he owned the place. He was one popular guy.

I had so many cameras to choose from so I did what I used to do when my life was good; I got one of the best. A Fuji S602 pro. It apparently had ultra high resolution, six million pixels, whatever that meant, and it could store hundreds of digital shots on one little 128 meg card that loaded straight onto a P.C. via a card reader connected by a USB cable. It also had a 6x zoom with good low light qualities and a silent shutter that could snatch five frames per second, and you could also make short videos with it.

'The dog's bollocks or what?' I said to Jimmy who agreed, but still wouldn't have used such an automatic idiot-proof device even if he had a gun to his head.

I also purchased a nice state of the art laptop. It was the smallest I could find. It had everything built into it, modem, sound card, CD re-writer, twin headlights and all that stuff. By the end of the day I would have blown almost one thousand dollars, but thanks to Jimmy the man I got the lot for just six hundred, which strengthened my opinion about 'Rip off a Briton'. I was now in business.

I always thought of The Big Apple as being an impersonal 'fall down on the street and get stepped over' sort of place, but being with Jimmy, who was obviously born and bred here, I began to feel differently about the city. There was still the crime and poverty that all big cities share, but a day out with a proper New Yorker made me realise that it was like being a member of a really big happy family. Never the less I had to get my head around to the reason I was here, and the particular people who didn't deserve to be members of the big family.

I packed my new Bergen with all the gear I calculated I would need to support what is known as hard routine observation. Warm clothing and a sleeping bag, ground sheets, water and Mars Bars and packets of sliced ham all wrapped in silent Clingfilm. I also had with me a large hunting knife, condoms, plastic bags, and a dark green balaclava, an aerosol containing pepper spray and some cam cream to disguise my eyes and mouth.

I had just finished filling the bag when with a crash Rees fell through the door. I immediately thought he had been on the piss, but on closer inspection he looked worse than I did after being used as a football. He was bleeding badly from several deep lacerations to his face and had obviously had a good kicking as well. I helped him into a chair and rushed to the sink for some water.

It must have been a Stanley knife or something similar by the look of the cuts. They were terrible, one had gone right through his cheek and was blowing red bubbles as he panted like a dog trapped in a sun-baked car. I tried to slow the bleeding with several tea towels, but the direct pressure made him shake with pain. He was going into deep shock. I had to get him to a hospital fast. As I pulled him up he struggled to sit back down.

'Come on Rees you need help and fast,' I shouted at him. Again I tried and again he resisted. After the fifth or sixth attempt he was almost out of it, he was spitting blood all over while trying to talk as I virtually dragged him down the stairs and past the scooter, slipping on his blood as I dragged him towards the door.

He raised his foot and pushed against the door so I couldn't open it while he attempted to draw something on the wall with his blood he was muttering. 'Ohf, oth, oth.'

I struggled with his constant refusals to move and managed eventually to get him through the door where I could hail a cab.

I abruptly found out why he'd struggled so much. Two men rushed from the shadows towards us. I was holding Rees upright with his arm held around my neck. My other arm was around his waist, holding him up the best I could. I froze as a flash burst from one of the men's hands, then I felt a sickening thud followed by a loud crack as the first bullet hit Rees, making me spin forty-five degrees from the force of the impact.

A painful blood-curdled gurgle escaped from poor Rees. At the same time his legs buckled, dragging me down with him. Another loud crack pierced the air and a stomach-churning thud followed as another high calibre bullet tore into him. I scrambled to my feet half-crawling half-falling towards the door. Another two cracks rang out. One splintered the doorframe close to my head; these guys weren't taking prisoners.

I hit the scooter painfully with my knee, knocking it over and falling onto it. I crawled over it like a madman. Clearing the bike I scrambled up the stairs. I could hear 'Shit' and other loud curses behind me, as they fell over the scooter like a comedy act, but this was no laughing matter.

I was slipping on blood all the way up the stairs then everything turned to slow motion. I rounded the corner at the top of the landing and shouldered the door. It was a big old house and it had big old doors. I had to slow down and get the key into the lock in one, a hard thing to do when you can hear the grim reaper clattering up the stairs to collect you. I concentrated and did it just as my peripheral vision registered movement. I slammed the door shut and slid the bolt across. Luckily there was enough light coming through the window for me to grab the Bergen. I snatched the laptop from the table and stuffed it into the bag. The door was getting the meathead treatment, but holding up. Then it exploded in a spray of splinters as bullets tore it to pieces. The bedroom was my only escape; I burst in and slid the window upwards. Just a black hole greeted me.

The alley was about twenty feet below and I knew people who lived here used it to store their refuse sacks. I'd seen them when I looked out the window during daylight.

The air rushed past me as I fell into the blackness, I sensed something closing then bang, my knees banged into my chin as I hit the ground and bags at the same time, knocking all the air from my lungs as small stars began darting in my eyes. Then a big star flashed above me joined by a loud ricochet, which bounced off the wall, similar to the ones in a cowboy movie.

I got up and ran for my life, bouncing from the alley walls like a ball, while stumbling over the rubbish bags. I exited the alley at the end of the block of buildings and ran towards Fifth Avenue as fast as my aching body would let me.

As I reached people I slowed down to blend in. My breath was gushing out in big white clouds in the cold air. A few minutes later my adrenalin rush slowly abated and I no longer looked like a two-legged steam engine, but I was trembling so much my muscles were aching and I was wet with sweat. I put on my new waterproof jacket to hide the blood that had come from poor Rees and stopped and got a burger and a hot drink from a van then sat down to recover. I felt so sorry for Rees. If I hadn't tried taking him outside he might still be alive. No wonder he resisted. He knew what was waiting for him in the street. Then again he'd have bled to death the way he was cut up. Either way I felt that I had fucked up big style, and let him down. I only hoped Jimmy would be all right. As I calmed down and nibbled nervously at my burger the area became alive with blues and whites racing towards Jimmy's place. I could certainly never return there.

My illuminated watch told me it was 3.30 a.m. New York never sleeps so they say, but it does slow down and it had done now. I stayed in the shadows as I approached the exit drive. At least I would see oncoming headlights if a car appeared. Eighteen careful steps got me into the shrubs.

Dense Christmas tree type firs and broad leaf bushes, possibly rhododendrons, hugged the soft soil making it ideal for a hide. Low lights illuminated the steps leading to the big shiny black doors, enabling me to find a position almost unreachable and right in the centre of the bushes. The better-kept accessible shrubs, the ones next to the drive, were trimmed back, allowing me a good view of the steps while remaining virtually invisible.

I scraped a shallow valley in the peat-like soil and then laid one of the ground sheets folded in half into the scrape, on which I laid out the sleeping bag I rolled out the second ground sheet over the top, ensuring a good overlap to keep out any rain.

I couldn't have asked for a better observation point. It had taken an hour to set up, working in complete silence while remaining almost flat out. I climbed in and immediately the warmth started to build up in this cosy cocoon. I decided to get some sleep. I was sure the house occupants weren't going to show their faces till at least mid morning. Despite being in someone's front garden I felt safe and secure.

A blackbird totally oblivious of my presence serenaded me from only a few feet away, as I quietly withdrew a couple of slices of ham for my breakfast, which I followed with a wrapper less Mars Bar from within the soft and silent Clingfilm. I finished off my grand meal with a few little sips of water. Eating had to be kept to the minimum. I didn't want to be shitting and farting.

I checked the camera and made sure that the spare battery was accessible. Now I was fully operational.

Rees kept jumping into my thoughts. The poor sod must have been in agony the way his face was shredded. I wondered who could have done such a terrible thing then I remembered Northern Ireland and some of the terrible things I witnessed there. It's truly sickening to see what a sadistic maniac can do with an electric drill and an angle grinder. It certainly kicks you into maturity while making you sort of numb inside, a feeling that never leaves you. Then an hour later you're competing in the cookhouse for the least rubbery fried egg on the hot plate for your army classic, the egg banjo.

I snapped out of my thoughts as the sound of tyres on gravel approached from my left.

The crooks' standard issue, a black car, pulled into view and the driver stepped out and slammed the door. His feet crunched on the gravel as he walked towards and up the steps.

I already had six shots of him before he scratched his arse, but he never turned so I only had his hairstyle to look at.

Another two hours passed then he appeared at the door with Larry. I gave them the five frames a second treatment. They walked towards the car and as Larry passed the bonnet, heading for the passenger door, I zoomed onto his long, unattractive face, which was smiling just as I remembered, reluctantly I captured it.

After the car purred away I checked out the shots in the Fuji's small colour LCD screen. Anyone who had been through what I had been through over the last few years could be forgiven for suffering from attacks of melancholy and looking at Larry through the crystal clear screen spurred one on.

I was basking in the sun with Larry and Laura for a few seconds and I was enjoying life to the full. My mind had released something that gave me the recollection of happiness. Then the camera clicked softly as the screen turned itself off to save power, and I returned to the cruel realism of sitting in the soil thousands of miles from what little home I had left and remembered that I was most likely on Interpol's top ten most wanted.

The door opened and out walked Laura. She looked quickly around, turned and looked back inside. I was in David Bailey mode again, keenly snapping away. Then I saw them. David Bailey suddenly wanted to do a Lord Lucan; I slowly lowered the camera and froze as two of the biggest black dogs squeezed through the door together. They only just cleared the gap.

They were huge and Rottweiler's; the biggest I'd ever seen weighed in at eighty pounds and I reckon these two bastards could have had it for breakfast. What pissed me off more is that my hard-earned money had probably paid for them. My heart was beating so hard I was afraid the dogs would hear it. Everyone who has ever done an O.P. fears this happening, but the thought of these beasts face to face, with me trapped under the low branches of a bush made me feel sick. I imagined them dragging me into the open, then tearing apart the sleeping bag while Laura watched on, amused until she saw who was being eaten. Then she would be even more enthralled and near to an orgasm at seeing who was being turned into dog shit.

I remained frozen like a rabbit in car headlights as they went about their business of spoiling the grass verges, while at the same time sniffing out every scent molecule that passed their big wet snouts.

There was little wind and thankfully I hadn't been far enough into the grounds to leave a scent trail for them. Five minutes passed like five hours, then Laura clapped her hands and they moved slowly towards the steps. Just before they entered the black door a bird flew into the bush and landed a few inches from me. It must have done the same thing lots of times before, it started scratching the soft soil while darting its suspicious eyes all around, then it saw me and shit itself. It flapped noisily while screaming out its alarm call, as it crashed suicidal into the broad green leaves.

I watched as the dog that hadn't quite reached the door stopped and turned to see what all the noise was about. Then it trotted back down the steps straight towards my vision tunnel. It kept coming and coming until it entered the thin trimmed edge of the bushes. It then stopped and sniffed around, turned and looked back at the door.

I slid deeper into the sleeping bag instinctively, without even a thought, but that was a fatal mistake. Its ears pricked up and it turned my way again, lowered on to its haunches and started a belly crawl straight towards me. I removed the cap of the pepper spray and held it in my right hand. My other hand steadied my arm. I placed my finger on the red plastic button.

Its breath was getting louder, as it closed in on me. It growled long and low. Still looking through the slit in the sleeping bag, I waited. The massive head stopped about eight inches away and growled so deeply that I could feel the ground sheet vibrate around me then it gave the confused 'head-to-the-side' look. I gave it a face full of mace. It squealed as if I'd jumped on all its four paws at once, while wearing hob nailed boots, and then it burst vertically out of the bush like a Polaris missile.

It landed with a crashing thud on its side still in my vision tunnel then scrambled upright and legged it like Scooby Doo, tripping on the last step it somersaulted through the open door.

I couldn't hide my smile, one second I was going to be dog food, the next I was watching ninety pounds of dog in a real life cartoon. I felt a lot safer with my tin of mace by my side; at least one of the dogs was no longer a threat.

I relaxed until Laura appeared again, one thing I had noticed is that whenever she left a building she always paused at the door, looked around carefully then adjusted her attire. While she did this I added more pictures to my camera's data card.

Two hours and forty minutes later she returned. This was exactly the same time it takes to walk to the Plaza spending two hours there, then walk back. Nothing else happened.

Larry hadn't returned and it was past midnight. I had nowhere to go, but I needed to stretch my legs. I had the proof that Laura was alive and happily cohabiting with Larry. It was obvious even to Simple Simon that he wasn't and never had been a widower. I was sure that if he had taken an insurance policy out on her I would have a valuable ally somewhere.

I decided to stay where I was. If I moved off I would have to come back before dawn to return unseen and if I didn't Scooby Doo's mate might get the scent of the stuff under the bushes and that would blow the whole thing.

I didn't fancy another doggy encounter, but it was almost inevitable that I would have one more.

I had a leak into a condom, tied a knot in it as you do, and put it in the rubbish pocket of the Bergen so there would be no excessive scent of me blowing around for the dogs to pick up, as dogs dedicate their lives to sniffing piss.

I slept quite well and remained pleasantly warm and dry despite the night being damp and cold with a heavy mist that caused steady drips to fall from the leaves as if it was raining.

Larry returned about 8.45 a.m. I snapped him and the driver, but again I couldn't clearly see the driver's face because Larry's big long head blocked him out, and whenever the driver left the car he always looked towards the black doors or at Larry as he joined him climbing the steps.

Nothing much happened for a couple of hours then the inevitable dog release occurred. The door opened and the dogs strolled down the steps. Scooby was hanging around a small piece of grass under one of the long windows. They kept coming into view then at times all I could see was their black and tan legs passing the gaps in the foliage.

Suddenly they started barking aggressively, which caused Laura to appear. She clapped her hands and they shot into the house just as a post van pulled into view. I placed the pepper spray back into the little hole in the mulch I had made for it and took a few shots of the van.

An hour or so later Laura and Larry climbed into a cab, which already had a person sat in the back seat. I zoomed in and fired off a few more shots before the cab's wheels spun on the gravel and disappeared.

I lay for another hour assessing my situation. I had lost the bike along with the jacket and helmet, somewhere to stay and the new clothes I had just bought. The police would have found lots of evidence, my fingerprints would be everywhere and it wouldn't take long for them to match them to mine. The only thing on my side is that I was most likely seen helping Rees by people in the street before they scattered when the gunfire started, hopefully the witnesses would have seen me being shot at while making my escape. I just hoped they would tell it that way.

It started to rain lightly, then the sky turned dark and it pissed down. Despite my good location the mulch was soaking up the rain like blotting paper and it was starting to squelch beneath me. As I supported my weight with my elbows they sank, letting in little rivers of water. A change of plan was needed, or I would freeze to death.

I carefully packed my Bergen and turned the sleeping bag 180 degrees. I covered the top ground sheet with dead leaves and twigs then retreated. The dogs wouldn't catch the scent of my O.P with all the rain falling. Housedogs when let out in the rain usually have a quick dump then shoot back into the warmth. I felt my hide would be safe.

At a different motorcycle shop I paid out another $350 for twist and go number two. This one came with a smelly helmet that matched the bike's paint job. It was an ex pizza delivery scooter complete with a back box, perfect for blending in. $15.00 secured a tired looking leather jacket. I was invisible and mobile again.

Chapter Ten

I arrived outside the New York Times building just as the rain reached my nuts.
I could see Patsy gathering her things as she prepared to leave the building, so I started the pizza express. She descended the steps while at the same time opening a flowery umbrella. I blew the horn that sounded more like someone imitating a horn while holding their nose. She looked up momentarily on hearing the strange sound.

'Patsy,' I shouted while beckoning her with my gloved hand. She stopped so I snatched off my helmet, made eye contact then put it back on. She placed her brolly over both of us and pushed her face to the helmet.

'Follow me.' I followed at a safe distance, as she pushed through the sea of umbrellas. Thankfully hers could be seen easily with its big yellow flowers.

She stopped to check I could see her, then turned down an alley the width of a car. I followed her until we came out of the other side where there were less people. I stayed about eighty feet behind her as she rushed along, occasionally casting a glance to check I was still following.

After five minutes she stopped to let me catch up, and when I did she turned to go through an arch that opened out into a small courtyard. She opened a door that led to another smaller area. There were several cycles and boxes resting against the paint-flaked walls. I pushed the pizza express in.

'It'll be safe here,' she whispered. I pulled it onto the stand and removed my helmet.

'Through here.'

I followed her through a door into a landing then up a flight of old, but clean stairs that creaked with disapproval as we climbed them.

Patsy flashed her big eyes at me as she led me to a door. 'This is my apartment,' she slid in a Yale key and pushed open the sticking door with the side of her thigh. Warm air, full of the aroma of cooking, greeted me. The place was tidy and homely in a girlie way. A well-rounded black girl appeared from the kitchen.

'This is Dee, Kris.'

'Hi Patsy.' Her face dropped on seeing me. 'So who's this?'

I must have looked like a vagrant. 'Hi, I'm Kris.'

'Oh, you must be that English guy?' she huffed indifferently. Patsy took my helmet from my hand and waited for my soaked jacket as I peeled it off.

'I'm sorry,' I spread my hands down my filthy mud stained clothes. 'I can explain.' Patsy's flatmate put her hand to her mouth and coughed. I looked at Patsy, who was trying to hide her amused face, but couldn't as her hands were full.

'I know I'm a mess, but it's not that funny?'

'Sorry, Kris, it's just…' she grinned, 'You look such a mess yet you talk so goddamn posh.'

I smiled, but I could not hide how I felt. My smile soon faded.

'I suppose you'll need the tub,' Dee said derisively and disappeared.

'Don't mind Dee, she only lodges here.' Patsy walked into the kitchen with my jacket then returned with a bottle of beer and handed it to me. 'You'll be safe here, Kris,' she said reassuringly.

I felt like a lost boy who'd just been found by some nice people. I tried to appear cool but my expression must have signalled my feelings and relief. Patsy placed a finger on her lips then pressed it on to mine. 'I said you're safe here with me.' I really liked the 'with me' bit.

I peeled the filthy clothes from my bruised body and placed them on to the pink carpet with the least dirty side down. Then I enjoyed one of the best baths of my life.

A half-snore, half-grunt I made woke me from my deep sleep.

'Are you hungry?' Dee's voice called from the half-opened door.

'Yeah, thanks I am a bit.'

'What's this 'bit' shit?' She walked straight into the bathroom. 'You're either hungry or you ain't.' I moved my hands. 'Don't bother, I looked in on you when you were sleeping, didn't want you to drown in there.' She winked, 'Not bad for a spook,' then she sort of frowned. 'I heard what's being going down, Kris. Patsy told me all about it.

New Yorkers are less tolerant about that sort of shit, especially after the 11th.'

A key grated into the lock of the main door and Patsy bounded straight into the bathroom. 'There you go.' She fussily dropped my holdall onto the floor. 'Everything's in there, just as you dropped it.' She gave me an accomplished grin between heavy breaths, her eyes quickly fluttered over my nakedness and she smiled while blushing.

'How the hell did you get it back?' I asked while covering my bits with both hands.

'Six kids in one bed, three at the top and three at the bottom. I could kick real hard and my pretend cousin Leroy still remembers every one of them. I kicked that boy till I was ten. We go back to the care home.' She looked pleased and proud and then her mood stiffened as she remembered the paper that she held. As she passed it to me her face transformed from a smile to one of pure innocence.

'*EX COP MUTILATED*

A distinguished ex New York police officer, Mark Rees, was gunned down last night on west 29th street off 9$^{th.}$ Eyewitnesses told investigators that a man who was trying to help Rees at the time of the shooting was also attacked; apparently he escaped and is now being sought by the police. Fifty-four year old Mark Rees was in the centre of a corruption investigation two years ago but the allegations he made to Congress fell upon deaf ears. Soon afterward he was forced out of the N.Y.P.D. Rumours are still widespread about the case, which has now been strengthened after scene-of-crime officers reported that before being gunned down Rees had been tortured during which there was a sordid attempt to cut out his tongue.'

I dropped the paper. 'Christ! No wonder the poor sod couldn't talk.'

Dee handed me a glass of scotch causing me to move one hand to receive it.

Patsy smiled and looked me up and down. 'Maybe you should have used suds, Kris?' She gave me a mischievous grin. 'Come on Dee, we're embarrassing him.'

The neat drink filled my head with wool after the first mouthful while in the other room the girls whispered and giggled which gave me a nice feeling of belonging as I relaxed in the warmth.

After the bath we had hot dogs and more drinks and talked till late then I vaguely remember being led to a bed where at last calm and comfort enveloped me.

Things were looking up for me. Last night I was sinking in dead leaves, cold, damp and without a bed, now I had a good-looking friend, another bike and a safe unconnected place to hide it. All my clothes and documents were with me again and I had photos of my prey, and further means of observing them. I didn't give a toss if they found my O.P now. The two ground sheets and a sleeping bag that I had left open and facing away from the house would be blamed on a dosser trying to seek shelter. Anyway, I reckoned Larry wouldn't soil his Armani suit crawling under bushes to have a look at it.

I was laid in the big warm bed juggling ideas when the door opened. I remained still and pretended to be asleep.

'Morning, Kris.'

I pulled the quilt from my face to see Dee holding a tray. She reminded me of a young Whoopi Goldberg.

'Hey, you shouldn't have.'

'Cut the bull, Kris, you need sustenance, not manners. Just you eat it all.'

I didn't expect such a big breakfast. I had fried potatoes, or hash browns as they're called, beans of course, bacon and four eggs.

'I didn't know how you like your eggs, so I done them over easy.'

'Soft, she means.' Patsy walked in and sat at the end of the bed smiling. 'How are you feeling today?'

'Fine, thanks to you.'

She studied me.

'Look, Patsy, it's wrong me imposing on you like this, you could be in serious trouble for harbouring someone who's on the run for... well you know.'

'You couldn't murder anyone, no more than I could see you alone and on the streets.' She sat watching me eating my breakfast. A thought came to me. Every man loves attention from a woman. It's primeval, but when a man is in real trouble and alone, it seems only a woman can truly help.

'You're not at work today?'

'It's Saturday, Kris,' she grinned, peeling her glistening lips back, revealing her beautiful teeth. I couldn't take my eyes off her. She was truly stunning. Each time I studied her face it looked better than I remembered, and she seemed to enjoy the long smiles we shared.

'We're off for some stores. Is there anything you want fetching?'

I dragged my jeans leg and reached into the pocket and passed her $100.

'Shit no Kris, I don't want that.'

'Patsy, take it please. There's some stuff I need anyway.'

Reluctantly she accepted.

The laptop clicked and whirled into life as its little green indicator lights flashed away and the screen lit up displaying several icons. I clicked the program icon that came with the camera and several small thumbnail pictures burst immediately onto the sharp screen.
There were some of Jimmy in his flat, taken the day we loaded the programs onto the laptop. I wonder how he was getting on after all that shit went off? I would have to get in touch with him. It shouldn't be too hard after all; most of the eastern seaboard knew him.

I connected the U.S.B. lead into the port at the back of the laptop then removed the small 128mb card from the Fuji pro and slid it into the card reader. Lots of numbered files appeared as if by magic all ending with the letters jpeg. I double clicked the first one. The neatly trimmed head of a man with his back to me filled the screen. The quality was superb. I could even see imperfections on his skin when I used the digital zoom facility. This gear was shit hot.

The next five shots were of the haircut. When *'No. 007.Jpeg'* flashed on the screen I yelled, 'Got you.'

The next twenty-four shots were of Larry and his unknown associate in split-second frames walking down the steps to the car, but when *'No, 031.Jpeg' opened* I could have screamed out. It was a perfect full body shot of Larry smiling. When I zoomed in I could even see the bastard's nasal hairs. If he had opened his mouth I would have been able to tell what the prat had eaten for breakfast.

Laura appeared next. I'd shot her as she looked around, prior to letting the hounds of death out. I had a perfect left, right and centre profile of her, even the wrought iron number 'forty' that was fixed on the wall was in the shot. I went back and clicked number 031 again. 'Yes!' I shouted, the number was clear in nearly all the shots.

Looking at Laura again I zoomed in. All of a sudden I felt strangely sorry for her; she looked happy; and totally incapable of doing what she had done to me. It was like looking at Doris Day when she was young. She was completely unaware that I was here, and that I was going to devastate her life the way she had devastated mine. It felt good taking something from them without them having the faintest clue, but I'd sooner have been able to travel back in time, back to my Lodge.

The shots of Laura were all very good and would be my evidence one day. Larry's return was recorded, but even with the aid of the digital zoom I couldn't see the driver's face clearly, every shot had something obscuring him.

I laid out the police file on Laura on to the table, and with the Fuji's versatile focusing copied them to disk. I opened the pack of CDs and inserted one on to the carrier, which dragged itself back into the laptop with a whirring sound. I made three copies of my new photo album, then pulled the wardrobe in my temporary room from the wall, and taped a copy to the back of it. I left one in the laptop, the other one I was going to send to my flat in the U.K. I sat back at the table feeling really pleased with myself. I still felt bad about Rees, but I'm sure his card was marked long before I arrived here. For the first time in ages, things were looking up.

Saturday night in New York is pretty serious. Patsy and Dee had press-ganged me into savouring the ambience. What they really meant was to have a good time, after all they were just kids, and after all the shit I'd recently been through, I needed to chill out.

Walking with the locals I experienced the same feeling that I had when I was with Jimmy. There seemed to be a big inner circle, who knew how to live and survive in this big metropolis,

We only had to walk fifty yards through a labyrinth of streets and alleyways to reach the next bar, and on entering we were received like long lost friends, which made me feel quite humble as drinks appeared from nowhere.

I looked at Patsy who was grinning and gleaming, as she rolled her shoulders to the music. Everybody was relaxed and enjoying the atmosphere. I started people watching. Why the hell was it that I always end up with women almost half my age? Vicky, who is always with me, was eight years my junior. Jenny Dean is sixteen years younger. And here I was with a gorgeous New York chick that I reckon could have easily been my eldest daughter. I wasn't complaining, but it puzzled me.

We danced while some 'guys' pranced. I'd never come across so many Transvestites. Gays and Goths outnumbered the normal people. I felt totally alien, dressed in my Levi 501's, black shirt and bomber jacket. I was eyeballed by several what I could only describe as total fuck-ups. When they saw what I was wearing, I was shunned as though I were the weirdo, much to Patsy's amusement. I noticed that throughout the night she was never more than two steps from me.

As Saturday turned to Sunday morning I was feeling the effects of the last few days, and the beers that had flowed constantly. Patsy, observant as ever, smiled her wonderful smile and gestured with a nod that we should make for the exit. Whoopi had met an old friend and was long gone.

We ambled our way through the district were Patsy lived, Alphabet City. My mind, with the help of the alcohol, was for once, trouble free.

'Guilty,' the foreman had said so confidently. 'Not guilty,' was now repeating in my ears like tinnitus.

'Hey Kris, what's with the serious look?'

'I'm sorry I just was thinking…. you know.'

She hooked my arm in hers and leaned on me as we walked. 'Kris, what you gonna do when all this is over?'

'Try and get my little piece of heaven, back in Devon.'

'Huh?'

'I'll tell you later.'

Patsy made two large glasses of scotch on the rocks and we sat in the warm apartment on a tired double settee that had knitted covers on its arms to hide the worn edges.

'Earlier you said heaven in…Divon?'

'The Lodge is what I want back.'

Patsy turned. 'Is that in…Divon?'

'It's Devon, not Divon.'

'Hmm yeah, sure.'

I smiled at her lovely face. 'Imagine a rugged coastline with high storm-battered cliffs that face the sun, and like a hidden world there's an inlet. Its sloping banks are covered in a green blanket of shrubs and trees. The angry sea can't get in and the wind can only shout or whisper from above, but rays of sunshine caress the area from dawn till dusk. There are a few houses and each one is unique, they are nestled among the greenery and overlook the blue water that leads out to adventure.

One place is special. It nestles almost on the waters edge and has uninterrupted views, it can only be seen from the water, which serenades it with gentle slapping of wavelets, the only other sounds you hear are from passing seagulls or the buzzing of bees that seek out lush flowers that decorate the inaccessible places. Old stone steps that have been worn down by pirates and smugglers through the centuries, lead to a small hidden jetty where the water is so clear you can see bass and mullet hiding among the waving weed. That's The Lodge.'

Patsy pulled her feet up on to the cushion, clamped on to my arm and rested her head on my shoulder. 'Jeez, I'd love to see it, Kris. I've never been out of New York. It sounds so beautiful. Like something from a fairy tale.'

'Yeah a fairy tale, which I once lived in,' I finished my drink. Patsy copied me.

'Well, I've plans to get up early Pats, so I'm going to get my head down.'

'Pats, you called me that the day we met, no-one has called me that for years.'

'Sorry, don't you like it?'

'I'm cool.'

'That means yes?'

'Uh, huh,' she nodded while staring blankly.

I left her deep in thought and walked to the bathroom. When I returned I felt a little sad to find she'd gone. I turned out the lights and walked to my room. I was taken aback to see Patsy standing in front of the window.

'Will you tell me more about your lodge in Divon Kris?' Her eyes sparkled questioning me. Strangely it brought back memories of how I felt in the early days with Vicky. Feelings of total desire tinged with apprehension. She sensed my nervousness and slowly moved towards me. 'Kris...let me stay with you tonight.'

Her warm lips brushed onto mine slow and tantalizing, my hand found the small of her back and I pulled her close. As our thighs combined her mouth opened and I felt the full strength of her desire. Her hand caressed the back of my neck then ran deep through my hair, tugging gently as her need for me strengthened even more. 'Take me to bed.' She whispered.

Patsy obviously liked me and I was enjoying being liked right now, so we spent most of the day like a couple of dating teenagers. It was like going back to my youth. She was incredible and the intense experiences we were sharing instantly cemented something special between us.

Monday morning came too fast and I had to get back to reality. The pizza express smoked a little in defiance then revved cleanly as I set off to take on New York's ruthless drivers. After being beeped more times than a female streaker, I arrived outside 40 East 68th. Thankfully it wasn't raining, but it was quite chilly.

I sat watching in the mirror for a little over four hours. I was becoming a bit depressed, until a car indicated its intentions and pulled into the drive. I was now freezing my nuts off. It started to piss down again. I felt like binning the whole escapade and becoming an illegal immigrant. At least Patsy liked my attentions.

The car pulled out of the drive, which caught me by surprise. I didn't make a move until it was a good distance away, then I took off like Carl Foggerty on one cylinder.

I kept a safe distance while weaving through the queues and on occasions I folded the odd wing mirror over with my elbows, which didn't go down well. Then the car stopped outside what looked like a museum or library type of building.

I pulled onto the kerb, got off the bike and pretended to struggle with the lock on the back box, but really I was looking at the car from behind the black visor.

Larry climbed out from the back followed by sexy Laura, who managed to show her stocking tops as she slid off the car seat. Then the driver's head rose above the door. I couldn't believe my eyes, or was I mistaken. It had been years since I had seen the man who was now pressing his central locking key fob. Was it really him? He looked older than I remembered, and a little heavier. I began to doubt myself until I looked at one of the information boards that flanked the steps.

The Institute of Marine Archaeological Conservation was the poster's heading. They were presenting a seminar and there was a list of the names of the people who were giving specialised talks. Half way down the list of speakers was the name Tony Banks. I was gutted. What was he doing here, with those con artists? Next to his name it said, 'Managing Director, International Salvage and Recovery.' Then it clicked, as I remembered that was the name of his company. I read on. 'Specialised subject: Modern search and recovery techniques of lost archaeological artefacts.'

I sat heavily on to the wall next to me as the pieces of the jigsaw fell into place perfectly. A flashback of the video that caught the burglars at The Lodge entered my mind's eye. That third head on the video must have been Banks. The three of them had stitched me up like a fucking cricket ball. They had the help of Ferret's local knowledge; he would have been an asset to them, but when he was no longer needed he became a risk, so he was callously fed to the same crabs he made a living from. They used one of the anchor chains from *Westwind*, which cleverly implicated me. I knew the *Madeira* salvage had pissed Banks off, but not to this extent.

I waited for them to enter the building then I entered the reception area and gathered up a pile of leaflets that promoted the seminar. It was obvious that they weren't going to leave town for a while yet.

One of the leaflets was promoting a company that was seeking new investors to fund a multitude of proposed recoveries, which would make every investor a lot richer. It was Banks company. I was witnessing the planning of one of the biggest scams to ever hit the marine salvage world. Tony Banks, after instigating the elaborate con which had ruined me, was obviously a new and welcomed member to this team of ruthless high flyers, and through the guise of marine salvage he had opened a whole new and untapped source of income for them.

I returned to Patsy's apartment and studied the promotion leaflet more closely, and was pleased to see a web site address for this 'new and innovative company' called ISR.com.

I scanned the massive phone book, but gave up. Then, with the invaluable help of my rough guidebook I found: *'Easy Everywhere 234 W42nd between 7th and 8th Avenue.'* It was a cyber café that was advertising some 800 terminals for accessing the Internet.

I was beginning to find my way around quite confidently now, and I located the Easy Everywhere cyber café on my first attempt. It also had a place for bikes to park, right outside the premises. In the safety of the enormous building I removed my helmet. Neat rows of large flat-screened monitors mounted on light wooden partitions filled the place.

An eclectic mixture of people played with their mice while staring with deadly conviction at the flashing screens, while hundreds of keyboards rattled away in unison. A tall orange vending machine seemed to be in charge.

'Pay here first' it said in white lettering. Various options of payment were available so I chose: *"Dynamically Priced Credit'*, which would let me logon a multitude of times until my credit expired. I bought ten dollars worth and was given a log on PIN number then I found myself a terminal and sat down between two Kevin and Perry look-alikes.

IRS.com got me straight into the American tax agency, so I retyped ISR.com and a professional looking home page flashed almost instantly via the fast Broadband link. There were a few pages, so I sent them to the printer, but before I logged off I typed in Jenny's old email address at the Uni in Plymouth. A blinking cursor asked me to type my message. I had to create an address for myself, so called myself something she would remember. Being called Woods, my nickname offshore was plank and she knew that, so plankadrift@easyeverywhere.com became my e-mail address. I asked her to check my mail for the CD I had sent and to put it somewhere safe. Then I briefly explained what I was trying to do here. I asked her to send me all the details on Ferret's reappearance, anything she could find, and whatever she could find out about my position with regard to the law. I pressed the send button then logged off, with $5.00 still in credit. I collected the pages from a bored looking youth manning the printer, which cost $2.00, then headed back to Patsy's.

Back at my safe house I studied the printed web documents. Even I was getting excited at the proposals that were on offer. Photographs of big expensive remotely operated vessels, similar to the one that visited the Titanic, were illustrated. Incredibly some of them were claimed to be the property of ISR

Other machines were apparently being developed and would revolutionise deep-water salvage. Pictures of gold bars, gold coins and jewellery made up the borders of the web pages. It all sounded so good that I almost believed it. With the help of Banks' years of experience they had researched everything thoroughly.

I had heard of some of the proposed wrecks they had on the list. They had scores of proposed sites that they had allegedly already found, using an array of multi-facet discriminating proton magnetometers in conjunction with a recently acquired high tech Russian bi-directional sub-bottom profiler. All of course was interfaced with twin multi headed side-scan sonar's. Whatever the hell they were.

All of this gear produced data that could be analyzed by a super computer which could produce near perfect-scaled 3D pictures of the seabed. Specifications weren't available due to the top-secret nature of the gear, as it was all recently acquired by ISR from the 'Russian military'. It read to me like the scriptwriters from Star Trek had been asked to invent the gear.

I knew it was utter bullshit, but it all sounded shit hot, and would appeal to any fatback sitting with a wedge in the bank, gathering sod all interest.

I almost wanted to join the team, it sounded so good, and how could anyone discredit them? Any criticism about the operation would be labelled sour grapes or commercial rivalry. The team surely was pleased with their future prospects, as the last page announced that millions of dollars had been invested already and applications from keen investors were flooding in.

A scale of percentages that would have pleased any accountant showed investment figures in black and the rewards they would gain in red. One flaw, and the only one I could find, was that there were no names of the directors, just a box number.

I was with Vicky and Janie for a few seconds, but even though I was asleep I knew I was dreaming, and tried hard to manipulate the dream, but I only saw them in fleeting moments before they slipped back into my memory. At least they were smiling and happy this time. I even managed to raise a smile when I woke up and recalled the dream. Thankfully those lonely depressing attacks were all but gone now.

I made a stir-fry and tidied the place. After a weekend of rushing in and out it really needed it, and I quite enjoyed picking up the knickers and bras that were strewn around. I placed Patsy's jacket in her dresser and couldn't help but notice that the wardrobe was almost empty. She only had a few clothes. She probably earned the minimum wage, and after the rent and all the other costs, would be left with little for luxuries.

I was watching Sky News when the key grated in the lock and in walked Patsy. She looked worn out, yet still radiated something that only a naturally beautiful woman can.

'Hi, Kris.' She stopped and sniffed. 'I can smell food,' she looked around. 'Wow, this place is spotless.'

I shrugged. 'You like stir-fry?'

After demolishing the chicken with hoi-sin and spring onion sauce, Patsy sipped her wine and thanked me for such a nice surprise. Then on a more serious note she reached for her bag and passed me a note. It said, *'Conservatory Garden Central Park 12.30 p.m.'* I looked at her.

'A guy called Jimmy gave it to me in the reception. He wants to see you, but he thinks he is being followed. He said don't ring him 'cause his phone has been cut off. He said he would wear his baseball cap backwards if he thinks it's not safe for you to approach him.'

'Shit Patsy this could be a trap. It would be impossible for me to expose those con merchants from behind bars. I would be totally finished…I don't think I could survive on memories any more, prison would kill me for sure.'

She studied me for a few seconds. 'I'll go for you and you can check from a distance if anybody is watching.'

I considered her idea for a moment then realised that if she was associated with all this, she would be in danger as well and I would be under the bushes again, and it wasn't getting any warmer as October was disappearing fast.

I left Patsy soaking in the 'tub' and went to the nearest pizza outlet and bought three pizzas, then returned to the apartment.

'You got be joking, Kris. I couldn't eat another thing,' I grinned at Patsy who stood wearing a bathrobe. She overlapped it exposing her trim, heavenly body for a second.

'Put yourself away before I lose the plot,' I turned and walked straight into Whoopi, who looked at the pizza boxes, then grabbed the top one.

'What a guy!' She opened the box and scooped a slice to her cavernous mouth. 'Don't ditch this one, Patsy. Cleaning and feeding, who knows what he'll do next?' She swayed her well-rounded arse from side to side as she disappeared into the kitchen. Patsy giggled.

'What did you get us pizzas for?'

'Come and sit down. I've got an idea.' She sat close and I could feel the warmth from her curvy thigh as it pressed against mine.

'I don't want you anywhere near Central Park tomorrow Pats, there's too many complications. Don't ring in sick, just go to work as normal. If you get seen with Jimmy anywhere but work we could be history. Do you understand?' She smiled nervously. 'We can only hope that Jimmy is one step ahead of them.'

Whoopi walked in. 'Hey man, you didn't clean my room like you did hers.' I laughed at her effort to join the conversation, but seriously wished the fat sod would just piss off.

Ten minutes later Dee switched on the TV and sat with a bag of crisps or chips as they're called here, despite having just demolished the big fourteen-inch pizza in less than three minutes.

'I will be fine and safer by myself, I can nip in and out of the traffic, making it hard for anybody to follow me.'

She nodded, making her ringlets spring up and down while exuding the homely aroma of a freshly bathed person.

'You don't have to do all this, Kris, you can stay here as long as you want... with me.'

Jerry Springer's bouncers were breaking up a fight.

'Did ya see that?' Whoopi shouted as she turned to us, spraying chips onto the carpet that I'd spent half an hour cleaning. 'That girl damned near scratched that guy's eyes out.'

I lay thinking about what Patsy said, it was happening to me all over again, was I just a sympathy case? Or did I have something that truly appealed to her? I wasn't complaining right now. Then a worrying thought suddenly unsettled me, was Patsy going to be someone else that I would have to survive?

I wanted to recce the area where I was going to meet Jimmy, so when I arrived there I'd know all the escape routes if I was compromised.

I purred along Fifth Avenue at 10 a.m. weaving in and out of parked and slow moving cars. It was dull and cold and occasionally the wind found its way through the monster buildings, chilling me to the bone, making me think of the warm cosy flannelette sheets I'd just left.

I passed the Zoo and got a whiff of mixed animal shit then I approached E68th where I knew a pack of more dangerous animals were holding up. I approached the Park's reservoir where even at this early hour runners were pounding the track that circles the expanse of water.

A sign told me I was at East Meadow. Conservatory Gardens was next. I hoped that I would be able to ride past and suss out the place, but it looked like something from the Chelsea Flower Show. Trees and shrubs, plant and flowerbeds covering at least six acres spread out before me. I stopped and chained the scooter to a tree, then had a stiff walk around.

Jimmy had chosen well. I nearly got lost in just five minutes. Trying to keep a tail on somebody in a place like this would turn into a scene from Pink Panther. There would have to be a man on almost every twist and bend.

I drove to Easy Everywhere to check for E-mail but there was none. Maybe Jenny wouldn't check hers for days, or even weeks, if she had gone away to sea early.

I had a coffee to kill some time, then at midday I buzzed off. I parked the scooter at the most northerly point I could inside a big bush. A well-worn path ran almost through the middle of it, which partly hid the scooter. I stopped and quickly familiarised myself with several landmarks that could be seen from most places, then picked out the pizza boxes from the shiny black top box.

I walked for about two minutes then made for the lower flowerbeds. I couldn't hold the pizzas under my arm. It wouldn't have looked right, so I minced along as a butler does with a tray, holding them in front of me.

The dog walkers were already out in force and I began to feel that I wasn't quite blending in. I wished I could have swapped the pizzas for a dog right now. Then I saw Jimmy and he had a dog with him that looked like canine version of a doorman pumped up with steroids. He was even carrying the obligatory plastic bag of crap. He was moving suspiciously, and looking around like a fugitive. Thankfully his hat peak was pointing forwards. He hadn't recognised me yet, or was acting in spy mode, so I pretended to trip and dropped the pizzas almost in front of him. He stopped as the muscle-bound ugly dog leaped greedily onto the pizza that had fallen out of the box.

'Jimmy.' He looked frantically around.

'Here ya daft sod,' I shouted. I was bent down trying to pick up the boxes he looked down at me.

'Shit, man, I never ordered those.' He shone a grin at me like a daft lad. 'Kris, is that you man?'

'Course it is.' I snapped up the visor. 'Listen carefully.' I was still bent down pretending to fumble with the intact box. The dog was savaging the other box, which had held the ham and pepperoni.

'Listen and remember this '*plankadrift@easyeverywhere.com*'.' I stretched my arm out, reaching for the other box and the nasty little dog sank its teeth into my hand.

'Ah! You fucker!' I screamed. Jimmy's face froze as I straighten myself up; he gulped then turned his hat peak to the back. 'What are you doing?' He twisted it around 360 degrees again grabbed the pizza box from me, and stuffed the dog lead into my hand, snatched my bike key from my other hand threw the bag of shit into the air and legged it.

I turned around to see what had spooked him, two men in black suits were running towards me, the pain suddenly returned. The dog still had hold of my gloved hand and was pulling at me using all the strength it could muster. I started running, but the dog had other ideas and started the growling while doing the defiant head shaking thing.

The men in black were only ten metres from me now; still dragging the dog I veered into a flowerbed. The dog wasn't that big and once I pulled it off the ground it lost its traction and I could move faster. I heard one of the men shouting orders to the other. Dog walkers looked on with horror as I ran through them swinging the dog in circles trying to dislodge the ugly snarling head.

Then a suite burst out of a bush and raised a gun at me. I instinctively used what weapon I had available and swung the dog at him. It was pretty pissed off by now and lost its grip on me just at the right time, causing it to land on the man's chest, spitting and growling for his face.

I left him with his new found friend and dashed into the bush where he had burst out. I had to slow down mentally now and ensure every step was distancing me from them. Then I heard the rotor blades thumping above me. It was a big area and I guessed by the pattern the helicopter was flying that they hadn't located me yet. Once they had, I was well and truly finished, as their heat-imaging camera would hunt me down regardless of where I was hiding.

I crawled under the bushes as the chopper made a closer pass. The men on the ground would be having a fag by now, and waiting for directions from the eye in the sky. The chopper had me like a rat in a tin bath.

I belly-crawled for another minute then came to the edge of a tree-lined pond. I remembered from my map that it was called the Loch. It had some reed beds and several floating duck houses, and appeared to be as secluded you could get in Central Park.

The water seized me with its death grip as the cold found every inch of my skin. It felt horrid, if there was anything equivalent to the opposite of sex this had to be it. I dragged myself through the shallow water until I reached the nearest duck hut. It was a floating raft made up of wooden planks. I pulled at the middle plank and thankfully it was soft, almost rotten. I immersed my head under, but the helmet was too big so I took it off and fastened it to my thigh. I tried again and after almost tearing off my ears got my head inside. I had to push hard to dislodge the eight-inch mat of wet and rotted nesting material that was inside, then I was able to get my hands through and pull it apart. I could breathe again.

I started to calm down and remain as still as possible, despite shivering severely.
I could hear the chopper searching relentlessly above for me, but the cold water and the thick layer of soggy shit and nesting stuff on my head was hiding my heat signature, and there were ducks all around me. If they picked a small part of my head inside the duck house they would dismiss it, as I was the last thing they would expect to find stuffed inside.

Diving was my job and I had spent thousands of hours in freezing cold situations, but now I was becoming severely cold and knew it. According to my illuminated watch I had been in the same position without daring to move for hours. If I hadn't been able to extract myself out of the water up to my waist I would have been in a sorry state by now. Despite the smell, the soggy nesting material had given a degree of insulation and had stopped hypothermia setting in, but my legs were numb and I found it almost impossible to move them.

It was now almost 4.30 p.m. and getting dark. The ducks were queuing outside and were quacking complaints while attempting to squeeze in with me.

Outside in the park they would have manned most exit points and linked the scooter with the pizzas and me, so any thought of getting the scooter back was a no-no. They had number two now. I'd certainly torn the arse out of that plan; they were most likely calling me the scooter killer by now.

It was darker and the chopper had long gone. I had to make a move for I was dying from the waist down. As I extracted myself from the duck house the coldness of the water hurt as it assaulted me again. All my senses were alerted to signs of movement as I crawled like the swamp thing on to the grassy bank. I had to start off on my hands and knees at first because I couldn't stand, then after five minutes the severe hot aches made me aware that my circulation was kicking in. Another agonising few minutes later I was staggering from tree to tree.

I rushed through the streets like a sober vagrant on a mission to find his next drink. I thought of where I would be now if I hadn't had Fido with me to gain those vital seconds of surprise that were so crucial. Poor Jimmy, they used him like a toilet roll and he didn't have a clue. He thought he was the man and now he's probably in the can.

Patsy sat on the well-worn toilet lid and carefully dressed the teeth punctures on my right hand. I watched her, thinking how beautiful her profile was as she repeatedly pinned her hair behind her ear. She was drawing small breaths through her lips and releasing them through her nose and each one fell softly on my arm like an invisible kiss. Even though I was bitter about recent events, I felt more relaxed at this moment than I had done for a long time, as the warm soothing water replenished my core temperature.

Chapter Eleven

The fact that the police didn't have a clue where I was gave me all the advantages. My entry visa was irrelevant now, and that gave me as much time as I needed to gather evidence to present to the authorities. I had to get it right because I would only have one chance. As soon as I gave myself up I would be in a cell. The police would no doubt have my face plastered in every car and precinct by now. I really needed to find some sort of disguise. The picture they had of me would be the one taken when I was charged more than two years ago. I was now a stone lighter and had a short beard and moustache, so with the right head attire, while behaving normally, I doubt that they would link me with their wanted man. It was bloody Larry and Laura that worried me. They would spot me a mile off. I had to think up a disguise.

'Stay still,' Patsy giggled, as she mixed the colours on a kid's face-painting palette as she brushed it gently on to my face.

'Hey Pats, I don't want to look like a Moroccan or a Jamaican.'

'You won't silly I'm giving you a sort of South American look. There isn't a chance of them making you with your new black hair and these neat face fins.' She pulled my moustache and giggled. 'That prickly beard didn't suit you anyway; it hid your bonny face.'

I felt pleased, hearing someone as good-looking as Patsy say that. It made my day. She stood back looking at me with the brush in her hand, like an artist looking at a canvas

'Hmm, just a shade here.' She was quite dedicated and within twenty minutes I was allowed to look at the mirror.

'Well?' Patsy stood back with her tongue curled at the side of her mouth.

'It's different, I suppose.'

'You can say that again.' She plonked a New York Giants cap on my head, and started smirking. 'What ya gonna call yourself then?' She put her hand to her mouth. 'Shaft?' Snorting uncontrollable through her nose she burst into a giggling fit, then creased up and fell on to the settee, jigging up and down holding her belly. I shook my head in the mirror just as the apartment door opened.

'Who the hell is this?' Dee shrieked in a high-pitched voice that caused Patsy to bury her head into a cushion using both hands, as she rapidly stamped her feet up and down. Dee took a closer look at me then screwed up her face like Tina Turner.

'Get the fuck out of here!' She hit me on the shoulder then laughing feverishly, fell with Patsy who was pulling a strained face as tears ran down her cheeks.

I opened a bottle of wine and poured three large glasses.

'Thank you, Jeeves,' Dee shrieked, spilling most of it as they turned to jelly again.

After an hour of relentless piss taking I was sitting down and under the brush again. This time Dee, who had worked as a make up assistant in the past, did the job properly and twice as quickly. I was pleased with the result. My appearance had changed enough to fool anyone, and I no longer felt I'd be more suited on the side of a marmalade jar.

'Thanks Dee.' Patsy moved the wineglass away from her mouth and pushed out her tongue. I put my bomber jacket on and they shook their heads like puppets.

'What?' Dee stood up.

'Walk to the door, Kris.' I did and they started giggling again.

'What's up now?' They laughed even harder.

'Whots up now luv?' Patsy mimicked.

'Ah, this isn't going to work, is it?' I took off the cap. 'I'm a Yorkshire man, not Dezmond fucking Decker.' I walked to the small window. They stopped sniffling and looked at each other nodding their agreement with me. Dee stood up.

'You can't even walk properly, man! You just ain't near, you haven't got any rhythm.'

Patsy smiled at Dee's remarks and gave me a wink.

I looked out of the window and down on to the street, then a melancholy thought about the view from the window in The Lodge made me sigh loudly.

'Why not dress as a woman?'

'Fuck off, Dee, it's not funny.'

Patsy joined me at the window and put her arm around my waist.

'Don't they have dark skinned people in…Divon, you know, where you come from?'

'Yeh, course they do but…'

She placed her finger on my lips. 'Well why not become a slightly dark skinned reporter from Divon in England? We get reporters from all over the world visiting on special assignments. You have you're cool camera and hey, I could get you a phoney press card. You could hang it from your neck. It will say who you are and where you're from.'

'Yeah man, then you can still walk around in that weird way,' Dee added.

The next morning Dee made me up again. This time I looked acceptable and not as if I had fallen off a Broadway stage, which I was more comfortable with. Patsy was complaining that her belly was aching from laughing more than she'd ever done in her life, as she dashed around getting ready for work.

The Alphabet City area appeared to be mainly Puerto Rican, and by the look of some of the new buildings, had recently been renovated.

I walked invisibly past police cars and locals without any reaction and found my way to a large clothing shop where I got some, in Dee's words, 'cool stuff'. The escalator down from the men's department passed through the women's department. I couldn't forget Patsy's empty wardrobe and how unselfish and honest she had been with me, a total stranger. She had never asked for a thing from me. A mere stir-fry and a bottle of wine made her beam like a kid on Christmas morning. Obviously she hadn't opened my folder. Even though she owned little, she had so much.

I picked lots of nice things, from underwear to some designer skirts and tops, jeans, jumpers and shoes. I'd sneaked a look at her sizes after she left for work. It was a struggle to carry the stuff out, even with an assistant, to the taxi outside. I also got my makeup girl some stuff. It was only fair, as she no doubt earned a pittance serving fast food.

I picked up some fillet steaks and lots of drinks. I intended to have a good night, for tomorrow I was going to be Christopher Dean, an English roving reporter attached to the New York Times, and Chris was going to spend every hour of every day gathering information, while hunting those ISR bastards down.

I didn't cook the steaks, but the starters, lobster-sized king prawns, champagne and caviar were laid out like a banquet on the wobbly old table. I'd even bought a nice tablecloth, which had a picture of the statue of Liberty and other New York landmarks. Sadly the Twin Towers was one of them.

I got a sudden wave of butterflies when I heard the door key grate. Dee burst in followed by Pats and her smile.

'Gee, what's all this?' Dee said, loud as ever. Patsy beamed a smile over to me as she bent her leg back to take off a shoe. She hopped around a bit while rushing.

'My God, Patsy, just take a look at this spread,' she threw a glance at me. 'You ain't robbed any of this?'

I smiled my answer as Patsy stopped at the table with her arms down by her sides, bending over as if studying something amazing.

'Wow!' She glanced at me, speechless.

'Come on then, sit down.'

I popped the champagne and passed them the plate with the caviar-coated crackers.

'This is a thank you for being real friends and helping me through this crisis I'm in.' Patsy's face dropped instantly.

'You're not leaving are you, Kris?' There was a sad urgency in her voice.

'No, no,' I was stuck for words. I couldn't say, 'yet'.

'Come on, let's live like kings tonight. We've got fillet steak for the next course.' They grinned as I pulled out the chairs.

After the starters Patsy stood up and went to the sink. She picked up a wipe then concentrated on a small food stain on her cream skirt. I placed the steaks into the pan and they sizzled loudly.

'I'd best put my denims on,' she said as she finished removing the stain, then looked at the steaks and licked her lips. 'Gimme two minutes.'

I walked through with more wine as loud screaming erupted from Patsy's room. Dee jumped up and ran to her. Patsy continued shouting something to Dee while I refilled the glasses.

The building was down W 40th in Midtown West near Bryant Park. I walked straight in and was stopped at the reception to sign a visitors' book. I signed my new name as I had practised and felt quite proud when I put 'New York Times' after it. The ID card that hung from my neck had 'PRESS' in large letters and looked the business.

The receptionist pressed a stick-on ID, with my name on to my jacket, and logged the time I had arrived, then I was pointed politely which way to go.

I pulled the peak of my hat down almost to my nose and made my way along the plush carpeted corridor where display posters and boards promoted International Salvage and Recovery. The corridor opened out to a large room. One side looked like a display area while the opposite one had rows of chairs facing a small raised platform, which had an overhead projector on it. Sitting on a table behind it was a large screen. There were people milling around reading pamphlets that were piled everywhere and detailed famous treasure ships. Others were studying the information that adorned the walls informing them how wealthy the investors who backed the salvers had become.

One such success tale was the 'Central America' that was found in 7,000 feet off Cape Fear. The salvage company who had the balls to turn a dream into reality had recovered almost **One Billion US Dollars**. Another, the 'General Grant' wrecked off Disappointment Island, Auckland, with over **Five Million English Pounds** worth of gold that had not yet been recovered.

All the amounts were larger and highlighted in bold text so when you looked around millions of dollars leapt out at you. They failed to mention the dozens of unsuccessful attempts to find treasure in the past at lots of these sites, but it sure looked impressive.

I had to smile when I saw the picture of 'The Legendary Salvage expert Dr Tony Banks PhD'. He must have been cramming his studies big time since he arrived in the States.

Suddenly I was rudely reminded why I was here. SS Madeira. **One million, five hundred thousand English Pounds**.

I swallowed my gum. Salvage expert Dr guess-fucking-who,

researched this wreck and found it miles from where it was believed to have sunk. He had personally supervised the successful recovery of over fifty thousand gold sovereigns…Blah, fucking blah. Then I saw it all by itself and looking so lonely. It was the identical gold sovereign that I had left on the wreck for a laugh, but my joke had now soured considerably.

'Christopher.' My heart jumped into my mouth. Laura was a mere eighteen inches from me. How the hell she had recognised me so effortlessly?

'Hi,' was all I could nervously muster. I felt utterly fucked. She looked at me suspiciously, then at my ID. She smiled.

'Let me show you around,' I swallowed down my pounding heart as I realised she must have got my name from the visitors book, or the ID stuck on my jacket. She put her hand on to my shoulder. I had to restrain myself from punching her pretty nose into her brain.

'Are you interested in treasure?' she paused… 'Christopher.' I had to answer her, but would she remember my voice? Voices stick in the mind.

'Sort of, gold is always alluring.' My accent was hopelessly embarrassing and shit.

'Are you Australian?' She looked at me with a humorous squint. 'Have we met before?'

She had either sussed me and was taking the piss? At any other time I would have burst out laughing. Then her eyes discreetly lowered and scanned the New York Times ID around my neck. 'Nah, my folks emigrated there when I was a kid, but it was to hot for them and we returned to England after a couple of years.'

'I see,' she sounded genuinely interested, but that was just her bullshit way.

'Can I get some shots?' I raised my Fuji, knowing full well that she would avoid it like the plague.

'Sure Kris, go ahead.'

I pressed away like a pro while she skirted my field of view, avoiding the lens. Then I walked over to the *SS Madeira* display and focused the lens on the small cabinet and then deliberately turned away.

She approached me. 'You don't like gold sovereigns,

Christopher?'

'Is that what it is?' I had lowered my lens and my plan worked. She walked to the small display.

'This is from your part of the world Christopher, you know, England.'

I restrained myself from saying, 'You don't fucking say.'

She softly stroked the cabinet like a model showing off a car. 'There's treasure everywhere, in all the seas around the world.' I was boiling inside.

A few people gathered around on hearing her, which caused her to mutate into a marketing monster. As she babbled on she constantly gesticulated with her arm towards the lonely sovereign.

In a split second I seized the moment, and photographed her. Her face suddenly burned into me with such evilness, like Dracula caught in the sun, and I was the one who'd just flung open the curtains. I felt uneasy, almost scared of her wicked aura, then she realised that people were still around her, and her visual molesting melted away. She managed to continue with her spiel, but I could tell by her heaving breasts she was still seething with rage.

I tried to discreetly slip away, but Laura saw me.

'Bye, Chris,' she shouted, her words were too poignant for me look back.

I sat with my cappuccino, trying to stop my strange-coloured hands from shaking, but inside I felt good. I had done well; linking the bitch with the *Madeira* was another major advance.

Easy Everywhere was flashing and clattering away as I logged on. A little message flashed, *'Collecting mail'*. I sat excited as I worked the mouse. Sadly it was just a welcome from Easy Everywhere, then the screen flickered and another little envelope appeared below the opened one. I immediately double-clicked it.

'We need to meet. Where we eat, we can talk, when dogs walk.'

Hell! It was from Jimmy. He must have got away from them. 'Good on ya, Jimmy,' I shouted which caused a row of heads to turn momentarily before snapping back to their screens, as if they were all attached by elastic bands.

His message was simple, clear and rather clever. We knew that through the big computer in the sky clandestine eyes and ears monitor all and every communication made on this planet, but I doubt 'eating' and 'dog walking' would activate the automatic word association program. Jimmy had done well. He'd been walking that vicious, nasty little shit machine at ten a.m., and Pier's place was the venue.

I hit the KFC and arrived back just before Patsy and Dee giggled through the door, looking smart in their new outfits. The family bucket was demolished. Dee grabbed most of it, and had a piece of chicken in each hand, gnawing from one to another. She certainly would never have a size twelve in her wardrobe ever again.

Half an hour later they were sitting in front of the telly, dozing like two tired kids. I was looking at the results of my morning's photo shoot and ten thumbnail pictures of Laura blinked on to the laptop. I remembered that I had changed the setting on the Fuji to rapid shoot. I was so pleased my face must have beamed and then I remembered the previous night when Patsy came out of her room sobbing her heart out, while holding a pair of red shoes in one hand and a red top in her other. Dee was shouting and hugging me so tight I could hardly breathe, as my eyes fell once again upon Patsy, stood like a lost orphan jerking up and down while shedding joyful tears.

I felt even more justified later that evening when we drank wine and talked in depth for the first time about Patsy's past. I couldn't believe Patsy Alvarez was almost thirty-five, which really phased me out. She looked at least ten years younger. She was born in Harlem. Her father was an illegal from somewhere in South America, and had left when Patsy was a mere two years old. Her Puerto Rican mother died shortly after from drug abuse. An old friend of her mother's helped to bring Patsy up, but she ended her life by jumping off the Brooklyn Bridge when Patsy was only eight. From then on Patsy was reared on trouble and violence. She was placed in numerous hostels and establishments until she was old enough to work. Through work she met her prince charming, he promised her the world and they got married. It only lasted one year, but in that short time she attended two casualty centres. Her third visit left her in the intensive care unit where she lost her baby; she was treated for a broken jaw, a broken arm and four cracked ribs. What she told me next sent a cold shiver through me. The bastard had deliberately beaten the baby out of her.

Dee had previously explained that being a man magnet had screwed up her life. One smile from her and men became hunters. She said Patsy seemed to have something special that men became addicted to. Dee also told me that she was just a scared kid inside, and that every man she's ever known had transformed into a horrible green monster. She said that while casting a forewarning stare at me.

Right now Patsy Alvarez was sleeping and had her head resting on Dee's shoulder. She looked like a beautiful Little Red Riding Hood in her stylish red top. Her red shoes were neatly placed on the worn rug, her faultless looks and silky Latin complexion, set against her black curly locks, contrasted perfectly. I could never ever turn into a wolf with one so lovely.

I returned to the laptop and moved the mouse to wake it up. The shots of Laura I stole earlier were quite affecting, watching her face transform with each frame from an attractive classy smile to a look that could only described as truly evil, was intimidating. She was one mean woman.

Pier greeted me quite solemnly; knowing Rees was a friend of mine. He was showing his respect. I ordered some coffee and read my Fuji manual while I waited for Jimmy.

He turned up when my cup was half-empty, wearing a crash helmet and a leather jacket. I stood up and offered my hand. He bypassed it and gave me a friendly hug.

'Hell man, it's so good to see you here and not in the columns as another victim.'

'Same here mate, what the fuck happened in the park, and where did you get mini jaws from?'

'I don't get it man. Those weren't cops, those spooks in black.'

'What do you mean?'

'Those guys weren't cops. They're the same spooks that killed poor old Rees, man.'

'Well…what about the police helicopter that was looking for me?'

'Rees had a lot of friends, good cops who are still on the case.

That chopper was after them or whoever wasted him. We just screwed up someone's surveillance, or trap, I really don't know, man.'

'Well I'm still being hunted, aren't I?'

'I suppose so, but there are dozens of murders here every week. I don't think one English guy suspected of murder three thousand miles away will be high on their priority list. Especially when Sumer's goons are killing ex-cops.' He looked around then back at me. 'Hey man, buy me a drink. I've brought yer wheels back for you.'

'You what?' he nodded, smiling, obviously pleased with himself. 'How did you manage that?'

'You passed me the keys man. I saw where you parked it. I thought that's what you wanted. Someone would have only stolen it if you had left it there.'

'No, no, that's brilliant mate, you did real well.'

'What happened that night…you know after I escaped out the back window?'

'Cops everywhere man, there was such a mess. They paddled blood everywhere I had to get all my rugs cleaned.'

I sighed and looked around. 'Hey, is that my old helmet?'

'Yeah, it's cool man. I'll get myself another one.'

'Why?'

'Your old bike man, it's a lot faster than the pizza express. That one is just about worn out.'

'Didn't the cops take it away for fingerprints?'

'Nah, they fired a few questions. All but one of the witnesses melted away into the night. I told them that you were an illegal and you were looking for work. Why didn't you come back, man?'

What a total cock up. I had almost assumed myself to death by thinking the British way, in one of the least Brit places of all, New York. I felt stupid.

Jimmy was talking to a subdued Pier, no doubt about Rees. The coffees were well gone, and it was almost midday so we continued our chat over a beer. 'Jimmy can you get me some photos of Sumers?'

'Sure, I have some already.'

'You said you think you were being followed, well that's what you told Patsy.'

'I thought I was, hey man, you with her?'

'You must have been followed, how else would they have found us in the park?'

Jimmy thought. 'They must be after you then, 'cause they've left me alone. They must be trying to get to you through me. They must think you can identify them or something.'

'No way, it was dark and they were shooting at me. They can't be that stupid.'

'Did Rees give you anything? The mothers had a good rummage around my place they were looking for something man.'

'No, the poor sod was in agony. They mutilated him with a razor or something.'

'Yeah,' Jimmy said sadly. 'So you're shacked with that Patsy chick?'

I just smiled.

'Your stuff is safe man. The bike?' He looked apprehensive.

'You keep it, mate. I can't drive two at once.'

'Thanks.' Jimmy nodded to himself and smiled. 'Thanks, man.'

There was a short embarrassing silence after Jimmy's burst of excitement about the bike. Then he asked me how my toy camera was working. I started to tell him how good it was, but his wry smile told me to shut up.

The next morning I zipped along on my reunited pizza express towards Easy Everywhere. It was almost November and it was getting significantly colder. I noticed everyone's steaming breath escaping as they hurried along the sidewalks.

I appreciated the warmth inside the cyber café as I entered my pin number and gave the big orange machine another twenty dollars. I had no mail and was disappointed that Jimmy hadn't been in touch regarding the photo of Sumers.

Jenny was fading from my memory by the day. For the past two years whenever I closed my eyes I saw her. Now Patsy was shouldering her away and appearing herself. I could have never imagined this happening to me a year ago. The brilliant lines from a

Pink Floyd song came to my mind.

'All you touch and all you see is all your life will ever be.'

International Salvage and Recovery had added more pages to their web site. They included details of sixteen investment opportunities. They were offering early investors the lion's share of the lucrative profits. Every investor could gain one hundred times his or her investment. This next line was very clever indeed. Only persons with substantial means were eligible. That one would attract all the bullshitters who have more money than sense, the type of fools that compete stupidly at auctions and would feel like social lepers if they missed out.

'This company's foresight into deep-sea technological development is equivalent to the space program.' That was a quote from leading politician Bob Sumers. At last Sumers, their ace card had turned up and joined the party.

Each project would be split into three stages of investment. The three R's: Research Reconnaissance and Recovery. Research units were $5,000 each, and investors would receive 10% on their investment. The Recon units were $25,000 each and would profit an investor 25%. The recovery units were also $25,000 and would also profit 25%. Each project had only a certain amount of units available, which was dictated by the individual value of the project.

ISR had an impressive list of targets in their 'Area One', which covered Mexico Bay to the Bermudas. The list was long enough, but incredibly there were another nineteen areas being researched. I wouldn't be holding my breath.

C.V. = current value.

TRINIDAD1540 Santa Ann. Cargo. Gold. C.V. $3.2m
SAN PEDRO 1569 Lost off Acapulco. Cargo Porcelain and Gold. C.V. $2.5m
SAN AGUSTIN. 1595 San Francisco Bay. Cargo. Gold. C.V. $3.2m.
HOOP 1600 Hawaiian Isl. Cargo. Gold Specie. C.V. $6.8m

*AGANA. 1686 Guam. Cargo. Silver Specie. C.V.
$2.7m*
*JUAN RODRIGUEZ. 1696 Guam. Cargo. Gold and Porcelain C.V.
$4.5m*
*ROSA. 1841 Located in the Pacific. Cargo. Gold C.V.
$3.2m*
*BROTHER JONATHAN 1865 Seal Rocks C.A. Cargo Gold Specie
C.V. $8.5m*
*CONTINENTAL 1870 Cape San Lucas C.A. Cargo Gold Specie C.V.
$ 4.7m*
*PACIFIC 1875 Cape Flattery. Washington. Cargo Treasure C.V.
$1.8m*
*GREAT REPUBLIC 1879 Columbia River Oregon. Cargo Gold C.V.
$15m*
*CITY OF CHESTER 1888 San Francisco Cargo Gold Bullion C.V.
$50m*
*COLIMA 1895 50nm Sth Manzanillo Mexico Cargo Gold C.V.
$9.5m*
*CITY OF RIO 1901 Off Mile Rock Golden Gate S.F. Cargo Gold
C.V. $14m*
*ATLANTIC PRINCE 1928 24.00N 155.00W Cargo Gold C.V
$25m*
*FLORENTINE 1951 22.30E 140.28E Cargo Gold Bullion C.V
$26.8m*

By chance I noticed in minuscule print, at the bottom of the contract page and hardly readable among the gold and treasure border, was a condition.

> *'All contracted investors have to maintain a code of secrecy. Any investor found to have breached the code of confidentiality would be putting at risk the consortium's investments and consequently would have to surrender their investment to the aforesaid consortium.'*

In plain terms if you told your granny about your little investment you'd be fucked over big style. What a truly fantastic opportunity for someone to make money from money. Who could refuse such a certainty? After all the research ISR had done and the millions they had invested to procure the top-secret state of the art search equipment. Who could resist investing? It read like a fairy tale.

These venal bastards would appear bulletproof to some idiots, and I'd learned from the college of life that there are a lot of rich tossers mincing around looking for armchair adventure.

The sheer fact that Bob Sumers had climbed so high up the slippery political ladder made him the perfect figurehead for ISR. To have reached those dizzy heights of moral transparency confirmed to me that he was the type who wouldn't bat an eye to eating a live baby while still maintaining the 'cheesy' politician smile. He'd do anything for the sake of the 'Party' or himself. The same thing really! He'd no doubt throughout his climb up the ladder lied, deceived and cheated like all politicians do to get to the top. Without a doubt he would genuinely believe himself to be a superior life form and outside of the law. I had some tough adversaries to deal with, but secretly relished the thought of seeking revenge on the bastards.

Jenny was with Paul, which pleased me and freed me morally as Patsy was becoming more than just a friend to me now, and I looked forward to the long evenings with her. She was also a good ally as she had access to lots of information. Her latest task was to steer me to the right public records department where I could discover who owned number 40 on E68th.

After a morning in the public records office I found that a property management company calling itself Phoenix developments owned the building.

My next port of call was the company records department where I had to pay $10 to access the records via computer terminal, and within two minutes I found the name I was hoping for. The president of Phoenix Developments was one Robert Oscar Sumers or 'Bob' as he obviously likes to call himself. It was no surprise that when I tried to find his address all I got told was '*Information withheld*'. At least I had a second link between Sumers and the Edwards!

I mounted the pizza express and drove back towards Easy Everywhere. It was a cold and crisp day and in small places the sun's rays had found the damp sidewalk causing it to steam.

I recalled the big sandstone slab at the top of the old steps at The Lodge; it too used to steam when the sun reached it in the morning. Then I remembered the time Jenny lay naked on it while sunbathing. I'd sneaked towards her to push her into the water, but she saw me and held on to a rail. As I held her naked squirming body my motives soon changed and we ended up making love on the warm stone. Several solitary rocks that protrude out of the sea along the rugged Devon coast are called Shag stones because Shags, black seabirds, perch on them to dry their wings. After our passionate encounter Jenny called the slab at the top of the steps our Shag Stone from that day.

A loud horn blasted me back to New York as a stretched limo with blacked out windows almost took me out, causing me to wobble through a small gap made by a Greyhound bus and a yellow cab. 'SREMUS' it read on its custom plate. I immediately thought it must be owned by a wealthy Arab with a name like that.

'And up yours too dickhead,' I stuck my finger in the air and worked it up and down. Hell, I was getting like Rees. Then about a hundred yards further on I saw the limo stopped at the kerbside. I pulled up behind it. I had nowhere else to go, as the traffic was bumper to bumper.

Its two front doors swung open and two meatheads climbed out, straightened their black suits and walked towards me. I tried with my legs to turn the scooter, but the steering circle was too tight. Just as I got the scooter sideways and needed only one more turn to make an escape when a strong hand fell firmly on my shoulder. I pushed it off, and in a flash I was kicked off my bike. I hit the ground hard, banging my protected head. I instinctively curled up, expecting the physical bad news. At least I had my helmet on, but nothing happened. I cautiously looked up to see the meatheads walking towards the rails of the flyover carrying my scooter between them. When they reached the safety rail they casually threw it over. There was a terrific screech of brakes, then loud crashing sounds. Lots of car horns erupted as the meatheads brushed their hands off. One of them gave me the finger gesture and smiled then they calmly got back into the limo and drove away.

I rushed to the safety rail and looked over. On the road below was a silver BMW roadster with a caved in bonnet, at least ten cars had shunted each other behind the roadster. My pizza express was totalled and lay like a dead cat in front of the roadster. Its irate owner was screaming at the car drivers behind him. I legged it.

Sat at the monitor at Easy Everywhere I still couldn't believe what had happened. The BMW was a convertible. The driver would have died instantly if he had been going a little faster. Those foreign goons didn't even look to see what they had done. I decided to curb my street manners and leave the abusive gestures to professionals in the yellow cabs.

I had mail. The icon flashed and the little paperclip told me there was an attachment.

> *'Hi, man. As promised, if you need more just mail for a meet. P.S. tread real careful man. J.J.'*

I double clicked the paperclip and I got a message asking if I wanted to open the document, another double click and suddenly I was face to face with Bob Sumers. He looked about sixty; his grey hair had turned white and was combed over a bald patch like a hinged flap. A white well-groomed moustache grew below his sharp large proportional nose, his eyes were slate grey and his eyebrows were also white and thick. In all he looked quite distinguished, a bit like James Coburn, but with a thinner, nastier face that was ideally suited for a politician or a lawyer.

It was late afternoon and I had a fair walk ahead, so I dumped the files to the printer and paid the bored kid at the reception and collected my brown A4 envelope.

It was pointless taking a cab. The traffic was so bad I was walking faster than the cabs and kept catching up with the same ones for most of my journey. I carried my helmet, but kept my riding hood on, which exposed only my eyes and mouth. Carrying the helmet justified my disguise perfectly.

I arrived back at Patsy's and was greeted with a warm blast of air as I entered and I received an even warmer smile from my new found Latin lovely.

'Hi, Kris how's your day been?'

'Progress,' I waved the envelope, 'I'm getting something every day. Today's been good. I've found out that Sumers owns the house where Larry and Laura are staying. I've found the name of his company and I've got good professional pictures of him, thanks to Jimmy the man. I'll have enough evidence sooner than I hoped the way things are going and then I can try and stitch them up.'

Ringing a clean, but tatty tea towel she lowered her head.

'Pats are you OK?' She nodded solemnly then walked into the kitchen.

I moved a warm plate aside that was set on the wobbly table that had all the varnish kicked from its legs, and placed down the envelope.

'Come and look at these.' I pulled out the pictures. 'Pats?' There was no answer, so I went into to kitchenette.

She was stood half-smiling while starring at the steaming saucepan then on seeing me she snatched the pan and banged it down on the small available space and started giving the potatoes a good hammering with the masher. 'So you're getting closer Kris, that means you are getting closer also to returning to England to your idyllic heaven in Divon.'

Her derogatory tone was supported by the way she hammered the potato masher repeatedly into the already soggy mash, which had ridden up the handle and was sliding awkwardly in her hand.

'Hey babe what's eating away at you?' I asked instantly regretting it.

She threw the masher into the sink and shot me a stare that would have stopped a charging elephant and then pushed past me knocking me off balance. 'Jeaz you sure ask some dumb ass questions.'

Thankfully big Dee had a night stay over somewhere so I had a chance to quell the atmosphere that had developed between Patsy and me. It had dawned on me that Patsy was obviously thinking that I had used her for a convenient shake down and that I was going to leave as quickly as I had arrived and that accusation surprised and hurt me. We spent the evening like a newly courting couple stroking, cuddling and kissing, there was no need for words as her doe like eyes smouldered at me once again. She eventually came around and by bedtime I had her laughing like she did when she had transformed me into 'Shaft'. The mood soon became serious when we went to bed and my earlier attentions were repaid with some incredible Latin loving.

At yet another shop I got bike number three for $470. Again it was a black one and in about the same condition as number two.

I rode around to number 40 and parked using a tree to hide most of the bike and myself. I moved the mirrors so that I could watch both driveways at once.

About ten thirty out walked Laura and headed towards the Plaza. I waited till she went out of sight, then drove directly to the Plaza, passing her on the way. I pulled up a fair distance away so she wouldn't notice me. As predicted she disappeared into the building. I set my timer and watched the joggers dragging their blubber around. While I observed the dog people, I thought again about that saying about dogs and their owners. Some of these people truly looked like their dogs. A longhaired blonde had an Afghan and a fat stumpy redhead had a pack of bulldogs.

Three minutes short of two hours she appeared on the steps. She stopped, gave the customary scan around then started walking back.

I set off again and followed her at a more than safe distance. A vehicle purred past me like a hearse. It was the limo that had a go at me the day before; I saw the silly number plate. I almost shit myself when the brake lights flashed on. There were no traffic lights around and no reason for it to slow down, let alone stop. I carried on driving and as I approached I saw Laura standing at the rear door window. I couldn't see in, but just before I passed an arm extruded holding small handbag. Laura smiled and fussed around a bit then it purred away again.

I decided to go to Easy Everywhere to check how ISR were progressing. A few minutes into my journey I sensed something behind me. I looked at the mirror and I felt a jolt shoot through me like I'd put my fingers in an electric socket. The number plate abruptly became clear. The mirror showed me that 'SREMUS' was

'SUMERS' backwards.

I turned left and the limo followed, but I was heading out of the little area I'd got to know and everything was getting less busy. I turned again and the limo turned.

The little bike did only thirty miles per hour and I couldn't distance myself from the limo. I shot a red light and heard horns blasting behind me as the limo did the same. I looked back and its lights flashed me. 'No way, pal,' I thought, after my last encounter. I knew they weren't running red lights to offer me compensation.

The road got wider and sank into the ground and became flanked by sloping shale banks on either side, which had chain link fencing at the top.

The limo sped parallel with me and the window started to open. I thought they wanted to talk. They weren't trying to knock me off or run me down, which they could have done ages ago. My stupidity suddenly became cruelly obvious as I saw a big, fat silencer pointing straight at me. Then my head kicked back and I swerved into the side of the limo. I instinctively braked and the bike skidded on the shale that had spilled on to the side of the road, and it high sided me into the air.

Dazed and hurting I pulled myself up and dashed to the little bike. I dragged it upright. I could smell the blue tyre smoke in the air and then I heard an intimidating screeching roar as the limo stopped.

The little engine thankfully buzzed into life. I was now going the wrong way and thought I was safe, but another look in the mirror told me different. The Limo was making a three-point turn and white smoke was belching from beneath it.

I would be crushed, and then finished off with two taps to the skull within sixty seconds if I didn't get off this bloody road. Then I noticed a concrete drainage gully about a hundred metres ahead. I flattened myself like a boy racer to gain maximum speed. Reluctantly I snatched a glance in the mirror. The Black Death was screaming closer and closer by the second.

I drove headlong into cars that were blasting their horns, flashing their lights and noisily swerving while braking. I was almost twisting the throttle off the handle bar to gain more speed and was nearly at the drainage gully when a searing pain gripped my right shoulder close to my neck. I had to fight the pain. I was so close. I knew they were close, as I could hear the roar of the big engine.

I bounced over a small grate. I was in the gully and travelling as fast as the little engine would take me up and towards the link fence. I heard another squealing roar somewhere behind and below. I braced myself as I approached the fence that I calculated to be about five foot high.

A split second before the front wheel hit the fence I sprang to my feet. Number three twist-and-go disappeared as if by magic; as it catapulted itself back down the slope.

I was now flying like Superman, but in my flight path was a big road sign, 'Welcome to Washington Heights'. I was about to experience what a fly feels like when a hitting a car windscreen.

After a loud painful thud I crumpled into a pile of fast food cartons that accompanied the thin bits of grass that were struggling to survive amidst the pollution. I was heavily winded and clawed for breath.

I'd landed in a road interchange; the motorists must have thought bloody Evil Knievel himself had just dropped in after being shot out of a cannon.

I hobbled as fast as I could towards some buildings, then along the edge of a park until I came to a sign that told me I was at Amsterdam Avenue. I could feel blood running down my right side, but felt no real pain. My adrenalin was sky high.

I took off my helmet to find a neat bullet hole on the left side just above my temple. A few inches further around the top of the helmet, where the bullet had exited, it was blown apart. It had bits of liner and casing flapping like it had been attacked with a chainsaw.

I quickly flagged a cab and hobbled inside. The driver didn't speak. He looked Spanish; he just nodded when I told him where I wanted to go.

As I eased down into the seat the pain rose up. It felt like a hundred bee stings all in the same spot.

Patsy was still at work but thankfully Dee was in, as she was working an evening shift at Big Mac's.

'What the hell happened to you?' greeted me. I was now feeling like shit and hurting.

'Help me with my jacket please, love.' Her mood changed as she realised I was in a state. She predictably screwed her face up like Tina Turner when she saw the mess.

'What the fuck has gone down, Kris, how come you find all this trouble?' she blurted.

A furrow the diameter of an index finger ran at 45 degrees across the top of my shoulder, starting from the muscle at base of my neck. On either side of the furrow the flesh had erupted and peeled back as the bullet tore across the muscle.

'This is a goddamn bullet wound,' Dee said with shock on her face. 'What is really going on, man, are you robbing banks?' I just asked her to get some clean water and pass the whisky bottle. I needed a drink.

Patsy walked in just as Dee was finishing cleaning up the wound. She stood with her little girl lost look.

'I'm fine, Pats, there's no problem, every thing's all right. It's cool, OK?' she gave me a suspicious stare, then picked up some cotton wool and started cleaning the blood from my chest.

'What happened this time?' she asked calmly.

Dee listened with her mouth hung wide open, and then blurted. 'Patsy, this guy's in deeper shit than Al Capone.'

'I was following Laura as I've done before and that black limo, you know the one I told you about,' she nodded. 'Well it somehow sussed me out,' she looked puzzled. 'You know, they made me?' She nodded. 'I can't see why or how?'

Patsy walked over to the door and picked up the crash helmet, she gave out a gasp on seeing the damage.

'Pizza Express,' she said, and then ran her finger along the vinyl lettering. I felt like Homer Simpson after yet another cock up.

'What a tosser,' I sighed.

'You can't think of everything, Kris.' I was gutted at making such a fundamental and almost fatal mistake. Sumers and Co was either getting payback after experiencing a traumatic pizza delivery at some time in their lives, or they knew I was watching them with a little too much interest. With me wearing the same helmet after their road rage outburst, I didn't need a bald head and a lollipop to guess which one it was.

I had bruises all over me and was aching everywhere. Even so, I was grateful for the strength of my bones. If I had broken a leg when my flight was rudely terminated they would have finished the job. I thought of when I was a kid and of my attentive mother who used to give me lots of milk and always said, 'It will give you strong bones son.' Bless her, she was right all along.

From what I could remember the goon who shot me was using a Heckler & Koch .45. An expensive weapon made from polymer plastic, with a silencer it is the perfect tool for a silent takedown. These guys hadn't just fallen out of the trees. They were pros. I was incredibly lucky that the helmet diverted the head shot, he must have realised the helmet had foiled his first attempt, as his second shot was aimed at my spinal column. He fortunately missed, but only by inches. They were quick kill shots from a pro. If they had used a sub-machine pistol I wouldn't have stood a hope in hell.

Despite my pain I felt fortunate to still be here and able to plan my retaliation. I really needed stitches to close the wound, and going to a hospital would be suicidal. Instead we sent Dee to get some light fishing line and a suitable needle. I placed a large ice pack on the stained dressing and applied direct pressure, it hurt like hell but after thirty minutes the pain subdued into heavy throbs. Either the ice pack had numbed the pain or it could have been the half bottle of whisky I had drunk.

Dee arrived with the line and needle, which we sterilised, then without any hesitation Patsy stitched me up. I was pissed by now and almost out of it. I remember grabbing Patsy's four breasts as she leant over to tuck me up in bed, there were two of everything by then, but two of Patsy was a bonus.

Chapter Twelve

I awoke and checked my watch. It was ten thirty and I felt like shit. I couldn't even climb out of the bed. I ached all over, and when I tried to move my arm I was reminded of the damage a .45 round at close range causes.

I painfully hobbled to the toilet for a piss. I steadied myself with the wall, but the pain was too much. I started feeling light-headed, and quickly sat down on the seat.

Something was digging into my back. I heard Dee's voice as I came round. I had fainted and was lying on the floor, preventing Dee from entering. I dragged myself up and she squeezed in. I was shivering and soaked in a cold sweat. Dee roughly towelled me down.

'Isn't all this getting out of hand? They almost killed you.'

'They stole my life. I've nothing to lose.'

'That's not true, Kris.' She meant Patsy. Her dark eyes cross-examined me for a response.

'I won't let her down like the others.'

'And how are you gonna do that? What if you do succeed and get back what you're after? Your gain will become Patsy's loss.'

I was expecting her to come to that, and I didn't have an answer.

'Hmm,' she stood up. 'She's fallen head over heels in love with you, Kris. I've never seen her so happy as she is now, you're all she talks about, you know.'

I sat in silence as Dee stood over me, then she helped me to my feet.

Back in the bed I started to warm up while Dee made me a coffee.

'She's like a sister to me, Kris.' She passed a mug to me and stared. 'Don't hurt her, she couldn't take it.'

'Don't worry, that's not my style.' Dee stared sternly at me for several seconds then left the room in silence.

I stayed in bed for the rest of the day and woke up to find Patsy sat staring at me.

'You looked so peaceful sleeping. You smiled in your sleep, were you dreaming?'

'Yeah.'

'Was it about that place, Divon?'

'Devon, Yeah, The Lodge, and you were there with me.'

Her face beamed. 'And me, I was there!' She glowed with delight and moved her face within inches of mine. 'Kris, why don't you forget about those hoods? They almost killed you, the next...' She looked into my eyes. 'I don't want you hurt anymore.' She stroked my face softly, which was sending me back to sleep.

'I've, err, I've got to clear my name, Pats. I couldn't live with myself knowing all I know now. Anyway, if I don't, I'll end up in jail for a murder they carried out.'

'Be careful, my English knight from Divon.' Her soft lips pressed on to mine.

'I love you Kris.' A flock of butterflies ascended in my stomach, my eyes must have shot out at her, but before I could speak she pressed a finger to my lips. 'Shhh, you go back to your dream and give your bruises time to fix.' Her teeth gleamed in the dim lighting. 'See ya later.'

Sitting with the laptop and a notepad I breathed a heavy sigh. I had come to a grinding halt and didn't know what to do next. Another bike was a possibility, but Sumer's meatheads were on to that one and no doubt would have told Larry and Laura what had happened. Now they all would be alert and suspicious of passing or parked bikes. Thankfully wearing a crash helmet on both encounters with Sumers and Co had given me the slight advantage of anonymity.

If Laura had a death policy when I drowned her they would have gained a bonus pay out, and with my assets and savings added to the kitty they must have felt like they'd won the lotto. If I could only find out which Insurance Company they conned I would be able to sit back and watch them flapping around like headless chickens as the shit hit the fan. The problem was there were thousands of possible companies worldwide and I couldn't sit here corresponding with those long-winded bureaucrats for years, so I decided that I would pursue that course only if all else failed. Right now, mentally and physically, I needed some extra protection.

You can buy a gun in the US as easily as buying a loaf of bread in the UK. That's as long as you are a US citizen and could prove it with the correct ID, which I didn't have. Buying a dirty weapon off the street could drop me in even more shit. I had to find Jimmy, the man. He would know where I could obtain some protection. I didn't go around to his place. Instead I took a long walk to Easy Everywhere with my Giants hat pulled down almost to my nose. I found a terminal and entered my pin number.

I sipped from the glass and forked up the last of my Spaghetti Bolognese while Pier gave me polite smiles and nods whenever he passed. I had asked Jimmy to meet me at 2.00 p.m. and it was now 3.25 p.m. and there was still no sign of him. I gave Jimmy till 4.00 p.m. then left Piers. I decided to walk, so by the time I arrived at the apartment Patsy would be there. Being alone with Dee was becoming more and more uncomfortable, as she wouldn't drop the subject about me letting Patsy down. I was beginning to feel that she was jealous of my relationship with Patsy.

I got back to the apartment just as Patsy arrived. I went to my corner of the table where I kept my ever-growing collection of pictures and notes, only to find them mixed up and not in the order I had left them.

Dee was out at work at the moment, but when I had left earlier she was still in her room; she had obviously gone through my stuff, but why? Patsy poked her head through the door.

'Want me to fix you something?'

I needed to clear my head and plan what to do next, and the thought of spending a night with the huffing hippo didn't appeal to me.

'No, but do you fancy going out for a chinky?'

'A what?' she grinned.

'You know, a Chinese.'

She looked amused and shook her head. 'Sure, love to.' She hurried to her room.

I collected my records and notes and hid them under the spare bed.

We took a cab to Chinatown where we found a place called the

Silver Palace. Riding the escalator towards a massive dining room, I observed Patsy; she was wearing a black backless top that sparkled with sequins. It hugged her waist and neatly overlapped the soft red leather skirt that showed enough of her shapely thighs to turn any man's head and they were turning all right. For thirty-five she looked stunning. Her naturally beautiful Latin features, olive skin and long black curly hair complimented by eyes that sparkled like black gems made me feel honoured to be standing with her.

'Why are you staring at me like that?' she asked, teasingly.

'I can't believe how lucky I was to find little you in this enormous city.' She smiled. 'And how beautiful you are.' She just stared back at me for a while through uplifted eyes then offered her hand as we left the escalator.

We entered the large room and were greeted by dozens of faces, mostly men's. We were guided to a pleasantly secluded table, which pleased me, quickly and politely we were seated on plush red chairs.

Dragon pillars supported the ceiling. The room was huge, and large groups of diners everywhere were competing for food on their revolving tables. I smiled as I saw the same obligatory peacock murals that were on the walls of the local take away back home.

We started with crispy Peking duck. After the waitress shredded the duck, leaving it like a pile of straw, I felt a little sad when Patsy sank her fork into the pile, then twisted the fork, dipping it into the bowl of Hoi-Sin sauce as if she was eating spaghetti.

'Hmm, this is tasty, but that sauce is cold.' She sank her fork into the duck again and I smiled. She instantly stopped chewing and gave me a 'Huh?'

I took the lid off the steamer and removed a pancake. Then I spread the sauce on it, placed on some strips of cucumber and spring onion, topped it off with some duck and rolled it up.

'Here try it this way.'

She quickly swallowed what she had left in her mouth and took the roll from me.

'Hmm, that's even nicer.'

For our main course Patsy had sweet and sour chicken that came served in a scooped out pineapple, she welcomed it like an excited child. I had Sea Bass with garlic and ginger. As I reached the bones I removed the whole lot on to a side plate. Patsy watched intrigued.

'You want some?' She opened her mouth and I fed her like a baby, she even ate sexy.

'That's wonderful. I've never had fish like that before, or duck.'

'You're kidding me?' She looked a little hurt, then embarrassed. I suddenly realised what a dickhead I was saying that. This girl had experienced a past life that made me look like a middle class spoilt English brat. I couldn't begin to comprehend what she had been through, regularly having the shit beaten out of her by jealous bullies, and always being broke. I poured some more wine.

'I'm sorry, Pats, I didn't mean to...' she smiled then crunched a piece of pineapple with her perfect teeth. As I watched her I began to feel that she was mine now. Her honest innocence that had caused her so much pain in the past I saw as an asset, despite having only recently defrosted my heart with Jenny's help. I was beginning slowly to feel something strong and deep inside me, was I falling in love with this undiscovered Latin version of Marilyn Monroe.

I had mail but I also had the foulest smelling guy sitting next to me. He can't have washed since he sprouted pubic hairs, and the woman next to him looked me up and down as though it was coming from me.

I pinched my nose and pointed discreetly with my finger next to my chest at Smelly. After five minutes they got up, and the woman shouted at me.

'Haven't ya heard of soap?' Arm in arm they left. I could still smell the fat pig when Jimmy's mail opened.

> *'Sorry I missed you, man. I got the message too late. I will be there between 3 p.m. and 4 p.m. today. JJ.'*

I was just about to log off when another little envelope appeared. I double-clicked it. *'My Dear Kris,'* Hell, it was from Jenny. I started to read it, but decided to get a hard copy when I saw the name Ferret. I was surprised to be asked for five dollars from bored boy and even more so when I felt the weight of the envelope, she must have written a novella.

Jimmy turned up as I approached Piers. He zipped past me and gave a wave.

I reached him as he took off his helmet.

'Hey man, where's the wheels?'

'Let's go in.' I nodded to the door. 'You won't believe what happened.'

Pier was pleased to see us and brought a bottle of wine.

'This one is, err, on the house.' He poured two oversized glasses then gave a proud smile.

'For Captain Rees.' He looked upset, then said, 'I'll a leave you the bottle. You want food?'

'No, man, I'm broke,' Jimmy blurted. I nodded to Pier and ordered for both of us. I started telling Jimmy about Sumers. As he chased the last piece of linguine around his plate he shook his head.

'Jeez, all this is getting out of hand. Rees and now you. Who do these lawless fuckers think they are, man?'

'Jimmy, I need a gun.'

'Agh, for God's sake, man, don't go that way, the war is over man, don't go there.'

'Hey, Jimmy, get real, those bastards are out to kill any one who walks on their grass, let alone someone who's trying to destroy their lives. Once they click on to what the pizza boy from hell is trying to achieve, do you think they'll put their hands into the air and get their chequebooks out? Fucking hell, Jimmy, you're a New Yorker, where's your renowned scepticism?'

Pier plonked another bottle of wine on the table and sat down with a sigh. 'What are you, an Australian here in New York, getting so involved with, eh?'

Even Pier was joining in now. He poured half the bottle he had just given us into an enormous glass he just happened to have in his hand.

'You, my Australian friend, are too tense. Every time you visit me you look like a racoon in headlights.'

Hell, even Pier was having a pop at me for looking guilty, but indirectly he was giving me good advice. I needed to collect my thoughts and quit the racoon look.

Unfortunately I succumbed to the crack, as Pier got more intoxicated and Jimmy recognised several friends who joined us, the inevitable spontaneous piss up unfolded.

I drifted as usual with the tide and before I knew it, it was 10.30. I was well pissed and swaying around to the music when one of the staff came and sat down next to me.

'G'day cobber,' she smiled. 'That's how you say it, isn't it?' She was in her thirties, pretty and bubbly. Then I remembered the only secure part of my life at present, Patsy. I wanted to go there and then.

'No, it's so long mate.' I told her in the nicest way I could, then I found Jimmy. He was groping a girl in the recess that was surrounded with shrubs.

'Jimmy, I need, you know!' He turned to me breathless.

'Yeah man, a shooter?' I was totally embarrassed; he was discreetly giving the girl one on the table we'd just eaten from.

I crashed into the room. I had rehearsed my entry to perfection while riding the yellow cab, but I caught my shoulder on the doorframe and it made me enter sideways, which caused me to spin out of control. I fell over the armchair and into Dee's lap. She pushed me off as if I had leprosy.

'Where's Patsy?'

Dee, dressed in her bathrobe, ignored me and charged to her door like she was part of a stampede.

I checked Patsy's room and found her lying in the dark. I concentrated really hard to talk correctly to her, but couldn't. I was too pissed and I stumbled to her bedside in classic drunken style.

'I'm sorry I, I'm so sorry. I chilled out and lost all account of time, everything felt like the past, I forgot about all the crap and just let myself go.' I dropped my head onto the quilt and sagged. Then small hands cupped my face.

'Kris, you're the only man I've ever known who has come home drunk and been nice. Climb in and give me a big hug.'

I must have slept instantly. I vaguely remember waking up during the night and searching for the toilet, but that was all I remembered.

Opening my eyes as the light streamed into the room I caught sight of Patsy. She was naked and bending down while searching through her drawers. It helped my hangover immensely. Then I succumbed to the warm sheets again and again. No one was sending me final demands and no one was ringing me. I felt a bit like a castaway, but my head felt like shit, and I would have to get up sometime and face the thuds.

As I left the toilet I walked straight into Dee.

She huffed and rolled her bulging eyes. 'Your true colours are showing, Kristopher.'

'Give me a break, Dee. I've done no harm.'

'Patsy thought you had gone…and left her.' She folded her arms and swayed her head at me.

'That's a load of bollocks Dee, all my stuff is still here. We had a really good time at the Chinese the other night and we talked a lot about our future. It's bollocks.' I could tell now that she was jealous, but of whom I hadn't figured out yet.

She eyed me with hostility. 'You took all your stuff with you!' She had obviously noticed that I'd hidden my records and told Patsy.

I wondered why she had done this as she strode past in a dress that I'd paid for. Why was she being so unreceptive? Then it dawned on me, if Patsy and I bonded and I whisked her away Dee would be homeless. Patsy had rented the apartment and had gained the rights to a fair rent under a protection scheme. If Dee had to relocate she would have no choice but to find somewhere where the rent can go up without official intervention. I would have to tread carefully, as in her eyes I was becoming a problem. I remembered what that word truly means: difficulty, trouble and complexity. I had enough of all of them at the moment and they were multiplying by the day. It was time to go back to the basics, less emotion and more common sense.

I sat at the wobbly table as Dee sat watching another crap chat show in which groups of enormously obese people hurled abuse at each other. I slid out the pages of the brown envelope.

'My dear Kris,
I have completed my contract on the survey ship and am going to spend some time at home for the winter. I've finished with Paul and want to be alone for a while. I talked to a policeman friend of my dad's and he confirmed that they have linked Ferret's death with you and that the chain that was used was the same type as 'Westwind' has onboard. So I went to Looe to see the guy who now owns her. He told me that the police took a sample of the chain, but I don't get it Kris. I had a look around and all the spare chain is still there so the chain that weighed Ferret down wasn't ours. It couldn't have been from the boat. So I went to The Lodge to check in the blue drum where you kept some new chain for spare and it was gone, Kris. How could you have removed it when you were in Guernsey?

I put the letter down, I often thought about how they had fucked me over so efficiently. It must have been Banks and Ferret who picked up Laura when she was supposed to be drowning. Then they disposed of Ferret so he couldn't tell anyone.

I had thought about such a possibility, but Laura's disappearance made the whole idea sound like wishful thinking back then. I was right all along. They would have used a boat, and on the way out must have stopped at The Lodge for the chain, the sneaky bastards. I continued to read.

You must be so lonely all by yourself in that big cold city and always having to look over your shoulder.
I tried ringing you lots of times but your mobile is never switched on. I was so pleased to receive your mail; you said we could always be friends, and right now you certainly need a friend. Paul and I drifted apart. He was not like you, Kris.'
Love Jenny.

Shit, I had done to her what I was afraid of. I was no shrink. In all probability I'd make a model patient for one, but she had received everything the wrong way round. She should be living all the experiences a young girl needs to gain knowledge while growing up. I had catapulted her years ahead of her time with my selfish fuck-it attitude. What worried me now was that she was talking about coming to New York and using the word 'us' again. Maybe she had burned her bridges and wanted to recapture the past with me, but I know from experience the past in your life only ever comes once.

The rest of Jenny's letter was equally worrying, as she had virtually written a novel about our time together, as if she had copied it from a diary.

Dee stood up and farted, then sarcastically apologised as if I shouldn't have been in the room in the first place.

I met Jimmy two days later at the Tompkins Square Park. He was wearing a big long coat and had its collar hiding the lower part of his face. Ironically he was wearing sunglasses even though it was pissing down. For good measure he had a black woolly hat pulled down to his nose.

'For fucks sake, Jimmy, you look like a cross between a tramp and a spy.'

'Do I, man?' he said grinning. 'Jimmy 007Bond at your service.'

We started walking. It was cold and miserable. Despite the inclement weather the dogs looked cosy, dressed in their personalised coats. However they still shivered while soiling the grass.

'Where are we going, Jimmy?'

'Friend of a friend, man, he's cool.'

'Jimmy, the weapon has got to be clean.'

'Hey, sure man, would I find you an old rusty piece?'

'No you daft sod, the weapon must be new and without a past history. Will you stop calling me 'Man'?' he shot a surprised, hurt look my way. I suddenly felt guilty for being harsh on someone who was unselfishly trying to help me.

'Sorry mate, it's just all too much sometimes.'

'I'm cool man, I'm cool.'

'Clean means the gun can't have shot someone, or I would be

walking around with a ticket to Death Row.'

'I'm with you now, man, they tell from the bullets.'

We walked for almost one hour. Jimmy walked a bit like a black guy; I suppose it was the 'New York strut'. We eventually arrived at a little hardware store. It had all sorts hanging from the ceiling, like you see in some backwater town in a TV movie.

An Asian-looking man probably in his late fifties nodded to Jimmy then looked at me.

'Hi there,' his accent didn't go with his face. 'What can I get you?'

Looking around the full, cramped store I thought the only thing I'll be leaving with from here was some cleaning stuff. I stood like a daft lad waiting for 007 to break the ice.

Jimmy pulled a piece of paper from his pocket. The man looked at it then picked up his phone, obviously to verify who we were.

'I know about you,' he pointed at Jimmy then he looked at me. I didn't have the time to plead my case and tell him how unfair the world was.

'I'm from Australia and on the run from some people. I need personal protection, but it's got to be clean.'

'What if I haven't such a thing?'

'I'll take a mop and bucket and start up a cleaning company.'

He studied me. 'Ex-Forces?'

I nodded. His look demanded more.

'Aussie SAS.'

'Green Berets,' he grunted. 'H&K .45, Sig P226, FF97 Glock 19, Browning HP,' he studied me for a reaction.

'An old faithful would be fine.'

Jimmy looked at me, then at the dealer, as if we were talking in a foreign language

'It'll cost 1000 with 20 hard tips, cash up front.'

'Shit that much? This is America isn't it?' I received an indifferent shrug. I pulled out an envelope and dragged out the notes then placed them on to the small space on the counter. He tucked the money into his trouser pocket. 'Come back in ten minutes,' he said firmly.

'Jesus, man, this is unreal. It's like being a goddamn spy.'

I ignored Jimmy and moved to a doorway to get out of the rain. I could feel where the money had been insulating my thigh and realised I would have to curb my spending.

Grand Central Station was crawling with humans imitating ants. I shuffled amongst them and headed towards the toilets. The row of doors inside was my target and one with a small felt tip circle next to the lock. I found it straight away, but someone was dumping inside so I washed my hands and went back outside and bought a paper and a polystyrene cup of muddy coffee.

Ten minutes later I was in the foul smelling cubical where the guy must have dumped his Vindaloo. I reluctantly felt around the back of the bowl and found a key attached with white duct tape. I washed my hands again then sat keeping the left luggage boxes in my peripheral vision.

There were too many people rushing around to be sure that the moment I opened the box I wouldn't be at the end of a dozen gun sights and surrounded by men wearing black suits and Ray Bans.

I moved around and repeatedly glanced at my watch as though I was waiting for someone. Then a woman managed to scream abuse louder then the ambient noise, which caused heads to turn.

I made my move and opened the box and pulled out what looked like a Christmas present the size of a shoebox. While I was admiring my red foil wrapped present the woman fought with the mugger and it looked like she was winning as she dragged him around in circles while he stupidly clung on to his next fix.

I moved out slowly and nonchalantly so I didn't look like a member of the mugger's gang trying to do a runner. Security guards dashed around like rugby players dodging around the people with their Smith & Westons pointing skyward. I was impressed with the present idea; I just hoped I would be equally impressed with its contents.

I was pleased that deceitful Dee had gone out and thankfully it wasn't a potato gun in my box. It was, as promised, a brand new Browning HP with a magazine wrapped in protective greasy brown paper accompanied with a small cardboard box containing twenty stubby nine-millimetre rounds.

I checked the weapon and found it was genuine. Known to many as the good old Browning high power, it has long been the mercenary's favoured personal protection weapon as it is accurate at ranges under fifty metres. The HP bit ensures that a hit in the right region will stop a man in his tracks. My new mate 'Bill Browning' made me suddenly feel a lot safer. The Asian American Indian had been true to his word and was sound as a pound. Using the gun was the last thing I wanted to do, but if I came face to face with one of those goons again at least I would have some bargaining power, Anyway, I would be long gone from this world if they had got their way. I had nothing to lose, and wasting one of those heartless bastards wouldn't give me sleepless nights. In fact I would probably have pleasant dreams about such a revengeful encounter.

ISR was, according to their web site, gathering more investors by the minute. It was apparent that their 'Only persons with substantial means were eligible' had hooked the punters. I wish I had thought up such a good scam. No doubt when the kitty was big enough Larry, Laura and Banks would leg it with the cash, then re-invent themselves somewhere sunny while Bob Sumers tore out in public what little hair he had left, claiming to have been cruelly conned, when secretly he had taken the lions share. There had to be something else going on. Rees never got to know about ISR, yet someone silenced him. Why was he so desperate to get to Jimmy's apartment that fateful night? Whoever was responsible had left Jimmy alone since, but they were still after me.

Patsy bounced through the door. My new little protector Bill, complete with a full magazine, was in my bomber jacket, within arms reach and well hidden.

After tuna salad we settled in front of the TV and drank cold Buds while Godzilla destroyed Manhattan.

Dee kept complaining that she had seen the film before and that Jerry fucking Springer and a crowd of Neanderthals were on the other channel. She was even pissing Patsy off with her constant distracting huffs and loud gaping yawns. Again she was impersonating a bored hippo with wind.

I decided to turn in just as Godzilla shrunk and started crawling along the drains. I was lying there, thinking about what I should do tomorrow, when the conversation in the living room started to get louder than normal. Then it became clear that they were arguing. I felt really uncomfortable, but Dee was bang out of order and insulting me more and more every day. I didn't want to intervene. It was their problem and I had enough of my own.

ISR's web site was looking even more tantalising to the investors. They were about to enter the second 'R' phase, as their research into area one was now complete. New pages of ships' details were available for inspection, along with more bullshit and lies than circulates in the House of Commons on a Wednesday afternoon.

Any dedicated wreck researcher could have compiled what they had in a few weeks but ISR's presentation, combined with Banks experience and their skilled deception, had the investors well hooked.

Dr T. Banks was earning his keep. 'Reconnaissance' is a big word that required big investments. At $25.000 per unit this was the phase when their hard deceitful work was going to start showing telephone number size rewards. Well that's what they would be hoping for, and the professional way they were presenting themselves, at this stage in the scam, they would probably achieve it.

Names of genuine dive vessels were being bounced around, and suggestions that hire contracts were about to be signed. Some of the vessels were in South America and finishing successful commercial oil associated contracts. Now was the time to commit to them so as not to miss next year's weather windows. In layman's terms, get your dosh out!

I had been witness to smaller, but similar cons like the one where a diver would find records of a ship sinking with a cargo of say, tin ingots. After researching what size and appearance the missing ingots looked like, they would have an identical one cast. The next step was to find a lonely sucker with a bit of money who loves the romance of the sea and befriend them. Then, when pissed and bitter at the same things the sucker dislikes, our man confides his intriguing romantic tale. Eventually after dropping hints they reluctantly divulge that they have already found the lost wreck and show the loss details and the manifest, which indicates that there is tons of cargo up for grabs.

Breathing through their teeth their next confession reveals an ingot; it's the only one they managed to grab before a storm chased them off the site. The sucker has it analysed and it is found to be pure tin and truly believes his new found benefactor. The next step is simple; the sucker sits clock-watching while Jack the lad drives to his next target area with a handsome amount of investment money and of course his alluring tin ingot.

The scam these seasoned pros were involved in could bag millions, and I had to be around when it was their pay day.

I decided to visit Easy Everywhere every morning as soon as Patsy had gone to work. I had purchased a large businessman's briefcase that had locks to store my papers in.

Dee knew enough already to compromise me so I had to be extra careful. I was politely blanking her and soaking up her increasingly nasty comments. She was getting worse by the day and was obviously jealous of my relationship with Patsy. I had told Jimmy all about her attitude and in his laid back way he suggested that Dee was probably a dyke and had impatient fingers for Patsy.

I sat staring at the monitor and at the words, *'Dear Jenny'*. What should I say to her? The more I thought about her, further memories unfolded in my mind, and I started to enjoy them. I realised despite falling for Patsy, the adventure and time spent with Jenny had affected my life. She was still my friend. Eventually I pressed the send icon and my message to Jenny all those miles away would be in the new computer in her bedroom within seconds, waiting for her to wake up while conducting her predictable wiggly stretch.

ISR were bragging big time and according to them location and identification of their latest target had been successfully carried out. They even had pictures of early investors being awarded cheques.

ISR were boxing clever, they were using some of their funds to good use. Mrs Collinwood from Ohio had invested $20,000 and received $30,000. Gaining a $10.000 profit she was over the moon and the sun was shining brightly for ISR

I then noticed I had new mail.

'Kris, I am being followed again. They are in a black Chrysler. It's got a crack across its front screen. Meet me outside the Met Museum at 4.30 p.m. we can hide behind the front pillars. They won't be able to see you from the road and it's always busy. Jimmy.'

It was only midday so I decided to take a long stroll towards Eighty-second Street on Fifth Avenue to the Metro Museum. The Met, as it's known, is located on the edge of Central Park itself.

It was another dull and damp day. I had my collar up and a woollen scarf up to my nose like a bandit, while my Giants' cap hid the rest of my face. I had to pass East 68th on the way, so I approached from the Madison Avenue end for a change.

I sauntered into 68th at about 2 p.m. and kept at the opposite side from the white house. Then I saw her. I couldn't believe my eyes. It was Dee. She was hanging around the entrance drive. She looked nervous and was wringing her black gloves and pacing around.

I stopped and positioned myself behind a tree. What the hell was she doing here? Then it dawned on me. She was going to or already had grassed me up to those three killers. If she had done already I was finished. I had no choice but to confront her and find out.

At a stiff pace I crossed the road, opened my newspaper and approached her. 'Dee, Dee.'

She looked as though she had just shit herself. Her eyes and mouth opened wide with shock just as the black Limo turned into 68th. Her eyes blinked and, behind her, the car indicator light began flashing back. Laura would see me at any second.

'Please Dee, no.' I pleaded with my eyes and received a scornful, threatening look.

'You leave Patsy and me alone, get the fuck out of our lives, you needy bastard.'

I had to nod; she turned and waddled away in quick time just as the limo made its turn. I pulled up the newspaper and headed for Madison Avenue.

I felt thoroughly weak. If I hadn't been there those few minutes they would have known my plans and had the advantages of surprise. Why would Dee do such a deceitful thing? My mind yet again was doing cartwheels as I walked in a daze to meet Jimmy. I had averted disaster by sheer luck, but that luck had created another problem, what was I to say to Patsy? Whatever I do will devastate her, but if I didn't do anything Dee would eventually blab and I'd be in even deeper shit. The bitch must have read all my stuff; she must know everything, she had me by the nuts big time.

Chapter Thirteen

The Met as Jimmy had said did have big pillars at its front, but they were flush with the building's walls and there was no way, apart from climbing up and behind them, to stay out of sight. Jimmy had cocked up, which was unexpected. Fortunately I was early, so I sat casually down on the long stone steps that lead to several entrances.

4.10 p.m. still no Jimmy, then a youth came from within the building and passed me a note.

'Go to the first phone booth, head north.'

North was to my left so I headed that way. Maybe he hadn't cocked up after all. I began to think he was acting in spy mode again.

I could see two phone booths ahead of me. To my left Central Park opened up. I arrived at the graffiti-decorated booth and within a minute the phone rang. All I could hear was a muffled sound then Jimmy.

'I, I'm sorry man,' he was sort of crying and then the phone clicked dead. I stood confused, suddenly panic banged through me as a black car squealed to a halt and two well-dressed men dashed out. I dropped the phone and was greeted with two discreetly hidden barrels.

'Inside,' one of them gesticulated to the car with his weapon. I reluctantly followed his request and within seconds I was sitting between them and at the end of the two gun barrels. No one spoke. I felt terrible. I'm sure if I'd farted my heart would have dropped out of my arse.

We drove in silence and within minutes I was lost. We eventually arrived at a big gate in some sort of industrial area. The gate rolled sideways on small squeaky wheels, and the big automatic accelerated in to a parking area and stopped abruptly, causing the soggy suspension to dip heavily.

Everyone got out and I was turned and pushed against the car, still with two guns pointing at me, I was frisked. His first pass missed my Browning, but the second didn't and Billy was snatched from me.

'What have we here?' I received the bad news to my kidneys before being grabbed by my hair and pushed with a gun digging into my back into a warehouse type of building that was full of empty Dexion shelving.

We passed between the dusty shelves into a smaller walled off area where I saw Jimmy. The poor sod must have resisted for a while. He was badly bruised about the face and his head was down and dripping with blood and snot. He tried to look around but his eyes had swollen shut and his face looked bigger.

I was pushed to my knees and a black hood was forced over my head. Having a hood numbing all your senses is so scary because you cannot anticipate assault.

I could hear whispering then I heard the squeaking wheels of the gate and several car doors slammed and then the sound of footsteps became louder.

I had been on escape and evasion exercises while serving in the forces, and had been knocked around a bit, but this was real, and I was shitting myself.

'You are good at hiding, my foreign friend. You have cost us a lot of man-hours.' I didn't relax; I had no idea who they were, but after seeing Jimmy I knew they were no doubt going to give me a good kicking and probably more. 'You've seen your friend I gather?' I didn't reply. I just nodded subserviently. The last thing I wanted to do was piss them off.

'We went easy on him, just a few slaps. You're a bit different though, a regular Houdini?' I said nothing, then all of a sudden I was seeing stars and hearing loud ringing in my ears, then I felt a searing pain in the side of my face.

'I said, aint you?' I nodded. 'You see, you have something we want, and we want it now.' There was a foreign ring to his voice. This was the bloody mob. What the hell did they want from me?

'I'm sorry, I don't understand. I have nothing of yours. What is it, anyway?' I heard a whooshing sound, but had no idea where the pain was coming from next then I felt a shoe hit my stomach. I instinctively tensed up, but I was too late, and was reduced to a coughing fit. Then a firm hand grabbed my hair through the hood.

'Do not fuck with us, you limey bastard.' I could smell garlic on his breath even through the hood. Then my head hit a wall. Another blow landed on my left eye then another on my right cheek then the scary whooshing sound presaged a solid kick to my kidneys.

'What the fuck do you want?' I screamed. 'How the hell can I give you something I don't have, for fuck's sake?'

They started laughing; suddenly the hood was pulled off.

'It doesn't matter my friend, dead men say very little.' The voice came from behind me.

Through watery eyes I could make out four men standing over me. At the back of the room sat an older man. He looked smart and well groomed. He studied me intently in between dragging on a big cigar.

He gave a slight nod and a foot swung towards me. I grabbed it twisted it causing the goon to fall among the dust, I attempted to get up, but punches rained down on me from everywhere. I was spinning around and felt sick filling my throat, then water soaked me. I was lifted on to a chair then my hands were forced behind me. I opened my fingers while being tied in an attempt to expand my hands and when I relaxed them the pain cased. This guy hadn't been in the scouts. His knot was shit and I started loosening the rope instantly.

'Why are you not telling us? It means nothing to you.' The old man spoke calmly. 'You see what you have is personal and important to me,' he paused and took a drag from his cigar. 'You come from over the pond and cause all a this trouble. What do you expect us to do, take you to a restaurant for a meal, or maybe a show, eh?'

'I don't fancy an Italian right now.' I slurred.

A solid punch to my jaw put me among the stars once again.

'You just don't get it, do you?' the big goon spat out at me.

'And you won't either if you don't tell me what the fuck you're after.'

The old man slowly walked over and stared down at me. 'What are you doing here? Ordinary visitors don't sneak around like you; they don't carry weapons, a clean one at that. Who…' He studied me closely with his mature sinister eyes. 'Who's paying you to go through all of this stuff, who are you working for, eh?'

I shook my head. 'It's for protection that's all. I got it in a bar.' Another blow to my cheek knocked me off the chair and back among the shooting stars.

As my focus returned I could see them gathered around the old man. After a heated discussion one of them walked over and sat me upright again.

'We will give you some time to think about a few things. Your friend, he showed no respect, just like you are doing now, and we had to teach him some.'

He walked behind me and clapped his hands, which made me flinch. I could feel his breath in my ear. It stank of stale tobacco.

'Now he tells us anything,' he moved his face inches from mine.

'We know all about your girl.' My eyes shot at him, which caused him to smirk in triumph. 'We know her name and where she works. I'm sure the well-being of your precious Dee concerns you.' He waited for a response.

I looked him in the eyes. 'You touch her and I'll kill the fucking lot of you.' Loud laughter erupted in the building. Even the Don liked that one. He grinned and shook his head, then looked at his men. He nodded towards the door and they all left but for ashtray breath, who sat in a revolving office chair, dragging from his cigarette and puffing out smoke, which was swirling into a haze and mixing with the dancing dust partials all around him.

It was now dark outside and the single light bulb that dangled on a long cord cast elongated shadows in the dull light. I estimated that they had been gone for about twenty or thirty minutes. My hands were now free and ashtray-breath was dozing.

I stood upright then froze; I ached all over and had trouble focusing, as my left eye was almost closed due to swelling. I slowly approached him. I was committed. If he stirred now I would get shot. I was within one metre when my shadow reached him; his eyes opened wide when he saw me. I threw myself at him. It was one of those chairs that rock backwards and it went right over backwards, with both of us grabbing for each other. He struggled to raise his gun as I connected my fist with his nose, but I hadn't had enough room to draw back my arm, and it did little to slow him down, so I grabbed his short greasy hair, trying to draw his head closer. I managed to get my left arm around his neck. I just had to bring my right forearm to my left hand then push his head forward with my right hand, but he was fighting like a madman as we squirmed all around the dusty floor. Then I managed to get to one knee and raise myself slightly above him, which enabled me to complete the grip.

He became still as I applied pressure, then he started to gag as he fought for breath.

'Smoking can kill you,' I said between heavy gasps for air. His hands clawed for my face so I tightened more and he lowered his hands in submission so I eased my grip slightly.

'Can you understand me?' He sort of nodded. 'Tell your Don or whatever the fucker is called that if he touches one hair on Dee's head I'll kill the son of a bitch and all his family and his grandchildren and their fucking pets and the pets' fucking relatives. Have you got that?'

He made a horse-like noise through his nose with anger. I tightened my grip again and he started gagging. I waited till he started suffering from lack of air then I rammed the bastard into the wall, his head gave a sickening thud, his legs buckled and he slid unconscious to the floor.

I searched his pockets and found Billy Browning and a fair wad of dollars, a set of car keys and my other belongings that he had stolen.

I dragged ashtray-breath to the centre of the room and hog-tied him. There was no way he was going to untie himself. In a small adjoining room I found Jimmy and untied him then helped him to his feet. He was conscious, but in lots of pain, we both were.

Outside I made a quick recce of the area then opened the squeaky gate. I helped Jimmy into the car and got in myself. Ironically I noticed the crack in the windscreen. I rushed with the keys, trying to find the right one. After what seemed like minutes but was seconds the big V8 roared into life. I stirred the column change and pressed the pedal and we shot forward and hit the wall with a jolt that made us both cringe in pain. 'Shit, sorry.' I pulled the column gear stick and tried again. This time we shot backwards towards the open gate. Just as we stopped to engage forward gear the black limo appeared, the stretch one.

'Fucking gear stick.' I cursed and then stalled the car. I had picked too high a gear.

I frantically turned the key and we lurched forward in gear, picking neutral again I turned the key and the engine roared into life.

The limo stopped and the doors flew open, I found a gear and pushed the accelerator hard down. We shot forward just as one of the goons popped up and drew his gun over the top of his door; a big thud left a plate sized bullet mark level with my head. The car hit his open door and he screamed as he was trapped painfully by his legs and chest.

We shot past as more confused goons poured from the limo.

'And fuck you too pal!' I shouted loudly as I gave them the finger, releasing all my built up tension. Then I felt sick inside as I caught a fleeting glimpse of Dee's terrified face. Bullets thudded into the rear windscreen as we tore away.

The big stretch limo would find it almost impossible to do a three-point turn in the narrow street. We had made it.

'Nice one man.' Jimmy struggled to say then patted my shoulder. 'Shit driving though man, you must have learned in a stick change.'

'Jimmy, what did you tell them? I must know everything you told them. Did you tell them about Patsy and where she lived?'

'No man, just about Dee and where she worked.'

'Hell of a move Jimmy, you're one crafty dude.' He attempted a grin, which caused his hands to hold his face. 'Nice one, pal. Traitor Dee deserves everything she gets. What about me though, what did you say about me?'

'Just that you lodged with me and you were on a holiday from England.'

'Excellent mate, but what the hell do they want from me?'

'I think it's all about something Rees had. That's all it can be.'

'When did they lift you?'

'Last night, man, after I sent you that e-mail. I went out, and they were outside waiting for me. I reckon they got pissed with waiting for your return, so they used me to get to you.'

As we disappeared into the night traffic, I began to relax and felt a lot safer. We must have looked a sight, we were covered in blood and snot. We needed sorting out, but dare I go to Patsy's place? I really had no choice.

After dumping the car we walked briskly to the apartment. I just hoped Dee wouldn't betray Patsy and tell them where she lived.

I entered the apartment. Patsy was humming a song in the kitchenette; I closed the door behind me.

'Pats, it's me,' she popped her head around the doorway. Her smile instantly dropped from her face. She rushed to us, holding her hands up while shaking them from side to side like E.T.

'Warm water, Pats, and some sterilising stuff.' She shot back into the kitchenette and after a lot of banging and clanging appeared with two steaming pans. 'You…have been in another fight, Kris?'

'Not really. It was a bit one sided. The mob lifted us. They think I have something that Rees had. God only knows what it is.'

'So they just let you go, huh?' She rolled her dark eyes.

'Hardly.'

She looked at me and huffed then turned to Jimmy. 'What do you mean, Kris, hardly?'

'I jumped their guard. I had no choice, Pats.'

'You did what?' She span around and faced me.

'I untied myself and sneaked up me on him while he was dozing, then had a fight with him, got him into a death grip, then knocked him out then tied him up.'

Her anger sank into despair. 'Gee whiz, Kris, this is getting crazy. Those mobsters run the city, Kris. It's just you and Jimmy,' she shook her head. 'It's all getting like something you see on the T.V. except, Kris, these guys use real bullets.' She dropped her head. 'Lots of them.'

Patsy, despite being upset, cleaned up Jimmy and me attentively. As she carefully dabbed the split bruises I thought about Dee. She wouldn't be returning from her shift at the bone grinders tonight, and we could get a visit from the Godfather at any moment if Dee betrayed Patsy. Fortunately it was a narrow corridor, and the door to the building was well secured. If they broke it down we would easily hear them, and I had Bill Browning, plus the advantage of being at the top of the stairs, but they would be well tooled up, I didn't relish the thought of an Eliot Ness shoot up with the New York Mafia.

Jimmy crashed in the room I used, while I sat on watch during the night. Although I rubber necked it most of the time, I would have heard them coming though the door. Also the creaky stairs would be unavoidable for them, and when they were halfway up the stairs I would have no choice but to drop them.

Jimmy looked a little better in the morning. His swellings had gone down a bit, and after Patsy reluctantly left for work I soaked and catnapped in the bath, while Jimmy watched the street.

Dee's absence was sinking in. Although she had almost betrayed me I felt sad. She was fine with me at first, but what the hell; she would have inevitably caused me fatal problems. She hated me now anyway; I just hoped she hadn't blabbed to the mob.

We spent the day licking our wounds, half-expecting Dee to burst in, but she didn't show. It was Patsy who returned, with a family bucket of KFC and some drinks.

We did the same as the night before, and thankfully no Don or Dee turned up. I felt a bit like a rabbit in a burrow waiting for a box of ferrets to come charging in on me, but I was sick of running and wouldn't hesitate to defend my new friends and myself.

Patsy was also voicing concern about Dee, but said she had done this sort of disappearing act several times before, and that they had fallen out anyway because Dee wanted me out of the apartment.

She was making me feel guilty each time she mentioned Dee, so I told her all about my encounter with her outside number 40 East 68th. She couldn't believe it, and she got angrier than I'd ever seen her. She spent the next hour packing Dee's belongings while cursing in Spanish, and some other language.

She eventually struggled through the bedroom door and waddled across the room with all of Dee's stuff, which she piled up in the hallway outside.

'That's that then,' she brushed her hands off. 'It's just us now.'
I looked across at Jimmy who looked a bit sheepish, like a guest trapped in a family argument. Patsy must have sensed his distress.

'It's all right, Jimmy, you can stay in Dee's room while things cool down.' His face smiled the best it could.

I could see Dee huddled in the small room; the same one Jimmy had been put in as the Don's goons turned on their own man: viciously kicking Ashtray's face around the floor. 'Did he say anything to you?' He coughed nervously then a gun pointed at his kneecap. 'Yes, yes but...' A hand cocked the pistol. 'He...he said if any one harms one hair on her head he'll take out all of your family, even your grandchildren.'

'Anything else?' he demanded. 'And he's gonna waste the kids pets for good measure.' The Don snatched the gun from the goon and fumbled it into his hand then rushed to the small room. A few seconds later, a loud bang echoed around the building. 'That Limey piece of shit will soon be joining her...soon.' The Don shook with rage then threw his cigar at the wall, which sparked like a firework in the dim lighting.

The bright sparks transformed into the bedside lamp. Patsy's hands shook me. 'Kris, are you OK?'

I stirred and rubbed my eyes.

'You must have been dreaming, Kris. You were kicking and moaning, and you called out Dee's name several times. It must have been the shock she gave you when you found her trying to betray you.' She placed her arms around me, and turned out the lamp. 'Go to sleep now. You're safe here with me.'

Patsy was so kind I didn't have the heart to tell her about the dream or of Dee's capture.

I had told Jenny via the e-mail that I should be coming back to the UK soon, so it wasn't worth her while to come all this way for such a short time. I lied and told her that things were coming to a head and that the police and insurers were closing in on them and it would soon all be over.

I then thought of the reality of my situation. I had one of the New York's Mafia families tearing up telephone books with rage after I had escaped from them. Sumer's goons were also in the queue and just as ruthless, but why me? We really needed to get away for a few days and lie low.

Only one door led to Patsy's, so I placed thin pieces of the fishing line, the one we used to stitch up earlier wounds, across the hallway at several different places. If anyone visited when we were away, we would know.

We creaked down the stairs with a holdall each then peered into the alleyway. It looked empty so we hurried along, stopping at every turn to check for the feared limo.

It was 9 a.m. and rush hour I reckoned the mob would avoid the heavy traffic.
Jimmy saved the day with his extensive knowledge of New York. He called a relative who lived in Brooklyn and came off the phone beaming. I had given him Ashtray-face's two thousand dollars, and he was becoming his old self again.

'Hey dudes, you'll love where we are going to stay for a few days. It's my uncle's place; he's going away on business tonight. He's a widower and has a big house, we're welcome to stay there man.'

'Thanks mate.'

Jimmy shouted down a yellow cab and we climbed in.

'Fourth Avenue Bay Ridge,' he shouted. The cabby nodded then with a jerk we joined the queues of beeping cars.

I was sitting in trance thinking about ISR and the past weeks and what my next move would be, when the soft familiar voice broke my thoughts.

'Kris, are you OK?' Her perfect small round face smiled somewhat hopefully. 'Hmm,' I nodded, but I wasn't getting off that easy.

'Kris, I know how you feel about what has happened to you. It's a terrible thing to lose so much, then have to go through all of this. You are brave and strong, but now you must recharge yourself. Let it all go, just for this weekend. Forget about everything and enjoy yourself with me.'

'I will.' I smiled back. 'We will.'

Bay Ridge could have been in a different country. Old wooden mansions with trees and yards that lined the shore gave it an Eden sort of feeling, away from all the hustle and bustle elsewhere. There were faces from all cultures smiling and taking things easy. The place had a laid back feel to it.

We walked up the path towards the type of house that would have been unnoticed in the set from Saturday Night Fever. The big wooden door opened and a smiling professorial looking man in his early sixties welcomed us wholeheartedly. The reception area was like a fifties film set, in fact the whole house looked like one, it was so homely and welcoming, and Uncle Edward, 'Eddy' he insisted, was a gent.

We were shown to our rooms politely and left to freshen up while Eddy made tea.

The room was beautiful. It was almost like being inside a dolls' house and the polished wooden floors creaked under foot.

'Look Kris.' Patsy pulled aside the net curtain to reveal a view of New York Bay and the Hudson River. I stood staring. Here I was with a great water view and a gorgeous curly haired woman again. My emotions were overloaded and I turned away to hide my feelings, then her small strong arms saved me.

Eddy fussed around us pouring tea like an English butler. The teapot even had a cosy, which had stains of use near the spout, just like the ones I saw as a kid when visiting my auntie's. I only hoped the dreaded tin of ancient cakes wouldn't appear next.

We enjoyed our English tea, I commented that it tasted as good as my mum's. My comment pleased Eddy so much that he made us another pot.

Eddy then gave us a tour of the old house, constantly referring to his loving wife, whom he was obviously still in love with. Jimmy remembered lots from his childhood visits. It was a nice homely day free from the fear and violence that I had inadvertently become used to during the recent difficult years.

Eddy left in his equally old smoking Cadillac about 4.00 p.m. and Jimmy disappeared, no doubt to find something unusual to smoke. I lay with my head in Patsy's lap and sank into a deep untroubled sleep.

Saturday morning at Bay View was easy. We showered, then had free-range eggs knocked into a tasty mushroom omelette.

I sprinkled a little salt on to my omelette. Patsy did the same and then stared into my eyes. 'Who is Jenny?'

'Jenny used to crew on *Westwind* when we took divers out.'

'You were talking to her last night in your dream, Kris.'

'Talking to her?' I paused. 'We had a relationship during the salvage of the gold sovereigns that I told you about.'

'So it was Jenny who was your partner in the salvage, not another man?'

'Yeah, and she worked on *Westwind* on the weekends.'

She looked troubled as I ate. 'Do you still love her, Kris?'

'No, but I still like her. We spent special times together and bonded a good friendship. She helped me after you know?' Patsy remained silent.

'I'm being open, Pats, I'm not hiding anything.'

'Will you go back to her when you leave here?' I noticed she hadn't started eating yet.

'Come on, Pats,' I nodded to her plate. 'It's going cold.' With that she jumped up and ran to the door and disappeared.

I got to the door and saw her running along the shore I chased her and was quite surprised how fast she could run. When I caught her up she dropped to her knees and her face disappeared into her hair.

'Patsy what's wrong?'

'You were dreaming about her. You… you said intimate things, Kris, inside you must still love her.' I pulled her to her feet.

'Look, I received an e-mail from her recently, she had just finished with her boyfriend and she must have rebounded back to me. She recalled our past as if reading from a diary. It brought old memories to the surface that's all. She's too young for me, Patsy. I still feel for her, but we could never be, it's over between us.'

She gave me a pout and with her chin on her chest, rolled her big eyes up to mine.

I froze in her searching stare.

'Kris, tell it to me straight, are you planning on ditching me?'

I shook my head slowly. 'Never, Patsy, never ever, never,' her mouth curved and her saddened face found a smile, slowly shaking her head she repeated, 'Never ever, never?'

Patsy's hair was blowing big and wild. I even saw her cute ears as our stomachs floated up once again as the Wonder Wheel carried us towards the ground, her infectious giggle started me off, and we held our aching sides at the sight of each other's screwed up faces.

When the big Wonder Wheel started to slow down she pleaded like a little girl for another go. We rode the wheel five times before Patsy admitted that she was beat and aching so badly she found it hard to giggle any more. We staggered away like two drunks, squealing at each other much to the amusement of the people around us. Then Patsy headed towards the Astroland Cyclone roller coaster and I was dragged along like a parent. I gave the attendant an extra five dollars and we got the front seat.

She jumped like a high jumper into the yellow two-seated carriage that had a scratched red interior, and almost trapped me under the safety bar.

As we clanked up the steep incline I used my Fuji once again to capture the moment. She was so excited all I got from her was snatched exuberant smiles and glimpses of her perfect teeth. Speeding down the track Patsy lowered her head and put on a serious face as if she was driving the thing and trying to gain more speed, then her serious look melted to one of pure revelation as the g-force gripped us. We turned and dropped rapidly, which caused another giggling fit from her, before her predictable postures started all over again. It was pure fun and she was brilliant to be with.

Our next stop was the Coney Island Emporium, which had the latest video games. We ended up on the Daytona Simulator and six other racers joined us, causing Patsy to turn really serious as she suffered what I joked was pre-race nerves.

The lights turned green and the seats bumped and vibrated as the track screamed into view. I took a look at Patsy. She was moving around as though the race was real. Her face was so funny I had to get a shot of her, and I did, just as she gritted her teeth before she entered a turn at a stupid speed. Her car spun all the way round and ended up facing the right way again. I couldn't believe it. She was in first place. She screwed her face up again and trashed a car that was attempting to pass her then another racer got rammed off the track. Patsy was a loony. I reckoned she'd learnt to drive in Harlem and in someone else's car. She finished first and started throwing her arm into the air as her opponents slinked away.

Searching for the exit we passed a row of basketball nets, where if you score three nets out of five you win a cuddly toy. I scored only one, much to her amusement. She called me a country boy, then scored five out of five and collected a teddy bear.

We ended up in the Cabana Carioca, a bustling and colourful looking Brazilian restaurant, which I felt was in keeping with the brilliant day we had spent here at Coney Island. We ordered Mariscada, which was a kind of seafood stew with a tomato base, and a bottle of Sagras each, a Portuguese beer that tasted strong, but great. The Mariscada came served in a sizzling black cauldron and we had big chunks of bread to dip into it. After more beers we took a steady walk back to Bay View.

'Hi man.' Jimmy was lying on a lounger in the wooden conservatory type building, with the doors open to the view and sounds of the bay.

'It's a cracking place this, Jimmy.'

'Yeah, I've lots of growing-up memories of this place and the parks and rides. I used to come here every year. It's sad to see Uncle Eddy alone after being married for almost fifty years to such a kind person as my Auntie Ethel.' He took a drag at his joint. 'How's your day been, dude?'

'The best I can remember.' Patsy's face lit up. 'I've seen a different side of Patsy today, mate.'

'Oh yeah, what's that then?'

'She's a speed freak and a giggling fanatic.' Jimmy grinned. I reckoned he was comfortably numb.

'Hey man, I got you some drinks.' He looked at his joint.

'Cheers pal.' I opened the bottle of brandy and filled two big glasses. 'Thanks for... you know, everything.'

Jimmy nodded to me. 'I would be part of some construction foundation, if it weren't for your balls, man.' I shrugged. 'And the money, that was cool man, mugging the mob, holy shit man, cool or what.'

Whatever Jimmy was smoking it sure was working. He was

floating somewhere in a world all of his own.

I caught a glimpse of Patsy struggling to swallow the brandy, so I topped it off with lemonade. She winked at me then slowly left the room. I finished my brandy while trying to make sense of Jimmy's one-sided conversation then shut the doors leaving him humming to himself while grinning at me.

I climbed into bed quietly and lay with a smile on my face as I recalled the brilliant day. I felt mentally refreshed and ready for action.

Patsy couldn't work out why the gear was still in the hallway. I didn't need to tell her what had probably happened regarding Dee, and how Jimmy had inadvertently saved us both from becoming bridge foundations.

No fishing line tell tails were snapped, even though it was almost five days ago, but I wasn't going to lower my guard. Dee would have surely blabbed to save her fat arse, or maybe my dream of her getting wasted meant something after all.

I had been escorting Patsy to and from work in between visits to cyber world, where I was keeping an eye on ISR developments. It was a cold damp evening, and mist had found its way down to the streets. Even the drains were steaming, making the whole scene look like a big fire had just been quenched.

I waited below one of the big globe lamps for Patsy, occasionally straining to look inside, expecting to see her at any moment, but I'd been there for almost half an hour and she hadn't shown. I waited a little longer then decided to go inside to find her. The usual security men were casting their suspicious glances as I stood at the reception.

'Hi, can I help?'

'Is Patsy still here?'

The girl gave me a stare then must have remembered who I was. 'I'm sorry she left early today, Kris isn't it?'

'She didn't say where she was going by any chance?' She shook her head and shrugged her shoulders at the same time.

I returned her polite smile and returned to the mist. Where the hell could she be? I waited for another ten minutes then decided to go back to the apartment.

Dee's bags were still there and the light was visible through the doorframe. I walked briskly in holding Bill Browning inside my pocket.

'Hi, Kris,' Patsy, out of character wasn't smiling.

'What's happened, where the hell were you? I waited as usual.'

'I'm sorry; I got a call from one of the girls where Dee works. No one's seen her, Kris. She's just vanished!'

I placed my arm around her.

'I...I know we weren't getting along too well, but I'm scared for her, Kris. What if she's done something stupid because of our argument?' Her words tumbled out punctuated by gasps of air. She looked hopefully for a favourable reply, but the phone broke the silence. Patsy nodded while holding the phone towards me. 'It's Jimmy.'

'Hey man, my place is trashed, all my pics are torn and the whole place, man, it's been totalled. Even my dark room man, my fucking dark room it's a holy place to me, all trashed.'

'Shit, they're still searching, but what for... what the hell could it be? Hey, you be careful Jimmy, where are you now?'

'At home, man, well, what used to be home? It's finished.'

'Shit, Jimmy what the hell are you doing hanging around there? Get out before... oh shit, Jimmy, they will have it staked out. You'll have to take the back way.'

'What back way? There's only the fire ladder out the front.'

'Get out through the back window.'

'Hell, man, that's far too high, man. I would get killed.'

'Jimmy you have to, just, just hang from the sill then drop. Do it now Jimmy. Have you somewhere to stay? You can't come back here, not for a while. They could be following you again. You're their only ticket to me.'

'OK man, I'll try.'

'Don't even think about trying, do it now!'

The phone went dead then my heart almost stopped as I realised that they could have tapped his phone, or worse, that through crooked associates they could have traced his calls.

'Patsy, you'd better pack your favourite things and anything special to you, documents and papers, you know, ID documents all that sort of stuff.'

She didn't need asking twice.

I fitted my life into a medium sized nylon holdall within minutes and then checked quickly around making sure I hadn't left anything that could compromise my previous investigations. A quick last glance around the room, that had been so good when all felt hopeless, caused a stab of sadness as the reality dawned; I'd never be back here, and would again have to find another pillow. I came here desperate and was now leaving desperate, and having radically disrupted these two innocents' lives made me even angrier inside.

Patsy stood holding two bags like a wartime orphan about to embark into the unknown. I grabbed a bag from her and caught her eye.

'I'm so sorry about all this, Pats.'

The corners of her mouth curved. 'I'd follow you into hell, Kris.'

I contemplated my reply, but could only smile it to her.

Passing Dee's life's belongings yet again put things into perspective. This was real. They had all the resources and advantages, and were probably waiting outside.

I carefully opened the door to the yard, holding my position to let my eyes adapt to the darkness as I held the 9mm with the safety off. After five minutes I slowly moved across the small courtyard towards the arched doorway that leads to the alley. If they were going to strike it would be soon.

It was shit or bust time. I didn't like being in the courtyard because it was a perfect trap. I told Patsy to crouch behind a big garbage container then rushed to the doorway, weapon at the ready. Still I heard no sound.

Despite being assassins, my enemies all wore designer clothing, including impractical leather shoes that skid loudly in gravel and stones, but all was silent.

I called Patsy and she was beside me within seconds. The air was cold and cut like a knife through our clothing as we rushed down the alley, hugging the wall. As we came to the end of the alley Patsy walked openly into the street and waved for a cab.

'For fucks sake, Pats, what are you doing?'

'Come on Kris this is dumb, let's just get out of here.' Suddenly a squeal of tyres followed by the roar of a big engine filled the air as the big limo accelerated towards us. Patsy was in the cab I dived in behind her.

'Conducir, conducir! Rapido! Rapido!' Patsy repeatedly screamed at the driver. 'Si senorita donde a.'

'Solo conducir rapido, rapido soccoro nosotros, por favor, rapido.' Whatever Patsy had said it worked, the driver floored the pedal and we shot along 42nd Street like bank robbers making our escape. The only problem it wasn't the good guys who were chasing us.

Patsy continued to shout Spanish at the perplexed driver while I watched the limo virtually crashing through the confused drivers. Hub caps spun from the frantic black monster as it rammed aside any thing in its path, a profusion and sparks flew into the dark each time the pursuer ruined some poor sod's pride and joy.

A big jolt made me pull my arm from my bomber jacket to keep my balance. I didn't have time to release the gun. Patsy's eye's widened, but the driver saw it as well.

'No, no.' He mounted the kerb braked to a stop opened the door and legged it.

'Shit.' I opened the door and pointed the gun at the limo, which was bearing down on us. Suddenly with squealing tyres we left the kerb with a series of jerks as the tyres struggled for grip, we were on the move again, and accelerating big time.

'Well done kid,' I shouted to Patsy. She turned quickly and acknowledged me. I had another problem now. She had that look in her eyes, the one she had when she raced on the Daytona video game.

We hurtled around street corners almost on two wheels, making roaring skids as the cab drifted sideways, then almost flipped over as she yanked the wheel from lock to lock. Through the mirror I saw her almost possessed gaze as she tore down some street on the wrong side like a loony playing chicken. Cars swerved and crashed as we entered an alleyway almost airborne. It was the garbage containers' turn now. They flew spinning into the air as if they were exploding. I'm sure Patsy was driving at them deliberately.

We crashed back on to another street, heavily bottoming out the suspension, causing Patsy to bounce off the seat like a doll as her hair flew from her shoulders. She landed and her foot hit the gas once again. We must have been flying along at eighty miles an hour or more then she hit the brakes and casually joined a steady flow of traffic as we crossed over a bridge.

Patsy scanned the rear mirror and her eyes fell on mine. 'Lost 'em,' she said and screwed her face into a thrilled grin as if it were all a game.

'Shit, Pats, where the hell did you learn to drive?'

'Self taught.' I saw her smirk reflect in the windscreen. 'I don't have a licence. I failed for speeding.'

'Yeah, that doesn't surprise me.' She shot a cute smile at me then started singing something in Spanish.

We drove for about half an hour. During the journey we kept getting hailed, which amused Patsy each time it happened. She gave a giggle and a wave to the disappointed pedestrian.

We ended up in Jackson Heights; Patsy obviously knew where she was as she drove through the area, which was predominantly South American. She pulled up in the car park of a diner, stopped the engine and turned, grinning.

'Driving always makes me hungry.' She grinned. 'That will be twenty dollars'.

'Hell, we've got to ditch the cab. Every cop in New York will be looking for us.' She jumped into the back with me.

'Kris, this is a gypsy cab.' I looked dumb. 'An illegal, Kris, no genuine licence, no insurance, you know, no records, no problem.'

I was learning more each day and was quickly realising that Patsy wasn't as green as I first thought she was. We ate at the diner. Patsy was still high on adrenalin and constantly smiled for no reason as she ate. Later with the help of her ID we got a room for the night.

Chapter Fourteen

Leaving the battered cab in the car park we started on foot for Easy Everywhere. After paying the motel tab I realised sadly my money was getting low. In fact I had less than one thousand dollars now, and we had nowhere to stay. To make matters worse the mob had clocked both of us, only in car headlights, but it was enough to make us extra cautious.

The orange machine was still in charge and I had credit left. I tapped the keys and waited as numerous little unopened envelopes appeared in a line. The first two were junk, but the next three were from Jenny. Patsy was stood over me. I had no options.

> *'Dear Kris, I hope you got my last mail, I feel so helpless here I want to help you. You're always on my mind. Tell me where you are staying and I'll fly out to you. I can afford it, but I can't afford to be without you any longer. Love Jenny.'*

Patsy grabbed the mouse and with shaking hands clicked the next envelope.

> *'Kris why aren't you returning my mail, it's been three days now. Please contact me and tell me where you are. Always yours. Jenny'*

'Always yours, huh!' Patsy clicked the next envelope then glared at me.

> *'Dear Kris, it's been more than a week now, in your last mail you told me not to come to you, but you not contacting me causes me concern for your well-being, so I'm coming to New York to find you. See you soon, love Jenny'*

'Oh shit.' I sighed loudly.

'Well, stud, what you gonna do now?' Her eyes searched for an answer.

'Nothing I can do is there? I mean, I haven't encouraged her, she's just stubborn and trying to help a mate.'

'Help a mate, sure that's a new way of putting it. Do ya think I'm a dumb-ass?'

I deliberately ignored Patsy's jealousy, which fuelled digs in Spanish as she voiced them with gusty defiance.

ISR was still boasting mega profits and lots of good home-loving folk were reaping the benefits. A list of Mr and Mrs Jackshits were boasting big profits, but there was no way of checking their stories. It was obviously a load of crap. Just how long they would carry on with this scam was my concern. I had been here now for weeks and the longer they stretched this con, the more exposed they would become and they would be aware of that as well. I had to be more vigilant.

I left e-mail for Jimmy making him aware of our situation then we logged off and had a coffee in the diner opposite. We ended up in a bar then later another seedy motel.

As Patsy approached the check-in counter a youth blushed embarrassingly as she spoke to him. He was obviously shy and taken aback by her good looks and her warm smile. After passing her everything upside down he dropped the pen between the desk and the wall and looked at us.

'I…I w…will g…get another f…from the o…f the off…' Patsy smiled and said Office for him.

'Mm,' he nodded then left through a door. I stood with my hand on my chin.

'What's got into you?' Patsy tilted her head to one side.

'I've got it, I've got it.'

The lad returned and as soon as she signed us in I dragged her outside.

'That lad reminded me, I should have known all along.'

'What, what should you have known?'

'That night poor old Rees was bumped off he was trying to tell me something, but they had mutilated him and all he could say was off or oth. He meant office, his office.'

'Yeah, but you went there and it was completely empty.'

'The wrong office, Pats, when we first met he took me to a bar, and guess what?

'What? What?' she was jumping up and down with frustration.

'He said. 'This is my real office.' Patsy lowered her arms.

'Jeez, is that all?'

'Don't you get it? Whatever the mob is after must have been left there.'

Patsy gave a shrill whistle, a cab pulled up and we climbed in.

'Where to?' Patsy looked at me.

'204 West 57th, please mate.'

I asked the driver to wait for us then we passed through a group of banished smokers hanging around the doorway, sucking deep drags from their cigarettes as if their lives depended on it. A few drinkers looked pleasantly surprised as Patsy entered, as did the barman.

'What can I get you guys?'

'I don't suppose you remember me, I came here with Captain Rees before, you know,' he nodded solemnly then took a long look at me.

'Sure I remember you,' he probably didn't, but I nodded acknowledgement.

'Rees told me previously that he'd left something behind your bar for me.' He eyed me for a while.

'He rushed in that night he didn't even stay for a drink. That's when I knew he was in trouble. What's your name, kid?'

'Kris, Kris Woods,' He reached under the bar and produced an A4 sized envelope.

'Here,' he passed it to me. 'Kris' was scribbled over the name Rees; it was the same envelope I'd seen the day Rees gave me Laura's file that he'd got from his police mate. I thanked the barman and we left.

I waited until we got back to the dingy room before I peeled off the numerous lengths of clear tape. I pulled four A4 sized black and white photos and a note from it. The note fell on the floor and Patsy picked it up.

'Kris if you are reading this, I've bought it. Bob Sumers is paying hired gun Joe Calesy to take out the local boss. It all started over a property deal that turned sour. Be careful, boy, it's your only way to that degenerate bastard. Use it well.'
Rees.

'Is that all?' Patsy sounded disappointed.

'Can't you see? Look!' I showed her the picture. Sumers was passing a thick brown envelope to some greasy looking guy. 'He's paying the guy who killed the son of the head of the bloody Mafia. This is his death sentence. The Don must have known that Rees had acquired the surveillance pictures, and obviously wants to find out who is to blame for...'

'The hit on him that killed his son,' Patsy said interrupting me.

'Yeah, and now they think I have the pictures.'

'Well you have ya big gavoon.'

'Yeah, but, shit yeah. Hell, Pats, as soon as they have the pictures Bob Sumers and probably whoever is with him will get wasted for sure. That would mean the end of ISR, and Larry and bloody Laura would disappear, and I would become an illegal.'

'Sure, I could live with that,' she smiled.

All night my mind in spite of the traffic noise was spinning with ideas, and the scenarios that could develop from different actions. I needed to talk to Jimmy if he was still in one piece. Pier's was my best bet.

Pier was pleased to see me and seated us personally. He then produced a bottle of Australian Chardonnay. 'To a make you feel at home, my friend.' I accepted with a smile. I'd given up on that one.

Patsy grinned even though she didn't understand the joke. Despite being short of dollars I ordered Piers seafood special as a celebration for having obtained a silver bullet for Sumers.

I asked Pier to join us and he accepted, and brought two bottles of wine. Before we started drinking I asked about Jimmy. 'Agh, he's at the hospital, he's a broken his foot.'

'Has he been in here then?' I asked.

'No...no he's, you know,' he winked. 'One of my barmaids, he sees one of them. I will find out for you. Now you must eat this splendid food and, err, drink all of this wine.' Patsy didn't need encouraging. For one with such a petite frame she ate like a horse. Cracking open shellfish with her perfect teeth and washing it down with mouthfuls of wine with big gulps, while constantly smiling. Pier was on one; he told us that he hadn't had any time off for months, and that on our arrival he'd decided to have the day off and spend it with us.

Unfortunately we never got to the hospital. We ended up in Pier's city apartment. After the fantastic meal we sampled the wine stocks and ended up wrecked. Patsy was speaking mostly Spanish, in between trying to talk with a Yorkshire accent, while Pier spiced the conversation with Italian. We talked away the day and by the evening I was beginning to feel multi-lingual. We had a scream and I felt I had found a real friend in Pier.

St Vincent's hospital on 7th Avenue was caring for Jimmy, so after a head thumping late sleep in, we headed there on foot. The traffic was heavy and the constant blasting of horns didn't help our fragile heads.

We found Jimmy in a private room.

'Hey guys, where have you been?'

'What happened mate?' I asked.

'The leap of faith, man, I screwed up big time. I hit a trash bin and took all the impact on one leg. It's all pinned together man, it's a mess.'

'Were they waiting outside as we suspected?'

'Yeah, you were right, man, there was a set of wheels in view, its windows were all steamed up. They were waiting just as you said. How the hell did you jump out the same window and not get injured, man?'

'It's a Yorkshire milk thing,' I joked. Patsy added a 'Luv'.

'You gonna be all right, Jimmy?' she asked, showing genuine concern.

'Yeah, sure girl, I'm the man.' He did the American fist and hand thing with her.

'I've got it.' I smiled at Jimmy.

'He's got it?' Jimmy frowned at Patsy causing her to giggle.

'Can I be the first to sign your cast?'

'Yeah, it'll be my pleasure babe.'

'Hey! I said I've found what the mob is after, aren't you interested?'

'Shit man, calm down, what have you got?'

'These.' I laid the pictures on the bed, Jimmy's face changed.

'Holy shit man do ya know what you have here?' I smiled.

'A silver bullet that will destroy Sumers.'

'No, shit man, but what good will that do?' he shrugged, leaving his mouth open.

'Their scam will end, and as soon as Sumers and his goons are out of the way then I can get Laura.'

'Then what, man?'

'I'm not too sure yet. I've got to think this over carefully. It's a one shot affair, shit or bust.'

'Shit or bust?' Patsy repeated with her face screwed up. 'Is that a Yorkshire thing too?'

'Hey you're getting too big for your boots, smart arse.'

'So when do you get out, pal?'

'A couple of days they said. The bones have to set.'

'I thought your phone had been cut off?'

'I need my phone man, you know, work and chicks. It's my lifeline. I paid the back charges with some of the greens you gave me.'

'Lifeline? Jimmy you've got to be more careful. It was nearly your deadline, and ours.'

After I described what had happened to us while he was limping among the bin liners and rubbish, Jimmy promised he would be more vigilant in the future. Ironically, shortly after he made the call to us, the car full of goons obviously left his place to come for us. Jimmy had jumped for no reason after all. That word 'hindsight' rang yet again in my ears.

'We'll come and visit tomorrow. Is there anything you need?' Jimmy made a list, which Patsy took from him.

'We'll see you tomorrow, mate.'

During the time I spent with Pier I had told him what had happened to me. He was especially interested and also quite shocked at Laura's cruelty. As we talked further about our totally differing lives, we began to realise how alike our ideals were. Despite our cultures we were similar.

He had kindly given us the keys to his city apartment and told us to treat it as our own, a generous gesture from someone I hardly knew. It couldn't have come at a more needy time, but it wouldn't be until later that I would realise there was a reason for his offer.

I needed to update my information on ISR, to find out what they were up to on the ground, but I couldn't follow them on foot and a bike was too dodgy. I was discussing the problem with Patsy and she bounced up.

'I can get us some wheels.'
'We haven't got the money, Pats.' She shook her head.
'Kris, you're so naïve. I'm a New Yorker - this is my hood. I may be small, but my brain is the same size as yours, you know, I won't be long.' She disappeared leaving me feeling strangely alone and concerned for her. I spent the next three hours almost in a state of panic.

Pier had a well stocked bar and he had told me in no uncertain terms to help myself, so I had a look. Jack Daniels wasn't an option then I saw the pirate Captain Morgan hiding at the back of the cocktail cabinet.

The next thing I was focusing on was Patsy smiling face.
'I've got us some wheels, Kris. It's a phone company's van. The guy's on holiday for two weeks. We can return it if it would make you feel better.'

I threw my arms around her and stared into her face, she looked a little confused at my response. 'I love you, Patsy.' Her expression froze. 'I said I love you, I love you to bits.'
'To bits, that's kind of cute.' She didn't say any more, but her kiss told me everything.

The small van was perfect. I didn't ask her how or where it was from, that would have been patronising. It even had the company hat and overalls in it, and they fitted me. It was as if a fairy godmother had waved her wand.

Patsy sat beside me wearing a baseball hat. Her hair in a band poked out from the back, she looked dead cool.

As Laura left the drive on foot I drove to the Plaza and parked next to a service cover on the footpath. I lifted the cover and erected a warning frame around it, then sat in the van with the back doors open. Laura appeared as she had in the past and entered the Plaza. I checked my watch and squirmed on the box seat.

'What are you looking for, Kris? I mean what are you actually looking for?' Patsy asked. I froze as a Blue and White cruised past, the cop nodded and waved, I sighed.

'I really don't know. Seeing her sort of reassures me. I need to know where she is. You know, find out what she's up to.'

Patsy got out of the van.

'What are you doing?'

'What you can't.' She walked briskly towards the Plaza and disappeared inside. I sat watching the entrance like a hawk for what felt like ages then Patsy eventually walked casually down the steps, followed by Laura.

'She's striking, Kris. It's hard to believe she could be so wicked.'

'What have you been doing? I was almost off my head.'

'I chatted to the reception staff.' She pulled a New York Times press card from her neck. 'I thought it might come in useful and it did. Sumers is staying at the Plaza, he hardly ever leaves, and when he does he has heavies with him. Apparently Laura visits him almost every day.'

'He's obviously shitting himself after the cocked up assassination attempt. He must know through his police puppets that Rees had the photos away and that the mob was hunting for them.'

It was all falling into place; he and posh la, la Laura were promoting ISR hard and fast to attain retirement finances before the mob took their revenge. It was all becoming a race against time and ironically I had the starting gun.

We drove to Easy Everywhere to check on ISR. I sat at the

terminal while Patsy shopped for our evening meal. ISR was still bragging, and Dr Tony Banks was now updating ISR progress on the Microsoft media player. I clicked the icon and watched my old adversary bullshitting his heart out. He was verbally reporting progress on numerous projects, vessel procurement, dive systems and personnel. To me it all sounded way too rosy. There were no photos or film clips, just Dr Tosser pointing a laser pointer at a load of figures, wreck names and the treasures they carried. To someone who had money and no idea about marine operations it would look a lot more lucrative than committing their cash to alternative low yield investments and with the recent expansive coverage of successful salvage operations being blasted out by satellite TV networks, who could resist?

A message flashed that I had new mail.

> *'Hi Kris how are you? You didn't return my mail did you? But it doesn't matter now. Love Jenny'*
> I was confused until I noticed the e-mail address.
> *djennyd@Easyeverywhere.com.*

'Hi Kris,' I saw her in the screen. Jenny was standing right behind me. I stood up and turned to face her. She smiled and put her arms out to me. There was an uncomfortable pause then I surveyed her face. Suddenly all the good times flooded my mind. I opened my arms and she moulded into me as she had done in the police station almost two years ago. Then over her shoulder I saw Patsy enter the building. A wine bottle exploded in a spray of foam. Other things bounced on the tiled floor as Patsy's small hands released their grip on the brown bags. Her face suddenly filled with dejection and betrayal then she ran out of the building.

I turned and pulled the pillow under the side of my face and then I saw her curly hair, it lay across her face hiding her good looks; I moved it to see more of her. She stretched then snuggled her head into the thick pillow. I watched the sun slowly tiptoe along the frilly linen and when it reached her face she slowly opened her eyes.

'Morning,' she smiled warmly as I pulled her into me and held her tight. Patsy pressed her warm lips on to mine. Yet again my mixed emotions had run amok, I had been dreaming again.

The heater blasted warm air on to our feet. It was getting colder by the day. Laura walked briskly ahead of us with her breath billowing out from her.

'She's not going towards the Plaza today, Kris.'

'I know. This is interesting.' A large removal wagon stopped and a man jumped out from the passenger side and held his hands up to the traffic while the driver attempted to manoeuvre the truck into a narrow alley.

'Shit, we'll lose her for sure.' Patsy slipped out of the van.

'I'll see you back at Pier's apartment,' she winked at me, turned and started running.

I kept moving to the window. She'd been gone for almost three hours, during which time I made a meal. Pier had an excellent kitchen and I took full advantage of it, to keep my mind from wandering into scary thoughts about Patsy cocking up and getting into bother.

The photos on the shiny table drew me each time I passed them. How was I going to get them to the mob after making fools out of them and crushing one of them in a car door? I'd get shot as the messenger for sure; they would have it in for Houdini big time.

The door burst open, making me jump up and grab the gun. Patsy dashed passed me straight to the big cast iron radiator and sat on top of it while stroking it with her hands.

'Brrr…it's freezing out there.'

'Your nose is red.' I rubbed her shoulders. 'And your cheeks are glowing. What have you been doing?'

'I followed her all over,' she shivered. 'She must be fit, she certainly walks fast. She went to the postal building where she picked up a pile of mail, and then she went to the bank, then back to the Plaza and back to East 68th. I ran from there back to here.'

'Well done.'

She grinned and pulled a piece of paper from her bomber jacket, and held it to me. Box No 4148.

'Just a minute.' I opened my file case and sifted through the papers. 'Here it is. I studied the ISR investment form. Look at this.' We read out aloud 4148. 'Well done, Pats, how the hell did you get it?'

'I queued behind her. She showed them her authority and they passed her lots of letters, enough to fill her big shoulder bag right to the top.'

'I bet those letters contain investors' cheques. They must be scooping a fortune. We will have to watch them closely. One day they will clean out their account. We must be around when that happens.'

'But what can we do against Sumers' goons?'

'That's all down to timing, and setting up Sumers just at the right time.' Patsy sniffed the air. 'I bet you're starving?'

She nodded. 'Something smells yummy.'

I was at Easy Everywhere. Patsy was discreetly watching over number forty from the warm comfort of the van. I suddenly felt a strange feeling and turned. I couldn't believe my eyes, stood leaning against the big orange machine with arms folded was Jenny. This time I wasn't dreaming. She looked a little thinner. Her hair looked just the same as I remembered; she was wearing her favourite combination of faded jeans, walking boots and a tight jumper. She looked good. She watched me with an amused smirk, and then she walked towards me swinging a black leather jacket she held in her right hand. She stopped a few feet away.

'Surprised to see me, Kris?' She cocked her head in an inquisitive manner.

'Yeah,' I nodded. 'Yeah I am.' She moved closer and I sort of stepped sideways.

'What's a matter, Kris, don't I even get a welcome cuddle?' The dream, or was it a premonition, had come true and I didn't want to complete it.

'Jenny you shouldn't -'

'Have bothered! Is that what you are trying to say, after all I've done for you, Kris?'

'Come. Let's go and sit down, and have a coffee.' It felt weird walking with her, just being so close to her confused my emotions. The last few years had transformed her from a student kid to a beautiful woman.

'You're looking good.'

'So are you, Kris. You have lost some weight, you're…' she looked me up and down, 'All toned up, eh.'

'Thanks, so are you.' She flashed her eyes at me the way she used too; in fact her body language was screaming out at me she was so confident, she knew she was intimidating me.

'What is her name then, Kris?' She sipped from her cup while uplifting her eyes as I squirmed in the chair.

'Let's cut all this small talk crap, Jenny, I told you not to come here and what was all that stuff you e-mailed me about?'

'You think you can come into my life with such a bang and then slip away as though nothing ever happened between us?'

'Manslaughter and jail is hardly slipping away.'

'You and I are destined to be together, Kris. All the adventure we shared! Nothing in my life has ever come close to all that excitement, not to mention the impression you have left on me, Kris.' I remained silent. 'So what's her name?'

'Jenny, you can't do this. Everything has changed in my life, and right now this confrontation is the last thing I need! I'm on the run for murder for Christ's sake; I'm sorry Jenny, we finished a long time ago. I'm just getting my head sorted and can see light at the end off the tunnel. I want to keep it that way. We did have good times but that's past. As I said before, the past only ever comes once.'

'Still the romantic, eh, Kris?' She looked sad. 'We never did really finish, you know. Come back to my hotel, Kris, come, if only for old times.' She held my hands.

I pulled away and stood up. 'I'm sorry, Jenny, you have grown into a beautiful woman. There are thousands of young men who would give anything to be with a girl as pretty as you.'

'It's you I want, damn it, we melted together, we belong together. We're forever friends.'

I remembered that determined look and the gritted teeth. It used to precede a temper outburst, but instead of losing it she stood up and passed me a card.

'I'm spending a few weeks here. Don't let a brief needy romance divide us, Kris. I didn't. When you get fed up of your American…fling, come around we've got a lot of catching up to do.'

'She's not just a fling Jenny, don't start kicking shit around.' She ignored me and continued with a smile.

'I knew there was another woman. My room number and mobile is on the back.' She walked slowly and deliberately out of the building, without glancing back. I was surprised at her resolve. A few years ago she would have been knocking tables over and shouting blue abuse at anyone who dared to look her way. I only hoped that her temper wasn't being channelled in other ways.

Patsy's bonny smiling face was good to see through the van window.

'Laura went to the mail building, and again to the bank. The limo visited number forty, but the windows are tinted and you can't see inside it.' She gasped for a breath while studying me. 'Kris, are you all right?'

I dropped my head and shook it slowly. 'Kris what is it… What's happened?'

'Lets go home Pats. I'll tell you later.'

Patsy passed me a large glass of rum, pulled her hair behind her ears and sat facing me.

'Jenny is here in New York.'

She turned her head to one side. 'The girl you used to work with and…?'

'Yeah.'

'That's no big deal.' She looked for my response. 'Is it Kris?'

'I didn't tell you everything. I thought there was no point. Jenny and I were in quite a strong relationship and it only sort of fizzled out when I was sent to prison. She got herself a boyfriend the same age as her, and that was that as far as I was concerned.'

'There's a 'but' isn't there?'

'Unfortunately she's a single-minded young woman and that's partly my fault. You know I told you about her e-mail, well I thought that was her last word, a sort of summary of our past.'

'So what now?' She sat back and folded her arms.

'Nothing, Pats, her presence just upset me, she can't let go of the past. I feel as if I've screwed up her life. I always knew this could happen, but I was so lonely back then and I just gave in.'

She moved close to me and placed her hand on mine. 'That's not a crime; we all do dumb things from time to time. There are things in my life that I wanna to forget.'

'Yeah, but Jenny can't forget, she wont let go and it makes me feel uneasy and it's muddling my mind.'

Patsy dropped her chin and turned away and gave a squeak.

'Are you laughing?'

She snorted and sniggered and then turned. 'I'm sorry, that funny Disney word you used made me laugh, 'muddling.' I'm sorry. Anyway thanks for being honest with me, Kris.' She pressed her lips on to mine and then grinned, 'I'm off to bed now, are you coming?'

The days were becoming a routine. Patsy would follow Laura and she was good at it, while I kept an eye on ISR's activities. The moment their web site became dormant would be the time to watch them twenty-four seven, but for now Dr Knobend Banks was still spewing out the bullshit. I suppose as long as the twenty five thousand dollar cheques were coming in they would be reluctant to end the scam, but they would have to, when their first project was exposed as a cruel and expensive hoax.

We finished our meal. Patsy had hired a film for us, she was just about to insert the D.V.D. when the doorbell rang, causing us to look at each other.

'I bet its Pier, it's about the right time for him,' Patsy said as she sprang up and opened the door.

'You must be?' Jenny's voice, which I instantly recognised, hit me like a hammer blow sending waves into my stomach.

'Patsy,' she replied innocently. 'Who are you?'

'I've come to see Kris.'

I moved to the doorway. 'What have you come here for, and how the hell did you know where I was staying?'

'Simple surveillance, the sort of stuff you told me you were doing.'

'You must be Jenny? Kris has told me all about you.' Patsy spoke calmly. 'You'd better step in.'

I was surprised at Patsy inviting her in. Jenny stood looking around the apartment. 'Not bad, not bad at all.' Her eyes fell on Patsy and then on me. 'You've done awfully well for yourself, Kris, all this in such a short time.' I could smell that she had been drinking

'This place is just on loan from a friend, he's helping us out.'

'Us?' Jenny said under her breath and then glanced at Patsy.

'Jenny, I know why you're here, and honestly you're wasting your time.'

'Oh you think so do you? Well I'm afraid Kris and I have unfinished business, which does not include *you*, so why not take a little walk off the balcony, Patsy?'

She emphasised the 'you' loudly through her teeth, which worried me.

'Jenny, just go now…'

Patsy interrupted me before I could speak. 'Kris has finished with you. You're just causing more problems for him and he's got enough right now, we both have.'

'*We both have*,' Jenny mocked rolling her head around. Her mood had swung.

Patsy walked to her and, although smaller than Jenny, grabbed her arm.

'Get your hand off me you thieving…midget,' Patsy pulled her towards the door then Jenny lashed out at her. I intervened. Patsy's chin lifted as she made a fist and drew her arm back.

I escorted Jenny to the door trying to avoid her eyes as she called my name over and over, then her resolve broke and tears streamed down her face as she pleaded for me to leave with her. Patsy opened the door.

'Jenny, please don't do this!' I stood on the stairs consoling her. Patsy stood holding the door open. She was biting her lip. She also had tears breaking down her face.

'Walk her home Kris; don't leave her alone like this.'

'I don't want your fucking sympathy!' She threw my arms off her shoulder and without warning swung her fist into my eye putting me among the stars once again, as blood ran from a new cut over my eye. Patsy rushed towards her and lightning fast landed a sickening combination to her cheek then another to her stomach.

'Stop it, for God's sake, both of you stop.' I pushed them apart. Jenny held on to Patsy's hair, I had to prise her shaking hand free.

Patsy stood with her fists clenched in a boxer's stance. Her eyes were wide and wild. Jenny was holding a lump on her face and weeping.

'Ah, Kris,' Pier shouted while holding up his arms, 'I've called to see how you are getting along.' Fuck me, not now I thought.

I ushered him past Jenny and into the apartment. Patsy lowered her fists and followed us. I went back out shortly after, but Jenny had gone. I felt sick and hopeless.

Pier stayed for a few drinks and I entertained him the best I could, considering the state of mind I was in. He reassured us that we were welcome to stay while we sorted things out then left as cheerily as he arrived. Thankfully, he hadn't noticed the fracas earlier or perhaps he was being discreet.

As I closed the door Patsy embraced me and started crying.

'Oh Kris, you must be hurting inside. I didn't mean to hit her, but she hit you first. Oh why did she come here Kris and spoil everything. Why?'

I felt crap, unsettled and downhearted yet again.

'Why couldn't Jenny accept things the way they are? I accepted her relationship.'

'I love you Kris, you stood by me, and she's a real looker.'

Jimmy hopped through the door dropping his alloy crutches with a clatter.

'Hey guys! The main man is back.' If I didn't know Jimmy and had my eyes closed I'd have sworn he was a brother. Patsy greeted him with a kiss. As I approached to slap his back his smile disappeared. 'Who the fuck did that?' I instinctively raised my hand to my bruised eye.

'Ah, you don't want to know.'

'Yeah, I do man,' he looked closely at my eye. 'Jeez that's a real shiner on top of your old one as well. He looked at Patsy. 'Not you babe?'

'His ex,' Patsy said then looked sheepishly downward.

'What!' Jimmy shouted.

'Ah, ah,' Patsy said while nodding to him impishly.

'Gee man, is your ex a prize fighter or what?'

I joined the conversation. 'Just half Irish.'

Patsy put her hand to her mouth trying to hide her nervous smile I knew what was coming next.

'Go on, have a laugh then.'

She shook her head almost like a shiver then turned her back to me, her shoulders hunched up as she tried restraining herself. Then, Jimmy cracked into loud laughter, which caused Patsy to turn on her infectious giggle.

I shouldn't have been laughing, but Patsy was funny when she did her giggle fit. We couldn't stop laughing. Each time one of them pointed to my shiner it started us off.

There were three of us now Jimmy had returned. He was going to wear the phone company's overalls and watch the bank. Patsy was watching for Laura on 68th while I checked out ISR. I had mail; it was from Jenny. I didn't want to open it, but it nagged at me.

'Dear Kris, I read everything wrong. I'm so sorry for what I did the other night; I don't suppose you will want to remain friends any more. I'm sorry I hit you and for all the horrid things I said. I hope you sort everything out and wish you and Patsy well. She is very pretty. You have chosen well, my pirate friend.
  Love always Jenny'

I needed some fresh air so I left the building and walked for an hour. I couldn't get Jenny out of my mind; she'd showed real guts writing the e-mail.

During that evening Jimmy coaxed me away from Patsy, we were in a small bar and chilling out. After a few beers I started spilling everything out to Jimmy, about Jenny and how bad I felt after the other night.

'Go and make peace with her man. If it's eating you up it will never leave you, and hey, you have to be focused right now man, or you'll end up dead, or locked away on death row. How about if I come with you man, a bit of moral support and all that, eh?'

I slowly shook my head. 'Nah, I'm not deceiving Patsy.'

'You won't be if you tell her, man.'

'Oh yeah, have you seen that girl punch?'

'It was only a suggestion; I didn't say you had to rearrange her spider legs, just part on friendly terms, man. She said she was sorry, man.' Jimmy was right; it was eating away at me.

We took a cab to the hotel and asked at the Reception. Thankfully she hadn't checked out. Jimmy was talking like an agony aunt as we walked along the plush hallway. I tentatively pressed the bell. We waited for about a minute then pressed it again. A noise like something falling onto the floor reached both of us, then fumbling noises and the door opened. The security chain stopped the door opening, and caused it to slam shut. Again it opened and Jenny looked through the gap.

'What… what, who is it?'

'It's Kris.'

'You're not Kris,' she slurred..

'I'm Jimmy, Kris is here.' Jimmy pulled me to the gap. The door opened and Jenny stared at us.

'What...' She was drunk. I instantly noticed a big bruise on the left side of her face.

'Can we come in?'

She stepped back and caught her Mickey Mouse slipper under the carpet, which caused her to fall; I rushed in and helped her upright.

'Come on, Jenny, look at the state you're in.' She didn't reply. Instead she tried pushing me away. I sat her on to the bed.

'I got your e-mail, thanks.'

Jimmy turned on the kettle that was next to the bed while discreetly moving the almost empty bottle of Grants out of sight.

'I just couldn't leave things as they are, Jenny, you still mean a lot to me.'

She let out a 'Huh' then turned to me staring through double-glazed eyes.

Nodding drunkenly she said, 'I...I still wan...wants to be friends still, you know.' I heard Devon in her voice, which made me feel even worse. She blinked repeatedly while staring at me and then raised her hand to my eye, opened her mouth and then she fell back on to the bed.

'Jenny?' I shook her.

'She's out cold man,' he picked up the bottle. 'Fuck man, she's drunk almost a litre of the stuff. You better not leave her like this, man. She could choke on her own vomit like a pop star.'

'Fucking hell, Jimmy, I can't stay, no way!' I paced up and down.

'I could. That's if you don't mind?'

'Why the hell should I mind?' There was a short silence. 'I don't mind.'

'I'll stay then, but I want you to put her to bed before you go. I don't want her to think I'd undressed her or any shit like that, man.' He moved to the door uncomfortably, shaking his hands at the thought of Jenny accusing him. 'I'll leave the room, man, you call me when you're finished with her, I mean got her in the bed, no! When she's in the bed. Shit man.' He left the room.

It was one of the saddest things I'd done for a long time. Her body was beautiful. She'd lost that youthful softness and now she was curvy, lean and firm. It saddened me as the reality that I would never hold her passionately again struck home. Vicky was gone and I had accepted that I could never again enjoy her company. I knew I loved Patsy now, but lying before me at this moment was someone I'd desperately craved for during that long lonely imprisonment. I could easily love them both, but that wasn't an option.

On returning to Piers I told Patsy everything and she seemed pleased for me. She agreed that leaving her alone in that state would have been irresponsible.

'Was it hard for you?'

'Yeah, her face has a big bruise, she looked a real mess.'

'Jimmy will cheer her up, Kris. He'll have her laughing within minutes of her waking up, and you never know?'

'Never know what?'
'Well Jimmy is kind of cute.'
'Oh yeah, that's what you think is it?'
'A bit jealous are you?' She widened her eyes at me.
'No, you're here with me aren't you?'
'I didn't mean me.'

Chapter Fifteen

We hadn't seen or heard from Jimmy for two days. Admittedly he was fast with women. My mind was boggling, but no news is better than bad news.

On arrival at Easy Everywhere I had second thoughts about the 'no news' theory. Normally after the weekend Banks always presented an updated presentation on the media player, but this Monday morning the one displayed the previous week was still showing. This was totally out of character, and looked suspicious. It wholly contradicted the recent ISR disciplined schedule.

I logged off and had a coffee. I thought that maybe they were updating the site a bit late. When I returned and logged on once again and I got the message.

'Web Site not found'

Were things about to happen? I had to meet with Patsy and find out what she had observed. As I walked out of the building the little van tore through the traffic towards me. It screamed to a halt.

'Get in Kris, quickly!' She was breathing heavily. 'Laura and that Larry guy were at the bank for ages. They went into the manager's office for about an hour and came out with two big leather bags. What do you think?'

'It's started. They're on the move, Pats.' Her face looked concentrated, as both our minds tumbled in silence with desperate ideas.

I got her to stop at a hardware store, where I purchased a packet of large tie-wraps, some heavy-duty duct tape, a road map of the States and other bits and pieces. We drove to East 68th and stopped in-between the drives. It would soon be afternoon dog release time. If Laura kept to her routine, we would have one slim window.

I kicked the panel that divided the cab from the back of the van and crawled through it, then back into the cab again.

'What are you doing?' I began telling Patsy my plan. She looked concerned.

'Shit, Kris, so much could go wrong.'

'Look it's our only chance. Once they leave here they will disappear for good and we'll be totally finished.'

'There is... still us, Kris.' I gave her a hard kiss then gestured to the door.

'Don't forget the safety, Pats.'

She fumbled with the gun while stuffing it into the pocket of her brown flying jacket, she then ran to the back of the van and opened both doors then as planned, she disappeared into the bushes.

I placed my crash helmet on, took a few deep breaths, then drove slowly into the drive signed 'Strictly No Entry'. Through the broad leaves I could just see the big shiny black doors. I glanced at my watch. She was late. My heart was pounding while my body shook uncontrollably as if I was freezing cold, but I was sweating. Then I saw the door open and the hounds of hell sprang out. I engaged the gear and drove into full view.

Laura's head rose from its shoulders like a meerkat when she saw the van. I passed her and stopped almost out of sight, just barely visible through the bushes. I got out and ran into her view. She whistled the dogs while pointing to me.

The dogs didn't need encouragement and bounded towards me growling and barking. I dived into the van and pushed down the panel, the van rocked as the first dog bounded into the back. It managed to seize the heel of my boot. Suddenly my leg was being shaken ferociously. I kicked out with my free leg, made full contact with its snotty wet snout, and it released me.

I was in the cab and leaving in a split second, a big head hit the glass as I slammed the door shut then I dashed to the back doors. Number two's arse was mooning at me as it tried joining its mate I slammed the doors shut as the second dog thumped heavily into the glass smearing it with snot and steam.

'What the hell do you think you are doing to my dogs?' Laura shouted while marching aggressively towards me.

'Stop right there.' Patsy stepped out holding the gun in shaking hands. Laura looked her up and down and almost smiled when Patsy repeated in a wobbly voice. 'I said stop right there.'

'What have we here? A dognap? You stupid morons get off my land, and release my dogs right away,' she hissed defiantly. I took the gun from Patsy.

'Walk, you bitch, back to the house and if you open that big mouth of yours I'll blow your fucking brains out.' Her face changed instantly. I pushed the gun hard into her back and she lurched reluctantly forward. 'Faster!' We climbed the steps and past the pillars. Patsy stayed behind me as planned. We walked in line behind Laura. The large reception resonated with echoes from our steps as we entered. The place was warm; it smelled of polish and wealth. I grabbed Laura's hair; she held her hands to her face. I was fraught and anticipating instant attack, but no one was there.

I forced my helmet to her ear. 'Where are they?' I twisted the gun into her neck, as her strong perfume found my nose.

'Who?'

'Don't give me that shit.' I placed her into a firm neck hold so she couldn't shout or run to warn them.

'Laura is that you?'

It was another voice I would never forget. I dragged her further behind the door. Patsy was close by me. My heart was beating into Laura's cheek like a drum.

The footsteps got louder then a long shadow cast from the lights in the room floated across the shiny tiled floor. He was now standing a few feet from us, looking and listening.

Laura squirmed and tried to bite my hand, which I had over her mouth.

Then Larry turned and saw Patsy. He attempted a smile on seeing her, but before he registered me tucked behind her, a large Ming vase exploded in his long face and a loud crash echoed around the big reception room.

He reeled back a few steps and took his hands off his face. Patsy's fist landed squarely on his nose, causing him to stagger back further while holding his arm out in shocked defence. Laura started struggling; I just manage to grab her free hand before it found my crutch.

Patsy bobbed on her toes then jumped while swinging her shoulders. Another sickening slap filled the room. Larry reeled back, half-staggering. She followed her attack with another lightning fast blow to his nose before he could bring his hands up to defend himself. He swayed then dropped to his knees. Another big swinging uppercut exploded from Patsy and he was out cold, slumped on his knees with his arse in the air and his face pressed on the tiles like a worshipping fanatic. I looked at the mighty atom as she stood over Larry. Her chest was heaving and she was panting heavily, she shot me a grin through her wild dark eyes.

I snatched a doily from a recess in the wall, causing a small figurine to smash on the tiled floor. I then rolled it up, and with difficulty forced it into Laura's defiant mouth and then taped it up. I nodded to Patsy and she did the same to Larry. Even though our situation was desperate I almost burst out laughing at Patsy, who because of the blood on Larry's face couldn't make the tape stick. She wrapped it over and over around his head until he looked like an Egyptian mummy.

I forced Laura's protesting arms behind her back and Patsy, without instruction, secured her wrists with two big white tie-wraps. She then secured Larry's arms and ankles the same way.

I forced Laura next to Larry while Patsy joined them at the wrists with another big tie. We had to find Banks now; my adrenalin rush was so high everything felt effortless like I was floating in a dream. I rushed into the main room, but no Banks.

'Kris, Kris,' Patsy whispered while looking through the open door to the utility room. 'The water boiler is working.' She passed the gun to me.

'Have a look around for the bags. I'll sort that bastard out.'

The big sweeping staircase made of Italian marble didn't make a sound as I climbed it. Nearing the top of the stairs I was guided by the sound of running water to a number of suitcases, which were positioned outside one of the ornate doors that lined the lavish hallway.

The noise from the shower got louder, I opened the door holding the gun and cautiously looked inside. The smell of expensive cologne filled the warm room, a pressed suit lay on the bed along with other items of clothing. I noticed a plane ticket next to an open suitcase alongside it and two others stood on a thick Persian carpet.

I scanned the room and noticed the fanlight was steamed up; I had Dr Bullshit where I wanted him. This was the man who had instigated my years of anguish. I was buzzing.

The water stopped flowing and I could hear movement. It became louder then the handle turned.

He flew backwards into the bathroom as I swung the heavy chair into his face; his blood splats decorated the shiny white tiles. The payback felt good. More blood ran from the split on his forehead into the thick rug on which he had landed. Splintered wood from the well-made chair lay all around him like firewood. He never knew what hit him.

I hastily dragged him roughly along the hallway and down the marble stairs causing his limp legs to make fleshy slaps on the steps.

'OK?' Patsy stood swaying.

'Yeah, did you find the bags?'

'Yeah, I got them all.' Patsy said in a loud whisper while looking over Banks' fat naked body. We secured him to Larry with two heavy ties then rushed out under the gaze of Laura's distressed eyes with the heavy bags.

Laura's pupils danced in confusion on my return as I fumbled through Larry's pockets and produced a set of car keys for the red and white Mustang that sat in the drive. They could keep the van! I must have been so wound up earlier I never even noticed it sitting there. We loaded the bags into the trunk. It must have been their planned getaway car; now it was ours. Then the thought of Sumers and his heavies arriving any second put me into panic mode again.

Laura tried to scream, through her nose, and kicked out at me as I cut her tether and got my arms under hers. Her hair was in her eyes and some of it was matted with Larry's blood. Larry moaned deeply as he started coming round, which caused Laura to make a more vigorous effort to resist my every move, so I dragged her along the tiles and down the steps. She was bucking and twisting and both her shoes flipped off as she shrieked rebelliously through her nose.

Patsy had pulled the seat forward so I forced her into the car with help from my boot and then Patsy climbed in the back with her. I pulled the seat forward and slammed the door. It suddenly opened again.

'Let me drive, I know my way around better.' She was right; the last thing we wanted was to get lost. I needed to keep my identity for now and driving with a helmet on was dumb.

We parked the Mustang in Pier's slot in the private underground car park. I took the heavy bags to the apartment via the lift then returned for Patsy and the human bag she was guarding. We manhandled her into the lift and across the hall into Pier's place without anyone seeing us.

Safely in the apartment we secured Laura's ankles and fastened her arm to the frame of Pier's king sized bed. We looked at each other with disbelief as we stood panting heavily with excitement and nerves. It had gone perfectly.

A screwdriver made light work of the flimsy brass lock on the first bag. We attentively peered inside as the zip revealed the contents. 'Mi Dios, Mi Dios,' Patsy shouted in disbelief.

'Jesus Christ, payback, with interest,' I added. The other bag contained equal amounts of cash, lots and lots of it.

'How much do you think, Kris?' Patsy asked, in a shaky voice.

I picked a wad of one thousand-dollar notes. 'More than a million, matey.'

She jumped up and down with her fists in the air like a celebrating football fan. I sank on to the floor with jubilant shock. 'Maybe two or three, could be more.'

Patsy dived on me, knocking me over, then grabbed my hair and pulled me firmly to her lips, but her giggling ruined her attempt. She just held me while panting with excitement. 'What a buzz that was,' she gasped. 'You really know how to show a girl a good time.'

I could only shake my head at her remark, but I felt ecstatic also, we had completed the hardest part and pulled it off in less then ten minutes. 'Hey, where's that one from?' I nodded to an expensive-looking briefcase.

'It was with the others, but it's empty, I think.' She picked up the small briefcase and opened it. 'Nah, there's nothing in it, but it's nicely made and it smells nice.' She dropped it to the floor.

The phone rang making us both jump and share a startled look.

'Who could that be?' Piers old-fashioned style telephone tinkled away. 'Pier, it'll be Pier.' Patsy stretched towards the phone and picked it up. It sounded like a call you hear in a cartoon from where I was sitting.

'Calm down and speak slowly. Kris… it's Jenny, she sounds in a right mess.'

'She, she's not pissed again is she?' Patsy shook her head vigorously.

'No, it's something to do with Jimmy, Kris.' I took the mouthpiece.

'What is it Jenny, what's wrong?' She told me what she'd heard. Although it didn't make sense to her it certainly did to me. They would kill Jimmy for sure. It was time to use my silver bullet.

Pier was at work thankfully and he was genuinely pleased to hear my voice. I struggled to get a word in edgeways as he was trying to get me to join him for a drink. He stopped talking instantly when I asked my question about the photos I had.

'Kris…Kris! No, you don't understand.' I pleaded with him. Then when I told him about Jimmy's dilemma, he told me to wait by the phone.

A few minutes later his voice sounded again. 'Kris, take the photos to the main entrance at Central Park Zoo and wait there.'

I took a yellow cab within minutes of the call. Five minutes afterwards I was standing sniffing ape shit. The inevitable stretch limo pulled up and I was surprised, but more pleased to see Pier step out. He looked anxious.

'Pier.' He looked up at me. 'Christ, are you with this lot?'

'Give me the photos, quickly.' He thrust the palm of his hand towards me moving it impatiently up and down. Then he rushed back to the limo with the envelope in which I had added Sumer's address. I stood nervously shuffling my feet while under the cold gaze of the two players who, only a week or so ago, were giving me a good kicking.

A minute later Pier got out and while the door was open I saw the head of the old Don, his mature hard eyes stared at me and then he half-smiled and he gave a slight nod of his head.

Pier said, 'I must go back now. I am short staffed.'

'What about Jimmy?'

'They will clean things up, Kris, I have their word.'

'You know them?' He smiled at me like a father does to a son. 'It is a family thing my English friend, a family thing.'

'But Rees?' As he climbed into the limo he turned.

'Sumer's men were responsible for that and they will now pay. You let me know when you find your peace my friend; maybe one day we will again drink fine wine together.'

'Thanks…for everything Pier,' He nodded as he pulled the door firmly.

Patsy and I discreetly loaded up the Mustang then tidied the apartment. We sat with hot chocolate drinks cupped in our hands, hovering close to the telephone, hoping desperately for some news about Jimmy. I now realised why Pier had offered us his place. It was the last place the mob would think of searching. He had protected us and enabled us to use our trump card without getting blown away at the same time. I even believed he'd changed my origin to protect me, as every one in his restaurant thought I was an Australian. He was more than just a smiling restaurateur.

At seven p.m. the ornate phone rang again and we pressed the earpiece between our heads. It was Jenny. We gasped with relief as she told us she'd received a call from Jimmy. He'd been dumped outside a hospital in which he was now being cared for. He had suffered concussion, a broken rib and severe bruising about his body, but he was going to be all right. The news was so refreshing, but I still had a couple of things to sort out before we departed this big city. I placed my hand over the phone. 'Patsy?' She nodded.

'Sure thing, Kris,' she said with a blink of compassion.

I took a cab to Jenny's hotel and all the way my mind was buzzing. So much had happened in the last few hours and I was finding it hard to take it all in.

Jenny opened the door with a smile. 'Come on in, Kris.' Even she was talking USA style now I mused, as I fumbled with a large brown bag. She must have been brushing her newly washed hair; it looked beautiful.

'Can you give this money to Jimmy, please?' She nodded without taking her eyes from me. 'There's quite an amount in there and, well...' I was hopelessly waffling.

'Well?' I looked at her awkwardly. 'Right now I've got a long and dangerous delivery to make.'

'You be careful, Kris.' I hung in turmoil thinking of how I could extend the conversation. 'Will you look after Jimmy for me? I'm going to visit him if I get time,' She gave me a half-smile, having sensed my vulnerability.

'He's looked after me exceedingly well, Kris, he's quite a gentleman. He stayed with me until I got sorted out; he even made a meal for me.' She paused and looked up at me. 'I like him; he's really funny and cool.'

'It's a good job you loaned him your mobile, or he would be in a body bag by now. You did real well, Jenny Dean.' She tilted her head and smiled at hearing me say that, but the smile faded as quickly as it appeared.

'When he's better he's going to take me on a fashion shoot, he knows all the magazine editors, he said I would do well modelling over here.'

'That's brilliant. I'm really pleased for you, I'm sure you'll be good for Jimmy.' She cast a half smile. 'You know what I mean.' She stared and slowly her face turned serious.

'Anyway, thanks for everything, Jenny,' I turned and reached for the door handle. A strange feeling of cowardice was rapidly welling up inside me, I opened the door and her voice immobilised me.

'Kris, I thought pirates were more idealistic, and fearlessly seized all opportunities.' I turned around and she approached me.

The kiss lasted almost a minute. Our bodies instinctively pressed together, our hands met and our fingers locked tightly. I began to taste her uniqueness again as her soft hair caressed my face. I was spinning and loosing my restraint too easily, I reluctantly pulled away, quenching our volatile desires. The hunger on Jenny's face burnt deep into my mind as she struggled to smile.

'I believed true pirates felt no remorse, Kris.'

'Maybe…I'm not a true pirate any more Jenny.' She lowered her head, which instantly filled me with a feeling of betrayal. I turned and walked down the hallway, she called out. 'Bye, Kris.' I just couldn't look back.

For the duration of the taxi ride back to Pier's apartment I willed a vision of Patsy into my mind. There was no going back.

Patsy handed me a brandy. 'Sit down, Kris.' I swirled the drink around the big balloon glass then took a sip.

'Everything went well?' she asked in a whisper full of anticipation.

'Yeah, Jimmy's a bit bust up apparently, but he'll be fine with Jenny caring for him.'

'That's not what I really asked, Kris. Did you say your farewells?'

'I gave her a last kiss, no hands though.' My joke fell flat as her eyes searched mine; I felt she was unselfishly sharing my feelings. 'Yeah, well.' I took another gulp of brandy, which sank warm inside me. 'How's Laura been?'

'Asleep most of the time. She's such a wicked person Kris, she tried to kick me and knocked me over when I offered her some water.' She stared away vacantly in thought.

'Pats, what is it?'

She replied, while staring into her glass, 'Sumers, his two goons and Banks, they're all dead, Kris, gunned down. It's been on the TV headlines; they described it as a gang war.' She looked up at me. 'But there was no mention of Larry! Kris, he must have escaped them. Let's get out of here now, with this amount of money on the streets he could buy anyone to help him find us. He could even hire bent cops.'

'The bastard will have to get his nose fixed first, Pats. Where the hell did you learn to fight like that? He's about six two, nearly two feet taller than you are and twice as heavy. How in hell, you were awesome.' I smiled at her, but she sat staring into nowhere.

'When in hell, Kris, you have to learn to fight…to stay alive,' she pressed her finger to her lips and looked up at me,' but that's in the past now, come on let's safeguard the future.'

'I've got to see Jimmy before we leave, it's the least I can do after all the help and support he's given us and then we get out of here.'

Jimmy was picking at his breakfast while trying to chew, with obvious difficulty.

'Hi man.' He gave me a high five. 'Thought you'd be long gone, man. Jenny said you called and told her you were leaving with your special goods.' He winked his bruised eye. 'Oh, and thanks for…you know.'

'She's been in touch then?'

'She's one lush red-haired chick, don't you think, and she talks real cute?' I felt a pang of jealousy.

'Yeah, she's a good mate, so what happened then?'

He pushed his plate away. 'Hell man, I thought I was one dead mother. I had left Jenny safe and sober and was struggling along Fifth Avenue on my crutches, hoping to find Patsy for an update and a lift back to the apartment. I stopped at a safe distance opposite number forty and carefully looked around. She must be at the other end of the row of trees I thought; changing viewpoints is a normal procedure for a field operator.' He looked at me. I couldn't hide my grin listening to his waffle. He continued. 'As I passed the house I saw the van parked right in the middle of the goddamn drive, man. Shit man, I thought, what's it doing there? So I moved closer like you do, man, and as I entered the driveway I noticed the van was rocking and then I saw movement inside.'

I shook my head; he was talking like an MI5 agent. Noticing my amused stare he paused.

'What?'

'Nothing, carry on.'

'I moved deeper into the driveway, man, and put my face near the steamed up window and called her name. Suddenly a big mother of a dog exploded against the window with its teeth snapping out barks. Shit man! I almost released into my Kelvin's! Then I fell back into the bushes. As I struggled to get to my feet car headlights appeared.' He took a sip of coffee.

'The next thing I know, man, is that two big guys are dragging me towards those black doors, man. Shit, I thought, the van was a trap, man, and we'd all been caught.

Inside the mansion that old silver haired guy Sumers was throwing a fit, man, he was one angry dude, he was kicking two guys who were tied together on the floor and sitting in a pool of blood. One of them was stark naked, man! Then he left them and went into another room. He came back even more pissed and was knocking chairs over and smashing pots and stuff.' He shook his head. 'The heavies untied the two bleeding guys, then the tall ugly one, I think he was that Larry dude, stood up and nursed his bleeding nose, while the other the naked guy remained on the floor. I could see several big gashes on his forehead. Then the old guy...' he paused in thought.

'That would have been Sumers,' I interrupted.

'Yeah right, well, he started screaming about some bags or cases, then that Larry guy told him that they had been robbed. He, Sumers that is, went ballistic, shouting out things like 'who would dare come into my house' and shit like that. He was well pissed. Then Larry told him all he could remember is seeing is a girl's face, then blackness, which caused Sumers to rant on and on at him, then he asked Larry where Laura was. Larry just shrugged.

Then he turned his attention to the naked guy who was shitting himself big time.

He said that he was leaving the shower room and that was all he could remember. Sumers then shot his angry face back at Larry, asking him more questions about the girl; he started accusing him and Laura of setting everything up until Larry told him he thought it was a Latino chick. That's when my heart sank. He continued screaming at them, things like 'You think...' and other stuff, like accusing them both, you know all that sort of shit.'

He gasped a few breaths. 'They were shitting themselves big time then he turned on me. I just told the dude that I heard dogs barking and thought someone might be in trouble.

'You expect me to buy that crap? he spat at me. He wasn't having any of it, and set his goons on me.

That's when Jenny rang, I felt the phone buzzing in my pocket and managed to press one of the keys though my Levi's, then I started repeating my story about the van and dogs. The boots started even worse than before. Even Sumers joined in. Shit man I've never been beaten up so many times since meeting you.   I must have passed out. The next thing I remembered was being here on a stretcher.'

'Thank God you're safe, I'm sorry for all this. Did you see Larry in-between your kicking?'

'I saw him at the beginning, but... no, he wasn't in the room later on 'cause I got a three sixty as they kicked me around.'

'He must have got away.'

'Shit man, if he's on the loose you'll have to watch your back.'

'Yeah I know. Anyway Jimmy, I've left you some compensation for all this. Buy a photo studio with it. Jenny told me you were going to try and get her into modelling.'

'She's got the looks and the bod. Hey, you don't mind do ya, man?'

'Not at all, mate, you deserve the best. Just watch out if she grits her teeth.'

'What?'

'You'll find out.'

We shook hands and nodded respect.

'Well I've got to go. Patsy is alone with you know who. Take care, pal, we'll meet up again hopefully, after I've sorted everything out.'

Patsy had searched Laura earlier and found she had nothing on her. She was wearing thin black slacks that had no pockets and a silky red top. Her shiny hair was still in a bob and perfectly styled, although the right side remained matted with Larry's dried blood.

I knelt close to her and slowly removed the black crash helmet and placed it on the floor. I had done this in my mind thousands of times, I turned and faced her.

'Remember me, Mrs Stevens?' Her eyes widened and her face suddenly drained of colour.

'No, no!' she stifled through her nose while sucking the tape in and out as she began to kick and contort to break free. 'No!' a frustrated cry again bled from her nose and filled the room, her face screwed up in shock while her eyes flashed desperately around like a trapped animal. Patsy turned with a disdainful stare, slowly shaking her head she walked out of the room.

'I've dreamt of doing that for so long, but it didn't feel anything like I thought it would. I shouldn't, but I feel sorry for her.'

'Don't, your reaction is a normal human one.' She cast a glance at the door. 'That thing in there is far from human Kris.' She shuddered noticeably. 'Don't ever forget she will try to kill us without hesitation, given the slightest opportunity.'

Chapter Sixteen

Our journey south started on Broadway with Patsy driving the forty miles to join Interstate Ninety-five. We had Laura trussed up in the trunk like a turkey, as the first one hundred and fifty miles were mostly toll roads.

We came to the first toll as we merged on to interstate ninety-five. I passed Patsy the money and like a good little wife she paid the toll. Laura sensing our halt started banging and making as much noise as she could possibly make, but the woman just smiled and wished us a pleasant journey.

Fifty miles further south we came off Interstate Ninety-five and joined Highway Thirteen. Laura had tried her hardest to attract attention at every toll, but Patsy's flashing smile and hiked up skirt distracted all the male toll collectors.

With a further sixty miles behind us we took the US-13 S ramp towards Norfolk, Virginia.

'I've never been this far from the Apple before, where are we going?'

I had no answer ready.

'Kris?' She stared, waiting for me to answer.

'South for now and as far away as we can before daybreak.'

'Then what? She'll need the john, Kris. I do.'

'We can't stop at a diner then drag her screaming to the bog.'

'Bog, huh?

We left the highway and drove for ten minutes along the edge of a pine forest then a cleared area came up on our right. Patsy pulled into the deserted picnic park where the tables and chairs made from pine logs rose out from the ground in the dim misty light like headstones in a graveyard.

The toilet block was dark and shut down. The only thing alive was a telephone kiosk. Its light shone dimly as if a weakening battery powered it.

I got out of the car and listened. Only the distant roar of the nearest highway broke the silence.

We stretched then I unlocked the trunk and the courtesy light illuminated Laura's head protruding from several twisted blankets. Her eyes squinted in the light then on seeing me returned to spiteful slits.

'I'm going to take the tape off. If you start screaming you won't even get a piss.' I quickly ripped off the tape and her mouth emptily chewed the air. I untied her from the frame and lifted her out; my arm became wet as I realised she was soaked in her own piss.

'Bollocks,' I gasped. Patsy looked at me. 'Have you got a tracksuit that might fit her? She's soaking wet.' She nodded and went to look.

Laura eyed me in the little moonlight that shone down. She was quiet and strangely composed.

'For pity's sake untie me.' She looked down staring emptily at the pinecones that covered mulch. I untied her ankles and she lifted her knees up and down as if marking time, then she bent over and clasped her ankles like a ballet dancer stretching, she must have done ballet at sometime, she was so supple. She sighed as she straightened herself then held her wrists out to me and shuddered in the cold air.

'I stink of piss, untie me.'

Patsy returned and stood holding a white tracksuit, a pair of pants and some thick black socks.

Laura looked at Patsy then huffed repugnance through her nose.

She pushed out her wrists to me once again. 'What do you think I'm going to do, damn you, climb up a fucking tree? Untie me so I can change with dignity, you bastard.'

I untied her and she rubbed her wrists while casting blame at me for making them sore. Strangely, her calling me a bastard upset me.

'Round here.' Patsy said coldly and placed the dry clothes on the roof of the car. She stood with her hands on her hips facing Laura. Laura was taller and looked down at her, hissing contempt through her every breath.

I stood at the other side of the car while she changed. When she was finished she stood defiant.

'Have you food?'

Patsy rummaged among bags and wrappers and pulled out a pack of sandwiches and a small bottle of water. Laura leaned against the car and fumbled with the wrapper then dropped it into the foot well. Before Patsy could intervene Laura had recovered it. She tore the triangular plastic container open and ate the sandwich hungrily. Swallowing the last piece she then took a swig of water from the plastic bottle dropping it with a defiant smile.

'I need a dump,' she said solemnly.

Patsy huffed at me, pulled some tissues from the glove compartment then led her into the woods. I followed close keeping out of sight. As soon as they returned I got rid of the putrid blankets and Laura's smelly clothes. I placed one of the two sleeping bags into the trunk.

Laura stood fast in her half-mast tracksuit bottoms as Patsy tried to push her closer to the trunk. She resisted and Patsy faced her and held up her fist.

'Move or I'll bust yer nose big time, bitch.' Laura smirked uneasily as Patsy's face hardened with anger and then she reluctantly obliged her

I was amazed to see so many familiar place names, there was even a place called Falmouth signed up ahead of us. We eventually arrived at Norfolk after seven hours and with three hundred and seventy-five miles behind us. Now we had to find somewhere safe to stay. It had to be a place where we could keep Laura hidden.

As we drove around town the streets were coming to life and the traffic was gradually getting heavier, so we headed east, towards the coast.

We arrived at place called Willoughby Beach, a spit of land where Highway Sixty-four crosses Chesapeake Bay via a bridge and a tunnel.

We passed under the two massive stilted slabs of highway and drove north along the edge of Willoughby Bay. Across the bay we could see what looked like a golf course, which ran to the edge of the sea. It looked so out of place among all the industry. Then I homed on to the marina. It was tucked in a sheltered corner and had six long finger pontoons, at least two hundred boats of all shaped and sizes were moored to them.

My mind was working overtime as we got closer; the place

opened out before us. I suddenly felt the presence of the sea and instantly felt a strange comfort seep inside me. It felt like when I was a kid and running down the beach towards the waves to escape everything behind me.

We arrived at the entrance and received a friendly wave as we drove through and past a barrier, we continued to a large brown dirt-parking plot.

I climbed out and leaned against the bonnet. Patsy stood by my side pulling her hair from her unwashed tired face, while squinting, with her head to one side into the bright morning sun.

'I've an idea Patsy.' She remained silent, while blinking. 'It could solve all our problems.'

'Kris, we wouldn't have any if we ditched...' she nodded her head towards the trunk, 'That evil bitch tied up in there, let's just get the money out and push the car into the sea.' I looked at her she nodded. 'I'd do it right now. With all this money we can go anywhere and buy anything we want!'

'I'm still the prime suspect for a murder that she committed. Without her I'm forever guilty. Patsy, if I can get her back home I can clear my name and live my life out with you.' Her face melted into the Patsy I first met.

'With me?'

'Yes you, but we would have to change your surname to Woods.' She thought for a while, then her mouth widened and her hands moved to her cheeks. 'Oh Kris,' she kissed me eagerly and pulled me into her. 'Patsy Woods sounds really cool, don't you think, like a pop star or an actor's name?'

Banging and muffled noises escaped from the trunk spoiling our little moment of smiles. Patsy was deep in thought; she turned with a worried look.

'Kris, how could we get through immigration though? A wanted man, dragging along a bound hostage carrying all that money and a gun,' she shrugged.

'A boat.'

'A what?'

'A boat, we buy a boat and sail to England with her.'

'Jeez, Kris, I'm no sailor, I've only been on the river ferry.' She paused as a smile grew, 'But you are, aren't you?'

'It's a hell of a long way, Pats, and the first leg would be against the trade winds this time of the year.' I thought hard. 'That's going from Florida. Let's get some charts.'

The banging was getting more frequent and louder. We had to find somewhere and fast. Laura was compromising everything.

'You stay in the car, Pats, try and appease her.'

'What?'

'Shut the bitch up! I'll take a look around and get some charts.'

I had a wad in my pocket and felt excited about my new idea. I walked briskly towards the mix of old wooden buildings that lined the water's edge, glancing at the boats as I approached the chandler's shop.

The shop smelt of fusty rope. A big fat man with sweat stained armpits wearing a blue sailor's cap smiled. 'What can I get yeh?'

'Charts. Do you have any?' He looked up to the wooden ceiling that had all things nautical hanging from it.

'Up in the loft, help yourself.'

I made my way up the creaky steps and into a low roofed room that had a big pine chart table in the centre. Around the table, butted up against the remaining walls were cubby-holes filled with rolled up charts. I noticed one wall had a sign made from a car number plate material. It read 'Passages.'

I got all the charts we needed, covering Chesapeake Bay to Bermuda. Then Bermuda to the Azores then the Azores to the south-west approaches of England and that one had the Channel Islands on it. I also got dividers and a parallel rule.

'You're planning a voyage?'

'Yeah.' I grinned at my next question before I asked it. 'I need a boat first.'

'Are you Australian?'

'Yeah matey, we do things the wrong way around down under. We fancy a holiday in Bermuda.'

'This time of year you need a good sized engine to push the winds, but things get better out there, that's if you get there. You've not heard of the devil's triangle?'

'Yeah, we've got one of them off Sydney.' The big man screwed

his face up.
I paid him and asked him if there were any boats for sale in the marina.

'You want Joe, two stores down; he runs a brokerage and has all the vessels within fifty miles of here on his computer.'

'Is he a native Indian?' His face contorted in confusion.

'You know, Joe Two-stores?' He stared blankly at me. 'Cheers pal.' I grinned and left him in thought.

'Jeez! Foreigners!' I heard him sigh, as I reached for the door handle.

I walked to the broker's only to find a note on the door.

'I'm on the Blue Marlin'.

Shit, that's a lot of help, which bloody boat is that? I scratched my head and looked across the marina. There were so many boats, and the gate had a keypad on it.

After five minutes a man walked up. I pretended to struggle with the stuff I was carrying.

'Hey let me.'

'Thanks.' He keyed C458 and we walked down the ramp. I hurried along the fingers looking hopefully for vessels with 'for sale' signs, but the only one I found was a wooden tub that was hardly safe enough for a kid's playground.

I walked back to the gate then I saw it, the *'Blue Marlin'*. It was a Fisher forty-six, a beamy sturdy motor-sailer made from fibreglass that could motor efficiently and economically, as they were usually fitted with a big diesel engine. The sails in the right conditions were an added bonus and could push the vessel along at a good seven knots. I knew that inside they were big and spacey and well fitted out, ideal for offshore passages. This was the type of boat we needed.

I approached the rounded man who reminded me of the cop character Frank Cannon. He was wearing the obligatory sailors cap.

'Are you Joe?'

'Aye, aye. Joe Smith brokers at your service,' he replied in a seamanlike way.

'I'm after a boat,' He studied my unshaven face.

'What type of boat?'

'This one would do.' My answer made him bounce into laughter. I stood and grinned with him.

'She's not for sale, son.'

'How much would you want for her if you decided to sell her, if you don't mind me asking?'

'Four hundred thousand dollars, maybe a bit more?' he continued, jokingly.

'I'll give you four hundred and twenty thousand in cash. No receipt, no tax to pay,' His face turned serious.

'Are you shitting me son?'

'Not at all, my name is Kris.' I offered my hand.

'Come aboard Kris,' He stumbled out of my way as I climbed onboard.

'Right, err,' he paused. 'This ain't a wind up, is it?'

'No, definitely not.'

Rubbing his chin he looked around nervously. This guy was no crook; but I sensed that the thought of all that cash was throwing him into a greedy turmoil. Then his manner became more focused.

'Well business is business,' he pondered. 'You are serious?'

'Yeah, I need a boat fast. My sister is terminally ill and has always wanted to sail around the Bermudas. She was left injured after an automobile crash in which her husband got killed. She got lots of compensation from the accident. It wasn't their fault; it was a drunken traffic cop on duty. He hit the passenger seat full on; her husband the poor sod didn't stand a chance. His share of a construction company in Boston fell to her then she became ill. My task right now is to get her a boat before.' I sniffed emotionally. 'I've just got the charts.' I showed him them. 'See?'

I could hear the wheels turning in his head; he was a broker and in the trade. He'd probably acquired the *Blue Marlin* for a song. He showed me around the cabins, three in all. The large galley was well found, with all the mod cons, and the wheelhouse had the latest state of the art electronics. She, as I thought, could sail at almost eight knots given the right conditions, and the six cylinder diesel engine could push her along at almost twelve knots, while using less than a gallon and a half of diesel an hour: even less at seven knots.

We got back on to the pontoon, where he explained the sail layout to me and the shiny well polished Oxford blue hull. There was a pause.

'Cash, you said?'

'Yeah, all of it.' He looked furtively around.

'No record of the sale?'

'Only between you and me. I would need a receipt to prove ownership, but you could have lost her in a poker game, couldn't you? I would confirm that, if any one ever wanted me to. Look, if you are serious I'll go to the bank and be back in an hour with the cash. Or I will have to go elsewhere, because Laura is getting weaker by the day.' I sniffed several times, rubbed my eyes and turned away.

'No, no son, that sounds fine, yes fine. Are you all right?'

I asked him for some tissue and he obliged.

'Four hundred and twenty thousand, are you happy with that amount in cash?'

'I'll go to the bank right now, do we have a deal?' He fumbled with his cap and then we shook on the deal.

'I'll sort out her papers,' he said as he forced his hair inside his hat.

I left the charts on the boat and ran as fast as I could back to Patsy.

At the car park I spun around searching, the car. It was gone. I scanned the area meticulously; I could see no sign of it. I began to think horrible thoughts, had Laura overpowered Patsy?

I sat on a bollard near the entrance to the marina for another half an hour in which time I began to feel depressed. Lost in thought I didn't see the Mustang come back through the gate. She parked it where I had left her, it was behind a large shed and it obscured my view.

I waited for another twenty minutes then started walking to the gate. A pip of a horn made me turn. The mustang's lights flashed and I ran towards her. She got out of the car and ran to meet me. She hugged me really tight as I picked her up off the ground.

'Patsy I thought you...' the relief on my face must have been apparent. She was shaking like a leaf. 'What's wrong, Pats?'

'I'm sorry, Kris, a cop car entered the parking lot and drove slowly around. They started looking at me so I had to leave. I slowly drove to the exit, but as I approached the underpass I checked the rear view mirror and they were following me. I took the same route we came in on, but every turn I made the patrol car followed. I was shaking so much, I thought they were going to pull me over. Then the blue and red lights came on and the siren. I nearly died Kris. I frantically pulled over and to a halt, fully intending to speed off as soon as the cops reached me on foot, but it passed me by, it must have gone on a call.'

We had tears in our eyes. 'Oh God, I love you so much, Kris.' She screwed her face up, smiling whilst crying. 'I thought everything was lost.'

'I love you more.' She mixed a giggle with a huff, wiped her cheeks and smiled hopelessly. We were both so close to the edge emotionally it was hard not to spontaneously burst into tears over the slightest thing.

We moved the car to a less exposed area and fed Laura a burger and a diet coke. We had chicken royales, which Patsy had picked up on her journey. Laura seemed subdued, but I noted she was staring all around. I assumed she was trying to find out where she was. We packed her away again, strangely with minimal objections, which concerned me.

I plonked the leather business case on to the counter. Joe locked his office door and drew the shutters.

'It's all there,' I commented as I reached for a paper cup. He lined the wads up on the worn desk with methodical thumps, each one contained fifty thousand-dollar bills and there were eight lined up, plus the twenty thousand. Joe frantically checked them by flipping through them like packs of cards.

Sipping the cool water I estimated the boat was about fifty 'K' overpriced, but what the hell, it was our ticket to freedom and if all went well I would probably get a handsome amount for her in the UK.

'Everything seems in order Kris. Here are the papers and the keys. You are sure you understand everything on board?'

'Yeah, the Gardner engine presents no mystery. I had a boat with one in once and the electronics I understand. The sailing part will be a learning curve, but as you showed me, it can all be done from within the wheelhouse.'

'Good luck, Kris, I hope your sister enjoys the trip.' We shook hands.

'Thanks Joe, I'm sure she will.'

I spent the rest of the day acquiring as many five-gallon drums I could lay my hands on and filled them with diesel. I stored them in every possible space below and along the deck all lashed together. I also acquired extra stores from the shops. Things we would need: fuel pump spares, engine oil, spares and filters, pump impellers, plastic sheets, all sorts of stuff. The local shops must have thought Christmas had come early. Patsy was busy making a list of the food stores we would need.

It was time to move Laura from the car to the boat. It was now dark and the place was mostly deserted, apart from the odd boat owners making their final checks before leaving their floating babies.

We had two big leather bags, one crammed full of money, so much that it was hard to pick up. The other was just over half full after Jimmy's wedge and Joe Two-store's hefty lump had been removed.

I had the half-full bag in my left hand while Patsy unlocked the trunk. Laura swayed unsteadily as Patsy untied the length of rope that held her ankles to the frame. She had chewed part of the tape off her face and looked like she had grown a moustache.

Patsy suddenly gave a shocked whimper. 'How did you get a hold of that?' Patsy stared at her mobile phone lying in the trunk. She grabbed Laura by her arm, but Laura started laughing in Patsy's face.

'Put your hands in the air!' I instantly recognised the deep voice. 'Nobody move a muscle or I'll waste you right here and now.' Larry appeared from the shadows of a building with his hors'y teeth gritted tightly. 'So it was you all along, eh! You decided to come and get us?' He swung a left uppercut into my face; his big fist split my lip as it hit me. 'You're a bigger sucker than I thought.'

'He's carrying,' Laura shouted. Larry's hand shot roughly into my jacket as I held my cut face in my hands and he pulled out my pistol.

'A bit too ambitious, Kris,' he quipped. 'Been scuba diving lately?' He enjoyed saying that one, his long face beamed with payback. I was so pissed off at not drawing my gun the instant I heard his voice.

'Untie me you bitch,' Laura shouted at Patsy.

'Jerk yourself,' Patsy hissed.

Larry held his gun, looking between Patsy and me.

'Oh yes, I'm looking forward to a bit of fun with you, my dear.'

Laura laughed. 'I'll really enjoy watching,' she smirked. He moved towards Patsy taking his eyes off me for a second. I saw my chance and swung the bag with all my strength into Larry's shoulder. He staggered towards Patsy, grabbing for her, trying not to fall. Patsy shot her fists out like a cat attacking a dog. As Larry fell to the ground she dodged nimbly behind the car.

Larry sprung to his feet incredibly swift for such a big man, he pointed the gun at me again and a sadistic grin reappeared on his long ugly face.

'Shoot him. Shoot the sneaky limey bastard,' Laura urged frantically.

I noticed something moving on the ground in the corner of my vision. Patsy was under the Mustang's front bumper. She had found the fallen gun and was crawling stealthy toward them.

'Sneaky! That's a laugh coming from you, you deceitful lying super cow.' I played for time.

A loud crack at my feet caused Larry to spin sideways, but he got a shot off before he dropped his gun. Patsy's shot had torn through his jacket, but failed to hit flesh.

He looked surprised at Laura, then at me. I was on my knees, collapsed over the bag; he rushed to the open door and grabbed the full bag. Patsy would only be able to see their feet now as the open door was obscuring her view. Laura was still kneeling on the ground, struggling with her bound hands to pick up Larry's gun. Patsy's voice screamed out.

'Don't move, don't move… or I'll shoot all of you…both of you!' She moved in front of me, legs wide apart jabbing the gun aggressively at them.

'The gun Larry, it's here.' Laura pushed the gun to his feet. He paused staring down at her for a few seconds then at the gun. It was like a western stand-off. He looked at Patsy's shaking hands.

'She can't do it Larry, she can't... come on man, pick it up!'

'Just try me, bitch.' Patsy answered calmly. Larry's eyes fell from Patsy onto the heavy bag he clutched to his chest then in a flash he dodged behind the car and vanished into the night.

'Larry, Larry' Laura screamed. 'Come back,' she cried loudly then slowly dropped her head to her knees. 'You bastard, you lousy rotten bastard!' Her perfect nails dug into the dirt as tears dropped like sweat from her bowed head.

Patsy rushed and grabbed the gun that Laura was now trying to reach. She stopped and looked up at her.

'So you were gonna watch were you?' She ferociously kicked Laura in the head leaving her limp on the ground.

'Kris. Kris.' I looked up at her as her energised puffs of breath hit my face. The pain erupted in my shoulder the instance I moved.

'The bastard shot me, Pats.'

I awoke in a strange place and felt a sort of rocking movement. I was on a boat. Her face came into view. She pressed her soft lips tenderly on mine.

'You've come back to me,' her face melted into a beautiful smile.

'Where are we?'

'We're on a mooring buoy in that Cheseka-something Bay. We've been here almost two days.'

'How did you? Where's Laura?' I asked, desperately trying to sit up then the multiple wasp stings returned in my shoulder and my head began thumping. 'Shit, did she get away?'

'She's locked in a cabin Kris. Everything is fine. I secured her then I helped you on to the boat along with the bag, don't you remember?'

'Hell, not really.'

'I returned and locked Laura in the trunk again. I had to get the bullet out of your shoulder. I'm sorry if it hurts. I could only find these!' She held up a pair of pliers. 'I got you steaming drunk. That was the easy bit, but you kept struggling with me and messing around so I… well that's why you've got that bump on your head. I gave you lots of antibiotics and painkillers first though and with all the booze you fell peacefully to sleep.'

I held my gaze on her, which made her look down and put on her impish, guilty look. 'What?' she paused looking away, trying to hide her amused face. 'OK, I'm sorry I sort of knocked you out, you were almost there anyway after the cocktail of booze and painkillers. I had to, you were drunk and misbehaving.'

I couldn't help grinning at her. 'Thank God you're on my side. So how did you get the boat out here then?'

'You told me what you had told Joe. So I explained to him that your sister Laura was under sedation and that it had become too much for you and you had got drunk. I told him we were meeting a skipper and pointed to the yellow round things called moorings on that map you got. I told him we had to get there and he brought us there. His friend followed in his boat, and Joe went back with him. Quite simple really.'

'Simple for someone as streetwise as you, Patsy. You're amazing.'

She shook her head. 'No, I should have shot him, Kris and I missed, I was going to shut that needy bitch up with a bullet as well, but I hesitated and missed the chance. None of this would have happened if I'd seen her take my phone, I ain't that cute.'

'You are, they're real pros don't forget, but at least we got away with her and you aren't facing a murder charge.'

Laura had her own little cabin, which had a telly-video, toilet and a shower. All we had to do was maintain her diet. It was a relief to have her safely locked up. Her constant demands over the next two days became less frequent as the hopelessness of her position hit home.

We managed to unpack the tender and rig the outboard for a run ashore to get the food stores we hadn't had chance to obtain earlier. The remaining moneybag, sadly, contained only about four hundred and fifty thousand dollars. Larry must have netted at least a couple of million dollars or more from the full one, which pissed us off big time. That money was our future.

Even if I succeeded in bringing Laura to justice, I realised now there would be no way of recovering what they took from me. It seemed that Larry had the last laugh after all. At least Sumers and Banks didn't live to enjoy whatever they had made from the ISR scam and from me.

Five hundred and eighty-five nautical miles, the global positioning system indicated, was the distance of our first leg to the Bermudas. That was about seven hundred land miles, but that was as the crow flies.

We cast off from the mooring buoy at 09:00 on a bright sunny morning. It was a Saturday, not that it mattered what day it was. To us it was day one. Our bearing was slightly south of east. I wanted hands-on with the boat for the first few days, to get used to the feel of her then the autopilot would take over, with one of us always on lookout for other vessels or floating obstructions, such as containers lost from ships, or floating ropes. Travelling at night was a risk, but one that had to be taken.

The wind was on our starboard beam and as soon as we left the protection of Cape Hattaras we met with a big ground swell. All of a sudden the boat felt really small as it rose up the wall of water only to drop down into a deep trough, leaving our stomachs in our mouths, before the next swell picked us up like a matchstick, repeating the feeling all over again. Patsy kept looking at me each time we fell off a swell; her eyes were showing concern that was apparent by her uncharacteristic half-smile.

'What's wrong?' She moved her eyes to the approaching swell.

'Them,' she said softly. 'They're huge. I'm real scared Kris. It's so wide open.'

I smiled and held her hand. 'Don't worry; it'll get better as we get into deeper water.'

'Deeper,' she repeated while bracing herself with both hands, as the boat lurched steeply. 'Ain't we deep enough?'

I unlocked Laura's door, expecting it to be dragged open as soon as the key turned, but nothing happened. We had placed her in the larger bow cabin, as we had the freedom to move around.

I looked into the well-fitted cabin and was surprised to find it intact. Laura was sitting wearing the tracksuit with her hair wrapped in a towel. She must have just showered.

'Are you all right?' Her head slowly turned like the scene from the Exorcist, exposing her intimidating eyes. She had wrecked my life, and although I was in control of her, she still had something about her that was menacing. Her eyes were more like an alligator's than human. I felt I was being stalked even though I was only standing at the door, her head turned away.

'Your plan is pathetic, stupid and suicidal.'

'My plan is...' The boat lurched and I fell in the alleyway, she dashed up and firmly slammed the door shut as I struggled to my feet.

Patsy was sat in the comfy pilot seat, which she had adjusted to its minimum resistance, so she could spring up and down excessively on its suspension each time a wave tossed us up and down. She smiled on seeing me. 'How is it?'

'Never mind her, how are you feeling?'

'This is great. It's not that fast but when we drop off a big one I get the rush, and this seat's a real gas.'

'Hell you really are an adrenalin freak.' She giggled. I stepped across to take the wheel, but she stubbornly held on to it.

'I'm having so much fun steering this thing Kris. Make us a coffee, luv.'

I poured two cups of water into the kettle; until we reached land water was now precious. I reluctantly added a third cup.

I was surprised at the traffic, there seemed to be lots of sails heading in the opposite direction to us and the commercial shipping was much heavier than I had anticipated. We had to keep a sharp lookout as the big freighters that looked like blocks of flats were crossing our path at more than twenty knots. I decided to use the engine during the hours of darkness so we could use all the facilities for our comfort while keeping the batteries charged.

Blue Marlin, I was finding to my relief, was well fitted out. Joe had told me her brief history. She had been commissioned by an ex US navy engineer while he was posted in England, hence all the equipment was familiar to me, especially the big six l.x.b Gardner that churned out 120hp at economically low revs. She also had an independent generator that could charge the batteries while powering the 24volt, and through an inverter could supply 240volts.

All this gear of course added to her weight, and she was no greyhound in the water at twenty-five tons, plus the extras we'd added, but we still managed a healthy ten knots at a smooth 1800-rpm, which was excellent.

The swell was still there, but was more spaced out, making it appear smaller and less steep. We appeared to have cleared the busy shipping lanes. I was starting to relax a little. The nervous knot in my stomach caused by apprehension and the scale of our task was slowly untying itself, as I began to feel at home again on the sea.

I decided, after a self-taught crash course of the area, that by travelling directly for Bermuda we should pick up the Gulf Stream, which would help our passage.

It was 1500 hrs and the plotter told me we'd covered 60 nautical miles. We only had another six hundred to go; hell this was different to the ten miles to the dive site stuff.

'Kris, look.' Patsy, with her skipper's cap nestled on her black curls, gazed astern at the spectacular sunset. 'It's so beautiful! All this is so exciting…' she paused, wiping a tear away. 'I'm so happy, Kris, I never thought life could be this thrilling.'

'It will get rough at times. I mean rough… rough,' she put her arms around me and rested her head against my chest and rolled those dark eyes at me. 'Rough, rough like the doggy in the window with the curly tail?' she grinned and held my face. 'Nothing can get to me as long as I have you to share it with.'

I had set up the autopilot during the day and it was working fine. Every few seconds either a small red or green light would flash followed by a whirring sound from the pump fixed somewhere behind the bulkhead. The plotter's track was dead straight; the sea had calmed considerably. All was well.

A sudden crash of a plate' then shouting in Spanish made me rush below.

'La vaca! La vaca!' Patsy was stood covered in beans.
'What the hell?'
'I took her some food and she went berserk and threw it at me,

who the hell does she think she is? I'm gonna punch her god damn lights out!' She turned to the door.

I grabbed her, which caused the wound in my shoulder to wake up. 'Come on, Beanie, don't lose it on that bag of spite.' She was shaking with rage.

'Beanie?' she snapped and then offered a smile, then snatched it away as she turned to the door to Laura's cabin. 'You better clean up your shit, or you'll be on a one hell of a diet!' She banged at the door as several more beans dropped out of her hair. 'Tu comar la comida para perros.'

'What the hell are you saying? She probably can't understand Spanish anyway.'

'I can say things angrier in Spanish.' I smiled somewhat haplessly.

'Do you want me to lick you clean?' She glared at me.

'I hate her so much I want to punch her face in!' She held her tight little fists in front of her then she grinned. 'You can hit it off with me against her door if you want...'

'Hey, hey, don't let her get to you, Pats. You're bigger than that. What did you shout at her?'

'Against the door and I'll tell you.'

I returned back on watch slightly bemused, but concerned that we had been at sea only one day and they were already trying to dismember each other.

We saw distant lights on the clear horizon, but the radar set on five miles didn't pick up any vessels, they were further away from us than we thought. Patsy stared in awe at the sky with all its twinkling stars; I was relaxed and nearly dozing when she almost knocked me off the chair.

'Look, look at that!' she pointed, but didn't need to. The biggest shooting star I'd ever seen shot across our bow, leaving a big green tail that looked like a sparkler. 'Make a wish, Kris, now make a wish quick,' she smiled, childlike. 'What did you wish for then?'

I stared at her lovely face. 'I'm sure you can guess.'

The dawn sun looked enormous compared to what I was used to, and thankfully the sea was still relatively calm. I marked our progress on to the chart as the sun shone its light and warmth on us.

We had covered 203 nautical miles which was fantastic, but we had achieved that under power. Now we had to sail. Patsy was cooking breakfast. We had stocked the fridge with bacon and eggs, which we calculated, would stay fresh enough until we made Bermuda. The smell wafted into the wheelhouse and I was hit hard again with past memories, this time it was all the people whom I had shared such fry-ups with, and there were lots of them flashing through my mind. I was powerless to avoid these ever-more-frequent flashbacks, and they made me feel uneasy. This quest was all I had left. I didn't want to be on the run all my life, stripped of all pride and dignity. There was no going back.

Patsy broke my thoughts as she passed me the beanbag tray. On it was a full plate with a piece of paper that read.

'One full Englis to be paid for later'.

She rocked her head from side to side cheekily then with her hip squeezed me out from the helm seat.

'You spelt English wrong.'

'You understood didn't you?'

I started tucking into my breakfast as she took the wheel. I had only eaten half a rasher of bacon when the boat lurched steeply.

'Kris, it's gone all funny,' Patsy shouted as she fought with the helm.

A gust of wind had caught her out causing the boat to heel over and broach as it topped a wave crest. The breakfast slid on to the deck and pans and stuff in the galley crashed around. I grabbed the wheel and brought her downwind.

'What happened? It went all wobbly.'

'No problem, Pats, we've just got to learn how to sail, that's all.'

I slipped the bolt on Laura's cabin and knocked. 'If it's the bitch, get the fuck away!'

'It's me. I've got some breakfast for you.'

'Come in,' she said quietly.

She had cleaned up the bean mess and was sitting on the port side sofa, looking out of the small porthole at the sun. She seemed quite subdued. I placed the tray on the unmade bed and backed off. She stood up and her dressing gown opened revealing her shapely body. She looked up at me; I'm sure to gauge my reaction. I looked away and left her.

Patsy was getting the hang of sailing. The problem she had was that when the boat listed in the wind as the sails filled; she leant with it as if she was on a motorbike, which caused her to slide off the seat on several occasions. However, we were getting there slowly but surely.

The wind had moved into the west a few degrees, and was now on our starboard beam, so I put out all the sails. For a motor-sailer she was impressive and we silently shushed along between seven and ten knots, and on occasions when we ran down a wave we clocked up to twelve knots. I felt safe with this capable blue lady.

Chapter Seventeen

Day two, 1500 hrs, we had covered 56 nautical miles under sail and averaging seven knots.

The gods were smiling on us; the sea and air temperatures were similar making it comfortable. The dreaded hurricane season was behind us and all seemed well until I found among the charts and navigational aids a small booklet called 'Visiting Bermuda' and started flicking through it.

'Look, look.' Patsy pointed like a kid at things bursting out from the waves like torpedoes. It was a large pod of White Sided Dolphins. Patsy was ecstatically pointing and jumping up and down each time one shot airborne from a wave. I had to take over the helm as she dragged a safety harness on and scrambled to the bow, showing off her shapely blue shorts. She clipped on then hung over the bow regularly flashing magic smiles back to me. Louder shouts from her filled the air as a group of Pilot Whales joined in on the wave-riding fun, as though welcoming us. They stayed with us until dusk then disappeared into the darkening water.

Patsy returned soaked to the skin while smiling vibrantly; she purposely stripped off next to me.

Being at sea, I felt safe despite the obvious risks, and having Patsy with me gave me added confidence.

> The sails were in and Mr Gardiner was pushing us along efficiently in the low following sea. The autopilot was in charge and the cat in the forward cabin had been fed and was secure.

I had barely got back to the 'Visiting Bermuda' booklet when Patsy slinked up the galley steps wearing suspenders, stockings and her skipper's hat.

'Captain on the bridge!' she shouted, 'I want you standing to attention.' She twisted around with her hands on her hips and grinned. 'That's both of you.'

I lost the next two hours in another world and was left exhausted at the helm. In all my mature years I had never experienced any thing as intense as I had in those two hours.

I picked up the booklet, but my hands were shaking too much to make sense of it. Moments later Patsy returned with a glass of rum.

'I need to sleep now babe, do you mind?'

'Where the hell did you get this dark rum from, you can't get it anywhere.' She smiled a tired smile then disappeared.

I spent most of the night in confusion after recalling what Dee had once said, 'Patsy has something special.' I think I had just experienced that something.

During the night I managed to read through the visitors' guide to the Bermudas and to my dismay for us it read like an invitation to Colditz.

All yachts calling at Bermuda must contact Bermuda Harbour Radio prior to arrival. A VHF radio call should be attempted at 30 miles from the island giving your ETA and details of any special requirements. Harbour Radio will request a description of your vessel, as well as details of certain safety equipment carried onboard. Assistance with entering harbour and obtaining HM Customs, Immigration and Health clearance is also provided. Details of any relevant shipping movements or other safety information will also be passed.

All vessels should enter St. George's Harbour flying code flag 'Q' (the yellow quarantine flag) from a conspicuous position in the rigging, and proceed to the Customs dock, which is located on the Northeast corner of Ordnance Island. This flag signal should remain hoisted until clearance has been obtained. Should you have any questions for HM Customs at any time during your stay, they may be contacted directly on VHF Channel 16 or through Bermuda Harbour Radio. A call to Bermuda Harbour Radio on departure is also requested in the interests of safety.

Yachts arriving between the hours of 0000 and 0800 local time should be prepared to anchor in the Customs area at Powder Hole, St. George's until Bermuda Customs is in a position to clear you. Bermuda Harbour Radio should be contacted when 30 miles from the island, and certainly prior to entering port for further information.

Anchorage and Berthing Facilities

Safe anchorage is available for yachts in both St. George's and Hamilton Harbours. Advice may be obtained at any time by radiotelephone through Bermuda Harbour Radio. Yachts must adhere strictly to berthing instructions on arrival and should not proceed to any berth or anchorage unless directed by Harbour Radio (VHF Channel 16) or the St. George's Dock master (VHF Channel 14). Berthing space alongside at the north side of Ordnance Island and at Market Wharf is restricted. At Somers Wharf and Hunters Wharf (east) berthing is available on a first come first served basis without time limit and is free of charge. Berthing alongside in Hamilton is restricted to yacht club berths, boat yards and marinas, and is usually chargeable. Charges may be obtained on application from the Dockyard Marina (a full service marina), the Royal Bermuda Yacht Club, the Royal Hamilton Amateur Dinghy Club, and others. Berthing for yachts is prohibited at all commercial **quays** and St. George's, except in an emergency.

Immigration, Customs and Health Clearance

All visiting yachts are required to obtain Immigration, Customs and Health clearance in the port of St. George before proceeding elsewhere in Bermuda. The Customs clearance facility is located at the eastern end of Ordnance Island. This facility should also be used for obtaining Customs clearance prior to departure.

Mariners should note that the Ordnance Island Customs clearance facility is no longer 24hr.

Yachts arriving in Bermuda from overseas ports are normally cleared with a minimum of formality. Arrangements for clearance should be made by radiotelephone prior to arrival. The yacht master should have available two crew lists, showing name, date of birth, nationality and home address of each member of the crew and passengers. Two stores lists showing details of consumable stores in food lockers should also be included. The Customs boarding officer who normally carries out clearance formalities for all three departments brings all other documents required for clearance on board. A clearance fee of $15 (in either U.S. or Bermuda currency) will be made for each person on board the visiting yacht. This fee is levied to defray, in part, the costs of providing the Customs clearance facility, the Bermuda Marine Rescue Services, the Search and Rescue Co-ordination Centre at Bermuda Harbour Radio and local aids to navigation. The Customs boarding officer will collect the fee as part of the clearance procedure. A Bermuda Government official receipt must be issued.

How the hell could a boat enter Bermuda with a kidnapped woman trussed up in a cabin, by an armed man on the run from Interpol with over four hundred thousand dollars in cash?

I wasn't only in deep water; I was also in deep shit. Bermuda was not an option any more. At first light I altered course to the north-east, while Spanish screams rang out as another female clash erupted. I was heading into the unknown with two loonies. Despite the rolling and pitching the boat was the only stable thing around.

Later I got comfy with a bottle of wine, while Patsy had another violent confrontation with Laura, and we'd only been at sea for three days.

I was aiming to pass Bermuda to the north, about forty miles north, so no officials would board us.

Patsy was a lot calmer after spending five minutes free time with Laura. I didn't interfere. We had a long way to go, and as long as Laura was alive at the end of the trip I didn't give a shit. Patsy seemed to have things under control. I had no desire to check on Laura whatsoever right now. I had weather on my mind.

The further you travel north this time of year the closer you get to the north-west drift, as it joins the Gulf Stream. All the books I had available suggested you shouldn't be there in a small boat this time of year. Contra to that, our course alteration surprisingly gave us better weather.

We had been at sea for five days now and the first day out had been the roughest. We were sailing along at eight knots, and had

Bermuda forty miles four points off our starboard beam. Patsy had seen lots of sea life. She was fascinated by the dolphins and whales, and was thoroughly convinced they were coming to say hello to us. It was calm and we were sailing comfortably. Patsy was on the bow, so I checked on Laura. She was in her bed. I started closing the door, she stirred and caught my eye and she sat up.

'Can I stretch my legs please?'

As Laura gasped the air Patsy turned her head.

'What is that doing on deck?' I felt awkward to say the least.

'Human rights.' Laura squinted at the sun while taking deep breaths. I noticed a few bruises on her face. Right now I was entering new ground. I had sided with Laura. Had I become soft?

I lashed her to the base of the mast then returned to the wheelhouse. Laura simply drew breaths of air while blinking into the sun, like a sad caged animal, she was still wearing Patsy's tracky bottoms and they were quite dirty, the sight of Laura wearing them strangely upset me.

Suddenly a thumping noise sounded all around us then a big black helicopter appeared as if from nowhere, it hovered just a hundred metres from the boat.

'Go to channel sixteen please sir.' An amplified voice ordered loudly. What more could happen to us, I asked myself. I picked up the handset.

'*Blue Marlin* on channel sixteen over.'

'*Blue Marlin* you are entering a navel exercise zone. Please proceed due north for twelve nautical miles then proceed east for a further ten nautical miles to avoid our fire zone. Then you can resume your present heading sir.'

Laura was having a fit and was kicking out like a Tiller girl on speed, but thankfully the ever resourceful Patsy dashed to her and pretended to comfort her, no doubt with a bit of gutter Spanish. Then as fast as it had appeared the chopper banked away and left us in silence, luckily the sails had obscured Laura's fit.

Patsy had tried to bring Laura back to the wheelhouse, but they were again fighting. Laura had somehow managed to get her legs around Patsy, and was attempting to get her into a headlock. I had to leave the wheel and separate them as Patsy's boxing ability had kicked in and she was landing hard punches like lightning. If I had got there a minute later I reckon we would have been committing Laura to the deep.

'Fucking hell, you can't kill her, we need her alive.'

Her hair was covering most of her face, but I still saw those dark eyes flash at me like a wild animal's.

'Pats, what the hell is wrong with you? Why have you turned so aggressive?'

'That devil bitch is suckering you big time. She's a threat and will kill you or me the first opportunity she gets, and I'm not giving her the chance. We agreed that she wouldn't be allowed up on deck, then the next goddamn minute she's blowing kisses to the freaking navy, so who's getting soft then?'

After calming down she brought me a hot chocolate laced with rum, which I sipped slowly, as we headed into the increasingly restless sea.

We noticed lots of Black Hawk helicopters and jet fighters zipping around for most of the day. Big ships appeared and disappeared with astonishing speed as the might of the USA played war games on our starboard side.

After we had cleared the inconvenient war zone I pointed the bow towards the Azores. I made a brief calculation, which was confirmed by the GPS that we had more than two thousand nautical miles to reach the Islands. If we were lucky we would arrive there in good health, but that depended on us. Water was now on ration, the tank level indicator read three quarters full. Good old Fisher boats: the tank was nice and big.

Patsy had stocked up with several boxes of spring water and soft drinks, and we had enough tinned food to open a corner shop.

'Patsy had stopped on her walk to the bow and was knelt prodding something.

'What is this skinny bird thing?' She prodded it again.

'It's a flying fish.'

'Get out of here, fish don't fly. It's some foreign bird. It must have hit the mast.'

'I tell you it's a fish, its got fins.'

'They're its wings.' I picked it up. 'Look at its mouth, that's a fish's mouth.'

'Ah, you're having me on, luv,' she mocked me, then moved to her favourite place and hung over the bow. I returned to the wheel and checked the gauges everything was fine.

We were now north-east of Bermuda and it was getting warmer, I calculated that we were just within the south edge of the main vein of the Gulf Stream, and benefiting from it as we were sailing at a steady seven knots in the now brisk north westerly.

'Kris, Kris.' Patsy dashed back to the wheelhouse in her excited-kid mode. 'I saw fishbirds, a whole gang of them just flew across, bouncing off the water, and there was some thing like a big gang of fish chasing after them. It was great, gang wars at sea, huh?' She had me creased up.

'What's so funny, huh? I couldn't talk - she was crazy.

I placed the dead flying fish on to the hook, watched closely by Patsy. Then I let the line pay out from the small fixed spool reel. The rod was about twenty pound class, with line to match. We waited in anticipation as the dead flying fish skimmed along in our hissing wake. Suddenly the line shot from the water and tightened up. The little reel sang as line was torn from it.

'Pull it in, pull it in,' Patsy urged me while jumping up and down. I carefully adjusted the drag and before all the line was lost I had slowed down whatever we had hooked, then I began the slow task of retrieving the fish against the drag from the boat.

About ten minutes later we saw something skimming along.

'Look, look its coming, it's big. Look, its blue and white.'

'I think it's a tuna.'

'Fantastic,' she clapped her hands. 'Tuna for tea.'

A dark grey fin popped up behind our struggling tuna, which was almost at the stern. Then a head full of teeth appeared and in a second we had only the tuna's head left hanging from the line.

'Mi Dios,' Pats said softly, which I knew meant 'My God.' She pulled her hair from her face and bent over shouting Spanish abuse at the shark, which was now following steadily behind us.

After feeding the shark another three fish, we managed to get one aboard, a Dorado of about twenty pounds.

We were like two kids until we had to clean it, with Patsy peering over my shoulder, pulling every imaginable face as I firstly gutted it then cut into good-sized steaks, which we grilled with butter and lemon juice.

It was late afternoon, and we sat together in the shimmering sunlight with a cold bottle of Chardonnay. We chinked glasses and admired at our catch, which almost covered the plate and was accompanied with peas and new potatoes. I cut into the fish steak and noticed Patsy had put a third steak under the grill. I looked at her.

'I'll take hers later.' I shook my head slightly.

'What?' she said with her mouthful then swallowed it quickly. 'No way, Kris, she's not sharing the table with us. Hell! She'd stab one of us to death with a spoon as soon as we turned our backs on her. She's committed cold-blooded murder you said that yourself, she is a desperate criminal, with jack shit to lose.'

'You're right, but I find it so hard to be cruel to…I, err, I don't know.'

'She has you bent round her little finger, Kris. It's a man woman thing, she is a looker and she uses it to her advantage.' I remained silent, looking down at my plate.

Patsy lowered her head with enquiring eyes. 'Do you fancy her?'

'No, no, but this trip is going to take weeks, if not months, and stuck in that cabin in this growing heat, I don't know whether I can see this through. I feel like casting her off at the Azores and sailing off into the sunset.'

'Oh, yeah, that's stupid cool! Then when we stop at any place as strict as Bermuda I lose you forever. Murder one, would give you at least twenty years in a cell, which would be smaller and a lot nastier than the comfy cabin devil woman is in. Get real, Kris!'

She swigged the glass empty and studied me. 'Is there something I don't know about you two?' She refilled both glasses and eyed me. Hell, what this girl lacked in fish ID she certainly made up in other ways. She looked betrayed at my silence, then got up and left the galley. I pushed the last piece of fish around for five minutes.

Patsy was watching the mesmerising phosphorescence. 'All those zillions of bugs Kris, they make the waves glitter.' She looked up at me. The wind was blowing her hair all around her pretty face. 'I'm sorry for earlier, the thought of you and her…' She returned to the bugs.

After a rough unsettling night the dawn broke somewhere among the clouds. There was no way I was going on deck to make sail; it was blowing a gale. The weather forecast said a low would cause it to freshen for a while, then move north and give way to high pressure. Right now we were in the middle of the tussle and getting a hammering.

We had things stored and secure, but they still managed to escape to the galley deck, making the place look as if it had been burgled a dozen times. The grey monsters continued to maul us, leaving us on a different course after each attack. I had relieved the autopilot it couldn't cope with this angry sea. Patsy had herself pinned on the couch next to me and was hanging on like a kid on a fairground ride with her hair rising and falling.

I maintained the best course I could and slowed our speed to the most comfortable, but that was near impossible as the sea was hitting us hard on our starboard side and trying to send us north all the time. Each time I turned her bow into the waves we dropped into the deep trough so hard I felt the mast was going to snap. It was like being inside a washing machine. What Laura up in the bow was experiencing did not bear thinking about.

Day seven and I could see a brighter horizon ahead of us. We'd had our arse well and truly thrashed. Everywhere was wet and the galley looked like a bombed Beirut café.

Patsy found Laura under her mattress and every thing else that wasn't screwed down. Her cabin was wet also, but we had survived, and what I heard on the radio was that a force ten gale had passed through where we were. Although massive swells rose and fell like big hills, the sun was shining and the deck was steaming its welcome.

We spent most of the day airing the damp bedding. Where the water had come in remained a mystery. After our busy day we had corn beef hash washed down with a few buds. We were on course and shipshape once again.

Remarkably the swell was all but gone the next day, and the sun shone like a big fiery ball. It was midday and quite hot. Despite our agreement to keep Laura below we relented and decided to let her exercise for ten minutes. She was doing her stretching thing, closely watched by Patsy. Laura wore only underwear due to the heat and Patsy kept shooting daggers at her each time she bent over displaying her trim body directly in front of me. She was regularly checking in which direction I was looking, so I deliberately looked away to keep the peace.

I had caught a nice sized tuna and was bent over washing away the mess after preparing it when I heard shouting again. I looked up to see Laura struggling with Patsy. Something must have sparked them off again. Then as if in slow motion Laura pushed Patsy, her bare foot slipped on the raised deck and she fell against the rail. Off-balanced, she totted precariously against the rail then to my horror Laura lifted her leg and kicked her viciously over the side.

I scrambled to haul her back aboard but to my dismay the line followed by the clip whipped over the side before I reached it, she'd forgotten to clip on. Laura started laughing loudly.

I rushed back to the stern and on to the small platform and leant as far over the water as I could. Patsy appeared with her arms outstretched, but I couldn't reach her. The sheer terror in those eyes I loved so much caused me to panic even more. I leaped into the tender we were towing, but she slipped further and further away from me.

I pulled the tender to the stern and jumped back aboard, grabbed a man over board marker and threw it over, then ran to the wheel and spun it hard over. The boat lurched, but the sails hampered the manoeuvre and made it impossible to turn. The engine, I needed the engine.

I fumbled with the key and pulled it completely out of the ignition, then stabbed it clumsily back in and turned it causing the deck to vibrate into life. Grey smoke belched out from the stern as I pushed the throttle hard forward.

We started turning despite the sails' protest and I could now see the marker buoy between the swells but no Patsy. I struggled to hold course, then I saw a fin, which filled my stomach with waves of anguish. Time froze as I searched the lifeless swells, then I saw splashing about fifty metres away. It was Patsy, wildly flailing her fists whilst trying to keep a shark at bay.

I screamed her name over and over as I got closer she was fighting for her life as more sharks started circling her. If I got this wrong I would have no choice but to join her.

Blue Marlin shook as I pulled the throttle fully back causing her bow to dip while a big wave crashed over the stern almost washing me overboard. The boat's appearance seemed to have scared away the sharks for the moment. I could see no fins, but I couldn't see Patsy either, she was gone.

I screamed her name over and over again as the seconds passed like hours then she burst to the surface gasping and coughing, the boat had blown right over her. Patsy's bleeding fingertips touched mine for just a second then the wind snatched the boat and me away. Her petrified face imprinted in my mind as we were torn from each other again.

I could see the fins closing on her again. I was just about to release the inflatable and dive in when I saw her safety line trail past. I frantically lunged for it and just managed to reach it as the shiny clip came into view. I snatched it out of the water and wrapped it around my wrist twice before my arm was viciously wrenched from me.

I held on the rail with my right hand, but I only had my finger ends on it because I'd stretched to the limit to reach the rope. My grip was gradually slipping off the shiny rail, so I squeezed a bare foot under the lower rail that ran down the stern and locked it by twisting it. Now I was able to grab the rope with both hands and began to haul it with all my strength.

Patsy's head popped up, desperately gasping for breath, but the strain was severe and I was struggling to pull her in.

'Laura! Laura!' I screamed. 'Help us, for pity's sake, help us!' Suddenly I saw her from the corner of my eye then I felt her thumping and twisting my ankle. She was unhooking my foot from the rail!

'No! No! Laura, no!' I screamed.

The water altered my senses as my screams turned into gasps for air. It all happened so fast. Patsy bumped into me hard then started moving towards the inflatable tender. As I fell in the water I must have dropped below the tender's bowline. The safety rope must have been above it; the tender I could vaguely see was now skimming sideways as our combined weight pulled at its bow. The line dragged Patsy steadily towards the tender, with me being bigger and heavier.

I watched helpless as she reached it then clung to the slippery round tube with one leg and arm hooked over it like a koala bear. She was desperately trying to climb in as the tender continuously dug under the water then burst out, swerving and slewing in the boat's wake like a bucking bronco.

I dare not pull on the rope for fear of capsizing it, then a wave crest lifted her up, washing her partly over the tube, she stabbed her leg further over the top and pulled herself into the bouncing dingy.

It was my turn now. I pulled with all my might. I was skimming on top of the water and couldn't see much, but as I got closer and closer I could see Patsy fighting with all her strength to avoid being dragged back over the bow line.

She held her position with her arm across the painter line and held it secure despite the pain she must have been in. I eventually reached the boat and struggled into it, gasping and coughing.

Patsy grabbed at me. She was hysterical and covered in blood. Then I saw her. Laura was climbing down the stern with something like a bread knife in her hand.

I pulled on the painter like a madman and I got there just as she did. She stared coldly.

'You just keep on coming back,' She shot me a wicked look. 'This time it is 'Goodbye Kris.'

I grabbed the rail and Laura slashed at my arm, making me let go, then I suddenly felt Patsy's blooded hands take hold of my shoulders. Then her feet pressed firmly on my back. She launched herself off my shoulder, like a cat pouncing on its prey, knocking Laura off balance.

Laura dropped the knife as she grabbed desperately to hold on, then within seconds Patsy was dragging her by her hair up the stern.

I released the line from my wrist then rushed aboard to find Patsy holding her cut hands under her arms whilst kicking and stamping on Laura's head and body. I tried calming Patsy, who was snivelling uncontrollably, and obviously sinking into deep shock as blood ran freely from dozens of horrific gashes on her hands and arms.

I watched over Patsy as she struggled to sleep in between attacks of panic, which caused her to sit up and attempt to fight off her invisible demons, with wild punches that were causing her cuts to bleed even more.

Each time I would hold her down and comfort her. Then she would look wide-eyed at me and burst into tears, holding her bloodstained bandaged hands to her face while violently trembling like a scared frantic child.

She was deeply traumatized, and who wouldn't be, after such a horrific experience. The thought of losing her was terrible enough, but to watch her beautiful body being torn apart had sent me into shock as well. I felt I was back in the badlands. I couldn't stop shaking. We were in emotional trauma, and it was all down to the bitch in the bow. Patsy had repeatedly warned me about Laura, and how right she was. I had all but lost another love of my life to the sea. Thankfully this time… I was there for her.

The following three days were probably the hardest of my life. Patsy's hands and forearms were badly lacerated. Fortunately no major veins were severed, but the sheer amount of deep cuts was frightening. The little finger on her left hand had its tendons cut through, and sadly she could no longer move it, and there was bone exposed at the sides of her forearms where she'd pushed out at the shark.

I bathed the wounds in sterilising solution every day then when the bleeding stopped I closed each cut and stuck it together with surgical tape.

She was in so much pain I resorted on occasions to getting her drunk. I was so lucky to still have her. If the shark had been bigger she would not be with me now.

Incredibly, despite not being able to swim, she had punched and fought that shark constantly for more than five minutes, and had been run over by twenty-five tons of boat in a moderated sea. No wonder she was in such a state. I had one extra special woman for sure and felt even more for her now than I ever thought I could feel for anyone.

Four days since the attack, and thankfully infection hadn't set in, her cuts were on the mend and her strong little body as ever was fighting to win, but she was deeply scarred inside.

It took a further eleven days before we saw grey bumps on the horizon. During that time thankfully the weather had been kind to us and never blew above a force five.

Although Patsy's hands were almost healed, she was still suffering mentally. I spent as much time with her as I possibly could, telling her stories about my life and the people I had met, but she would drift off in a trance, staring vacantly. Then when I tried to leave her side she would plead with me not to go outside, and hold tightly on to me. At times she would almost go hysterical until I returned and calmed her down again, with lots of hugs. The nights were the most daunting. As soon as she fell asleep the nightmares would descend on her, causing her to fight ferociously. She often wet the already sweat-soaked mattress during these fit-like attacks. I eased the problem by giving her sleeping tablets, but they eventually ran out.

She had hit me so many times with no knowledge of it that I looked like I'd been sparring with Mike Tyson. She could hit incredibly hard for someone so petite. That's what had saved her, but I felt like shit. I really needed help with her. I was totally exhausted and had almost no sleep for days.

I could not face Laura; I had dragged her to the cabin soon after and pushed a load of stores and bottles of water in with her. She hadn't made a murmur, how could she?

We could now see the volcano Pica, the highest point in the Azores, quite clearly and all the other islands were slowly appearing as grey bumps, then one by one they became bigger and slowly turned green. Patsy was thankfully showing some interest and looking a bit more like her old self.

'We'll soon be in the harbour, Pats. We can go for a nice meal and get fresh supplies.' She nodded and stared blankly at me. 'Hey, how about a smile?' She smiled for me, but the look in her eyes said it all. Time would be our only ally, and fortunately we had plenty of it.

The smell of land found our nostrils and the sky seemed full of birds flying busily in all directions. We had a pod of about fifty dolphins with us for most of our approach. Sadly I couldn't coax Patsy to the bow to observe them closer.

After taking a long seawater shower she stood naked on deck while I poured a precious bucket of warm fresh water to rinse her off, then as she descended below, she looked over her shoulder at me watching her. She pursed her lips and blew me a kiss then smiled a thank you. She was getting there.

Chapter Eighteen

We arrived at the marina De Horta on the Island of Faial in the Azores twenty-seven days after leaving Norfolk Virginia, and had logged two thousand six hundred and thirty nautical miles, which makes an average of approximately ninety-eight miles per day. Not bad for the first time I had handled this boat.

I slowly nosed into the harbour and drifted opposite the marina section. It felt strangely closed in after being in mid ocean for all those days. Then a member of the marina staff called us to come alongside the reception pontoon.

I was flapping big time as I steered *Blue Marlin* closer to my possible capture. 'Welcome to Horta, senor.'

He looked pleasantly surprised when he saw Patsy emerge and I must have as well. She was wearing the most revealing bikini I'd seen her in. He nodded respectfully with a luring smile.

'Senora.' She re-arranged her freshly washed hair that was glinting in the sunlight, smiled sweetly then replied, 'O seu pais e muito bonito.' He smiled broadly at her.

'Como se chama senorita?'

'Patsy Alverez,' she smiled out.

'Senorita Alverez e…muito bonito.' Patsy giggled and blushed.

'Muy amablede suparte,' the man smiled genially.

After flirting with Patsy he passed her a form. He told us to wait, as the customs and immigration would see us next, a remark that put me into helpless panic.

Patsy smiled at me then whispered discreetly. 'Leave it all to me.'

The customs officer arrived within a few minutes. He had the appearance of a policeman. He was wearing a well-pressed blue grey uniform. He looked grumpily at me, and then Patsy whooshed past me. All the men around stood openly ogling her.

'Bom dia Como esta?' His chubby face screwed into a pleased smile.

Patsy sat swinging her lovely legs over the side while he asked her questions in Portuguese. He was struggling to concentrate on the form. Despite his dark shades I could guess where his eyes were concentrating.

He completed the formalities without even stepping onboard. Immigration was next. I noticed the marina's workers were hanging around as if we had a VIP on board and then two younger men again in grey blue uniforms approached us. Patsy spoke first and they gushed out flirting smiles. They were almost pushing each other aside to kneel close to Patsy. Eventually the higher-ranking official knelt, staring at Patsy's slim model figure while balancing a form on his knee.

He passed the form and a pen to her. She said something then put her hands out and they looked at her scars. I could see him gesticulating to her with his own hands.

Patsy's face became more serious as she obviously struggled while recalling to them what had happened to her. They all knelt in silence with shocked faces, shooting stunned glances at each other and occasionally at me. Then one of them filled in the form for her.

They spoke like old pals then the smiling returned and they laughed and joked once more among themselves.

Without one of them coming aboard we had sailed through the checks, thanks to Patsy's brave front.

It was the off-season and the marina was almost empty. We were told to moor on a long pontoon that was clear except for two white-hulled yachts. I slowly berthed *Blue Marlin* with her bow into the warm breeze on her port side, and at the extreme end of the pontoon, so no one would be walking past and possibly detect Laura, who was for the moment bound securely and gagged.

'So what was all that flirting about? I didn't know you spoke Portuguese.'

She blinked her eyelashes, which made her hair move, then smiled. 'There's a lot we don't know about each other, Kris.'

'So what did you say to them?'

'I told them that they had a beautiful island, that's all.'

'Oh no, the younger of the two, he said something back, though.' Her eyes sparkled like the girl I remembered then she exposed her neat teeth in a lovely smile.

'He told me the same.'

'What, about... you know?' She nodded with a vacant gaze.

'I couldn't hold the pen very well so I told them a little about it.'

'You did well, Pats, you saved me this time.'

She slinked down below like a model and returned a few minutes later looking frumpy, dressed in slacks and a tee shirt with a cardigan covering it. She turned to me, now serious.

'Kris, I need to go somewhere.'

'Where?' She looked tired after her effort to appear normal. 'I won't be long, Kris,' she puffed out firmly. She stepped off the boat and walked a bit wobbly down the pontoon and disappeared into the town, leaving me a bit gob-smacked.

I opened a bud and sat feeling quite smug at achieving two legs of the trip in one. Then I remembered our cargo.

I entered the door to Laura's cabin. It was hot and the air was stale, so I unlocked and opened the escape hatch. The breeze rushed in like a warm welcome from the Azores.

She followed me with her eyes while snatching short breaths through her nose; her hair was uncombed, making her look like a young Debbie Harry. I stared deep into those sea green eyes, her breathing stopped in anticipation.

'I honestly feel sorry for you, Laura, but to forgive you for the things you have done to Patsy and me is impossible.' Her eyes flickered. 'You have something special about you, yet you have spent your life hurting people. Was it your idea to set me up back in England and ruin my newly rebuilt life?' She focused unblinkingly then almost without moving gestured her head to a no. We locked eyes then a single tear rolled slowly down her cheek. I left the cabin immediately.

Laura wasn't going anywhere. I had her bolted to part of the boat's frame with a piece of chain, like a biker does to secure his wheels; she was as well tied up as humanly possible. I also had a crepe gag on her so I decided to explore around for a while.

The village of Horta is a lovely place with white painted houses that all have neat-looking red pantiles. It was the type of place I could live. The harbour walls had painted pictures and notes from the thousands of sailors who had passed through this vital oasis. It felt so welcoming, especially after all those days at sea. I walked for thirty minutes and bought some fresh milk and something I had been dreaming of, freshly baked bread.

As I walked back towards the marina nibbling the crust I saw Patsy coming out of a church. I didn't think she was the church type, but what had happened to her could turn anybody religious. Still I was pleased for her. I thought she might feel a bit better inside for it.

I deliberately ran to the boat to beat her back. I didn't want her to think I was spying on her. I had bread and butter then some toast soaked in more butter. We had lost weight, Patsy more than I. She needed feeding up.

When she returned I suggested we go out straight away for a meal at one of the waterside restaurants, where we could still keep an eye on the boat.

While she got ready I unshackled Laura and gave her a meal. The problem with having her tied up was the toilet thing, so I left her loose and locked her door then stood guard over the escape hatch while she went about her stuff. I had purchased a Brit newspaper and sat reading it. Some guy who was married to three women at the same time was pleading insanity; another headline was about a group of clergy who were administrating a young boys' football team and the price of fuel was increasing again. The usual crap the poorly led Brits have to live with.

Then through the hatch came Laura's voice.

'Kris, it wasn't me.' There was a pause. 'I am sorry,' she said softly. 'Larry has dominated me since I was a little girl, he turned me into what I am he will never let me go.' I got up and moved back aft to Patsy. Although sympathy was the last thing on my mind her words made me feel sad.

She spun around. 'What do you think, Kris?' I got a big attack of butterflies.

'God, you look wonderful!' She had a small red leather skirt hugging her bum and a stylish skimpy top that consisted of a lattice of strips that barely covered her full breasts. It was very Latin. I felt really proud of her, and then I noticed she was struggling with a chain clasp behind her neck so I pushed her thick heavy curls up to help her. The scars on her little hands were still pronounced and giving her difficulty holding the small chain.

'Here let me.' I fastened the chain then flared her hair back into place, noticing how good it smelled. She turned and smiled. I didn't mention the gold crucifix hanging above her cleavage, but I fully understood why it was there.

I had the unpleasant task of securing Laura again. Her eyes never left mine all the time I was there. It was as if she was trying to read my thoughts, I was pleased to get out of the cabin.

We had a wonderful meal, with Patsy speaking the lingo we got treated like locals. We were grinning at the massive ice creams that lay in front of us. Patsy sank her teeth into a big strawberry, but suddenly stopped chewing. I followed her stare to the boat where one of the marina staff was stood trying to call our attention. Patsy stood up.

'You stay here Kris. Let me handle this,' she walked briskly, turning heads as she went.

A few minutes later she had drawn the man away from the boat and they were slowly walking back to the marina gate. Patsy arrived back and the waiter liberated her ice cream from the cooler.

'What did he want?' She leant towards me, pulling her hair back as if about to share a secret.

'He said someone had called on the telephone in the marina office asking if a boat called the *Blue Marlin* had arrived.' She sounded and looked scared.

'Shit! Well, what did he tell them?'

'It was his assistant, he told whoever it was that we were here, he said that it was procedure to announce on their web site the names and passage plans of all visiting vessels, so that friends and families can check on them.'

'Did he say if the guy sounded American?'

'No. Apparently he's just a kid and doesn't speak much English.'

'Did the marina guy suspect anything, do you think?'

'No I told him the truth.'

'You what?'

'I told him we were runaway lovers.' She smiled then crunched a piece of fruit.

The marina office was small and well used. Patsy walked in and both the occupants almost stood to attention. She broke into conversation firstly with the older of the two, who ogled her while sniffing her sweet perfume as he listened, and then all eyes turned towards the young lad.

He shrugged his shoulders. I heard the word Americana, followed by a pause. The lad thought, holding his finger to his cheek trying to remember then he nodded.

'Sim, sim senora.' Patsy smiled, looked at me and rubbed her finger and thumb together. I passed her ten euros, which she gave the lad, causing him to blush as she thanked him.

We walked along the waterside in silence and then we spoke together. 'No, you first.'

'I can't bear the thought of sailing at the moment, Kris. We need time to re-charge and psyche ourselves up.'

'That's what I was going to say.' We walked to a bar still within sight of the boat and ordered beers.

'Flights from America to here can't be that regular.' She called the barman who was serving a customer; she started talking so fast I couldn't pick a thing up.

He walked over babbling back to her and I ended tipping him as well.

Ever resourceful Patsy had found out that there was no direct flight from the U.S. and that all flights to Horta were via Lisbon in Portugal. More importantly they were always on a Saturday. Today was Tuesday, so at least we had time to replenish our stores. If we could only freeze Laura then defrost her later, life would be a lot simpler.

We had more beers then wandered back to the boat, feeling quite tipsy. Patsy discovered a big bunch of flowers with a card attached. I picked it up, but it was written in Portuguese. I recognised the Senorita bit only. She read it and smiled at me, blushing slightly.

'What does it say then?' She smiled at me teasingly this time.

'Come on then, tell me.' She picked up the card and started reading it in Portuguese.

'Oh no, in English.'

'May we compliment you on your bravery and your beauty and

wish you a speedy recovery from your ordeal. From the marina, immigration and customs staff.'

She sniffed the flowers. 'They're beautiful, Kris, that was so kind of them.'

'I bet the women on those other boats didn't get flowers.' She grinned and blushed. 'Still those other women don't look as good as you, Pats.'

She spread the flowers in the vase I made from a plastic lemonade bottle and turned to me.

'You're not upset are you, Kris?

'No, just proud.'

I released Laura from her shackles and she once again burned her green eyes deep into me. I couldn't begin to imagine what was going on behind them. As I left her she wished me good night, but I ignored her.

Later on that evening, for the first time since the shark attack, Patsy came on to me. Whether it was mental release or the alcohol, or even the flowers, I don't know, but she again took me to a new level of pleasure.

The next day I got up early. It had been a hot night so I slipped into the cool water and had a snorkel underneath *Blue Marlin*. The anti-fouling was a bit patchy and she had a bit of growth, but nothing detrimental. I also checked the prop and cutlass bearing for play, but they were sound. The rudder's lower bearing was a bit worn, probably due to the use of the auto pilot's constant adjustments, but it would easily last the trip before it needed attention.

I had breakfast then headed into the village to get a chain and some fittings for securing the escape hatch. On return I fitted a chain stopper to the hatch above Laura's cabin and secured it with a heavy stainless steel padlock. Now she had fresh air and we didn't run the risk of her climbing out and legging it. I also obtained a pair of bondage handcuffs from a novelty shop as Laura's wrists had become sore. The handcuffs were pink and furry and had a length of chain fixed to them. I clipped them on to her wrists and she sighed disapproval.

'I heard you and her last night.' I ignored her as I finished off the hatch. 'I could give you a lot better than her. You can remember how it was, I know you can by the way you look at me, we would be good together. We were,' she stood up and held out the cuffs. 'I couldn't stop you, I'm bound in these and she's out. It's been a long time for me I'm so hungry for it.' I couldn't believe her gall.

'Not a chance Laura, you don't even make the cut.' She lunged at me kicking out her feet.

'You bastard, how dare you? Even the fucking sharks spat that Latino whore back out.' I clenched my teeth with rage and drew my fist back. 'Go on hit me again, you fucking coward, you wait till Larry gets his hands on you and your black haired witch, he'll skin you alive.'

I lowered my fist and she kicked me several more times before I was able to grab her legs and hold her ankles together, I managed to get two turns of tape around them as Patsy entered in the doorway.

'He's just raped me, the bastard,' Laura screamed.

'Oh yeah.' Patsy said coolly, 'Add this to your list.' A sickening crunch filled the cabin and Laura slowly stopped struggling and let out a painful groan. I turned to Patsy who was stood holding her hand as blood dripped from an opened wound. I finished taping Laura's ankles then joined Patsy in the galley.

'You've opened a wound up, you crazy sod.' She winced as she unmade the fist. 'It was more than worth it,' she said flatly and then eyed me inquisitively. 'What the hell's a sod?'

After we calmed down we sat at the galley table with a coffee. A dilemma was unfolding in my head. If Larry were on his way would he bring heavies with him? He obviously had the money to hire muscle.

We made a list of things we would need for our last leg, which was the most daunting yet. Although not as far as the last trip, which had us one thousand miles from the nearest land. The seas around there at this time of year can be mountainous and there's the cold factor, misty days and long dark nights. We still had a lot to go through.

The shops were not as expensive as in England and the mooring charges were about one third of UK costs. Having supplied thousands of passing vessels, the few shops there had the right equipment on the shelves and all the stores required for long voyages. We got more music CD's and lots of paperbacks.

It was Thursday night and we had fuelled the boat and all the drums and stored every empty space with food and everything we forgot to include on the last trip. This lifestyle was not cheap though. We must have spent a few thousand dollars, but we were better provisioned than the last time.

The weather was good and the five-day forecast predicted fresh westerly winds perfect for us.

We planned to sail first thing Saturday morning. The flight wouldn't arrive until late Saturday, so we would be well gone by then and Larry would have wasted his time and wouldn't dare go on to Guernsey.

We had a fantastic meal at the same restaurant and ended up a bit drunk on the fruity Azores wine, but that didn't stop us from romping around till the early hours.

Patsy went to pay our dues at the office for our extra stay, and she no doubt was going to thank them for their pleasant gesture. I busied myself making final checks on the long list we had prepared and almost every item had its tick turned into a cross. I had serviced the faithful Gardiner diesel engine during the past few days, but still had one job left.

I squeezed myself under the deck and alongside the big engine; I had to lie along the hull frames to service the greaser on the propeller shaft. I pressed the flexi-hose of the grease gun on to the nipple and pumped it until I saw the grease oozing out and around the prop shaft.

I felt the boat rock slightly as Patsy came back onboard then I jumped up banging my head as the engine access hatch slammed down heavily.

'Hey, I'm down here. Open the hatch, Pats.' I banged the grease gun loudly on the deck above me. 'Open the hatch, Patsy.' I waited for several minutes, periodically banging the deck, then I felt the boat rock slightly again.

Patsy must have got off for a while, not realising I was down here, but why had she locked the hatch. Then I heard a muffled scream above me, doors banged and feet shuffled everywhere.

I struggled to the hatch and tried lifting it with my shoulders again as the boat rocked some more.

Suddenly a deafening noise exploded next to me as the starter engaged throwing me into panic as the big engine roared into life. I tried to push up on the hatch again, but it was still locked from the outside. The boat's movement told me we were underway. Someone was stealing the bloody boat! Then I abruptly realised I could stop the engine by pulling the stop solenoid.

The big engine shook as it slowed then stopped, leaving my ears ringing. Then it started up again so I stopped it again.

This went on for a few more times then I disconnected the power to the solenoid by pulling off the spade connector and left it in the stop position. The engine turned over a few times, but wouldn't start.

A minute later light filled the small space and the sun dazzled me, but before I could spring out I saw a big shadow. I felt a sickening blow to my head.

I was spinning on a dentist's chair once again, as blurred shapes began to appear. Why was I looking up at the underside of the galley table? I tried moving, but I couldn't, I was tie-wrapped to it. What the hell was happening? Then behind me I heard her.

'Hi Kris, surprise, surprise.' Laura's foot found my groin then I saw Larry's ugly face grinning down at me.

'I had to wait until you replenished your stores before I joined your little party, Kris. When I called the Bermuda immigration they informed me that you hadn't shown. Hardly rocket science to predict you would arrive here eventually, so I chartered a suitable plane. It's quite handy being a multi-millionaire.' His spit fuelled voice landed on my face as he expressed himself jubilantly. 'I've really enjoyed my stay here and now Laura and I are going to enjoy having a bit of fun, before we dispose of you and your slut for good.'

He sat opposite; staring at me then pulled Laura to him. They partly undressed each other and had sex on the seat in front of me. Laura's eyes stared at me after each lustful gasp as Larry thrust roughly into her.

We were slowly heading out to sea on the autopilot. I felt so helpless and I didn't even know where Patsy was. After their sick show Laura moved next to me.

'You see what you've been missing, Kris.' They dressed then Larry pulled me up and on to the settee where they had just sex.

'My, my, my, how the mighty have fallen.' Larry paced up and down. 'I've been planning what I would do when I caught up with you the moment your little slut bitch broke my nose. And now it's all come together perfectly. What an escape plan! I have to hand it to you, Kris. You don't give up like some of the suckers we've worked over the years. On the contrary, you came after us like James Bond himself, covert surveillance, following us around, not bad for an English hick.'

He lit up a big cigar and blew the smoke into my face.

'Where is Patsy?' Larry didn't crack his face.

'I've been sitting in the sun sipping bourbon and watching you and your, how does one say in English, slapper, running around like termites. One call to the marina office informed me of your plans. You're not as smart as you think.'

'Where's Patsy, where is she, you sick bastards?' I struggled in vain to break free.

'Now, now, Kris, please stop interrupting me. I've planned this moment for a long time and you're fucking spoiling it for me.'

He kicked me hard in my kidneys, causing me to cringe in agony.

'Where was I?'

Laura moved close to me. 'Would you like me to give you head, Kris, it's the least I could do for you after you looked after me so well.' She tugged my shorts down. I squirmed and bucked, but my arms and ankles were tied to the boat. Larry kicked me again. 'Show some goddamn manners, boy.' She took me into her mouth causing me to squirm violently then Larry held me by the hair, forcing me to watch as she expertly continued, at the same time rolling those inhuman green eyes at me. Despite having my hair almost torn from my scalp and the dilemma I was in, she was causing my body to betray me. I could not believe it.

'Get off me you bitch, you fucking devil, get off me.' I screamed and squirmed more violently.

She smiled up at me. 'It must feel real good, you're getting nice and horny, Kris.' She continued shaking me. 'I told you what you were missing, just a few more minutes of this then I'm going to have you.'

'We'll bring your slut to watch. Would that excite you Kris?' Larry added.

I managed to draw my knee up and knock her sideways; she gave me a pout then carried on. I tried struggling again, but she moved with me. In sheer desperation I drew a mouthful of blood and snot and spat it at her. It stuck obscenely in her hair then dripped on to her face. She shot her head up.

'You ungrateful fuck!' she cursed, then a pain rocked me like no other I'd ever experienced. It surged through every nerve in my body as she bit me sadistically down below. She sneered and spat blood into my face then for good measure she punched my groin. I curled into a ball the best I could as Larry moved closer.

'There was no need for that, she was enjoying herself. Now look where it's got you. Patsy will miss out on the show now.'

Laura, obviously still aroused, licked her bloodied lips while she randomly kicked me. I'm sure she was getting off while doing it. I lay panting with pain and watched with disgust as Larry licked her bloodstained lips. I was being beat up by a nymphomaniac suffering from schizophrenia, who was controlled by a complete nutter.

'I thought we would have a cruise around the islands before we release you both.' He paced up and down looking for a reaction. 'For a little swim that is. Laura told me your little slut likes to swim with sharks.'

'Where is she, you freak?'

Laura crouched down and cupped her hands on my face. 'Don't worry about Patsy, my darling Kris, I've been comforting her for you, although she did get a little upset when I told her about how big the sharks are around here. She was, how do you English say…Oh yes, distraught, I believe one says.' She licked my face like a cat then pouted like a clown. 'But she was rude to me, so I had to punish her somewhat.' She smiled. 'You know Kris, like she regularly did me; she can be so ill mannered. It is a real shame she had such a pretty face.'

'I should have killed you a long time ago.'

'You did Kris, remember?' Her broad smile changed to laughter.

'Well you had your chance.' Larry stood up and looked around with a smug smile. 'Now it's our turn, but we have some added bonuses. This fine vessel and the remainder of the money, but there's the crème de la crème which I'm so looking forward to.'

I looked up at him. He leaned over me as if sharing a secret. 'Her butt,' he grinned. 'It's so petite and desirable just the way I like them. I'm saving it for dessert, but before we have a bit of fun, Kris.' His voice changed. 'Where is the rest of the fucking money? I can only find this!' He shook the bag that held all we had left.

'That's all of it.' He slowly knelt down then shot a hard punch into my stomach.

'I'm disappointed, Kris. I kind of…liked you. I know Laura does. She told me in detail what you did to her in Guernsey. I could only listen to you both back then.'

'Haven't you had enough from me, you degenerate parasites?' He shook his big long face and started talking to me as if I was a kid.

'Big words for someone in deep shit. You ruined years of work, just for your pathetic name. You caused the death of my friends and associates, you've tortured my wife.' I could see his mood changing, I should have known better than to piss them off. He grabbed my hair and dragged me back on to the deck where four feet painfully pounded into me until I could take no more. I started vomiting and became dizzy as I was forced into darkness.

The cool saltwater woke me abruptly then the sun warmed me as I came round. I was covered in blood and vomit, and my head was thumping. Then I saw her. Immediately I tried getting up, but I was tie-wrapped, with my hands behind my neck, to the bilge pump, which was located aft of the wheelhouse bulkhead. The handle was digging painfully into my back.

My heart then sank even deeper; I was within full view of poor Patsy. They had stripped her naked and had her spread-eagled over the small table, face down. They had her positioned so that I could see her and would witness whatever they had planned. Banging and crashing sounds were coming from below. They were looking for more money, I assumed. Then Larry appeared with the Fuji and the laptop, which he'd turned on. He sneered angrily at the photos as he realised I had been following their every move for much longer than they had anticipated.

It wasn't a good thing. He was getting angrier as each picture appeared on the screen then Laura appeared with the briefcase that contained the photos and all my stuff.

'My, my, what a busy boy you've been.' She slapped the folder on to Patsy's bottom, using it like a desktop as she studied the contents of my treasured file, commenting on each photo before tearing it up and throwing it over the side. I helplessly watched all the evidence I had taken so long to acquire disappear before me. Then she studied the New York Times press pass, along with the snaps of her with the sovereign.

'You bastard,' she knelt down beside me, teeth gritted. So, Mr fucking Do Goody Woods, you condemn us for deceit while all the time you were sneaking around our godamn grounds deceiving us!' She folded the ID card in half then stuffed it roughly past my swollen lips, cutting my gums.

Larry launched the laptop into the sea after smashing it up with the Fuji.
After all my stuff was gone he ran his hand along Patsy's thigh, while grinning at me.

'Touch her again and I'll rip your fucking head off,' I screamed as I tried violently to break free. Laura threw my empty briefcase over then slowly pulled down her skimpy pants and moved to Larry and began rubbing up against him.

'All this excitement and violence makes me so damn horny. You could be joining in if you weren't such a weirdo. It's a shame, that nice cock is wasted on you.'

Larry smiled down at Patsy.

'Don't you dare touch her, you deranged bastards.' I constantly strained desperately to get free then I heard a slight crack and felt one of the ties loosen slightly.

Laura knelt in front of Larry and without taking her eyes off me pulled down his Bermudas. I looked away, and at Patsy she was shivering and whimpering. I couldn't see her face, only her thick hair, as it hung swinging with the slight boat movement. I could see blood steadily dripping, adding to the large pool below her.

Laura took him into her mouth while predictably rolling her eyes at me. I was in a living nightmare again. I had to escape from these two freaks.

She pulled away from him then moved nearer to me; her face was now inches from mine then it pressed roughly into mine as he entered her with a hard thrust.

I tried frantically to nut her and bite her, but she simply smiled at my desperate attempts. Her moans and gasps fell on my face as her body jolted and rocked.

'Just lubing up, Kris,' Larry gasped. 'See this tight little bud here.' He slapped his hand hard on to Patsy's small bottom, making it quiver and her moan. 'I'm going to enjoy stretching it while she squeals like a Latin hog.' His words sent Laura over the top she started moaning loudly as she reached a grunting climax within less then a minute. She then rolled on to her back, smiling contentedly like a cat for a few seconds before standing up.

'Now Larry, do it now, make her squeal Larry, stretch her butt!' The sick bitch moved closer to Patsy and placed one hand on her buttock, pulling it further apart, while her free hand stroked his thigh.

They had placed several thick tie-wraps through what I could feel was the two upper mounting feet of the plastic bilge pump, which was fixed on a vertical panel. I was sure one of the feet had cracked from my earlier struggles, so I pulled with all my strength. Laura was occupied urging Larry as he began squaring himself up between Patsy's splayed legs.

He snarled at me, through his long crooked teeth. 'Here's some real Texan pork …you Latin hog.'

The plastic cracked as I dragged myself up, then the hose attached to the pump snapped at the clip, freeing me.

I swung the shattered pump over my head as hard as I could. Larry, still holding his member, turned, bearing a look of pleasure, which instantly turned to shock as I wheeled the shattered pump in-between Patsy and his ugly penis.

The sharp jagged plastic landed with all the force I could muster, ripping a big gash in the end of Larry's pride and joy. Blood pumped and sprayed into the air as I shouldered him towards the rail. He was still holding his blooded pride as I pushed the bastard over the side.

A knife blade suddenly seared into my shoulder, causing me to slip on the blooded deck. I tried to grab the rail but my hands were still fixed to the bilge pump and I fell hopelessly out of control. I struggled to my knees.

'Say goodbye to your bitch,' Laura screamed, while holding Patsy's hair with one hand the other held the knife to Patsy's throat.

'For God's sake, stop all this now.' She turned for a second searching astern for Larry.

I shuffled on my thigh, closer to her, which prompted her to pull her arm tighter; the knife pierced the skin on Patsy's neck, causing blood to run along its blade.

'Laura, please no more.'

Larry's scream caused Laura to look aft again. I lunged at her legs, knocking her over and she fell on to the sloping stern.

I grabbed her ankle as she squirmed to break away. There was no way I was going to lose her now. Loud agonising screams made us both to look where Larry was, time seemed to slow down.

Poor little Patsy's trail of blood had not gone to waste. About twenty metres astern the water boiled as a sea full of grey fins snaked around Larry's flailing arms. A few minutes later only rolling lumps of pink and red flesh could be seen in the boiling red circle of water, which was shrouded by an ever-increasing flock of diving seagulls.

Laura lashed out hysterically with the knife, trying to stab Patsy as I dragged her back up the stern. I had to resort to hitting her arm with the pump until she dropped the knife, then I sat on her while I freed my hands, before dragging her screaming and kicking to her cabin.

The sisters at the Catholic mission let me visit Patsy every a day. Laura had badly beaten her pretty little face; she had concussion and bruising everywhere. She'd lost blood and was dreadfully weak.

At our request, ranks closed among the sisters and no one asked any questions, after we told them it was my jealous ex-wife and her brother who caused the grief. Thankfully with Patsy speaking the lingo she was treated very well.

She had once again lost the glint in her eyes. They were red and bruised and, as her injuries peaked, she looked like a traffic accident victim. She couldn't see properly due to the swelling. The poor kid even had a deep nasty cut on her buttock, caused by the lifesaving bilge pump, as well as one on her neck.

I regularly shivered deep down inside at the thought of what would have happened if the plastic legs hadn't broke away when they did. That big ugly devil was within an inch of her gentle body.

I was also sore and hurting everywhere, more so down below as Laura had proved she has strong teeth, but I had the time to heal, and right now sex was the furthest thing on my mind.

All that was left of Larry was his Bermudas. He had been converted into shark shit and with him permanently out of the game I felt a lot safer, but I still had to contend with my psycho captive, whom I reckoned could effortlessly play the leading role in any gory horror film, without the need of a script.

We were in no rush now, although having 'the thing' on board was a risk. Larry's shark feeding technique had hit her hard. She now knew that he wasn't going to appear from the shadows and help anymore and that had affected her severely. She was acting like a classic schizophrenic.

I had spent hours cleaning away all the blood and snot from the forward cabin and had to get new sheets. All the time I was under Laura's one-sided gaze, she was silent, and whenever my face met hers she would turn away. Whether it was because of Larry, or her conscience, I really didn't care any more.

As the days passed she changed though. One day she would say nothing and sit in silence, staring at the bulkhead, another she would frenziedly attack me, always from behind, while screaming obscenities and on occasions she would try it on with me. I was concerned that by the time we got home she wouldn't have enough marbles left in that pretty mixed up head of hers to stand trial.

Saturday the 13th December Patsy stepped back on board. She looked so thin. Nevertheless she was smiling and I received a long firm cuddle as soon as she dropped her case and bag. We held each other whilst holding back our emotions.

Her bruises were now pale yellowish blotches and the cuts had healed. Her pretty nose was still a little swollen. Laura had cruelly concentrated on breaking it. Thankfully her strong teeth survived undamaged.

Her past years training and sparring at the boxing club I'm sure had helped her. No way, were we sailing on the thirteenth, so we had a couple of bottles of wine and lots of cuddles while watching one of our new videos.

Day one of our last leg home started well. We saw lots of whales and dolphins. The wind was blowing a steady force four from the south-west and useful to us as we were sailing along in a north-east direction.

We cleared Sao Jorge Island then past Graciosa on our starboard beam, the last island we would see in this beautiful chain. After changing course for home I began to relax as I saw the green bumps on the horizon turn grey and slowly sink into the shimmering sea behind us.

Although our visit had been near fatal, the place had an aura of adventure about it. Thousands of mariners had passed and replenished their vessels there over the decades and it felt so alive and special. The Portuguese had fought hard to keep their flag flying there and were now reaping the rewards.

I had all of the sail out and we were humming along at a healthy eight knots. The sun was out and Patsy was lying on the long seat, soaking up the warm rays. I had modified the rail around the cockpit by adding strong tight meshed nylon netting. It made the area feel safer and filled all those gaps where fins could appear and scare her. I noticed with regret that as soon as the sun dipped it felt a little cooler.

The sun was gone now and it was getting dark so I reefed the sails to the minimum and started the engine. Now with the help of the sail we were making a good eight knots and occasionally ten. We had made the longest leg with fuel to spare, so I didn't have that doubt nagging away at me this time. I set the radar approach alarm on, and left the autopilot in charge.

We had steak with jacket potatoes and fresh salad. Patsy enjoyed it and left nothing on her plate, which pleased me. Then we had pineapple chunks with cream all washed down with fruity Azores wine. I had the unpleasant task of caring for Laura. She had the freedom of her cabin with the en suite toilet and seawater shower that was heated by the engine.

To help her avoid cabin sickness I returned the TV/Video to her cabin. I didn't do it for her pleasure; I just didn't want to arrive with a mental case that would be whisked away by the anoraks. It fitted in its own little recess and had a steel band, which held it securely.

She looked at me indifferently before I closed the door and secured it with both locked bolts that I fitted in Horta, for extra security. We always cut up her food and served it in a wooden bowl along with a small plastic spoon. There was no way I was going to lose her after everything that had happened to us. She was at such low ebb right now she wouldn't hesitate cutting her wrists to spite us. She'd no doubt enjoy doing it.

We sat in the wheelhouse; it was comfortably calm so I pushed in a video. Three hours of Faulty Towers had Patsy in tears, she hadn't heard of it. And each time Manuel got harassed by Basil, her body would shake as she giggled. It was music to my ears. The flashing screen occasionally lit up the wheelhouse, and I caught flashes of her amused face. She was one incredibly tough cookie and was recovering faster then I could ever have hoped.

Day two was bright and breezy. The weather update showed a big low, circling on the borders of sea areas Fitzroy and Biscay. It was right in our path, but we had a fair way to go till we reached the area.

Horta was now one hundred and twenty six nautical miles behind us and we were still slipping along at eight knots. I was getting a little apprehensive as I thought through in my mind what I was going to do when we arrived at St Peter Port. Patsy would have to clear customs and I would either visit the policeman who arrested me or take Laura to him. I thought bringing him to the boat would be the best solution. Dragging a screaming American through the streets would get me arrested as the villain. I still had to convince them of my ever-so-implausible sequence of events. It wasn't going to be easy.

We saw a sail around midday and got a call on channel 16. It was a Dutch yacht heading for the Azores. The skipper informed us that they had experienced bad weather caused by the big low hanging off Biscay. We told them how quiet it was at Horta and made a bit of small talk then we wished each other a safe passage.

If the low moved east we would miss it, but if it stayed where it was we would have it on the bow. Thank God we had a big engine. For now we were untroubled, apart from finding something to pass the time away.

We played cards for a while, pontoon. We each had a bag of smarties to bet with, but Patsy kept eating them as we played. Then I saw several ace cards poking from under her bum. I confronted her, but she smirked at me then grabbed all the sweets and legged it below and before I could catch her, she had hidden them somewhere in our cabin.

I noticed over the weeks that she was really good at hiding things. It must have stemmed from her past struggles when she was younger; she had hiding places all over like a squirrel and had even managed to beat Larry in his attempt to find more money. 'I spy' died a death, she cheated by changing her chosen item and I never got one right.

I made an omelette with the last of the ham pieces and included chopped tomatoes. Patsy spiced it up with some chilli, but she put too much in and made it far too hot for me.

I gave Laura some bread and vegetable soup. I didn't want her ill from the spicy omelette. Patsy showed off by eating a raw chilli after I indicated my mouth was on fire. The wine came out and we got comfortably drunk. She was so funny when she was like this, so I opened another bottle, which she swigged away at like an old sailor.

One hour later she was speaking in three languages to me, but saying nothing intelligible. I'm sure it was her own way of healing herself, and when I helped her into bed her strong little arms hung on to my neck and she slurred, 'I love you, Kris Woods, you're my guardian angel.'

I spent what was left of the day maintaining the engine and repairing one of the sails that was starting to tear slightly. We had at least one thousand nautical miles to go, so everything had to be kept in top condition. I was stitching far enough along the good canvas before drawing in the tear, when I looked through the forward hatch. Laura was sitting staring at the bulkhead. She had the same blank expression that Jack Nicholson had after he was lobotomised. She didn't look up despite the noise I was making. Again those damn pangs of pity hit me. I plainly wouldn't be continuing a career as a bounty hunter after all this. If I never had met Patsy and only Laura and I were here on this boat, I fear I would never had made it this far before weakening before her manipulative feminine persona. I would have in all probability ended up as mad as she was, but she was here and had nearly cold-heartedly killed Patsy and me more than once. I was pissed off with myself for even thinking about the callous bitch. Sod her anyway, my knob was still throbbing the wrong way.

Day three. Patsy had a hangover and spent the morning in bed. I used her absence to try to catch a fish for our tea, using the new tackle I acquired at Horta. It was a thirty-pound class rod with a strong looking multiplier reel full of fairly thick line. I dropped the lure astern and waited.

About ten minutes later the rod bent encouragingly and what looked like a big tuna leaped out of the water then I saw the dreaded fins again. The line went so tight I could hardly hold on. Suddenly the biggest shark I've ever seen, at least four metres long shot out of the water with my tuna in its mouth. I adjusted my position then suddenly the rod was wrenched from me. It disappeared forever.

'Hi Kris, what you doing?'

'Err... just sorting the rod out. I thought we might attempt a bit of fishing when our fresh food gets a bit low, but...' Before I could tell her I'd lost the rod she shook her head.

'Nah, I don't want to do that, thanks.'

'Yeah, I can understand that, Pats. Hey, I wonder how Jimmy is getting on with Jenny?'

She came and sat down next to me, dressed in the boy's pyjamas that the sisters in Horta had given her. They had red and green racing cars on them; not that Patsy cared. She leaned forward and looked at the GPS causing the crucifix to fall out from her collar. It swung, glinting in the sun like a hypnotist's pennant and I drifted.

As I stuffed the belligerent and distraught Laura into her cabin I could not believe my eyes. There was blood splattered everywhere. The bed looked like a butcher's block. In one of the many pools of blood I found her crucifix. Patsy slid off the table and into my arms. She was cold and barely conscious. I cried uncontrollably as I peeled away the blood-matted hair from her smashed face. How could they have done such a wicked heartless thing? We had roughed up Laura a bit, but she was half dead, unrecognisable.

'Kris. Are you all right?' I snapped out of the daze and held her small, scarred hands for a few seconds, while wiping a tear that had appeared.

'I am now that I've got you back in one piece.'

''One piece', is that another English saying?'

'Uh, huh,' I replied, grinning. She pulled a funny face at me.

'That didn't sound right. It was far too posh, it's 'uh uh!' Like that.' She said it loud and brash. She sounded so funny, but in truth, despite all she'd been through, she was also helping me recover.

We had in the last twenty-four hours covered almost one hundred and seventy nautical miles, a personal best for us. We had travelled in total, three hundred and ninety-six nautical miles since leaving Horta. It was certainly getting colder. The wind had eased to a mere force three, so I decided to use some of the extra fuel we had stored in drums all over the boat, which had caused the whole vessel to smell of diesel. I wanted to use those stored below first so we could get rid of the stink. It would still leave us with forty containers lashed on deck, which equated to two hundred gallons, in addition to the three hundred in the tanks, giving us a total of five hundred gallons.

I pushed the throttle forward till the revs reached fifteen hundred and our speed jumped to ten knots. At this speed we would be in the UK within four days, but as the day grew older I could see dark skies ahead of us and we were still according to the plotter eight hundred and four nautical miles from St Peter Port.

During the night the wind freshened to force seven and the sea was hitting us on the nose, causing *Blue Marlin* to shudder each time a wall of water threw itself at us. It was like being hit with a big hammer. I couldn't sleep, so I kept a lazy watch while lying on the long seat.

I was at The Lodge snuggled between the warm flannelette sheet and the thick quilt. The wind was blowing noisily above and playing forlorn tunes in the telephone lines, while the rain lashed against the window. Then the alarm clock started beeping in my dream.

I awoke startled as reality thumped home. It was the radar alarm that was beeping and warning that something was within five miles of us. I reduced the range to three miles, but still at the centre of the screen remained a big green blob. I reduced the gain, but it was still there then an incredibly loud blast shook the air all around. About one hundred metres directly in front of us was the bow of a massive ship. It had lit itself up like a Christmas tree to warn us.

I spun the wheel, but she didn't alter course, because the autopilot was still on. I quickly pressed it off and swung the wheel hard to starboard and she responded just in time as the massive bulbous bow pushed past within ten metres of us, like a silent monster. I could even see the Plimsoll line on its hull.

Then the radio crackled and a foreign sounding voice spoke. 'That is a sure way to die, my friend.' I pressed the handset several times in acknowledgement. I held the wheel tightly while shaking all over. That was too close. We would have been crushed and pushed under like a balsa wood toy. I had learned another vital lesson the hard way.

I steered manually till the grey dawn arrived, before switching Mr Autopilot back on.

Chapter Nineteen

The wind continued from the north-east for days and with it heavy rain. I encouraged Patsy to stay in bed as much as possible and sleep away the dark hours, which were increasing every day, but every time I checked in on her she would drag me into her den like a spider. I had no complaints about that. It helped pass the time as well.

A check on the latest weather forecast had become almost an obsession now, as the sea was getting bigger by the hour. The report was not good. The low pressure was dominating the sea areas we were heading for, and the tightly packed isobars indicated gale force winds from the north-northwest. If I had wanted to create the worst weather scenario I couldn't have done better. We either had to hit it full on or head to the side and hope it stayed where it was, but that meant a diversion of miles. Go east and we could end up off Portugal or Spain. Go further north and we would end up off Southern Ireland.

We had the last of the bacon between slices of bread that was barely edible. Laura was suffering in the bow cabin. When I took her some food her cabin was a mess and she was getting launched into the air each time the bow dipped severely. Her glare indicated her feelings as I replaced her uneaten meal with a fresh one. She was either on hunger strike or found it impossible to keep the food down. I was not going to ask her and get involved. She was just live cargo to me now.

The little black box again printed the weather map with the noise of a parking ticket machine. It looked like some bored child had held a spirograph and spun it repeatedly without moving. The low was still there and looking even bigger than on the last update, so I altered course four points to north. We were pointing towards Ireland now and with the sea on our starboard quarter the ride was a lot softer.

I checked on Patsy and found her on her front, spread out like a starfish; no doubt she had found lying like that stopped her from rolling about. She was fast asleep. Considering this was her first time on a boat she had done incredibly well not to get seasick.

I attempted to read, but found it impossible. My head was full of weather thoughts, so I spent the night on watch and saw a few ships pass by within a mile of us.

The next day dawned and to my surprise the sea calmed to a steady force four, so I took a position fix and marked it on the chart.

Steaming at ten knots had achieved a brilliant two hundred and thirty nautical miles but we had been travelling further north and we had actually only gained one hundred and ten nautical miles closer to our goal. We still had about seven hundred to go.

I slowed to fuel the tanks while Patsy appeared and asked if I wanted some breakfast. We all had scrambled eggs and surprisingly Laura passed me her empty bowl and thanked me. Maybe the calmer weather had appeased her. When I told Patsy she shook her head angrily.

'She's trying to soften you up again, Kris, that's all, she's so cunning, she told me about you and her, you know,' she looked for my response. I remained silent. 'She said you banged her three times a day for a full week.'

'That's a load of shit, Pats. We all got pissed and Larry fell asleep. She came on to me full on we just had a quickie against the bulkhead. I was that pissed I can't even remember how it was.' Patsy looked a little hurt.

'She certainly can, she repeated it in detail over and over as she beat me up. She said you told her you loved her.' The corners of her mouth curved for a fraction of a second.

'You just added that on, you little sod.' She grinned. I held her head against my chest. 'Pats, she was hurting you deliberately. It was just a drunken encounter, which I seriously regret.' She looked up at me.

'What do ya want for lunch?'
'How about New York pâté?'

We made two hundred miles a day steaming at eighteen hundred revs, while averaging eight knots. All the inboard fuel had been used and we were topping up the tanks from the deck containers. Patsy worked like a trooper. She disinfected and scrubbed where the fuel had been stored and the smell was gradually retreating.

The weather was changeable, as we were between two weather fronts. A few hours would be reasonably calm, then the wind would gust and stir the sea into steep walls, but we were getting closer all the time, which was making me more and more nervous. I had been shot twice and stabbed twice and had the shit kicked out more times then I can remember and had my knob almost bitten off. I had witnessed Patsy being attacked by sharks, beaten half to death and close to being sexually abused in the worst way by that big ugly bastard and we had survived relatively strong minded, but the thought of walking into that police station scared me completely shitless.

The thought of being in a cell for twenty years and missing life with Patsy almost made me dump Laura overboard and turn back to Horta on several occasions.

Patsy sat down next to me with the briefcase she had taken from Sumers. She delved inside. She used it as a handbag for keeping her personal things safe. She pulled out a rosary and stood up.

'Do you mind if I put it here for luck?'

'Of course not. Put it where you want.' She wrapped it around the throttle control and sat back down.

'Sister Maria gave it to me for luck. I think it's working, Kris, those big waves have gone away.'

'Are you very religious?'

'No, but sometimes in your life you need something extra, being with the sisters reminded me of when I was small and when my mom disappeared. Similar people cared for me then. They were kind and gentle just like those on Horta. They fixed me up when I was broken, Kris, and like you they are caring and gentle.' She looked at me mischievously, then pulled a bag of smarties from the briefcase and started giggling.

'I've eaten all the rest,' she laughed. 'I saved you a few.'

Shipping was becoming more frequent now, so I switched on the heating system that ran off diesel and blew warm air through a series of vents around the cabins. It also kept the windows demisted, which would be useful when we entered the English Channel.

It was now day six and according to the GPS we had a little more than one hundred nautical miles to go. The shipping was almost constant now and inside I was becoming a nervous wreck. I was getting waves of anguish rushing through me each time I rehearsed in my mind what I was going to say. Even Patsy had noticed my apprehension and was sitting close to me most of the time. Whenever she took a watch I just lay sleeplessly tossing and turning.

On sighting the French coastline we opened a bottle of wine to celebrate what to us was an epic voyage. Patsy sniffed the air like a puppy.

'I can smell garlic,' she joked. I found it hard to smile with her.

'Hey, come on Kris, everything is gonna work out fine, listen.' She held my chin and turned my head. 'You have the best weapon of all, truth.' I nodded slightly. 'Just remember that and it'll all go fine. Whenever I got busted I told it as it was and it always worked.'

She instantly went red with embarrassment.

'Busted?' She had her head down then rolled her eyes up to me like a naughty child.

'GTAs, that's all.' I shook my head. 'I took a few motors when I was a kid. It means grand theft auto. It's no big deal.' I grinned. I didn't give a shit if she'd shot the Kennedys, our pasts were irrelevant now, but the future wasn't.

It was dull and misty. I kept close to the coast to avoid the busy shipping lanes and we ended up anchoring in the Gulf de Saint Malo, tucked in close to the coast. The wind was light and from the south-east and the sea was flat calm, but the smell of the land strangely demoralised me.

It was Thursday night; I wished it were a Monday instead. Going there on a Friday would probably mean being locked up for the weekend, but if the customs searched us, which no doubt they would, it would go against me having held Laura unnecessarily longer than I had to. What type of trumped up tale she was going to tell them didn't bear thinking about. She'd had plenty of time to make up a story and she had that excellent pedigree for lies and deceit. I didn't sleep and spent most of the night pacing around the wheelhouse rehearsing the final encounter, which every hour was getting nearer and causing me on occasions to tremble like a scared puppy.

I set off during the early hours, as I wanted as much of the day as possible to explain everything, but I knew they would be well pissed off at having to work over the weekend and I couldn't imagine them asking me to pop back on Monday.

As I steered towards St Peter Port I woke Patsy up. I needed her by my side. I was shaking inside and out. I hoisted the yellow Q flag up the mast then we slowly pulled into St Peter Port and moored on to the visitor's pontoon at the Victoria marina.

A young customs officer holding a clipboard walked military fashion along the jetty towards us.

'Good morning sir. Where have you come from?' Patsy appeared holding her briefcase. 'Madam.' The customs officer tipped his cap.

'I'm British. Patsy is American. We've just sailed over from the states.'

'Your passports please.' I shook my head despondently. Then Patsy produced them from her case. I looked at her and received a smile.

'Just the two of you, no pets or any goods you want to declare? I felt weak at the knees.

'I err… I need the police.' He looked at me, confused.

'Pardon sir?'

'I made a citizen's arrest and I need to see the police right away.' He looked at Patsy.

'No not her. Look, will you call or bring the police for me? I can't begin to explain, I have to talk to the police.' The young man stood up and took several paces back. 'The police you say?'

'Yes from the police station. I want them here and now please.' He turned and ran down the jetty. I turned to Patsy. My teeth were chattering.

'You're doing fine Kris, you're doing fine.' I held her close to me. I felt so afraid of losing my freedom, the freedom to hold her whenever I desired.

A few minutes' later four men arrived, two policemen and two customs officers. They walked briskly along the jetty towards us and stopped several metres from the boat.

'What is going on? Why have you requested police assistance?'

'Do you remember a woman being lost off a dive charter boat almost three years ago?' One of the policemen whom I vaguely remembered nodded.

'Yes I do, American holidaymakers, the woman drowned. The skipper was drunk, yeah I remember, he got charged for...' He paused. 'It was you wasn't it, you're the one, yeah.' He held his neck. 'You almost strangled me.' He had lost weight, but I remembered him now, he was at some of the meetings I had with my crap advocate.

'Look, they set me up. The woman who called herself Laura Stevens was not lost at sea at all. It was all a set up.' They moved towards us, each one looked quite baffled.

'Well, lad, you'll need more than some trumped up story. You'll need hard evidence. And if I'm correct you are under suspicion for the murder of a fella from the mainland who was trawled up off here recently.'

I passed the bag containing the last of the money and the gun. 'This is part of the evidence, there's also a firearm in there.' The police officer crouched and opened the brown leather bag; he blew a short whistle at seeing all the banknotes.

'I've got more evidence.' He looked at me. 'I have the woman who disappeared, the one I supposedly drowned. She and an accomplice are responsible for the murder of the man nicknamed 'Ferret,' the man who you just mentioned was trawled up, the one I am accused of murdering.' He stared around even more confused.

'You said you have the woman?' He looked again at Patsy.

'Yes, she is in the forward cabin.'

'In this boat?'

'Yeah.' I could almost hear his mind whirling.

'So where, how did you find this woman?'

'In New York.' He rubbed his stubble.

'You... you sailed from New York to here with a woman,' he struggled for the correct word but failed, 'hostage?' He looked at me in disbelief then back at the other men standing behind him. They all smiled doubtfully.

'She's not a hostage. I made a citizen's arrest. Come aboard. She's in the forward cabin.'

Their smiles turned to frowns as the policeman stepped aboard *Blue Marlin*, followed by his cautious colleagues. I stood beside the door.

'Look, she's a professional con artist, her NYPD records are…shit,' I cursed as I remembered Laura had disposed of them. 'You must prepare yourselves for an onslaught of lies and deceit. Are you ready?' They looked nervously at each other then the older of the policemen nodded to me.

I opened the cabin door and Laura predictably rushed like a greyhound leaving a trap, straight into the policeman's arms, hysterically sobbing her eyes out, whilst screaming accusations of rape and abuse at me. She'd torn her clothes off and her bra was ripped and covered only one of her breasts. The only other item of clothing she had on was a pair of soiled and torn pants. She'd obviously changed into them to look even worse. I didn't want them to see her trussed up like a turkey, so I'd left her untied and right now I regretted my decision. She'd purposely made herself look abused.

The men looked on with horrified glances at Laura, who was now on her knees clinging to the policeman's legs, trembling.

'Get another car,' he ordered his colleague over the din of Laura's hysterically spouting accusations, which she repeated with her head buried in his groin.

The policeman looked at me sternly. 'I hope you can explain this abduction, son, or you'll be Her Majesty's guest for a long, long time.'

I sat alone in an interview room while people moved around outside. The door opened and a man in his forties entered, followed by a younger man in his late twenties. The older man sat on a chair while the other leaned against the wall.

'I am Chief Inspector Roy Proctor and this is Chief Constable Pat Cook.'
I nodded as he turned on a tape machine, told it the time and who was being interviewed.

'Well, Mr Woods, you have some explaining to do. The allegations made by Mrs Retch are serious indeed. We had to call a doctor to sedate her. And we've informed the American Embassy on the mainland, they are already pushing us for more information. Your friend Patsy Alverez handed these photos over to us, can you explain them?'

Thank God Patsy somehow had held onto four of my pictures.

'A Brit called Tony Banks with the help of Laura and Larry Stevens set me up. I now know they are really called Retch. I told you before that I had a file from N.Y.P.D. on her.' The detective nodded.

'What about him?' He pushed a photo of Larry in front of me, frowned and sat back folding his arms in a defiant gesture.

'He, he's...dead.' My answer made him stand up heavily scraping the chair.

'Yes we know, Mr Woods, according to Mrs Retch it was you who murdered him.'

'No, I'll tell you what happened.'

'We already know what happened!' He walked around and then turned and faced me. 'You cut off his genitals and then trailed him behind the boat with a noose round his neck and as his blood enticed the sharks you cruelly cut the rope, didn't you?'

'Yeah, then we fried his nuts off with some garlic. For fuck's sake!'

'You fed him to the sharks to ensure that no trace of his body would ever be found,' the younger one added then looked at his superior like a dog that just caught a Frisbee.

'That's a load of bollocks. I didn't do that; He was going to bugger Patsy. I only defended her, as I've told you in my statement. I did what any normal person would have done.'

'A load of bollocks? Hardly, more like a loss!' His crap joke was out of place. He continued to pace up and down for some reason.

'Mrs Retch has never been to the UK, she told us you repeatedly beat and raped her during the weeks you held her prisoner.'

'Yeah right, then I brought her over three thousand miles to end up locked up here. That's a bit dumb, don't you think?'

The younger one sat on the edge of the steel table. 'Where did you get your... non existent police file from?'

'The same guy who wrote that article I told you earlier.'

'Would he confirm your story?'

I sighed, 'He's dead too, Larry Retch's partner, Bob Sumers had him shot.'

'Sumers you say, who's he?'

'He was in on the ISR con; it's all in my statement.' I pointed to his folder and he looked at the photos.

'Is this Sumers?'

'No that's Larry, that one is Sumers.' He looked at the photo again.

'So where can we find this alleged con man, Sumers?'

I had to answer him despite knowing what reaction it would bring. 'He's dead as well.' They shot astonished looks at each other.

'What about this guy you have down in your statement, the British guy. Banks, Tony Banks. Don't tell me he's dead as well.' I nodded a yes.

Their mouths dropped open and they looked at each other. 'My God, does everyone that comes into contact with you get shot or eaten? This takes the body count to five, with the guy who was trawled up and you've only been here for four hours.'

'It was a Mafia gang who killed Sumers and Banks. And as I said Larry fell overboard while holding on to his dick.'

'What?'

'Hell, I just told you he was about to bugger Patsy! What would you do if someone beat you and your wife within an inch of your lives, then was about to kick her back door in right in front of you for good measure, eh? Would you ask him politely to stop it please? For fucks sake, they were going to kill us anyway.'

'You took their money?'

'Yeah, what about me, they took everything I owned. I was only taking back what they took from me.'

'It was other people's money?'

'They had it as well as mine. What's the difference? I seized an opportunity. It was payback that's all.'

'Payback, five murders?' He sat back down and there was a long silence.

'She's a good-looking woman. I suppose if we were given an opportunity...'

'You'd what?'

'You know?' He winked at me.

'Fuck off, you idiot, you really believe that I fancied her and... bollocks! You surely can't be that naive? Anyway, Patsy is my only concern. That sick bitch Retch tried to kill her and me. Laura's the one you want to be grilling, she's a fucking psycho.'

'Immigration records confirm that a Mr and Mrs Stevens did visit the UK but only Mr Stevens returned to the U.S.'

'Check to see if a Laura Retch returned to the US. That would confirm I'm telling the truth because that's her real name. How can you call yourself a detective with a head full of naivety?'

'Mrs Retch believes you mistook her for a look-a-like and her husband followed you all the way to the Azores to rescue her, but you mutilated and murdered him there.'

'She's hardly going to own up, is she? Anyway don't you think it's an unlikely coincidence that Larry Retch has a wife who's got form and is the double of the supposed Laura Stevens? Give me a break.'

There was a silence.

'You said you had a file, where is it?'

'They threw all my evidence into the sea.' I suddenly remembered the CD I'd sent to the flat. 'I have a CD that will link them all together on the mainland.'

'How did you come by the boat? Did you steal it?'

'The boat has nothing to do with it. The CD I just mentioned is far more important.'

'How did you obtain the boat?'

'I won the boat in a poker game.' He sat back and gave an exasperated shake of his head while eyeing the room. 'This gets better,' he said, sarcastically. 'Where the hell do you conjure up these incredible lies?'

'It's true, call the guy who owned it, Joe, err...he'll confirm it. His details are... fuck it; they threw the details in the sea with the rest of my stuff. He's called Joe err... A voice in my head kept saying 'Two-Stores', 'Shit, he's the marine broker at the Willoughby Bay marina.'

'You think?' The detective shook his head, told the tape recorder the time and that the interview was suspended then they left the room.

I was panicking big time; it did sound a load of crap and unbelievable. I spent the night in the same cell I occupied the last time I was a guest here, and I felt the same hollowness seeping into me again. The food remained on the plate as I lay looking at the featureless ceiling.

I was still rolling as if at sea when the dawn filtered into the cell. Breakfast came, but I couldn't eat it. Then the door rattled and opened and I was lead to the interview room once again. I saw a fleeting glimpse of Patsy as she entered another room. Her eyes called out to me then she was gone. I spent the rest of the day going over and over what had happened. Forensic experts were apparently testing the gun. Thankfully it had only been fired once, and hit no one. Laura was sticking to her story of rape and wrongful identity.

I was appointed an Advocate to defend me, but he was about as good as the last one I had and my story only seemed to confuse him. They had the magistrate's court turn out on the Saturday to grant them a further thirty-six hours detention time for questioning us. They also kindly informed me that Patsy was going to be charged with being an accessory to murder and aggravated kidnap, whatever that meant. Their ploy to demoralise me was working and I felt even more depressed. We should have stayed in sunny Horta.

Monday came. It was cold and damp outside and I felt the same inside. There were three police men in the interview room this time. I realised that the newcomer was from the mainland, because he started asking me questions about Ferret. I told only the truth. It was Laura who was doing all the lying and my only hope was that she would slip up.
I told them what I thought had happened, that Banks had recruited Ferret to go with him and pick up Laura and that they had drugged me with something they put in the coffee. I could tell by their faces that they didn't believe a thing, until the mainlander asked me how I knew about Ferret's disappearance. I told him that it was Jenny, who'd informed me, when I was in New York, he nodded.

'You mean Jenny Dean?'

'Yeah we…'

'I know all about you two, and the gold you recovered from the shipwreck.'

'Yeah, that's why they set me up, to get their hands on my assets, and the money I received from the salvage.' He nodded and I felt a ray of hope about his manner. He whispered something and they left the room.

About an hour later they returned this time, with a mug of tea and a penguin biscuit. Their attitude seemed friendlier.

'Was it a good crossing?'

'We had some bad weather, but generally it was blowing between fours and sixes most of the time. The hard part was controlling Laura… the bitch.'

'Joe Smith in Norfolk Virginia confirmed your poker skills,' he gave me a wry smile.

'You got in touch, thanks.'

'Not that it does you much good, Kris.'

I gave him a thin smile and nod of acknowledgement.

'I also spoke to some of the townspeople back home, and a few remember the American couple. Mike Walker remembered Laura quite well.' I looked at him somewhat confused.

'The barman from the Ship Inn,' he studied my face as I was hit with happier memories. 'I've sent for him to fly over'

I snapped my head up to him, my mouth open in surprise.

'Your tourists left a trail of unpaid bills in the town. It wasn't until a while after that I made more enquiries and I found they were using forged credit cards. They were long gone by then.'

A uniformed policeman tapped, and popped his head round the door. 'Telephone, sir.' The mainlander left the room.

'You see, I told you she was bent.'

'That is not the same woman, Mr Woods. I'm afraid our colleague from the mainland is mistaken.'

'He's not. I know exactly who she is and he's on to her.' They both left the room then the mainlander came back alone.

'D.C. Len Ferguson.' He held out his hand, he looked

experienced and must have been nearing the end of a long career.
'I've read your statement Kris, some ordeal you have been through. It would make a good film.'

'The CD, I made contains all the evidence, and will back up my statement. It should be at my flat near the harbour back home. It'll be with all the mail.' He nodded.

'That was pretty smart, Kris. That's if it's still there.'

'How's Patsy?'

'She's fine. Look, I spoke with Fred Ireland's sister. He had told her that he was going to do some work with an outfit from up north. An old friend, Bill Dean, asked me. I found out later his daughter Jenny had requested him to find out all about Fred's disappearance. Then Jenny told me herself her theory about Fred.'

'Fred?' I asked.

'Ferret, every one called him.'

'I'm with you now. Banks is from Hull, you know?'

'Yes I know. These Island police don't like scandals on their doorstep. I made my own enquiries. The shopkeeper who sold Larry the whisky remembers them. They fleeced him as well with their phoney credit cards. He told me something these guys missed.' He looked pleased with himself.

I was listening to his every word intently.

'Larry and his woman purchased the last bottle of J.D. whisky he had in stock the morning of the day Laura Stevens disappeared. He had the date of the transaction. That one was fraudulent as well.'

'He always crushed the top with his foot when he opened a bottle, but I vaguely remember when the policeman brought it from the wheelhouse on *Westwind* the top was still on it. Anyway no one drank that early, especially after the previous boozy night. They must have poured it on me.'

Loud shouting from some other room echoed through the building, interrupting us. I recognised Laura's American voice. She was demanding release.

The younger of the two local policemen returned into the room. 'She's one angry woman, and who can blame her. We may have to release her soon.'

'No, you can't. She'll disappear like a puff of smoke.' I protested.

He gave me a condescending nod. 'She won't be allowed to leave the Island until we have charged you, then she'll have to stay for the Magistrate's hearing.'

'You really think she will hang around? You nugget. It's she and Banks who murdered Fred thingy…Ireland, she's conning you big time.' He stared down at me.

'A sophisticated American's word against an ex con's, I don't think so.'

Len looked at him.

'We have an extension of one more day. I strongly recommend she be held until then. May I remind that I am the chief investigating officer in this case?'

'Depends on our chief,' he said petulantly, almost childlike as he left the room.

'They don't like having you on their patch do they?' His mature grey eyes studied me.

'You believe I'm innocent, don't you?'

He huffed somewhat sadly. 'We need something more, the barman's word is not enough to charge her.' He got up and left the room. I felt my hope dissolve into fear as the door closed.

I got the third degree from the local boys for a further two hours. The Advocate hardly spoke. I figured like most in his lofty profession he was just there for the money.

It was the early hours of the morning. I lay on a thin mattress, depressed at being locked up again. I was tired from lack of sleep, and after hours of repeatedly turning over I eventually dozed off.

It was virtually pitch black. The only illumination was from a few small green emergency lights that lead to the whimpering few that were close to death, and were slowly slipping below the freezing water. I was climbing down a rope screaming for my loved ones, I landed on bodies, which rolled in the water as I stood on them. I strained in the dim lighting then Vicky's face appeared. She looked strange and quite different to how I remembered. She was so pale. She held something in her hand and was trying to lift it out of the water. It was small and round like a mat or something. She smiled sadly up at me then uttered softly 'goodbye'. I grabbed desperately for her, but she dissolved into the water.

I woke suddenly as I always did after one of those haunting visions. I hadn't had one for years. I was scared that if they lock me away I would lose myself forever. Being back in here was obviously affecting my subconscious more than I realised. I sat in the dark scared to fall asleep. I was anxious and disturbed at the thought of slipping back into those nightmare days again. I sat uneasily fidgeting until the light joined me, then I must have dropped off.

My arm was being shaken. 'Breakfast, then clean yourself up, you look terrible.' He placed a yellow plastic razor with some washing stuff on the mattress. The food and tea was steaming hot for a change, and I felt hungry.

The repetitive questions were fired at me over and over again, but because I was telling the truth I remembered each answer without faltering, which was frustrating the local boys. Laura had obviously worked her charms on them. Maybe she was giving them blowjobs by now. That thought made me remember the pain. I stood my ground then Len Ferguson thankfully relieved some of my worries. He had the old school attitude, and wasn't going to be swayed towards anyone's opinion.

'Our barman has made a statement, which has for the time stopped Laura from getting early release. He is positive it's her. Apparently she had words with him over a spilt drink. He remembers her shouting about it.'

'Yeah, it was white wine and he caught the stem on the edge of the table and spilt some on her 'pants' as she called them.' Len sat back and smiled.

'Spot on, but we need more. She's pulled the hood over the other detectives' eyes with her articulate style and aggression.'

A haunting feeling descended over me as I recalled the strange dream. There was something nagging at me. 'Say that again please.'

'What, that she pulled the hood over their eyes?'

I closed my eyes and dropped my head into my hands and thought of the dream. Then I saw it. It was a diving hood Vicky was holding in the dream, and she was trying to pass it to me. 'A hood,' I gasped, feeling a deep shiver run through me. 'You just broke my dream.' Then I thought about Vicky, how the hell? I felt faint. Len looked bewildered at me.

'A hood?' He repeated.

'Yeah.' My mind was racing. 'We lost Laura's dive hood when she was here diving, you know the day before she disappeared.'

'So you lost a hood.' He didn't get it.

'Can't you get DNA from hair? Dive hoods always pull out a bit of hair out when you take them off, they're quite tight fitting.'

'Yes, the follicles hold DNA, but you said it was lost.'

'It was, but someone found it. It was Alan Bennett who runs the charter boat *Vagabond*. He operates around the Islands. He called me and told me he'd found a hood floating in the water near to where we were diving that day, and it fitted the description of the one we had lost overboard. He said he would keep it on board for me.' Len was scribbling details down on his little black notepad. Then he moved, almost dashed out of the room.

The useless advocate shrugged at me then the locals returned and continued with their ineffective double act. I was in another dimension now. If only Alan had kept the hood.

The rest of the day dragged along with more questions. They were getting well pissed off with my correct answers. I reckoned Laura would be talking gobbledegook by now and finding it hard to remember the many lies she'd told, which was obviously making things hard for them. I eventually got locked in the cell again and was sitting there feeling hurt and helpless.

D.C Len Ferguson walked into the cell at about six p.m. He shook his head. 'Mr Bennett is on holiday in Florida for two weeks.'

I slumped, with rounded shoulders.

'Nevertheless, he has a crewman, and I tracked him down. He leant over a bin liner and produced a clear plastic bag which held Laura's lost hood

I hung my head and thought about the dream. 'What date is it?'

'Dec 22nd,' I smiled as I remembered Dec 22nd was the day Vicky and I got married. My subconscious was either doing somersaults or somehow inexplicably she had helped me.

'Are you feeling all right?'

I sniffed as my eyes filled with tears. 'Yeah, I am now.' I smiled while wiping my full nose with a tissue. 'I am now.'

Chapter Twenty

We were sat around the galley table. Patsy passed the glass of rum to D.C. Len Ferguson and we chinked them together.

'To Len Ferguson,' we toasted. It was Christmas Eve; he had come for a celebratory drink before flying back to the mainland. The DNA test had proved Laura's downfall, in addition to the evidence *Vagabond's* crewman gave. He had seen a big orange inflatable leaving the area where Laura had supposedly been swept away. He even recalled seeing it through binoculars picking someone out of the water, but didn't think anything of it, as the area is busy with divers through the summer. If only he'd told someone.

Len had also acquired the copy of the CD. I had forgotten that I added her police record to the disk, which supported our cause and sealed the coffin lid for Laura.

She had apparently fought with the police in a futile bid to escape, and broken the nose of the younger CID officer, by head-butting him whilst he was reading out several charges from an ever-growing list of offences. I didn't like him anyway. The F.B.I. was showing interest in her as well. Apparently Len found out from them that Larry and Laura and company had been linked with several cases of drug-facilitated rape charges using a drug called Rohypnol.

Len read from the printed e-mail. 'The drug can mentally and physically paralyse its victim. Individuals may experience a slowing of psychomotor performance, muscle relaxation, decreased blood pressure, sleeplessness, and/or amnesia. Some of the adverse side effects associated with the drug's use are drowsiness, headaches, memory loss, dizziness, nightmares, confusion, and tremors. It takes fifteen to twenty minutes to take effect depending how much is ingested and its effect can last up to twenty-four hours.' He looked sheepishly at me before reading out the next bit. 'The drug's metabolic properties are detectable in urine for up to seventy two hours after ingestion.'

He hung his head, and muttered. 'What can I say?' I stared blankly as I recalled all the things he just read out happening to me.

How things would have changed for me if only they had taken a simple blood test!

Len told us that we would be contacted in the future to give further evidence, but it was a complex international case and could take months to get to court. Laura was still stubbornly denying all the charges. He shook our hands and reassured us that it was over for now and we could go home.

I smiled at Patsy who had a thick polo-necked jumper on, which almost reached her knees and made her legs look like skinny sticks poking out. Then it started to sink in that we had retrieved only the boat from all those millions.

'Well babe, what now? We have no money and I owe for rent back home.'

She pulled a wad of euros from her beloved briefcase. 'I hid them in one of my hiding places, I changed them at Horta. There's six thousand euros here. That will pay the rent and some of it can make our first Christmas a good one. Go and get changed, we are celebrating tonight with a meal.'

'Where is your hiding place, then?

'Every woman needs a few secrets, Kris.' She winked then mimicked a kiss to me.

Two days later we were approaching the entrance to the river. We did not speak as we passed The Lodge. Patsy looked in wonder at the hideaway, which sadly had a sale sign piercing the small lawn. I felt even sadder when I saw the empty oak bookshelf through the bare curtain-less picture window. Then we passed the old mooring buoy, the letters had faded, but *Westwind* could still be seen.

The weed that covered its base waved in the clear water like Jenny's long hair in the wind. I felt I'd died and was visiting my past life. All I wanted was to stop and tie up to the buoy and go home.

We eventually moored to the same jetty where I used to pick up the divers. We secured the lines then I introduced Patsy to some English fish and chips, followed by a pint of cider. This intro to my heaven in Devon wasn't what I had planned, and I felt that I'd let her down terribly.

Then we went to the flat, only to receive a rather cold reception, I reckon my reputation was well and truly shot after all the gossip that must have been going on. I paid the rent arrears and was promptly asked to vacate as soon as possible. Apparently one of the landlord's relatives wanted to move in. That's what they said anyway.

The press harassed us as we moved my few belongings over to the boat, but none of them asked about how we felt. Only the gory bits interested them and we eventually escaped into the private marina.

By New Year's Eve we were living permanently on the boat with my meagre belongings stuffed into the forward cabin. I had accepted that we would never be able to return to The Lodge. They were asking six hundred and fifty thousand pounds for it.

Even a small house in the area was no longer an option to us as all the prices had soared, due to the second hand car dealers turned estate agents, who were falsely hiking up the prices for their own gain.

We had become boat people. Paying insurance for the boat, which we had to produce to obtain a mooring, which in turn had to be paid for in advance had left us almost broke. I counted up and we had less than one thousand pounds left. I gave a forlorn sigh.

'Sorry Pats, you lost your apartment, your job and your friends. I dragged you through living hell, bringing you all this way for what? Just look at us!'

'Well at least we've got each other, and this boat to live on, and you've cleared your name. I would say we've done well. Anyway I'm used to making ends meet, Kris. We'll get by.' She stood with a glass of wine and smiled sort of hopefully. I wondered how long her happy smile would last during the cold dark winter days, sitting in a boat with no money and little to do.

She sat down and opened her briefcase, pulled out a small gift-wrapped present and walked over to me.

'It's not much.' I opened it to find a gold St Christopher pendant on a chain. 'It has your name on it and will bring us luck.'

I wasn't one for jewellery, nevertheless I put it on. I didn't have the heart to tell her St Christopher had been sacked. I thanked her with a snog.

We were sitting watching the TV. Patsy was fiddling with the expensive briefcase that looked like it could be made from some unfortunate alligator or snake. She had adopted it and kept it with her all the time. Perhaps it reminded her of life in the US.

I flicked disappointedly through the five channels. The reception was poor and every channel was showing people lost in a snowstorm. Then unexpectedly Patsy gave out a surprised, 'Huh?' I turned to see what had alarmed her; she had her head on one side, inquisitively looking inside the case.

'Take a look a here,' she requested, sounding so American. I moved next to her and she opened the case wider.

'Look, a secret hiding place. I turned this round silver badge that's got BOS on it and it made a sort of click sound somewhere inside, hey and take a look here.' She pushed it towards me.

I could see a thick pile of documents inside. I reached in and pulled them out. They were sort of old looking and had small writing and fancy scrolls covering them all over.

'Pay the bearer', Patsy looked at me with her mouth open, then back at the papers, 'one hundred thousand dollars? No shit,' she said cynically then started counting them. I studied one, noticing it had detachable coupons, each one with dates stamped on it. Also it had lettering on the main part of it declaring something about seven years then I saw the word 'Bond'.

'Jesus, Pats, they're US Bearer Bonds.'

'Is that good? Gee I hope it is, 'cause there are fifty of 'em.'

'Fifty,' I stood up, 'Fifty?'

'Uh, huh,' she stared at me as though I was mad. 'Here you count them if you don't believe me, there's forty-nine here.' She wafted them like a fan. 'Fifty counting that one in your hand.'

'Don't you see? I mean... do know what this means?'

She looked a little irritated at me. 'No I don't, just old bank notes aren't they, a collection maybe? They're all smelly; anyway.' She dropped them onto the table and brushed her hands off. 'What's got into you, Kris?'

I grabbed her shoulders and pulled her to her feet. She looked shocked.

'We're sodding millionaires, Pats! These bearer bonds are as good as international cash.' She bounced back on to the seat as her eyes began darting wildly around the galley in disbelief.

'You mean those things...' It had sunk in. 'Tha...That,' she stuttered. 'That's...' I was nodding along with her then she broke into a fit of nervous giggling. Suddenly she froze. Her eyes and mouth slowly widened at me then we shouted simultaneously. 'Five million dollars!'

Chapter Twenty-one

The first time Patsy stepped from the dinghy on to the worn steps leading up to the paved jetty she fell in love with The Lodge. She spun around the small lawn, beaming out smiles like Mary Poppins, and when she entered the well-fitted country kitchen she held her hands to her mouth in pure joy. We then moved to the room with the view, which caused tears to well up inside her. I felt the ever-present tension fall from me like a lead veil as it sank home that I actually had my special home back. It was one of the best days of my life.

Months had passed since we first arrived together in Guernsey. The police had made lots of visits and taken statement after statement, but telling the truth had paid off big time, well, nearly all the truth. Sumers' share of the con, the hidden bearer bonds disappeared via an anonymous Internet broker, who made a healthy profit for handling the sale and for arranging a Swiss bank account for us, which now safely holds our rosy future. Sumers' share of the ill-gotten gains was now our hard won gain. We deliberately got a mortgage on The Lodge with a local bank, where we were maintaining a modest account. Patsy's red Mazda RX8 was in the garage. She also had a wardrobe full of gorgeous clothes, after we spent a brilliant week shopping and sightseeing in London.

I'll never forget how excited I was while I filled the oak bookcase with my beloved books for the last time, under the flickering flames of the log fire that crackled and made homely sounds while casting that warm orange glow around the room.

It was dusk again and 'Mrs Patsy Woods' was sitting in the same warm glow, watching the fishing boats returning. Each time one disappeared from view for a few seconds behind the *Blue Marlin* she moved her head, and waited like an excited kid for it to reappear at the other side.

The New York Times newspaper lay open on the table before her, showing a number of pictures of New York's up coming models. One title read 'English rose with a hint of shamrock'. Jenny Dean looked truly chic in her trendy clothes while posing for her boyfriend, top fashion photographer J.J. 'the man' Jones. I smiled. I never even knew his surname was Jones.

'Hey, that blue one's late, Kris, the one called *Curlew*.' Patsy smiled and turned back to the window, then took a sip of coffee. Her little finger remained straight as she held the small cup, our constant reminder of how close we were from eternal separation.

Patsy had fully recovered and forever shed those horrid dreams. She was so much fun to be with, always laughing and joking. She had such a lovely personality, and there were the nicer personal things that she was also good at. She had learnt to swim and, knowing that no sharks prowled our waters was looking forward to learning to dive during the approaching summer, which pleased me immensely.

On the table near the big bookshelf lay the plans for our summer cruise back to Horta, where we were going to buy a second dream home. Everything was perfect, well almost, till the next morning.

The big frame of D.C. Ferguson stood at the door. 'Just a few last questions,' he said ominously. He started by informing us that the case had spilt over to America, and the shit had hit the fan big-time, and how sad that the only person left alive to take the rap was pretty Laura. She had been placed on remand here for the murder of Fred Ireland. There were other charges of deception and fraud. It would take years for all the escalating charges to be answered, but we didn't give a ten-ton shit about her. Then he started delving. He looked out of the window at *Blue Marlin*, then around The Lodge.

'You certainly have got back on your feet quickly, Kris. It must have been one hell of a poker game...' I looked at him, then at Patsy. 'Was it Texas hold 'em, or seven-card stud?' I could feel myself going red.

'It seems a long time ago. I forget.'

He smiled then Patsy interrupted. 'It was Omaha wasn't it, Kris?'

'Yeah, yeah, Omar...ha, yeah, I just got lucky for a change. After all those years of crap.' He looked at Patsy then back at me again.

'There is still a lot of ISR money unaccounted for, Kris. The Americans who lost money are making all sorts of accusations, and pulling strings in high places. The issue has reached Congress, and even the President himself has voiced his concern to our parliament, and it's fallen on me to get a result. Not something I wanted at the eve of my retirement. I'm one of the old school Kris, if there has been a crime committed there's always someone guilty of committing it. I suppose you don't know what really happened to those missing millions do you? Laura, as you know, has accused you both of taking the money.'

'We told you that when Larry shot me he took nearly all of it with him. Anyway I've told you all this before.' He walked to the window holding his hands behind his back. Patsy and I looked at each other in silence.

'I like your new sports car. The one in the garage, Mazda RX8 isn't it?

'Yeah, I promised Patsy that when it was all over I would treat her, but she's got to get a licence before she can drive it.'

He picked up the picture of Vicky holding little Janie and stared long and hard at it before placing it back on the windowsill.

'Twenty two thousand pounds is some treat. That's what they cost, I believe.'

'After what she went through it's not nearly enough. Anyway I got it on the knock.'

'Not according to my records, Kris, and I don't think I've made a mistake. You know I think that is the first untruth you have told me, Kris. Is it?

'No, I borrowed the money from a friend called Ronny, he's in Scotland. I'll give his number so you can check. I'm paying him back monthly, you know on the knock.'

He raised his eyebrows, showing his disbelief. I started to feel bad about this visit. He walked over to the bookshelf table.

'Are we under investigation again?' He deliberately ignored me.

'The Azores, hmm, he moved the chart, exposing a list of properties for sale in Horta, which made me feel even worse. 'These are expensive properties. Surely you're not thinking of buying one, you were cleaned out financially, weren't you?'

I laughed. 'You must be joking, unless...' I paused with my finger on my chin. As I began to feel threatened my defensive anger started rising. 'Unless I sue the police for my wrongful arrest, and the loss of my profitable business, and all the lost earnings I suffered because of it, and there's this place, which I have to repurchase, and the compensation money I received after cruelly losing my family. Oh yeah, and what about my good name? That surely must have a fair price to it as well.' I deliberately stared stern faced at him. 'I'm sure a good barrister would dig up a lot of mistakes the police made.' There was a long silence then he smiled.

'Are you planning on going down that road Kris?

'I think that depends on you, Len. Through gross injustice and poor policing, the system cost me the best part of two million, I reckon, and there's other things everyone conveniently forgets.' I removed my shirt revealing the nasty scars from the two bullet wounds, and the two stab wounds. I then held Patsy's hands up. 'Take a good look at these. You see, we weren't considered for compensation. We weren't even offered fucking counselling after all we endured. All we got was shit from 'This Great Britain.' We haven't even received a fucking apology from the police. We were treated worse than animals, even when I was almost dying of Rohypnol poisoning in that fucking police cell. I was dragged around and treated worse than a manky dog. You go ahead with your pride-motivated enquiries, Len, and we'll sell our story to those pestering press people you so strongly advise us to avoid. All that on top of this further harassment will make the front page for sure; they would in all probability print it in weekly instalments. Seventy-two hours they had to test my blood! The barristers would like that one don't you think? We sorted the bad guy's. I even pulled the Mafia, you lot couldn't or wouldn't so, bollocks to you lot.' I had lost it.

'I see.' He walked back to the window and stared out.

Patsy walked to him. 'They committed all the crimes. All we did is survive them. Kris lost everything because of those con artists, and with almost no help. He should get an award, not this constant persecution. I took the money that's missing, OK, if it makes you feel good. I gave it to a charity in Horta, so arrest me and I'll make a full statement. That should feed your holy pride.'

He stared at her sullen face then smiled a fatherly smile. 'You're a lucky man, Kris.' He gave another deep sigh while shaking his head and then walked to the door and then turned to us.

'As long as the case is open there'll be questions asked, even after my retirement.' He shrugged bearing a troubled look as he fought with his morals.

I walked over to him. 'Why not have a vacation in the Azores, Len? Horta is a beautiful place.'

He looked at me strangely. 'Are you taking the rise out of me, lad?'

I shook my head and moved nearer to his ear. 'I'm sure there's a hotel somewhere in Horta that is holding Larry's belongings in their left luggage room.' I didn't have to elaborate any more, as his naturally suspicious face transformed into a big nodding smile.

'Well!' He grinned, obviously pleased and relieved. 'I see no reason for any further investigation here. I should, if things work out, eliminate any link with you two regarding the missing money. Right now I've got a little trip to make. See you around and the best of luck in the future.'

Patsy held me with her head buried into my neck. 'Do you think he'll come back again, Kris?'

'No, not now Pats, he'll be able to end his long career on a high note.'

'He was wrong, though, Kris.'

'Yeah well, I'm just thankful the way things have worked out.'

'No, I mean wrong about us two.'

'What do you mean, he's wrong about us two?'

She turned her head to one side and smiled and then pulled up her top and placed my hand carefully on her belly, she flashed her captivating dark eyes on mine.

'He should have said, 'you three,' Kris.'